THE BURNING WITCH

THE BURNING WITCH

Volume 1

Delemhach

Podium

This book is dedicated to you, readers, and those that have chosen to follow my writing career. You have all been instrumental in changing my life for the better, and I wish you all the best in thanks. You are absolutely wonderful, and I am an incredibly lucky author to have people like you giving my stories a chance.

Cover design by Podium Publishing

ISBN: 978-1-0394-2991-8

Published in 2023 by Podium Publishing, ULC
www.podiumaudio.com

THE BURNING WITCH

CHAPTER 1

PINS AND NEEDLES

Troivack was a brutal and traditional kingdom.

With its five cities lying between its mountainous northern and southern borders, its prize jewel lay nestled in its belly—the vineyards.

Since the Tri-War, Troivackian wines and moonshine had become infamous amongst the nearest two kingdoms of Daxaria and Zinfera, and this was thanks mostly to the Daxarian hero Finlay Ashowan, the house witch. The man had gone from peasant cook to a viscount, and he famously bested Troivack's chief of military, a fearsome fire witch who had brought his dragon familiar to Daxaria's doorstep, though it was common knowledge that Finlay Ashowan's own familiar, a cat named Kraken, had been the major catalyst in the success of the war. The house witch had married a beautiful former Troivackian noble—a woman who had introduced to her husband the moonshine that boomed in popularity in Daxaria as a result.

The Tri-War had been a terrible loss for Troivack, one that took the life of their previous king, Matthias the Sixth, and which left his young son, Brendan Devark, on the throne.

Despite the odds, King Brendan Devark not only had survived his childhood as a ruler, but he succeeded in bringing about an age of prosperity and peace under his strong yet fair command.

He even managed to lay aside any temptation to carry a grudge against the kingdom of Daxaria, and fell in love with their one and only Princess Alina Reyes, a choice that was not well received by all in his land . . .

It just so happened that it was their wedding day.

By midday, the late summer heat simmered over the earth, but the mornings had notably begun to cool—a sign autumn was on its way. The wedding would take place, and shortly after, before the seasonal winds made the trip too rough to travel, King Brendan Devark and his new bride would safely cross the seas to his kingdom for Princess Alina's coronation.

A select few Daxarian knights and servants would join the princess to ensure her transition to the new land would be a smooth one, though there was one extra guest accompanying the newlyweds back to their kingdom. Alina Reyes's best friend would be present . . .

Lady Katarina Ashowan.

Daughter of the Daxarian hero, Viscount Finlay Ashowan.

And little did the people of Troivack know, it was Katarina Ashowan who should have been their true concern all along.

Katarina scowled at her reflection in the lengthwise mirror as the maids buzzed like bees around her, pinning and humming as they worked.

The princess of Daxaria was being sewn into her wedding dress in her own chamber, and even more excitingly, her brother, the crown prince of Daxaria, had reappeared after years of a mysterious absence . . .

Rolling her ethereal golden eyes to the ceiling, Katarina cracked her neck impatiently, her long wavy red hair rippling down her back as she did so. With the air brimming with excitement, standing still seemed horribly arduous.

Her gaze flitted to two maids huddled in the corner of her chamber, whispering and giggling amongst themselves.

"Something interesting?" Kat asked, her tone bored but her eyes unable to disguise a glint of interest.

The pair of maids straightened and glanced at each other guiltily before turning and curtsying.

"We were merely saying how . . . how beautiful you will look in your dress today, Lady Katarina." The pair curtsied a second time for good measure, and consequently missed Kat's sardonic quirk of her eyebrow.

"Oh really? Are you sure it isn't anything to do with Prince Eric returning?" Kat's lips curled upward in a wolfish smile.

The maids visibly gulped before unconsciously grabbing each other's hands and stepping forward.

"W-We wondered i-if His Highness was going to . . . to stay in Austice," one of the maids spluttered as Kat continued to smile with a touch of deviousness.

"I see. What if he *does* choose to stay in Austice once his sister is wed, hm? Are you hoping to wait on a new queen?"

Both maids curtsied until their knees touched the floor. "F-Forgive us, Lady Katarina, we only—"

"I'm teasing. Please don't stress. I'm sorry for making you worry." Kat sighed, her smile dimming.

She'd learned from a young age always to treat those of commoner birth with respect and consideration. Her father's former status as a cook had never been forgotten during her childhood, especially with many of the fellow noble children taunting her over her "sullied blood."

Despite her reassurance, the maids didn't resume their previous discussion. They instead refocused their attention to completing Katarina's dress.

The garment adorning the abnormally tall redhead was made of a dark blue silk with gold trim around the hem, sleeves, and neckline.

Not that Katarina particularly cared that much about what she wore. She tended to escape her noblewoman duties as the princess's most senior handmaiden and instead would seek out a good bit of fun somewhere else while donning trousers.

A knock at the chamber door startled the maids and slowly drew Katarina from her thoughts of escaping the wedding reception as swiftly as possible.

"Lady Katarina? The princess requests your presence in the council room," Ruby, the Head of Housekeeping for the castle, called out breathlessly.

The woman was getting on in years, and had never exactly been the pinnacle of health . . .

Already fidgeting out of desperation to get moving again, Katarina forced herself to stay put as the maids hurriedly made their final adjustments and allowed her to step down from the stool she had been perched on.

Striding out of the room with a quick wave of thanks to the servants over her shoulder, Katarina languished in the feeling of moving once more.

Sitting still was not a strong suit of hers by any stretch of the imagination. Everyone knew, and worried about, this fact when she joined the traditional Troivackian court in assisting the princess for a year . . .

Upon entering the council room, Kat wondered why in the world her friend was there and not sipping sweet mead with her long awaited brother and father in the king's private study.

Half expecting yet another full-blown meeting amongst nobility that was nothing short of torture to Katarina as she prepared to go abroad, she was grateful beyond measure to the Gods when she found only the princess in the room.

Her delicate brows were furrowed, her wavy dirty blond hair arranged beautifully, and her wedding dress already complete, Alina Reyes looked angelic and entirely out of place in the musty old council room. She sat in her father's chair that dwarfed her small frame, yet there was a strange coil of power within her rigid posture that belied one's initial impression of the princess.

"Alina?" Kat called out, grinning.

The princess's hazel eyes snapped up, though her frown remained.

"Oh, Kat . . . thank you for coming . . ."

"I'll have you know that when we first met, I would have seriously reconsidered becoming friends with you if I'd known that even on your wedding day you'd be summoning me to the Godsdamn council room." Kat ambled over to Alina's side and plunked her willowy form down gracelessly in the chair to her friend's left.

The princess's gaze was already lost in thought when she let out a halfhearted laugh.

Katarina felt her eyebrow rise, and her index finger begin tapping the table impatiently.

"So why did you summon me here? You should be sharing tears and feelings with your family before marrying your beloved rockhead."

The princess shot her friend a flat, irritated glance at the insult toward her groom, His Majesty Brendan Devark.

Katarina had never hidden her lack of fondness for the Troivackian king, who was built like a mountain—he even dwarfed some of his fellow Troivackians. Brendan Devark had made it perfectly clear the feeling was mutual.

"Alright, I'm sorry! I know it's his wedding day too . . . I'll try to be . . ." Kat trailed off, her expression growing pained. After another beat of silence, she decided to give up on offering a false promise. "So why am I here?"

Closing her eyes, Alina frowned again.

"I just . . . I need to talk . . ."

Kat blinked several times before jumping to her feet. "You're having second thoughts about marrying him? Fantastic, alright, I've got a horse and a donkey ready with supplies to take us to a small holding my family has along the coast. From there we can maybe travel down to the southern islands; it'll be difficult for people to—"

"Kat, shut up. I love Brendan and I'm marrying him. Today. One more bad word about him and I'll be having you writing all of my correspondence for the entire time you're in Troivack."

Kat's expression morphed into horror as she stiffly seated herself back down. "No need to be so drastic."

Alina sighed, though her irritation with her best friend wasn't so easily dissolved, and she turned sternly to the redhead. "It's about my brother."

Kat leaned back in her chair and folded her arms across her middle, her head tilted expectantly.

"He's been gone for years, and while I'm unbelievably happy to see him again, he is . . . changed. It's like he's an entirely different person. Then your father around him . . . I've never seen the viscount so . . ." Alina's gaze once again grew distant, and her head began shaking subconsciously.

"What about my father around the prince is so strange?" Katarina asked with a tilt of her head. The infamous house witch could be rather terrifying to someone who angered him, but he was generally known to be irritatingly charming and good-natured.

"It's clear the two of them are furious with each other, and it's almost as though . . ." Alina hesitated before she let out another frustrated breath. "Almost as though he expects Eric to do something to vex him. Meanwhile, my father can't stop crying because he's so happy to have us both home."

Kat's golden eyes moved to the ceiling as she pondered this tidbit of information.

Her father had been a close friend of Prince Eric Reyes since he had been a peasant cook and the prince a young boy. That is, until four years prior, when Queen Ainsley, Alina and Eric's mother, had passed away.

Something had happened between Finlay Ashowan and the Daxarian prince, and it had been the subject of an array of rumors ever since.

"Have you had a chance to speak to your brother alone?" Kat queried after considering her friend's concerns.

"Not yet. I'm hoping tomorrow morning I'll get a chance," Alina cited, though her wandering stare indicated her thoughts were already shifting.

"You think you're going to be leaving your bedchamber the morning after your wedding to meet with your brother?" Katarina asked with a roguish grin.

At this, Alina's attention returned as she blushed and opened her mouth to retort but found herself unable to make any kind of reply.

"Well, that is your business. I'll keep an eye on my father and your brother at the reception to see if I can weasel out any information." Katarina slowly stood back up from her seat and reached her arms high above her head in a satisfying stretch.

"Thank you, I appreciate it." Alina managed wearily as she, too, rose. "It feels like, despite Eric being back, I have even more questions than I did before."

"I'm sure there are perfectly good reasons why he was away and why my da's so annoyed. My best guess is he saw the prince be rude to a commoner or said once king, he'd deny my father's proposal for publicly funded education. Then the prince probably stayed away to gather more information or something . . ." Kat began moving toward the door as Alina followed at her own unhurried pace.

"That is a very specific guess."

"I'm just saying, it could be a number of simple things." Kat shrugged as she waited for the princess to stride ahead of her.

"I don't know . . . I have a feeling there was a bigger reason for it all . . ." Alina's frown was returning, prompting Kat to seize her shoulders as she passed and give her a gentle shake.

"Oyy, if you want me to be the epitome of a happy, supportive friend as you marry that giant ass—I mean . . . the Troivackian king, then you have to be happy too; got it? Come on! It's your wedding day! Great food, and I hear there are no less than *five* musical groups your father hired. We both know how excited you've been to hear them," Kat reminded, knowing full well that her friend's deep love of music would cheer her up, if only a little bit.

The tension leaving her shoulders, Alina dropped her chin to her chest, finally succumbing to her beautiful smile.

"You're right . . . I can worry about this later."

"That's the spirit! Even *my* brother has returned! Tam could help try and needle our da about what's going on as well if you'd like?" Kat asked while reaching for the door handle.

"Tam is back? Gods, it's been so long since I've seen him!" Alina's surprised yet pleased tone floated out to the guards, making them stand to attention as the two women passed.

"He has indeed. It's been nice not having his mopey self around, but ah well, I guess if you want to see him, I can put up with him." Kat huffed dramatically.

Alina linked her arm with Kat's before nudging her friend gently with her elbow. "You're happy he's home too, admit it."

"Pffft." Kat shook her head with a jesting smile. "He's just another person nagging me not to drink too much moonshine or go for night rides."

Alina laughed before turning a questioning gaze up to her friend. "By the way, you weren't serious about having an escape plan for me, were you?"

At this, Kat's expression grew suspiciously innocent. "I would never, *ever*, doubt your *sincere* heartfelt feelings toward the Troivackian king."

Eyes narrowing, Alina gave her friend a final stare before facing forward again.

"Well, I won't need any of your wild ploys. Now come along; I think it's just about time I walk down the aisle."

Kat's smile returned as she guided her friend back toward her chamber, where her maids undoubtedly were frantically awaiting the princess to add the finishing touches to her wedding attire.

While not exactly thrilled at having to hang around the reception longer, Katarina Ashowan couldn't deny that she was a little curious about the task Alina had set for her. Not to mention she hadn't seen the prince since she was a young child . . .

All she could remember of him was his wavy dirty blond hair like his sister's and an image of him waiting in the distance with a sword at his hip . . .

Ah well. One way or another, I'll figure out what happened. Though maybe I should try to tell the stablemaster to unpack our getaway steeds after the ceremony . . .

CHAPTER 2

LUCK'S MISFORTUNE

Katarina stood at the altar and beamed as she watched her best friend be escorted down the aisle by her father, King Norman Reyes of Daxaria, who was barely containing his tears.

The nobles whispered in awe over their princess's loveliness as golden sunlight filled the room with warmth and set the colorful jewels worn by the noble guests sparkling.

Even Troivack's stoic and stern king, Brendan Devark, was smiling dazedly as his bride floated down the aisle toward him. If anyone present had had any doubts about his love for Alina, they found themselves realizing it was a ridiculous notion, as it was clear to see that the mountainous man was deeply enamored with Alina Reyes.

The king's brother, Prince Henry Devark, stood at Brendan's side, completely aglow as he watched his sibling's uninhibited happiness—which, given the Troivackian nature of hiding one's emotions, made the sight all the more poignant.

When Alina finally reached the altar, it was the newly appointed Coven of Wittica leader, Leia Atkines, who stood in ceremony to wed the couple.

Norman kissed his daughter's cheeks as she smiled serenely at him, her hands gripping his own trembling ones before he turned and stiffly handed Alina to Brendan Devark. The groom's size easily dwarfed the princess's, but the gentleness in his eyes somehow made even their size difference seem endearing. Alina gave her bouquet of white roses to Katarina, then faced Brendan, placing both her hands in his.

Katarina was shifting back to her place on the step of the dais, when she noticed out of the corner of her eye the king leaning toward his son who was seated at his side.

Curious, Kat turned her chin slightly, only to have her gaze land on the crown prince of Daxaria, who was listening to his father's whispers.

A strange jolt in Katarina's stomach startled her. A rush was running through her that had her temperature spiking . . .

The shock had her swiftly turning her attention back to the ceremony, though she couldn't easily hide the tint of pink burning along her cheekbones.

Prince Eric didn't look anything like she had imagined he would.

She knew he was around nine years older than her, but she had expected a polished princely aura that made young women swoon: his wavy dirty blond hair gleaming, his gaze imperial, his face kind but firm . . .

Instead, Prince Eric's wavy hair looked bright and mostly blond, as though the sun had bleached it from time spent outdoors. It was long enough that he had tied it back in a small ponytail, and while it was clear he had shaven that morning, his face was weathered and tan. Unlike the large noble presence Kat had been anticipating, he was incredibly lean, but muscled, as though he hadn't eaten regularly but had worked physically hard for years . . .

All of these observations tripled the redhead's intrigue over where the prince had been, but what made it increase yet another tenfold was his eyes.

His hazel eyes, despite being the precise shape and color of her best friend's, were completely different. Although the prince's eyes were fixed on his sister, Kat could see a hardness in them. A possible glimpse of his true nature was nowhere to be seen. Furthermore, there was a depth that ended somewhere unknown, but Katarina had a strange sense that it wasn't somewhere good.

She understood then what Alina had been talking about with regard to her brother no longer being as she had remembered.

No . . . the prince was nothing like the stories she had heard. He could've passed for a sailor, or an underemployed mercenary . . .

"Kat?"

The whisper jerked the redhead from her thoughts.

Alina was staring at her friend with a bemused smile. "The ring, Kat."

Giving her head a shake, Kat hastily thrust an emerald green velvet pouch that had been clutched with the bouquet at the princess, making a number of nobles in the room chuckle at her awkwardness. Alina's hazel eyes danced with laughter and happiness as she accepted the rings, and she gave her friend a lingering look of appreciation.

Turning her attention back to the couple announcing their vows, Kat decided not to risk another look at the prince. She could already feel her excitement over investigating him begin to make it difficult to stand still. Without realizing it, she was gripping the bouquet in her hands a little more tightly, and the heat radiating from her was rapidly softening the stems. Her thoughts were practically humming, and she couldn't wait to begin her assigned task.

I do love a good mystery . . .

The ceremony ended with everyone standing and cheering, flower petals and birdseed cast in the air over the happy couple as they strode down the castle corridor to the great front doors, where they would stand on the stoop and wave to the crowd outside the castle that had gathered, having trickled all the way down the great slope of Austice to the harbor. The city was bursting at the seams to celebrate the royal wedding, every heart of its citizens overflowing with joy and exuberance for their princess.

After greeting some of the commoners and bestowing tokens amongst them of coins, candy, and flowers, the newlyweds would proceed to the banquet hall, where their presence would herald the beginning of the wedding feast.

This meant that there was a blissful break for Katarina to slip away and burn off some of the magic that was making her skin begin to itch.

After being escorted back down the aisle by Prince Henry, she hastily excused herself, claiming to need refreshing, and moved as quickly as possible to the west castle entrance that would lead her to the knights' barracks and slightly beyond to the stables.

She still had to finish bribing the stablemaster not to tell anyone about her crafting an escape plan for the princess . . . so it worked to her advantage to walk as quickly as possible, and hope that everyone had departed to witness the new couple greet their awaiting public, save for a few key members of the royal staff.

As Kat moved around the training ring that was normally teeming with knights and their squires, she eyed the vacant space wistfully. She had always dreamed of becoming a knight, or at the very least, learning how to wield a sword, but her parents had forbidden it. Despite their liberal and often accommodating ideas on education, the viscount and viscountess were incredibly careful about how often Katarina was permitted to enter into potentially dangerous situations, especially if she were the one who would be armed . . .

As she rounded the barracks, Kat found herself careening into someone, almost knocking herself onto her backside.

A strong hand grabbed her arm, keeping her upright.

"Ah! Lady Katarina!"

A young knight Kat had seen around the castle smiled at her kindly. He looked as though he were the same age as her, but the silvery chainmail over his black tunic told Kat he was in fact one of the elite knights . . . which meant he had to be in his late twenties at the youngest.

"Sorry about that, sir . . . ?" Kat grinned while offering her hand to shake his.

The blond knight with kind pale blue eyes and a soft smile looked at her hand, then back at her golden gaze as he carefully reached out, turned her palm downward, and bowed.

He failed to notice her good-natured smile fade as he greeted her as he would a proper noblewoman. "I am Sir Hugo Cas of the elite knights, my lady."

It was when he straightened again that Sir Cas noticed Kat's expression had grown shuttered.

"Nice to meet you; I'm just on my way to . . . the stables . . . for a walk . . ." the redhead began side-stepping the young man and started to worry about being stopped from proceeding with her plan.

"Without an escort? My lady, perhaps you may permit me to—"

Kat hastily interrupted as the point of concern began to develop itself. "Oh, don't worry about me, Sir Cas! I'm sure you have important duties to attend to today! If you'll excuse me, I will just be there and back quite quickly—"

"My lady, I'm afraid I must insist. It is my duty to protect the nobility today. In fact, I was just on my way to relieve one of the knights in the banquet hall for such a task. Forgive me." The knight's apologetic tone and sweet smile only succeeded in annoying Kat.

"I really won't report you, I swear, and I . . . er . . . Godsdamnit," Kat muttered as Sir Cas bowed and gestured toward the stable. The man was clearly resolute and also kind enough not to react to her cursing. That, or perhaps he hadn't heard anything.

Grumbling to herself, Kat continued walking as Sir Cas matched her harried pace, which, given their similar heights, wasn't as easy as it should have been.

"Is there a reason you are in a rush, Lady Katarina?" Sir Cas asked pleasantly.

It only made Kat want to shove him.

"I'm trying to burn off my magic and take care of . . . things," she finished lamely, not wanting to admit to her petty crime of bribing the stablemaster.

"Ah, I heard you are a mutated fire witch! What does 'burning off your magic' entail?" Sir Cas queried with sincere interest.

Kat let out an aggravated sigh. Didn't knights who escorted nobility normally not talk? Why was he so chatty?

"If I don't burn off energy, my magic grows stronger and I get . . . moody," she explained while an unpleasant memory threatened the edges of her mind.

"Hm, that must be difficult for you," Sir Cas mused aloud while nodding sagely.

Kat shot him a wry look out of the corner of her eyes before once again increasing her speed and picking her skirts up a little higher as the mud began to deepen as they neared the stables.

"What happens if your magic gets too pent up then?" Sir Cas asked as he clasped his hands behind his back casually, despite once again increasing the length of his stride to match the noblewoman at his side.

For a moment, Kat's expression grew stiff, and her eyes became lost as the vivid recollection of her hands growing sticky from warm blood snapped into her vision . . .

She gripped her skirts more tightly.

"Nothing much," she lied at last. "You seem unafraid of asking me personal questions. Not that I usually mind, but have we met before?" Kat shot back as she half leapt onto the cobblestone entrance to the stable.

"Oh, well, I've just heard that you are a good-natured noblewoman who, if you're frank with, is easy to get along with. I'm sorry if I've offended you, my lady." Sir Cas stopped and bowed to Kat once more, making her teeth set themselves on edge. "I merely wanted to build good rapport with you, as we will be journeying to Troivack together."

Kat stilled as Sir Cas straightened and smiled again at her.

Once faced with him properly, Katarina could see that he had dimples.

He really did look the pinnacle of innocent and well-meaning . . .

Kat sighed inwardly. She couldn't justify being snarky with him for just doing his job.

"Don't worry. Sorry that I'm being a brat. I'm sometimes not on my best behavior when I don't get my way, and I was hoping to come here alone is all." She managed to shoot him a friendly grin before she moved her hands to her hips.

She was still burning with magic, but at least the itching had lessened thanks to the walk.

"Excuse me then, Sir Cas, I need to have a private word with the stablemaster." She bobbed her chin while beginning to turn away from the knight.

"Ah, pardon me, my lady, but the stablemaster is actually part of the celebrations at the front of the castle."

"Son of a bitch," Kat blurted out while throwing her hands in the air and closing her eyes in exasperation. She didn't witness the startled look on Sir Cas's face followed by his nervous smile.

Sighing, Kat trudged off the cobblestones into the mud.

"My lady, perhaps pick your skirts up so they don't—"

Sir Cas's words were cut short when Kat managed to trip over her own hem. For the second time that day, the knight reached to catch her, but unfortunately, he was not as successful as the first time. Both the lady and knight wound up splayed across the mud, Kat along her side before flopping onto her back and Sir Cas straight onto his back.

"My lady! My lady, are you alright? I'm so sorry I wasn't able to—" Sir Cas was unable to finish his sentence as he righted himself into a seated position, having found that Lady Katarina was laughing.

At first it was a small chuckle, but soon she was clutching her middle, and rolling even farther into the mud.

"Ahh . . . that's more like it," Kat finally wheezed before she sat up and wiped tears of humor from her cheeks with the backs of her wrists.

"Forgive me for saying this, my lady, but you are almost exactly how everyone has described you," Sir Cas said while getting up to his feet and offering his own muddied hand to her.

Kat's smile brightened as she clasped his forearm instead of his hand and allowed him to haul her up to her feet.

"I thank you kindly for that." She flicked her long, dirtied hair over her shoulder. "Well, I better get back and see what I can do about this."

Sir Cas chuckled, though he looked a little nervous. "Will you be in a great deal of trouble? I'm truly sorry, again, that I didn't catch you in time."

"How is my clumsiness your problem? Come now, I'll take the servants' stairwell by the west corridor back to my chamber and no one will suspect a thing."

Sir Cas nodded his head and slowly followed the redhead he was beginning to suspect was perhaps even a little more bizarre than even the rumors had suggested. Meanwhile, Kat resumed her swift pace, heading back up the gentle slope that would take them to the barracks once more.

This time, Sir Cas didn't try to endear himself further to her, as he still felt rather embarrassed over not preventing their fall; Kat didn't seem to mind, as she hummed happily. It was as though she felt more like herself and less confined when she no longer had to mind her dress.

Upon reaching the barracks, Sir Cas bowed to her once more. "I-I'm sorry, again, my lady."

Kat only laughed again. "Sir Cas, if you're to see more of me in Troivack, I suggest you get used to seeing me like this." She then proceeded to gesture to her dirty dress, unaware that she had also smeared mud on her cheek earlier.

Sir Cas couldn't help but wince, but Kat pretended not to see it.

Then, without another word, she spun on her heel and left the poor knight behind as her arms swung gaily at her sides.

The best part of her taking an untimely—if predictable—fall was that she would have the perfect excuse to be late to the reception, or miss it entirely, which meant she could filch a bottle of moonshine and find her own amusements. A favorable turn of events indeed!

So tickled about this fortuitous development was she, that Kat had forgotten about her promise to keep an eye on Alina's brother.

Kat was just about to skip the rest of the way to the west entrance, when she passed by a small group of knights huddled together. Some smoked cigars, and all were laughing and seemed in fine spirits. That is, until they noticed her presence.

Kat waved without looking at them. "Sorry, lads! Carry on!"

"M-my lady!" One knight called out hesitantly, making the redhead stop and turn while still wearing a smile.

She didn't mind explaining that she was unharmed or in any distress; it would even help spread the story of why she had to be excused from the reception.

However, when she laid eyes on the group, she realized the knight hadn't been drawing her attention to ask if she were in fact alright . . . It was because she needed to curtsy to the Daxarian crown prince who stood amongst them.

Of . . . bloody . . . course, Kat couldn't help but think as her golden eyes officially met with the hazel pair belonging to Eric Reyes.

He regarded Kat's ethereal gaze indifferently before he surveyed the rest of her mud-splattered self. By the end, his only reaction was a raised eyebrow and a drag from his cigar, his lined face unreadable.

Feeling all kinds of oddities brewing within herself, Kat reacted as she often did when faced with unfortunate circumstances.

Dramatically.

Throwing her arm straight into the air, she swept down into an outrageous curtsy before straightening.

"Good day, Your Highness! Please excuse me, I have mud down my arse!"

Then she turned and swept away without waiting to see his response, though she did walk a little faster.

She had just placed her foot on the bottom step to the castle entrance when she noticed a familiar dark shape in her periphery. Her stomach flipped as she slowly, with sagging shoulders, turned to face the figure she knew all too well.

Viscount Finlay Ashowan, a legend in his own time, stood leaning against the castle wall, and he was looking properly furious at his daughter.

Smiling at him with a grimace mixed in, Kat once again couldn't help but speak before thinking.

"Shit."

CHAPTER 3

TUB TALKS

Kat waited as her father strode over to her, his blue eyes already glimmering with magic—which often happened when his emotions were running a little high.

"What happened, Kat?" Finlay Ashowan asked, his voice low.

All too aware of their audience of a handful of knights and the prince of Daxaria nearby in the training ring, Kat's smile grew strained as she responded through her teeth.

"I went for a walk and tripped. Honest accident, Da."

For a beat of silence, the viscount looked as though he were going to embark on a horribly long lecture, but instead, he closed his eyes and let out a small breath, though his shoulders remained stiff.

"Go order a bath; your mother's already looking for you. We will talk about your behavior shortly."

"But Da, it really was just—"

There was a sharpness in the viscount's face when his eyes slid back to her that had Kat shutting her mouth firmly and turning slowly back toward the castle entrance.

For some reason, her father already seemed angry about something, but given their witnesses, it wasn't the time or place to pester him about it.

So, Katarina resumed her trudge back up to her chamber, leaving Finlay Ashowan to turn, his expression hard, to stare directly at the crown prince.

Eric let out a plume of cigar smoke as the knights began to shift uncomfortably around him.

Striding over to the group, his hands easing into his pockets, Finlay never let his gaze leave the prince's.

"Your Highness," he greeted flatly.

The knights began ambling away from the two nobles as the air practically crackled with tension.

Or perhaps it *was* crackling. It tended to happen with the infamous house witch at times . . .

"Viscount, is there anything *else* you'd like to say that wasn't mentioned on the trip here?" Eric asked with a cold half smile.

Finlay's expression remained unchanged as he continued staring darkly at the prince. "How are you enjoying your sister's wedding?" he asked with feigned casualness.

The hostility in Eric's eyes wavered, and for a moment, anger and sadness flashed across his features. The display of emotion did not last long, and soon it was replaced by a bitter, resigned smile.

"She looked lovely. I trust Alina made a decision she believed would be best for herself."

Finlay tilted his head over his shoulder, his blue eyes electric and intent. "Did you even read her letters?"

Eric glowered. "Once again, Viscount, you've overstepped your boundaries."

"Not as a friend."

"I thought we stopped being friends a good few years ago."

"I'm still friends with your father, and my children, to the princess," Fin replied calmly, though his posture remained rigid.

Eric let out a harsh laugh. "Amazing how even your kin manage to weasel their way into important positions. Tell me, have they already figured out how best to backstab my sister?"

"I never backstabbed you." Finlay's eyes shone brighter as he watched Eric barely resist a jeer.

"Right. Even though it was you who told me friends don't abandon each other." Eric's voice had turned hoarse, but his stare remained icy.

Watching the prince for another tense moment, Finlay finally shook his head, the pain and disappointment in his eyes potent. "I merely refused to let you use me. Now, I'm going to return to your sister's wedding reception, but don't think I won't be watching you. You will not hurt the princess or your father today of all days. You've done that enough."

Finlay turned his back to Eric, his shoulders beginning to round against the furious stare he knew was boring into his back.

"You've your part to play in this mess as well," Eric called out before taking another puff off his cigar.

Stopping in his tracks, Finlay turned his chin so that only part of his profile could be seen by the prince.

"No, Your Highness. I don't. I've excused myself from the consequences of your choices." The viscount continued walking away, but as he moved, he called back loud enough for anyone near to hear. "Besides, Your Highness, I am the lesser demon you will face. Your sister is no longer the type to keep quiet about wrongs done to her."

Eric glared at Finlay's back as his former friend disappeared into the castle's darkness.

Once the house witch had disappeared completely from his sight, Eric returned his attention to his cigar and resumed consumption of his vice, though the pleasure it usually brought was dampened. Despite not wanting to harbor an ounce of care toward Finlay Ashowan, the exchange with the man he had once held the utmost respect and reverence for brought a heavy weight over his heart.

After all, the viscount had been a man Eric considered as one of his closest friends and confidants since childhood . . . Giving his head a small shake, he tried to free the growing sense of loss. He didn't need to worry about past wounds today of all days.

"Honestly! Falling in the mud? Are you a child? How in the world did you manage this?" Annika Ashowan's exasperation yielded a disconcerting lack of reaction from her daughter. A fact that made the servants present feel all the more uncomfortable.

Kat was in the process of attempting to blow the bubbles off the tip of her nose, allowing her eyes to cross as she did so, completely nonplussed by her mother's disapproval.

"I was going for a walk to take care of the magitch. I didn't mean to trip!" Kat finally managed to say once catching sight of her mother's raised, expectant eyebrow.

"Don't think for a second you can use your magitch as an excuse every time you want to avoid your noble obligations." Annika slowly folded her arms across her middle.

"Mum, I went for a walk and tripped. Do we *really* need to go on and on about—"

"Why were you on a walk by the stables?"

Kat's mouth froze for a moment while blowing bubbles, then her expression shifted to one of innocence as she became interested in flicking small droplets of water up in the air.

"Katarina Ashowan . . . what did you do?" Annika's warning tone was known to make hardened criminals sweat and tremble.

Her daughter, however, squinted up at the ceiling as though she were struggling to count each and every stone.

"I . . . was . . . taking care of something I had prepared just in case . . ."

Annika's arms fell to her sides, her eyes narrowed. "Everyone, please excuse us. I'd like a private talk with my daughter."

The maids nearly collided with one another as they sprinted toward the door in an unceremonious herd.

Once safely alone, Annika strode over to the foot of the tub, her stare boring into her daughter's profile as Kat actively avoided making eye contact with her mother.

"You arranged an escape plan without the princess's consent, didn't you?"

Kat bit down on her tongue. She didn't have the gall to lie to her mother when she'd guessed the truth so pointedly.

"For having crafted the plan, you have my regards."

Shocked, Kat's golden eyes flew to her mother's face and saw that a corner of her mouth had lifted.

"However, it was sloppily executed. You should have had someone you trusted disband the evidence. Or at the very least, been disguised. You are too noticeable, and infamous. Discretion is your best friend, Katarina."

"I feel at this point in my life, we should try to find a new best friend for me instead of 'discretion,' given my personality. We both know I'm too much like Da . . . I can't hide my nonsense."

Annika sighed before stepping closer to her daughter and kneeling beside the tub.

"It's accurate to say that you cannot hide your true intentions and thoughts . . . you burn too brightly for that. However, because you are like your father, I know all your mischief comes from a sincerely good place. It just lacks refinement or—"

"Discipline." Kat groaned. That word had become the bane of her existence.

"Precisely. Kat, do you know how you will be protecting Alina while in Troivack?" Annika rested her elbow on the edge of the tub before folding her hands together.

"By annoying courtiers who act like arses toward her?"

Annika took in a deep breath while her eyes closed for a moment, clearly forcing patience to reenter her body.

"No. You are to be the perfect assistant to her. Her handmaiden who doesn't have a hidden agenda. You are to be loyal to her and look out for any precarious situations around her. I have no doubt that there are many who are displeased with the Troivackian king choosing her as his bride. You will need to be on alert at all times, and for the love of the Gods, my girl . . . do not act impulsively. Otherwise, you could hurt those around you."

Resisting the urge to slouch back in the bath, Kat instead managed to force herself to reach up and clasp her mother's hand. "I'll do my best."

The viscountess surprised her then as she leaned forward and kissed Kat's forehead.

Annika Ashowan was not usually an affectionate woman.

"Katarina Ashowan . . ." Annika trailed off for a moment, her face unreadable as Kat tried her best to discern what her mother could possibly be thinking. "I love you, my only daughter. You, who have kept me awake and tested my sanity since the day you were born . . . Please. Please remember if you lose your way, you'll remember where you hail from. It's easy to lose ourselves in new places."

Kat stilled as she lifted her gaze to her mother.

"Did you get lost when you first came here to Daxaria?"

Annika's face grew sad for a moment before a smile lit her features. She had been known as the most beautiful woman in all of Daxaria when she had first arrived to wed a man decades older than herself.

"I was probably more lost than you'll ever be. I had no idea what a proper family or home was, and I never thought I would want such things for myself. It wasn't until I married my first husband, Hank Jenoure, and we became friends that I even realized how alone I truly had been."

"So, after Hank died, you knew what you were looking for? When you met Da, you knew right away?" Kat asked interestedly. Her mother was a private woman, and to hear her admit such personal things was a rare treat.

"Gods, no. Hank died, and for the first time ever, I felt lonely. Even though I had been that way before, it felt different because I knew what it could feel like to have someone there for you. But a friend is not a husband or even necessarily a substitute for family . . ." Annika's gaze became distant as she stared at the bathwater, lost in memory.

"Your father annoyed the living daylights out of me when we first met, but . . . despite everyone else gravitating toward him, and him seeming like he knew the right answers to everything, he was just as alone as I was. Yet when we were together, it felt as though there was finally someone who was the same—and different—in all the right ways. We complemented each other's weaknesses and strengths, and brought out sides of each other we didn't know we had. Next thing I knew, I had someone with me who I could always count on."

A small flush crept across Annika's face, and Kat's mind fell quiet as she witnessed her mother's obvious love for her father.

The viscountess was an impenetrable, mysterious woman who Kat still felt like she barely knew could have such a side, and seeing such an expression humbled her a little. She felt like a little girl again, watching her mother do something that seemed beyond her own scope or capabilities.

"Ah well. Enough reminiscing. I suppose it's because I'm getting old that I'm prone to such moments." Annika gracefully rose, though she winced when her knees cracked.

"Mum?" Kat spoke up as a question she had been wondering about for years surged forward.

"Hm?" Annika asked while gracefully stretching her neck.

"Does it ever bother you that Da is aging a lot slower than you?"

The viscountess's eyes drifted down to her daughter, her features once again schooled. Regardless, it was clear there was a calm underneath their surface.

"I get scared for the day when he won't be by my side anymore. Your grandmother's curse on your father may be helpful in preventing him from being sick and healing his wounds instantly, but . . . it is called a curse for a reason. We will have to accept the pain we are due. The gift from the Goddess of bringing him back alive came with the added magic your grandmother bestowed him, it is not a power to be taken lightly. We always knew that grand gifts come with grand prices."

Kat felt uneasiness broil in her stomach. Everyone had heard of how her grandmother, Katelyn Ashowan, a mutated witch with extraordinary healing abilities, had sacrificed her life in exchange for her son to return from the forest of the afterlife. However, when a witch dies after overusing their magic, a curse is formed.

When Katarina's father had returned to life, he had been cursed, but it had been easy to forget until the wear of the years showed on their mother but barely on their father.

"You do not need to worry about your da and me just yet. For now, you need to finish growing up." Annika smiled kindly down at her daughter as she strode over to the door, signaling the end of their conversation.

Kat felt her thoughts idly sift through her mother's wisdom while once again relaxing in the soapy water. At least the rest of her night was going to pass in a far more pleasant manner. The redhead happily recalled her stash of moonshine under the fireplace woodpile of her chamber.

"By the way, I had a backup dress prepared for you for the wedding reception. Just in case you had any plans on missing it to drink moonshine alone and go out on a night ride," Annika called over her shoulder.

Kat sat up alarmed, her eyes wide, bathwater splashing to the floor.

How did her mother *always* know her plans?!

CHAPTER 4

GARDEN GREETINGS

Dusk had settled over the castle, and thus the night's activities were only just beginning.

While dancing, drinking, and merriment poured out of the banquet hall, most of the attendees of the royal wedding remained within its four walls—the evening far too young to think about bed or sneaking off for a secret tryst.

However, a certain redheaded noblewoman had already claimed one of the stone benches in the castle courtyard. It was tucked away and difficult to see between two flowering shrubs with blooms of pale blues and purples.

Leaning her head back against the cool stone wall, Kat could feel her index finger restlessly tapping against the stone. The brilliant greenery was dotted with lazily drifting fireflies that revealed small bursts of color amongst the beautiful space, but despite the crickets being the only sound in the otherwise still night, Kat didn't feel peaceful at all.

She desperately needed to move again, or to consume an impressive amount of Troivackian moonshine. Otherwise, she was likely to get irritable after being forced to behave properly for so long . . .

Lowering her gaze to the dress her mother had prepared in advance for her, she grimaced. It was a mint-colored gown with lighter, breezier material . . . a color and style Kat typically tried to avoid since it tended to make men assume she'd be the blushing type, for whatever reason.

Of course, her mother had arranged the backup gown as a punishment for whatever her daughter would do to ruin the first dress.

While glumly looking to the heavens above her, Kat was about to force herself back to the reception, but the sound of someone's footsteps drew her attention.

Peering through the shadows effortlessly, her eyes already magically gleaming, Kat easily spotted the crown prince of Daxaria striding into the courtyard by himself.

She raised an eyebrow and straightened her shoulders interestedly.

It was the perfect chance to watch and see if the future king was up to anything suspicious.

The prince suddenly stopped in his tracks and turned around several times as though looking for someone . . . and that was when he noticed Kat. His tense expression immediately shifted back to one of indiscernibility.

For a moment, neither of them moved, and Katarina was beginning to wonder if she was about to get in trouble yet again, when the prince tilted his head over his shoulder and raised an eyebrow briefly before strolling over to her casually.

"Not enjoying the party, Lady Katarina?" he asked while moving one hand into his pocket.

Kat eyed the prince from head to toe. He was dressed in a crisp black tunic with a white coat, white trousers, and black boots. He had discarded his ceremonial mantle, and oddly, he didn't wear any other finery. He dressed the part of the dashing prince, but his worn face and deadened eyes indicated a different character beneath the clothes.

"Just biding my time, Your Highness," Kat finally responded ambiguously.

Despite waiting a moment to see if she might expand on her answer, the prince didn't receive any more information.

"Feel free to call me Eric when we're alone," he announced casually as he continued studying Kat in turn.

"Sure thing, Your Hi—er, Eric. Would you like to take a seat? Or would you like me to leave you alone? Or—" Kat began, unsure of what he was thinking. His eyes had a strange calm and his face bore no emotion as he watched her . . .

"I think I'll take you up on that seat now that you've mentioned it." Sitting himself down smoothly without a moment's hesitation, Kat couldn't help but shift slightly at his sudden nearness.

"So, what brings you out here, Your—I mean, Eric?" the redhead asked, while noticing her heart beating a little too quickly.

Letting out a long breath before stretching out his legs, the prince leaned back against the stone wall.

"I'm not used to being around everyone again." He paused, gaze cast down to the ground and lost in thought, before he let out a small chuckle.

"Though I'm glad Lord Dick Fuks is still doing well. He was always one of my favorite people."

"Yes, I'm really glad his grandson, Ass Fuks, seems to be taking after him so well."

Eric went rigid, his head snapping up to stare at Kat before he let out a bellow of a laugh. "Gods, I had forgotten about his grandson! I never realized his nickname when they'd named him Aster . . ."

Kat grinned. "Yes, Lord Fuks pretended to be on his deathbed in order to get the naming rights . . . his son, Les Fuks, should have guessed something was amok."

"So, when did our beloved earl let his son know about the planned nickname?"

"Oh . . . he gave them a good two years of bliss before he called him Ass. My guess is it gave Les Fuks's new wife time to settle down after the birth."

Eric smiled and nodded to himself. "Our elderly earl is a master strategist after all."

Kat's smile widened as she, too, slumped back against the wall while noting the hard lines of Eric's profile. She then observed his crossed ankles, a sign that he had no intention of leaving soon.

"So, where've you been all this time?" Kat blurted the words before stopping herself.

The prince stilled, then glanced at her expectant face out of the corner of his eyes.

"I've been around. Wasn't really in one place, so it was hard to send letters and the like—just in case you were about to ask why I hadn't written my sister."

Without missing a beat, Kat asked the next most prevalent question on her mind. "What did you fight about with my da?"

This time Eric didn't bother hiding his incredulous, wry expression over her candid question as he faced his interrogator more squarely.

"You know, I haven't heard much about the court since I've been gone, but you are definitely living up to what I've heard about you in the ten hours I've been back."

Kat shrugged nonchalantly. "If you had a chance to ask someone who had disappeared all kinds of questions without an audience, wouldn't you want to?"

Eric stared at her in mild awe for several long moments until, at long last, she blushed.

Sighing and shaking his head wearily, unable to stop a small smile of amusement at her shamelessness, he slumped forward to rest his forearms on his thighs.

His humor over Kat's bluntness faded then as his mind turned to the inquiry. "I suppose I'll be getting these questions a lot. Honestly, your father was always a terrible liar. I'm shocked he's kept quiet for so long."

"We all are," Kat muttered before she mirrored the prince's style of sitting and rested her chin in her hands.

Eric laughed bitterly. "Well . . . in answer to your question . . . your father, Finlay Ashowan, more or less told me once he stepped down for your brother to take over as viscount, that he would go back to being a cook. He didn't want any work befitting nobility. Nothing with regards to being a diplomat for the coven, not as an advisor, absolutely nothing. I took exception to that, given how when I eventually take over as king, I'd been hoping to at least have a friend there to help."

Kat's eyes widened as she sat stunned in disbelief.

"W-What? My father said that? But . . . But that doesn't make sense! Why would he—"

"Ah, ah. I think I've been plenty generous in my answer. That was a rather personal question after all, so I think it's only fair you answer some of mine."

Kat clamped her mouth shut and did her best to stop herself from further exclamations. She desperately wanted to find out why on earth her father would do such a thing . . . It wasn't like him to abandon a friend . . .

"Your eyes are glowing. I know you're some kind of fire witch, but can you actually see in the dark?" Eric asked interestedly as he once again turned to face her golden gaze.

Unable to stop the agitated sigh from leaving her, Kat slumped back into her original position against the wall.

"Yes, yes. Mutated witch here. I'm not a pure witch who can make and control fire, but I can eat a lot, see in the dark if I want, stay awake longer, and I am never really cold."

Eric nodded slowly in understanding. "Those are all incredibly handy attributes."

Kat didn't bother replying. She was used to every response in the book.

"What was this I heard from the other knights about you having a 'magitch'?"

At this she smiled. "Ah. Another little side effect about my magic is that my body burns energy constantly, so it's hard for me to stay still for long periods of time. I've called it my magitch because if it gets to be too bad, it feels like my skin is itching something fierce."

Eric leaned back, his eyes fixed on her once more. "I'm surprised then that you aren't dancing up a storm at the reception, with an affliction like that. I've no doubt you have a small horde of suitors after you, so finding a partner wouldn't be difficult."

Kat blushed again and failed at hiding her small, wolfish grin of pleasure at his words. "Well . . . I do have a few willing to brave an interaction with me . . . but to be honest, I find it hard behaving properly. So, I often try to escape."

Eric leaned toward her conspiratorially so that his face was only a few inches from her own, and all at once, Kat felt a different kind of heat than she was used to spreading through her body.

"Believe it or not, I'm the same way. I prefer to invite whoever I like to such events so that we can all behave comfortably." Eric's voice had quieted and turned slightly hoarse.

Kat's gaze dropped to his lips that were beginning to turn up into a small grin. When she leaned a little closer, however, blinking slowly, Eric hesitated.

"Lady Katarina, I suggest you go back into the reception before I misunderstand this . . . exchange." Despite his words, the prince was shifting even closer to her still . . .

He smelled of cigars and ale, but the night was filled with the smell of warmed earth and flowers around them.

The burning in Kat's belly was eroding away any rational thoughts she had on the strange situation . . . So instead of trying to cool herself down, she followed her impulse and kissed him first.

Eric's shock lasted all but a second before he closed his eyes and kissed her back.

His one hand reached to cup her face, while the other gently squeezed her upper arm.

The hungry flame in Kat began to burn brighter as she slanted her body instinctively closer to his, her entire being awash in sensations she didn't know she was capable of possessing.

She didn't know how long they sat kissing, especially once it deepened. All thoughts had vanished, and all that remained was the heat under her skin and a type of desire entirely new to her . . .

When the two finally broke apart, both were slightly out of breath.

"Listen, you are quite spectacular, but . . . you are only . . . twenty . . . and still unwed. This . . . could spiral badly." Eric inclined himself away from her, then cleared his throat as he slightly rounded his shoulders over his middle, his eyes fixed on the ground.

"Oh, don't . . . don't worry. I've done . . . things . . . to some extent before." Kat informed him awkwardly before chastising herself internally.

She hadn't meant to sound so . . . wanton.

Eric chuckled dryly, still unable to meet her stare. "Right. The daughter of Finlay Ashowan not being one of the most protected and cherished women on the continent? Pardon me, Lady Katarina, but I don't buy that for a second."

Kat rolled her eyes. "You've been back, say . . . ten and a half hours? Yet that's all the time it took for this little development. Perhaps don't underestimate my ability to— "

Eric turned and faced her, his expression once again schooled. "Ability to what exactly?"

Kat fumbled her words under his intense stare. "I-I just meant I'm not as coddled as you may think. I— "

"Lady Katarina?!" A woman's voice interrupted the couple, which subsequently dismissed Kat's argument.

Eric shot her a clear *I told you so* expression, which she pointedly ignored for the sake of her pride.

"Oh, at least it's just Hannah," Kat remarked glibly while peering through the dark at the silhouette who had appeared in the well-lit doorway to the courtyard.

"Hannah? You're father's old friend and former kitchen aide? I thought she would've gone to work at your parents' estate by now."

"Ah, we've offered, but she's refused countless times. Though given that she's in line to take over for Ruby once she retires, it was the right choice in the end." Kat stood up and turned to face the prince whose expression had once again become distant.

"I'll go. You stay here for a bit. Don't worry, I won't expect marriage or something . . . but . . . I did enjoy our time. So . . . thanks!" Kat scurried out of the brush, already trying not to cringe over her graceless farewell.

Once Hannah heard and turned toward the rustle of the shrubbery, Kat picked up her pace. She strode purposefully toward the doorway to the castle corridor where the petite older woman with blond hair streaked with white stood with her hands on her hips expectantly, though there was the unmistakable glint of fondness in her dark blue eyes.

As soon as she was within reach, Hannah grabbed her by the arm. "Alright, you. I appreciate that you didn't leave the castle grounds this time, but come now. Even your brother is managing to stay through the reception. I admit he looks like he is being pricked with a hundred needles, but he's there!"

Katarina laughed while moving away hastily from the courtyard to minimize the risk of Hannah asking if she had been with anyone . . .

Though as she walked, she couldn't deny that she was feeling all sorts of strange over what had just transpired.

She had been kissed before, and more than once, but . . . never had it elicited such a response from her.

Furthermore, what had the prince been doing out there to begin with? Even if he wanted a break from the reception, unlike her, he could have gone outside the castle grounds freely.

As her brain whirred back to life, another thought prevailed upon her. Why had her father refused to help Eric once he took over the throne? And even more frustrating, once again, zero information had been gleaned about where in the world the prince had spent the last four years.

CHAPTER 5

HAUNTED HALLS

Eric sat in the darkness for a long while after Katarina Ashowan had been whisked back to his sister's wedding reception, his pulse still thundering, and his nerves still rattled.

He had not intended for things to go so far with her.

"Must've been the ale. Needed a distraction," Eric muttered to himself nonsensically while rubbing his eyes.

Reaching into his pocket, the prince pulled free a small, worn leather pouch.

I knew Sir Smiths hadn't straightened himself out completely just yet, Eric thought to himself idly about one of his former acquaintances. As he began to loosen the pouch ties, his lips curved into what some could misinterpret as a smile, were it not for the soullessness in his eyes.

"Running away so soon, are we?"

Eric froze.

Slowly, he lifted his face up to see none other than Finlay Ashowan staring down at him in the darkness, his blue eyes glowing and magical as ever, with his hands placed expectantly on his hips.

"I believe the courtyard is still castle grounds. Hardly running away." Eric moved to place the pouch back in his pocket while pulling free a cigar from the other side of his coat.

"I warned you that I'd be watching. Now, I think that bag in your left pocket should be disposed of elsewhere, don't you think?"

Eric hesitated in drawing out the spill he had stowed to light his cigar, and instead removed the vice between his front teeth while rising.

"Mind your business, Viscount," the prince warned coolly.

Fin's eyes shone brighter. "It is your sister's wedding. She has not seen you in years, and believe me, she missed you. Now go back into that reception, leave that bag with me, and we will forget this happened."

Eric chuckled darkly. "I know for a fact you can't magic another's belongings off their person. You're jumping to one too many assumptions, Viscount, and if you continue to cross the line, I'll—"

"You'll what? Call the guards?" Fin stepped closer to the prince, his fierce gaze boring down on his former friend who stood several inches shorter than himself. "Go ahead. They'll be very interested to hear what I have to say, especially once your father is summoned."

Eric momentarily glared up at Fin without a word before shouldering past him roughly. Fin didn't bother calling the prince back or getting angry over the aggression. He knew better.

After watching Eric once again place the cigar back in his mouth as he retreated to the castle, Fin turned his attention toward a brushing movement against his ankle.

"Did you get it?"

Finlay's familiar, Kraken, gazed up at him. His fluffy black fur almost perfectly blended into the night save for the dash of white on his chest.

"*I did indeed*," Kraken meowed, then batted the small leather pouch onto Fin's boot.

"Thank you. Annika saved some fat from the beef tonight for you; you'll find it in your bowl at home." The viscount bent down to grab the pouch, his brow furrowed.

"*An adequate reward for my efforts. Tell me, does the mostly grown kitten still need my spies on him?*" Kraken chirped while falling into step with his witch as Fin made his way back toward the reception.

"'Mostly grown kitten?' Eric is older than I was when you and I first met," Fin informed his familiar, his tone weighted from his apparent weariness.

"*You weren't fully grown either, until my own guidance*," Kraken retorted glibly.

At this, the viscount laughed while pressing his hands into his pockets. "I suppose you're right about that. Problem is, Eric's not a witch, and I can't think of anyone who can help him right now. He just keeps running and hiding from everything in any way he can."

"*Why not take away all guidance? Leave him no one to blame but himself.*"

Fin stopped in his tracks and rounded on Kraken, who stared up at him with his pupils wide in the dimly lit corridor.

Lifting his chin to stare at the courtyard doorway Eric had just exited, Fin let out a somber breath, then dropped his gaze back to his familiar.

"I think I know what you're suggesting, Kraken . . . and . . . maybe. Maybe it'll work."

Eric continued puffing on the cigar and cursing himself for forgetting that Finlay's familiar was perfectly capable of picking anyone's pockets.

"That Godsdamn cat is lucky he's cute," he grumbled to himself as he stormed the darkened, empty corridors of the castle.

He needed time to clear his head before returning to the reception. Though, as he continued to explore his old home, he realized it had been a terrible idea.

At least at the reception there was Troivackian moonshine, wine, and ale . . .

Eric shook his head.

His sister and father were watching his every move, making him feel as though he were suffocating. The nobles all wanted to shake his hand and speak with him, and every single one of them were trying to glean any nugget of information regarding his whereabouts the past four years . . .

He almost laughed when he realized Katarina Ashowan hadn't been any different.

Though, at the very least, she'd been direct and fun about it.

Eric felt his frown ease slightly as he thought more about the daughter of his former friend.

She was incredibly beautiful and striking at the same time. She was tall like her father, her blazing red hair another similarity, but those golden eyes . . . they were wild, and unlike anything Eric had ever seen before. They looked like they were made of pure magic.

Yes, it was clear that she was a bit of a troublemaker. He thought about her bowing ridiculously and announcing for all to hear about the mud down her arse.

Eric sighed with a shadow of a smile on his face. He could see that she had been raised under privilege and protection—her every move screamed that she was a young woman relishing in the fun of a supervised rebellion.

The prince's mood turned grim again. *Which is yet another reason why I shouldn't have had that bit of fun with her. It's bad enough that she's Fin's daughter . . . not that it's her fault what happened between us . . .*

Stopping in his tracks and closing his eyes, he let out a long breath to ease the guilty ache in his chest.

Well, she did technically kiss me first . . . and she'll be leaving in three days with Alina, so I'm sure this will all become a distant memory. At least right now, she doesn't seem cunning or manipulative, and even if she becomes that way in Troivack, I can ask Sir Vohn to keep an eye out.

Eric opened his eyes again and searched for a sconce in which to dispose the cigar butt he no longer had use for. Only then did he take a proper look around where he had stopped, and he felt his heart plummet into the icy depths of his soul.

He stared at the chamber door that belonged to his parents.

Unbidden memories flooded into his mind before he could silence them.

Do I have to say goodbye?

Mom!

She's not working, she's dying!

Friends don't leave . . .

You're the only one your sister has right now.

"Shut up, shut up, shut up," Eric bit out to himself quietly before knocking his knuckles against his temple.

He started to walk again, quickly and blindly. It was as though he could still hear the shouts of those terrifying days all over again, then the heavy silence that had followed, his governess begging him to calm down . . .

Eric rounded the corner and lunged at the first door he could find and banged it shut behind himself, his breath ragged.

The fireplace was already lit in the random chamber . . .

Just where . . .

Lifting his eyes, Eric fell back against the shut door.

His mother stared down at him.

Her soft, wide brown eyes were smiling and warm as ever.

"Oh . . . Gods . . ." Pain tore through Eric's chest and strangled him.

He had forgotten the room the staff had arranged for him to get ready in wasn't his actual chamber.

Tearing himself away from the portrait of his family, he stared at the bed and felt another stab of emotion when he noticed above the bed hung the sword Captain Antonio had presented to him when he had officially become a sword master.

"Why did they send that here?" Eric's voice rasped desperately, his hands trembling at his sides.

After another torturous breath, darkness began closing in around him. He was being keenly reminded of the familiar pit that had grown larger and deeper in the passing years . . .

Turning, Eric threw open the chamber door and slammed it shut as he launched himself down the castle corridor yet again, all too eager to distance himself from his ghosts.

He needed a distraction.

And he needed it now.

Silks whirled, musicians played tirelessly, everyone drank, and everyone laughed.

Kat leaned her chin in the palm of her hand as she surveyed the dancers with a deceptive calm while her knee bounced relentlessly under the tablecloth.

"I'm surprised the silverware isn't rattling," Tam, Katarina's twin brother, remarked with a hint of amusement.

Turning her gaze to him, Kat regarded Tam flatly. "You haven't changed at all since you were last here. Aren't you supposed to look more like a noble ready to take over a viscount house these days?"

"Missed you too." Tam snorted while keeping his dark eyes fixed on the table in front of him, his long black hair curtaining his features from sight as usual. Despite being her twin, for all of Katarina's bright red hair and golden eyes, her brother was dark, like their mother. Ebony hair that touched his collarbones and often shrouded his features, his dark eyes fixed either on the ground or surface nearest to him, unmoving.

He was unreadable, quiet, well-read, often unmovable . . .

In other words, Katarina's antithesis.

That didn't change the fact that they had been best friends growing up, though recent times had changed the nature of their relationship.

"What were you doing these past few months again? Coven work?" Kat's bored tone told her brother she didn't really care about the answer.

"Don't worry about it." Tam sank back farther into his chair as a pretty, young brunette passed by and shot him a coy glance under her lashes, her invitation clear.

"Tell me, did you just go along as extra baggage for Likon to take care of?" Kat copied her brother's position while folding her arms over her middle.

"Our dear lifelong friend and my assistant didn't suffer in my presence. A welcome change from when he's home around Mum, Da, and you," Tam fired back curtly.

"Ahh, so he was cursing your name every time he went out to do your work for you. Got it." Kat nodded sagely. "Did you see anything interesting? Or are you still just as scared of open spaces and crowds as before?"

Tam cast his sister a brief, sardonic glance before rolling his eyes. "I'm working on it. How goes keeping your arse in a chair and not in trouble?"

Kat stuck her tongue out at her brother.

She loved him, she truly did, but much had changed between them in the past year. They no longer were constantly at each other's sides and talking about anything and everything, sometimes without words, as their understanding of each other ran deeper than most siblings.

No, now there was a gap . . . ever since the events of last summer . . .

Tam sighed and reached for his goblet. "So, where did you disappear to earlier? Hannah found you relatively easily. Were you in the king's moonshine cellar again?"

Kat frowned and was about to make another cutting remark when a young man stepped forward, interrupting them.

"Pardon me, Lady Katarina, but might I . . . that is, would you perhaps like to . . ."

Shifting her expression to an apologetic one, Kat smiled politely. "I'm sorry, Lord . . . ?"

"Rell." The poor young man already looked resigned to her rejection.

"Lord Rell, I'm catching up with my dear brother whom I haven't seen in ages. Perhaps another time?"

Bobbing his head but not bothering to give a proper farewell, the young Lord Rell shuffled back into the crowd.

"I was unaware you have another brother who you feel is so 'dear' to you. I must tell our mother; she will be oh so thrilled." Tam smiled into his goblet as he took a mouthful of wine.

"I'm just tired of being pleasant today is all. It's not that poor fellow's fault." Kat shrugged, her eyes falling to the table.

She wished she were still in the courtyard with the prince. At least there she'd been able to talk about things that mattered instead of "appropriate" topics.

"I think I'll head to bed. I've been here long enough, don't you think?" Kat stood with an exaggerated stretch.

"Mum's already watching you," Tam pointed out lightly.

"Godsdamnit," Kat snapped under her breath, when she, too, noticed her mother eyeing her pointedly. "What if I really am just going to bed, hm?"

Tam glanced up at her. A glint of humor in his expression made it clear no one was going to buy that load of nonsense.

"Fine. I'll just take a quick walk!" Kat blustered while plucking up her skirts and stepping around her brother's seat. "Honestly, I'm heading on a boat to a whole other continent without Da or Mum in three days; it's just pure ridiculousness that I'm treated like a prisoner right until the end."

"Kat?" Tam called out, his tone serious, making his sister turn to stare at him aggravatedly. "Seriously . . . don't do anything. At least for tonight. Alina looks really happy."

Kat's eyes flew up to her best friend, and for a moment she stilled as she watched the princess laugh hard enough to snort, then whisper something in the ear of her new husband, whose expression lightened at whatever delightful quip or observation she had made . . .

Dropping her stare for a moment and swallowing with some difficulty, Kat turned back to her brother, for once looking appropriately sincere.

"I won't do anything. Promise."

Without another word, she turned and exited the banquet hall.

She strode hastily toward the courtyard where she had left the prince perhaps two hours before, but she remained hopeful he was still there given he had not yet returned to the banquet hall.

She just wanted to talk with him a little bit more—that was all—maybe convince him to return to the reception, and they could continue conversing where it was brighter and deemed more acceptable. Or at least talk a little on the way there . . .

When Kat strode into the courtyard, she immediately headed toward the bench she had last seen Eric on, and when she caught a glimpse of white trousers, felt excitement rush through her all the way to her fingertips.

Then as she finished rounding the shrub that had hidden her earlier, she had the unpleasant sensation of excitement flip to sickening shock.

There was Eric, wrapped in a passionate embrace with a noblewoman Kat recognized as a young widow . . . Baroness Pinen. There was a degree of undress already in the works, and thankfully, also a degree of unawareness to their surroundings.

Numbly, Kat stepped backward, then hastily but quietly retreated into the castle, her heart thundering in her chest and her temperature rising rapidly.

She had not been overly attached to him over a simple kiss, nor was she a fool who fell in love over a small moment, but . . .

It was still embarrassing, and that alone stung, which in turn, made Kat angry.

Incredibly, horribly, borderline violently, angry.

CHAPTER 6

A FATHER'S INTERFERENCE

Kat was halfway up the grand staircase to her chamber, her skirts clutched in a death grip in her hands as she thought of several ways she was going to beat the prince within an inch of his life.

It was either that or escape the castle for a night ride, or a very, *very* long walk if she were to avoid rotting away in a cell for causing his death.

Kat was mildly aware that there was a faint orange glow around herself, and she knew that it was a sign that her magic was beginning to build.

I need to calm down . . . calm . . . down . . . she managed to narrate to herself despite imagining cutting off the prince's stupid ponytail when he wasn't looking.

"Kat?"

Halting in her tracks, the redheaded noblewoman waited.

She saw Kraken before she saw her father, and the little familiar let out a prolonged "*Meeeeooooooooooooow*" before he began to wind himself around her legs.

When Finlay Ashowan appeared in his daughter's vision, he noted the aura around her with a worried crease between his brows.

As was the norm for the cook-turned-viscount, despite wearing a rich navy-blue coat with black cuffs and black trousers, the former house witch had already disposed of the matching black cravat, allowing his snowy white tunic to remain loose at the throat. It always succeeded in giving him a comfortable, casual image, and it usually worked in helping even his daughter feel a little more at ease in formal situations.

"What's wrong, Kitty Kat?"

"Nothing! I just haven't been able to burn off any Godsdamn magic because you and Mum keep my arse chained to a chair!" Katarina snapped angrily, the magical aura around her growing.

Fin's expression turned to one of pained worry, adding a sense of guilt to the whirl of emotions Kat felt.

"Would you like to go on a ride?" Fin asked, his eyes turning up in a small smile, though sadness still lurked around his mouth. "It'll probably be the last time you and I can go before you leave for Troivack."

Kat stilled, and the flicker of magic around her dimmed as she remembered that she soon wouldn't be around her parents every day . . .

Letting out a short, heated breath, she felt a sliver of her anger dissipate. "Alright. Can you make the horses fly again? That was a lot of fun."

Fin coughed and cleared his throat while glancing around nervously. "Maybe—and remember that's a secret between you and me. Your mother would kill me."

Kat smiled brilliantly and nodded in response, the glow surrounding her dwindling to something that could be written off as a trick of the eyes.

Stepping forward, his loving gaze lightening his daughter's burden unbeknownst to him, Fin offered his arm to Kat.

Accepting his escort happily, Kat did her best not to bring up the image of the prince carrying on with another woman so soon after their own time together. Instead, she wanted to enjoy one of her few remaining nights with her father, who was the only person in the world she felt some semblance of understanding from. It was the first time since it had been arranged for her to journey to Troivack that it truly began to sink in that she would be leaving everything she had known in her twenty years of life . . . and soon . . . she would be alone.

When she turned and gazed up at her father, who gripped her hand a little more tightly, she felt her heart ache.

"Da . . . after you met Mum, were you ever tempted by other women?" Kat asked as they continued to descend the stairs.

Fin's happy expression faltered as he turned to stare at his daughter with a mask of delicate control.

"Why ever would you ask that, Kitty Kat?"

Katarina had heard her father's quiet voice before and knew that if she told him the truth, there would be a probable chance the crown prince would go missing once again, but this time into a deep hole in an unknown location . . .

"Earlier, Mum was talking about when you first met," Kat replied hastily. Fortunately, that was the truth . . . If she had to make up a pure lie on the spot, she would be ousted immediately.

Fin relaxed slightly. "Your mother was and, in my opinion, still is the most beautiful woman on the continent. Not to mention I was too invested in my work to notice or be drawn to anyone else. She just kept badgering me until I took notice," the viscount recanted while smiling fondly to himself.

Kat felt her mouth turn upward. "Really? 'Cause Mum says you were the annoying one."

"Ha." Fin shook his head. "Next time you see her, ask her which of us kept showing up in *my* kitchen."

Kat raised an amused eyebrow as they set foot on the first floor of the castle. "I once heard rumors that she had asked you to be with her twice before you gave in. Is that true?"

Fin chuckled before his eyes sobered. "Absolutely. Though, it isn't a point of pride. I hurt your mother both those times out of my own cowardice. Gods know I tried not to, but . . . sometimes fate doesn't take kindly to being ignored."

"When did you know you'd fallen for her?" Kat asked as they approached the castle's front doors.

Fin stopped and turned to face his daughter squarely. "Kitty Kat, you're beginning to worry me with all of these questions about love and marriage."

"Well, it could happen to me someday I suppose . . ." Kat sighed glumly. Seeing his daughter's sincere displeasure over the thought of marriage did wonders in helping Fin once again relax.

He resumed escorting his daughter through the castle doors into the pleasant, cool night air, where two guards nodded to him as they passed.

"Well . . . when it came to your mother, it was funny. It was like we kept orbiting each other, growing closer and closer, until we couldn't resist anymore, though your mother is far smarter than I and worked it out that we should be together a lot faster."

The father and daughter stepped down onto the gravel of the castle drive, and Fin summoned a steward to request two steeds.

"Huh . . . I doubt I'll be able to dance around in orbit to anything . . ." Kat chuckled dryly to herself.

Fin cast a sidelong glance at his daughter after sending the steward off.

"You know, Kat, for whoever your partner is meant to be, it'll simply feel as though it is easy to be yourself with them. In all your forms."

At this, Kat stiffened as she turned her gaze to her father, her apprehension over his meaning clear.

Rather than dwelling on the glimpse of an unspoken but understood fear of his daughter's, Fin concluded his insight with one final thought.

"Aside from that, my advice would be not to have any expectations. Sometimes the people we are meant for are ones we grow into belonging with."

"Hm." Kat's golden eyes surveyed the city of Austice that lay before her. Music and shouts of jubilance rang up to them as its citizens celebrated the royal wedding.

"Don't think about marriage just yet, Kitty Kat. It's hard enough letting you go to Troivack for now." Fin nudged his daughter's ribs gently, his tone affectionate, which in turn made Kat smile.

"I'm still amazed you trusted me to go by myself," she remarked with an impish glint in her eyes.

Fin groaned. "Gods, you better write to us. I don't think I'll be able to sleep this entire year. Do you know how much moonshine I've had to order for your mother since you've begun your lessons with her?"

Kat laughed. "It'll be alright, Da. I'll only annoy a *couple* nobles. I'll choose them carefully."

Feeling a squeeze from his daughter's hand once more, Fin continued smiling as he began to lecture her again about not bothering seemingly unpleasant nobles, though it was clear by his tone he wasn't being too serious . . .

Turning to watch the horses being led toward them, Kat realized something important that evening . . . something she knew would stay with her for the rest of her days . . .

Whoever I end up loving, should love me back as much as my da loves my mum.

Kat sat at the kitchen table the morning after the reception. As she finished off the apple in her hand, she idly scratched the back of Kraken's neck, who lay peacefully in her lap.

Most of the castle's occupants were still in bed following the wedding reception, and no one was up save for a few members of the kitchen staff, who were beginning to tidy the banquet halls in preparation for the late breakfast for the nobles.

The royal cook was a former kitchen aide of Katarina's father, a man named Peter, who was in the middle of slicing strawberries in the quiet morning while she sipped her tea and began thinking about the last items she should pack for when she would set sail to Troivack in another two days.

All was peaceful when the door leading to the gardens by the castle opened with a bang and in stumbled two drunken knights who were laughing and holding each other up. The door nearly banged into their bent heads as it bounced partially closed again from the force of their entry.

Peter glanced up at them with a hint of levity on his face before he turned to the kettle and set it over the fire—he already knew they'd be requesting coffee.

Kat shared a conspiratorial smile with the cook before turning to stare expectantly at the men, knowing that it'd be amusing when they eventually realized they were in the presence of a noblewoman.

Sure enough, the two knights straightened as soon as they caught a glimpse of Katarina's blazing red hair, and one stumbled but remained upright enough to perform a sloppy bow while the other fell over.

"My lady!" the man who remained standing slurred in astonishment.

Kat didn't respond but instead stared at the man lying in a heap on the floor. When instead of rising, a rumbling snore resonated from his chest, Kat returned her attention to the knight, whom she recognized as elite by the shine of his silvery vest. His shoulder-length wavy brown hair had been neatly tied back at one point, but in the morning humidity following an obvious night of revelry, it had been thoroughly mussed. His face was stubbled, his bloodshot brown eyes downcast. Oh yes, he was having quite the morning.

"Good morning, Sir . . . ?" Kat asked lightly.

"Vohn." The knight hiccupped.

"Sir Vohn." Kat smiled, her eyes dancing with mischief, that is until the third man tripped over the threshold, knocking the slightly ajar door fully open. The third interloper clutched onto its side in an attempt to hold himself up and stop from crashing into Sir Vohn.

"Your Highness," Peter greeted, stunned, his shoulders straightening in shock as Eric attempted to right himself but nearly hit himself in the face with the door as he peered around the room.

"Mornin'," he greeted Peter with a dramatic nod while stumbling farther into the kitchen. Thankfully, Sir Vohn caught Eric before he completely fell over.

Kat felt her anger from the previous night brewing in the pit of her stomach.

Her index finger began rapidly tapping the back of Kraken's neck, making the feline's green eyes open in irritation. Not in the mood to be bothered, he leapt down from her lap and sashayed over to the nearest patch of sunlight on the stone floor.

"Y-Your Highness, perhaps you may wish to retire to your chambers before breakfast. Lady Katarina here was just having a cup of tea . . ." Peter began with a strained, apologetic smile.

Sir Vohn was already beginning to look a little green as his knees buckled under the prince's growing deadweight.

Eric finally managed to shuffle his right foot under himself and straightened back up with a slight sway as he squinted at Kat.

"Either I drank that last bottle all myself or there are—*hic*—now *two* Lady Katarinas." The prince tried to smile but a sudden wave of nausea seized him, and he threw himself out of Sir Vohn's hold just in time to vomit right outside the garden door.

Kat's expression of disgust was not lost on Sir Vohn or Peter. Slowly, she stood and eyed the other kitchen aides present: two young lads who were glancing at each other nervously.

"Sir Vohn, perhaps you can escort your fellow knight here back to the barracks with the help of the aides. The Royal Cook can summon more help for His Highness." She managed to say this innocently despite a particularly devious plan emerging in her mind.

Fortunately for her, Sir Vohn was still heavily inebriated, and so he was far less astute than he normally was, otherwise he may have noticed the cook's face pale and his gaze hesitantly swivel to the lady. Peter, on the other hand, had come to know Lady Katarina quite well over her twenty years of life, particularly during this last year while she had been serving as the head handmaiden to the princess . . .

"I-If you insist, my lady. We'll take our leave now." Sir Vohn bent down, proceeded to stumble once or twice, but eventually was able to pick his comrade up before throwing his arm over his shoulder and hauling him out of the kitchen with the two young kitchen aides rushing forward to steady both men.

As they retreated down the garden path, Kat eyed the prince's white pants that were still visible just to the left of the garden door. She could see that he must have fallen asleep on his stomach, as the tops of his feet were pressed into the warm earth, and the rest of him was rather motionless.

Katarina's wolfish smile made Peter inch away from her even though there was the entire cooking table between them.

"Peter?"

"Y-Yes?"

"Please do me a favor and fetch Prince Henry of Troivack. Tell him it's a secret, but that Katarina has summoned him with regards to a certain debt."

Peter stiffened, unsure of whether he should obey her. He debated telling her parents . . . or perhaps the coven leader, who would have enough power to possibly subdue her.

"Peter." Kat turned her unnatural golden eyes to him, and he saw that they were already aglow. "Don't worry. You won't get in trouble."

"Lady Katarina, keep in mind he *is* the crown prince of Daxaria . . ."

"Are you sure? Hard to tell with him being passed out face first in the basil patch. If you're worried though . . . perhaps he got up and . . . stumbled off by himself before help came." Kat formed a delighted smile directed toward the garden door.

Peter winced. He didn't like where this was going. "Lady Katarina . . ."

Kat turned back around to face the cook more directly, but when she saw Peter's expression, her devious thoughts faltered. After a quick breath that restored her composure, however, she accepted and respected his unspoken discomfort.

"Peter, how about you go find some aides to help carry the prince to his chamber? I think some stewards are most likely awake and preparing to tend to the king; why not ask them?"

With a sigh of relief, Peter nodded and gave a quick bow before striding from the room.

Kat's grin returned. "Now he can honestly say he saw nothing," she announced to Kraken, who was already asleep in the sun.

Picking up her skirts, Kat moved toward the garden door with a jaunty skip to her step.

"Good thing the Troivackian prince is known to train early by the barracks, and the king's stewards aren't even out of bed yet."

Katarina had been disheartened before when she hadn't been able to plot some sort of comeuppance for the prince. However, the world turned perfectly right again as she set to executing what, in her mind, was the best revenge for the slight Prince Eric Reyes had dealt her the previous night.

CHAPTER 7

A REDHEAD'S REPRISAL

Katarina Ashowan, for once, was sitting still. Her restless legs, resting, and her normally *expressive* face, settled into one of pure tranquility.

Alina, the king of Troivack, and the king of Daxaria stared at the redhead as though she were an animal about to go on a deadly rampage.

"Has she been like this . . . all day . . . ?" Alina asked her father slowly while eyeing her friend, who appeared every bit as graceful and controlled as a noblewoman should be.

"From what I've heard, ever since this morning, she has been . . . well . . . like this," Norman, the king of Daxaria, responded while shifting uncomfortably in his seat.

"I don't like it." Brendan scowled, his arms folded across his barrel-sized chest.

"You don't like anything," Norman muttered under his breath.

"I like your daughter more than a little," Brendan bit back.

"An odd time for a sweet comment, but . . . does no one truly know why she has been . . . like *this*? Did someone give her a weapon last night? Or were there any fires in Austice?" Alina asked after giving a brief smile to her new husband.

"No fires have been reported, and no peculiar deaths either . . ." Norman replied with a frown.

Placing her porcelain cup back in its saucer, Katarina lowered the dishes to the table in a languid movement.

"I'm assuming you all know I can hear you."

"So will you tell us why you're acting like a Godsdamn lady?" Brendan Devark of Troivack growled.

"Your Majesty!" Katarina's hand flew to her chest, her wide eyes the epitome of maidenly purity. "I am a respectable woman of the infamous house witch's home, a viscount's one and only unwed daughter. Of course I am acting as a lady!"

There was a flat beat of silence.

Norman turned to his daughter. "I'll ask Ruby to check and make sure there aren't any farm animals wandering the halls."

"Farm animals?"

"That happened *one* time, and it was a pure accident!"

Both Katarina and the Troivackian king had spoken at the same time.

Brendan's face grew incredulous as he opened his mouth to ask a follow-up question to what was clearly yet another wild story the redheaded noblewoman starred in. However, it was interrupted by a knock at the door.

"Your Majesties, the viscount and viscountess have arrived."

"Ah, your parents are here." Norman breathed with some measure of relief.

"Parents . . . ? I thought I was helping Alina record the gifts received from everyone?" Kat's spell of calm was tentatively cracked by her alarm.

"It's okay; it's a good thing, I promise," Alina whispered with a warm smile.

Kat smiled back until she noted the natural glow around her friend . . . one of happiness . . . of wholesomeness . . .

Somehow, it made the redhead feel a shadow of distance between herself and her friend.

When Finlay and Annika Ashowan walked through the door, all eyes swiveled to the infamous couple. They were well-known throughout the kingdom for their striking appearance thanks to the viscount's tall, lean stature and magical bright blue eyes, which were contrasted with his short Troivackian wife, whose beauty had been spoken of thoroughly in Daxaria's four cities and the small towns in between. Even as they advanced in age, they had done so gracefully (particularly the viscount thanks to his late mother's curse).

"Viscount, viscountess, I thank you for joining me this afternoon," Norman stood with a warm smile for his friends.

Brendan Devark gave a respectful nod, though his expression grew guarded. His *tentative* trust in the Ashowan family was well-known amongst those present.

Alina rose from her seat, beaming as she stepped forward and nodded regally to the couple. In return, the viscountess smiled beautifully as she curtsied and straightened while her husband bowed.

"We are surprised to receive your summons so soon after the wedding." Finlay's eyes flitted to his daughter, who was looking somewhat pale and guilty.

"Ah, no reason to fret. We had hoped to have this discussion before the wedding, but the viscount's delayed return had us postponing this." Norman drew Fin's eyes back to him, his hands raised to help ease the couple's obvious trepidation.

He gestured for them to sit, which they did, one on each side of their daughter, who for whatever reason, was pointedly looking anywhere but at anyone present.

Annika eyed her daughter with feigned casualness.

"Lord and Lady Ashowan, the reason I have summoned you here today is because of a matter the Troivackian king and I discussed nearly a year ago. We waited to address this, as we wanted to see how Lady Katarina faired during her lessons and duties with my daughter for her time in Troivack," Norman began while plucking up his goblet of water and nodding at Brendan Devark to take over.

"Your daughter has incredible potential to be a skilled knight or scout, and I was thinking we could train her for one of these roles while in Troivack."

Katarina's spine straightened as her eyes widened with excitement.

"No. I told you my answer last year, Your Majesty. We are not putting Katarina in danger." Fin's firm voice resonated loudly in the otherwise quiet room.

Kat swung around to look at her father pleadingly, but he didn't spare her a glance while his attention remained on the Troivackian king.

"We would not be placing your daughter in any more danger than she is already while in Troivack. The training would mostly be to her benefit at the princess's side, if the events of last summer are any indication," Brendan pointed out evenly.

At this, Fin remained silent.

"Pardon me, but I must ask . . . on what basis were you judging my daughter's capabilities for such training? I realize you mentioned the classes before, however, my opinion of her performance was never requested," Annika interrupted calmly.

Both Norman and Brendan glanced to Annika, each sensing a careful line to tread.

"Your daughter's performance during the lessons, while not always to the standards of nobility, were completed. She endured council meetings and was able to fulfill her duties pertaining to the princess's schedule and needs."

Annika didn't immediately respond to Norman's answer, allowing her silence to speak for her.

"I think knight training could help me! Just think! It could help me burn off some of my magic," Kat interjected earnestly. It was clear she desperately wanted to pursue the endeavor.

"That's what you said about learning to ride a horse like a man and archery. However, it has done very little from what we can see," Annika countered evenly, her expression calm and unaffected by her daughter's pleading.

"That's because both those things were easy. Being a knight is a completely different lifestyle," Kat reasoned quickly.

Annika opened her mouth to counter that argument when her husband leaned forward and spoke.

"I will permit this only if it is for the sole purpose of defending the princess. Katarina will never bunk with the men, never go out *drinking* with the soldiers unsupervised, and last but not least, she will never be purposefully placed in life-threatening situations. Her training should be limited to survival as a last resort in the worst kind of situation."

No one said anything for a while, until Kat threw her arms around her father's neck and crushed a kiss into his cheek.

She could've screamed and danced for days, she was so elated!

Before anyone else could further the discussion, however, a knock on the library door interrupted them.

"Your Majesty! There is an issue with the prince!" Mr. Howard, the Daxarian king's personal assistant, called out to the occupants of the room, his voice strained.

Norman's face became worried, Brendan frowned, Alina looked confused, the viscount exasperated, and the viscountess . . . well . . . unreadable as usual.

Meanwhile, Kat was pretending to be grossly interested in picking imaginary fluff from her skirts, a detail only Annika and Alina noticed.

Mr. Howard entered the library looking mildly under the weather—the man was notorious for overindulging in wine or moonshine whenever the opportunity presented itself.

"Your Majesties, viscount, viscountess, Lady Katarina . . . Perhaps I should share this with His Majesty King Norman, and as much as it pains me to say this, Viscount Ashowan alone." The assistant's gaze roved over all occupants of the room while obviously pained.

Fin rose, as did Norman, though the man moved more slowly than the witch, who was more than a decade his junior.

Alina and Brendan departed soon after to resume what should have been a day spent alone in their chamber, though Alina couldn't help but glance once more at Kat as her giant husband gently ushered her from the room, the uncertainty in her eyes palpable.

Kat smiled and waved to encourage her friend to relax. This left her alone with her mother, who was already rounding on her daughter to question why she was acting as though she had, once again, done something wrong.

Kat sat at the banquet table, her brother on her right-hand side, as she listened to the conversations around her and pointedly tried to ignore Prince Henry, who was staring at her in a desperate attempt to get her attention.

Instead, her leg bounced under the table, though it was still without its usual fervor, and she watched all the guests of the castle mingle excitedly amongst themselves.

So immersed in watching everyone in the room was Kat, that she didn't bother looking at whoever sat down on her left-hand side until her brother shifted in his chair suddenly.

"Your Highness! Or is it Your Majesty now?" Tam blundered while bowing from his seat.

Kat's head snapped around, her heart in her throat until she realized it was Alina who had seated herself beside her, wearing a particularly lovely cream-and-gold colored gown for the second night of her wedding feast.

"Wonderful to see you again, Tam. I won't be a queen until my coronation in Troivack, so 'Your Highness' still applies for the time being." Alina smiled, but her face was wary as she eyed Katarina, who was taking a long draught from her goblet. "I would love to hear about your travels, but I'm afraid I have something to discuss with your sister privately."

Taken aback, Tam eyed both the princess and his twin, but then let his shoulders sag forward with a half sigh, half chuckle.

"I knew it. She did something. She's been far too reasonable all day. Alright, Your Highness, feel free to punish her however you see fit." Tam stood and gave a formal bow, which Alina quickly waved off before looking to her friend who was taking her time meeting her gaze.

"How did you do it?" Alina's voice had quieted, her formerly polite expression gone, as she stared at the redhead directly.

"Do what?" Kat asked, genuinely interested to see how much the princess had been informed.

"Don't give me that. They found Eric passed out, face down, arse in the air, in the pigpen this morning."

Katarina gasped, barely suppressing the smile on her face. "Oh my! Well, I hear it is a great way to cool down in the heat. Duke Iones was telling me about it last summer, how pigs do it all the time by rolling in mud." She proceeded to reach for her goblet yet again and take a healthy gulp of wine, while her eyes returned to the ceiling to better fight the urge to laugh.

"Kat." Alina's volume rose ever so slightly. "Kat, he didn't have his pants on. He was face down, and *bare*-arsed."

A cough mixed with a garble and choke seized Katarina, making her hand fly to her chest, and her lips pursed in her greatest effort ever to not snort out her wine.

Turning to the princess, her eyes widened, she finally dared to speak. "What. A. Pity."

Alina let out a long, careful breath as though she, too, were trying not to laugh, however, she was far better at masking her true feelings than Kat was.

"Listen, it could be a very serious offense if he gets churlish about it. I'm guessing you had someone help you, and I don't know what in the world Eric did that could have upset you, but if you tell me, perhaps we—"

"Why do you think he upset me?" Kat's voice was a little too sharp.

Alina stilled at the reaction, her eyes narrowing skeptically at her friend.

"You don't pull pranks like this unless, in your opinion, someone was being a prat and deserved it."

Quickly taking another desperate mouthful of wine, Kat hastily waved her friend's remark aside, though her eyes were a mite too shifty.

"Well, I've had no dealings with His Highness Prince Eric, therefore, I have no reason to be motivated to orchestrate such an occurrence. Perhaps the prince merely lost his pants another way." Kat paused for a moment, another thought seizing her. "The Pantsless Prince. Has a nice ring to it."

At this Alina let out the smallest of snorts before quickly regaining control of herself.

"Kat, don't you dare go around saying that. Besides, what do you mean no dealings? I told you to watch him and try to glean some kind of information!"

Thankful of the reminder, the redhead recalled the helpful tidbit of information she had gathered from her time with Eric, and hastily turned to face her friend.

"Actually, I did learn something interesting! Apparently, my father and the prince fought because my father said once Tam takes over as viscount, he wants to return to being a cook. He doesn't want *any* formal duties. Not as a diplomat, advisor—nothing."

Alina's face paled. "Kat, are you certain of that? That is . . . that is a very worrisome claim. In fact, that is something that involves many powerful people. I cannot believe the viscount would just step away like that while my brother is preparing to rise to the throne. He has never said such things before. I need to bring this to my father's attention at once and—"

"I haven't confirmed everything just yet! Please don't say anything until I check with my da!" Kat grabbed Alina's arm as she had begun to rise hurriedly from her seat, already looking for her father, the Daxarian king.

Alina's gaze then cut to Kat, and the redhead tensed. She knew she'd made a mistake.

"Where did you hear this then, Kat? If it wasn't from your father, and you *claim* you had no meeting with my brother the prince?" Alina's tone had begun to turn authoritative, which in Kat's case was not a good thing.

Deciding she would have to risk lying, she doubled down on her innocence.

"Alina, I have not spoken to your brother, I—"

"Well, that isn't quite true, now is it, Lady Katarina?"

Kat's heart dropped to her stomach at hearing the newcomer's voice.

She turned, her teeth already gritting, to stare up at Prince Eric Reyes. She nearly winced at the hardness in his eyes, and it was then she could tell that the man was already relatively certain about the details regarding how he wound up half naked amongst pigs that morning.

CHAPTER 8

A PEST OF A PRINCE

"Your Highness, I'm sure you are—" Kat's mind was scrambling to recover from the shock of the prince's sudden appearance.

"Mistaken? How could I be; there were several eyewitnesses." Eric tilted his head over his shoulder, his tone light but his gaze fixed on the redhead who was already squirming in her seat.

Kat couldn't speak. She knew anything she said would be to her detriment, and her heart was pounding too violently, her temperature rising too quickly.

Alina glanced at Kat slowly. Given that she was within a foot of her friend, she could feel the telltale surge of heat.

"You greeted me just after the wedding in front of the knights. Outside by the barracks, remember?" Eric smiled charmingly as he watched Kat let out a small breath of relief.

Alina stared at her brother with a frown, then back at Katarina. "Was that really all?"

Eric's smile brightened as he placed a hand on his chest and bowed to his sister. "Of course. Now, dear sister, perhaps you wouldn't mind consoling our father. Someone mentioned how you most likely wouldn't return for a few years, and he seems to be dangerously close to an emotional display."

Staring at her brother suspiciously, Alina didn't move until she glanced at Kat and noticed her friend had slumped back in her chair, the air surrounding her notably cooler.

"We aren't finished talking," Alina murmured so that only Kat could hear. She stood and gave a nod to her brother, then headed toward her father.

Once the princess had returned to the king's side, Eric looked back to Kat, his eyes glinting in a far less playful manner than moments before.

"Mind if I sit beside you, Lady Katarina?"

"I think I'll actually go find my own brother now, Your Highness, so—"

Eric hopped up onto the long table and swung his legs over to the other side, making a few nobles raise their eyebrows at his lack of decorum. He then proceeded to seat himself on her right side, his face still a mask of pleasantness.

"Care to share what it is that I did that brought your wrath upon me, Lady Katarina?" Eric's quiet voice didn't hide its coldness.

"I don't know what you're talking about, Your Highness." Kat's anger began to tickle her chest.

She didn't take kindly to him toying with her when he'd been the one to act promiscuously, then following it up by behaving like the best of the town drunks.

"Oh really? So my state this morning had nothing to do with your feeling disappointed that I stopped our activities?"

Kat's expression darkened, and the heat emanated from her yet again.

Eric pulled back ever so slightly out of surprise at the flare from her that felt similar to when the door of a hot oven is opened, but he quickly regained his former control.

"I don't know why you believe I would be upset, Your Highness. We've only had the pleasure of meeting yesterday in the training ring, as you kindly mentioned." Kat's tone was unassuming, but the predatorial shine in her eyes made Eric's own calculated smile fade.

"Ah, however, Sir Vohn, a very good friend of mine, happened to inform me that you were the last person to see me this morning. He reported that I had been quite pleasantly asleep in some lovely grass, which is not where I woke up later today." Eric's expression had become firm, but his eyes were dancing as he pulled at the loose threads of Katarina's story.

"You drunkenly stumbled to a new spot, I suppose. I had long gone by the time help was to arrive for you, Your Highness. I didn't think it proper to bear witness to you in such a . . . *poor* state," Kat replied scathingly. She turned to face him more directly in her seat.

Eric's eyes narrowed. "I don't know how you did it, but on the note of what is all good and proper, I'm surprised an *innocent* noblewoman like yourself was comfortable removing a man's pants. Did you satiate your curiosity then?"

Kat's smile froze, her right eye twitched, but then she got ahold of her sensibilities again and let out a breathy laugh.

"Your Highness, what interest could I have in looking at you as a man? Of course I would *never* dare to humiliate you in such a way. I'm surprised you are so willing to talk about your indiscretion so openly; thank you for trusting me." Kat bowed her head gracefully, her body tingling with the excitement of their thinly veiled battle of words. It was rare she got to cut loose to such a degree when properly annoyed by people outside of her family.

Eric, on the other hand, frowned. Kat's barbed insults and ire toward him was more than a little troubling, mainly because he didn't quite understand where they were stemming from.

"You were the one to say you weren't expecting more of our time; I'm not sure why you're acting as though I—"

Kat's back straightened and her hands gripped her skirts as she willed him to stop talking by casting him a look of alarm.

". . . Right." Eric stared at her, still confused, before the realization dawned on him. "Ah . . . Is this revenge in some misguided way because you believe I upset your father?"

Kat blinked, stunned. What was he talking about?

"That seems all the more likely for an Ashowan family member. Your father always did have a righteous streak that often got out of hand. Like father like daughter, I suppose."

Kat folded her arms across her middle, her anger lurching beyond passive-aggressive banter and reaching a whole other level. As a result, she was making herself glow with sweat.

"Well, now that I know you aren't so different from him, I'll be sure to warn Alina. However, I want you to keep something in mind, Lady Katarina," Eric continued while leaning forward, startling Kat with the wash of physical excitement it caused.

"I give as good as I get. So don't think I buy for a second you weren't behind what happened this morning. I'll be sure to pass back the kindness you dealt me."

Rising to stand, Eric gave a small bow of his head, which Kat could do nothing but glare at. She was too rattled by the physical reaction she'd had to his earlier proximity.

As she watched him stalk away to greet yet another noble that wanted to shake his hand and cozy up to him, Kat's index finger began tapping impatiently.

I'm not still attracted to him. I'm just angry . . . That's all this is. He's a philandering arse. He probably made up all that stuff last night about my da just so I'd like him. And why would he warn Alina about me? Doesn't he know about last summer? He should be grateful about me rescuing his sister. Now he wants to pit her against me?

Kat snorted to herself while shaking her head. *Pointless thoughts. He's not worth my time. I'll be leaving soon to Troivack anyway. Maybe I should try and become a full-fledged knight there, despite the agreement with my parents, or perhaps I marry a Troivackian so I never have to deal with Eric Reyes as my king.*

With another grunt, Katarina stood and made her way toward the banquet hall doors, blissfully unaware of her father's and mother's stares as she left. The viscount and viscountess noted Kat's departure and then glanced to each another in wordless communication from where they stood engaged in separate conversations. They both had witnessed the prince talking to their daughter, as had almost everyone in the room, though no one had any clue what the two could have been discussing.

The prince seemed aware of the attention but was pretending not to as he joined Earl Fuks's side.

Fin hadn't liked how comfortable Eric had looked with his daughter, nor had he liked how coldly he had stared at her. Kat was clearly angry as well . . .

He needed to address whatever was happening there. Especially given the plan he had finished formulating with Norman earlier that day . . .

Kat was just finishing the annoying paperwork involving what Alina would bring with her to Troivack. The ship was to set sail the next day, and she had finally been told the number of trunks the princess would be able to take with her.

Katarina had parked herself in the castle courtyard to make the work slightly less suffocating, but it wasn't as effective as she'd hoped. The castle was quiet, and its nobles and staff alike were still in sunny spirits as everyone continued their celebrations and rejoicing in the new royal couple still being amongst them.

The beautiful blue sky was dotted with lazily drifting wispy clouds. Leaning back in her chair, languishing in a well-deserved stretch with her arms reaching skyward, the lady's peace was interrupted.

"Lady Katarina!"

Kat sighed pleasantly as she dropped her arms back down. She'd once again been caught behaving in an unbecoming way. *Oh well.*

Her easy-going mood was disrupted, however, when her gaze landed on Prince Henry Devark. His face was strained as he glanced around to ensure the only maid present stood beyond earshot.

"Your Highness," Katarina rose and curtsied while Henry bowed hastily. "Would you like to take a seat?"

Henry pursed his lips. He was clearly in a rush but was too kind to ignore proper decorum, so he plunked himself down in the white-painted wrought iron chair while Kat seated herself across from him.

"Lady Katarina," Henry began in hushed tones, his eyes once again sweeping around the perimeter. Troivackian nobles were notorious for being incredibly careful in discreet conversations, as their political climate was often a savage battlefield.

"Yes, Your Highness?" Katarina asked brightly, though her stomach was already roiling.

"You didn't tell me that it was Prince Eric we were moving to the pen!" Henry whispered with a pained expression.

"Oh, I see. My mistake! He could've passed for any drunk servant though, I mean . . . you met him just that day, and even you didn't realize who he was in that state."

"That's because his head was down, and with his pants off, I wasn't particularly eager to get an eyeful of him! You said that he deserved it, but that is a very serious crime you committed," Henry whispered urgently while leaning forward.

"Being a prince doesn't change the fact that he deserved it," Kat remarked icily, her eyes drifting down to the paperwork in front of her, and growing lost to the memory of her anger.

Henry stilled and his cheeks became tinged with color. "My lady, did he . . . did His Highness . . . are you . . . by chance . . . compromised . . . ?"

Kat's gaze snapped up to him. "I am still an innocent if that's what you're asking, but there is more than one way to offend someone you know."

Henry sighed, partly in relief but partly still uneasy. "If you could just tell me what he did, I'd feel a bit better about being your accomplice. You know I have my family to think of now."

"Ah, that's right. I forgot to congratulate you on your marriage and your wife's pregnancy. Forgive me, Your Highness." Kat smiled kindly at him. She'd always liked Troivack's prince. He was friendly and considerate despite those traits making him wildly unpopular in his own kingdom.

Henry couldn't help but smile back at the mention of his wife. "I look forward to you meeting Kezia. Most of the Troivackian nobles have been more than a little unkind to her since our wedding—mainly because she was a commoner before, which firmly nullifies the possibility of our family inheriting the throne. So, your open-mindedness will be welcome."

Kat nodded. "I look forward to it; she sounds like a wonderfully interesting person."

Henry's grin broadened. "She is. Kezia is the most gifted storyteller, and her singing? I have no doubt Alina—pardon me—Her Highness will enjoy singing with her."

Katarina chuckled. "I must admit, I've been so focused on packing and helping with the wedding, I forgot to get excited about going to Troivack."

Henry's warm smile faded as he regarded Katarina far more somberly. "I hope you are prepared. Things are quite different there."

Kat gave a half shrug. "I've completed all the lessons, so don't worry too much. Besides, it's beautiful weather, and I'd hate to waste my last full day in Daxaria stressing."

Henry sighed, but his good-natured expression returned to his face as he bobbed his head in agreement and braced his palm against the table to stand. Suddenly, a frown crushed his brow and his backside down.

"Wait a minute. We were talking about you and Prince Eric."

Kat let out a moan. "Please . . . please . . . can we let it rest? Besides, we're leaving tomorrow, and you most likely won't have to see or hear from him directly for years!"

Henry tilted his head over his shoulder in confusion, clearly taken aback.

"Lady Katarina, did you not hear?"

It was Kat's turn to grow wary, a sense of foreboding bubbling up in her gut. "Hear what?"

Henry visibly winced in preparation for her reaction.

"The crown prince of Daxaria . . . Eric Reyes . . . is going to be joining us in Troivack. For an indeterminate amount of time."

Kat's jaw dropped, her hands fell limp on her lap, and her golden eyes rounded.

The shock lasted for several moments, but once she blinked, she dropped her forehead violently down with a bang onto the table in front of her, making Henry jump in concern that she had hurt herself.

He quickly recoiled, however, as she let out an earth-rumbling bellow.

"SON . . . OF A GODSDAMN BITCH!"

CHAPTER 9

CATCHING UP

Father, you can't be serious," Eric spluttered while he slumped back in the council room chair.

Only Alina and his father were present for the meeting, and at first the prince had presumed it'd be a friendly family gathering . . . only it wasn't.

It was a bloody ambush.

"We aren't saying it'll be forever, possibly just through the winter, and we will see how you are faring afterward." Norman replied to his son's outburst calmly, though Alina noticed he was gripping the armrests of his chair a little too tightly.

"That meddlesome viscount you're so fond of kept saying I needed to return to begin taking over my duties here, and now you're saying you're immediately sending me to Troivack!" Eric's exasperated response was earning him a calculating stare from Alina.

"It'd be good for you to ensure your sister is settled in, and it will serve the kingdom well if our ties to Troivack are further strengthened. With that under your belt, it'll make the work in assuming the throne far easier for you," Norman explained patiently while pointedly ignoring his son's odd resentment toward Finlay Ashowan.

Eric let out an aggravated sigh as he shifted restlessly in his seat.

"You know, we could use the time to catch up; it's been a long time since we've seen you, Eric," Alina interrupted quietly, which instantly softened her brother's face as he turned toward his sibling.

"I know it's been a while, Lina, but you're married now. You don't want to waste your rosy newlywed days catching up with your annoying older brother," Eric reasoned while calling her by her old nickname, his voice far gentler than it had been moments before.

Alina continued staring at him, her expression poised, which made Eric's eyebrows twitch.

When had she grown up so much? It had only been a few years since he'd last seen her, and she had never known how to make such a stony expression. Composed and pleasant, always, but never firm and judging.

"Eric, where were you?" the princess's voice remained hushed, but it still pierced both her father's and brother's hearts easily.

"I was doing mercenary work in Sorlia, traveling around and getting a real sense of the kingdom—I was even aboard a ship for a while. At one point, I was in Zinfera for a few months . . ." Eric explained carefully, though for some reason, both to Alina and their father, it felt like he wasn't saying everything.

Alina didn't speak for a long while, and Eric noticed she swallowed with difficulty. He could see how hurt she was . . . and a sharp ache began in his heart as a result.

"Why didn't you write to me?" Her voice came out as a croak, and Eric had to strain himself to resist kneeling and begging for her forgiveness.

"I was all over the place. It was . . . difficult to find the means to. I'm sorry, Lina."

Alina's chest was rising and falling a little faster, and anxiety knotted Eric's stomach as he remembered how terrifying her breathing episodes could be.

"You . . . You made us worry. You left us without a word, and no one knew a thing except . . . except for Viscount Ashowan. Just what was so important you couldn't bother telling us you were alright? Hard t-to write a letter? At some point over the four years? Y-You've got some . . . Godsdamn . . . *nerve*." Tears were falling down Alina's face, and Eric felt his insides rip apart.

His own throat felt swollen, and when he risked a glance at his father, he saw that the man had his head bowed into his hand, unable to look at his son. Eric found himself wishing he had never returned at all.

Alina stood without another word while wiping tears from her face and left the room.

After a moment of anguished silence between he and his father, Eric rose awkwardly and followed his sister.

His long steps easily caught up to Alina's small ones, his hand reaching out and gently touching the loose sleeve of her dark navy dress.

She turned partially, her eyes cast downward, but when he opened his mouth to speak, he realized the Troivackian king was standing at the end of the hall. His eyes were ablaze, and his thick arms were crossed as he regarded his crying wife, then Eric, darkly.

Letting out a small breath of annoyance, Eric leaned down and spoke quietly.

"Lina, I'm sorry. I really am. I . . . I needed some time after the epidemic and mother's passing, and I'm glad that the Troivackian king seems to genuinely care about you. I just think you two need your alone time as a couple without your kin around. Honestly, if I didn't trust him, I'd have obviously insisted on going with you, but that isn't the case. You don't need me in Troivack, and I don't say that lightly knowing how close you've become with Katarina Ashowan—"

"What is that supposed to mean?" Alina's furious stare jumped up to her brother's face as she stepped back from him.

Eric glanced at the Troivackian king, who had visibly tensed at his wife's movement.

"I just meant the Ashowans aren't to be trusted to always have your back. Look, I can tell you more about that, though maybe in private."

"No. I don't want to hear another Godsdamn word. The Ashowans were there to help make things right around here after you abandoned us. You know nothing about what they've done or about Katarina for that matter. Did you say something to her about her family? Is that why she already thinks you're an arse?" Alina snapped accusatorily, her eyes still red but her tears now dry.

Eric faltered. He had never seen his sister confrontational, and it was yet another difference between the sibling he had once known in childhood and the married woman in front of him.

"I didn't say anything about her family until after she pulled a nasty little move that I shouldn't have been surprised about." Eric let out a dry laugh while pressing his right hand into his pocket. "Though I suspect you already knew it was her behind yesterday's . . . event. Honestly, given what the knights have said about her, I'm—"

"One more bad word about her and I might have to admit she was right to punish you the way she did." Alina's voice had turned frigid and hard.

Eric fell quiet, as he couldn't help but be taken aback

Alina let out a humorless chuckle. "Though I don't know why I doubted her in the first place. She's proved herself time and time again. While mischievous with an uncanny ability of getting into trouble, Katarina Ashowan is a good person. I don't know that I can still say the same about you."

"Lina, I never meant to be hurtful. I just—"

"I don't think I can listen to your excuses right now. My husband is waiting. Excuse me." With a curt nod of her head, Alina turned from her brother and walked over to where Brendan Devark stood looking as fearsome as ever, that is until Alina rested her small hand on his arm and said something Eric couldn't hear.

Then, like magic, the bear of a man's face turned tender as he grasped her hand in his own and kissed her fingertips.

Watching the loving scene between his sister and her husband had the strange effect of making Eric feel even more out of place than ever, even though he had been experiencing that sensation ever since arriving back in his boyhood home.

Turning around and retreating down the opposite side of the corridor, Eric decided a trip to Austice for a bit of fun was just what he needed.

They wouldn't send him to Troivack . . . there was no way. His presence clearly was upsetting Alina, and only his father seemed truly motivated by the idea. Once the inner council met about it, they would dismiss this plan, he was sure of it.

Eric stood on the docks of Austice, hungover and in a foul mood, as stewards marched by him with everyone's luggage. The sun was burning hot, and a warm offshore wind heralded idyllic weather for the first day of their journey to Troivack.

"Your Highness? Excuse me? Hi, my name is Thomas Julian; I'm to be your assistant while in Troivack!"

Eric's eyes slid to a young lad with a mop of sandy brown hair that kept falling into his brown eyes that stared up at him eagerly.

"Gods, how old are you?" the prince asked wearily as he leaned on the nearest docking post.

"I-I'm to be fifteen later this year, Your Highness!" the boy replied nervously.

"My father assigned you to me?" Eric asked flatly.

"Y-Yes, Your Highness! Because your departure was so sudden, a-and I was recently rejected to be a squire but have high marks from my tutors, so I was asked to accompany you. Once you return to Daxaria, a new, proper assistant will take my place if . . . if I do not meet your standards." Thomas Julian bowed apologetically to the prince, and the boy was nervous to the point of trembling.

Eric closed his eyes, trying to remember what patience felt like.

Why had his father assigned a mere child to him? To a hostile kingdom of all places . . . ?

"Lad, are you sure you have your parents' permission to leave for Troivack for however long I'm there?" Eric finally managed, hoping to hear a way out of the strange arrangement.

"O-Of course! My father is a knight with land outside of Xava! H-He was really disappointed when I wasn't accepted as a squire here in Austice, but he was so proud when I t-told him I'd been selected to serve you, Your Highness!"

Eric grimaced when the boy's voice cracked for a second time during his speech thanks to puberty.

Of course the lad has a sad backstory . . . This makes him impossible to dismiss.

"Very well. Mr. Julian?"

"Yes, Your Highness?" The young man beamed at the prince, clearly too thrilled at having been accepted to care that it was done so begrudgingly.

"Please go find where my cabin is located."

"Yes, Your Highness!" The boy was practically jumping up and down.

Once his new assistant had disappeared in the crowd of people flooding to the boat, Eric reached up and wiped the sweat from his brow. He was cursing his familial duty for the thousandth time when he spotted a large, fluffy black cat trotting over to him.

"Well, well, well. If it isn't the flea bait that betrayed me two nights ago." Eric greeted the feline with a halfhearted scowl.

Kraken meowed at him, then proceeded to rub his head against Eric's knees.

"Your fluffiness doesn't work on me anymore, you old bother," the prince announced despite reaching down to pet the cat's cheek, his thumb massaging Kraken's ear the way he knew he liked it.

"He's missed you."

Eric felt his teeth clench as he lifted his furious gaze to Finlay Ashowan, who wore dark pants with a white linen tunic and lightweight cream coat. As usual, he forwent any finery aside from his wedding band.

"Kraken, why do you associate yourself with such poor company, hm?" the prince asked as Kraken proceeded to wind his way through his legs once more before sauntering over to the viscount.

The familiar meowed up to his witch, and finished with a chirp.

Fin raised an eyebrow at the feline before rolling his eyes. "He says the food is good and the rent is free."

Eric couldn't help it, he smiled when he spoke to the cat again. "A lazy life. Good decision, Kraken. You even chose not to have kittens to keep your life to yourself. Very wise indeed."

The familiar meowed and chirped a couple more times, making even Fin let out a wry chuckle.

"He says it's Emperor Kraken now, and that you've missed a lot, but that you're welcome to pet any of his subjects."

For a moment, Eric wasn't certain if Fin was joking or not, then the familiar turned his head to stare interestedly at a set of pigeons that had landed on some stacked crates nearby.

"Still just a cat," Fin teased his familiar.

"You never know, perhaps they're planning a 'coo,'" Eric mused while grinning at the birds.

Kraken gave a small chirp again and Fin's good humor dropped. "Wait . . . seriously? What do you mean every pigeon has to die?"

Eric blinked, caught between a laugh and concern. Had the viscount started going somewhat mad . . . ?

After another tense moment of Kraken eyeing the birds, he gave one final meow.

"Gods, don't jest with me like that. We just settled the rat negotiations." Fin rubbed his brow tiredly.

Eric watched the viscount blankly. "I don't particularly like you these days, but perhaps for the sake of the kingdom, you should take a vacation."

Fin sighed and shook his head. "I'll have you know there is a record low of rat infestations in Austice thanks to Kraken and me."

Eric didn't bother responding; there was no use getting entwined with such insanity.

"What brings you over here, viscount?" the prince asked instead, his unfriendly tone returning.

Glancing over his shoulder, Fin's eyes fell on his wife, daughter, and son who stood farther away on the dock. Lady Ashowan looked as though she were giving her daughter a lecture of sorts that Lady Katarina was struggling to receive, while Tam grinned tauntingly at his twin from behind his mother.

"Whatever animosity you hold toward me, don't apply it to my daughter as well." Fin turned back to Eric, whose weathered face had gone stony. "I don't expect you two to cross paths often in Troivack, but when you do, there is no need to be impolite. She's not as tough as some people think, and she isn't exactly going into friendly territory."

Eric pushed off from the post he was leaning on to stare levelly into the viscount's eyes. "Are you asking me for a favor?"

"No. I'm reminding you to be a decent person and not be antagonistic toward my child because of what is between you and me." Fin's voice was hard, but the gentleness in his gaze when he spoke about his daughter nettled Eric. Most likely because it reminded him that Finlay Ashowan was not an evil man, he was just a shoddy friend.

"Fine. You have my word I won't go out of my way to be unpleasant. Though if she picks a fight with me, I will not let it stand."

Fin's eyes narrowed. "Why would my daughter pick a fight with you? She never picks fights for no reason."

Eric rolled his eyes. "I've heard that, and yet, it is entirely possible, Viscount, that she does. Besides, wasn't it you who filled her head with warnings about me? She's most likely motivated by hearing your one-sided tales."

As Fin stood blinking and frowning in confusion, it dawned on Eric that Katarina's malice toward him had nothing to do with anything her father had mentioned . . .

"Eric, I haven't told anyone *anything*. Nothing outside of what I said I would."

Growing more uncomfortable over the way Fin was staring at him suspiciously, Eric decided he had once again endured enough of his former friend's company. So, moving one hand into his pocket and straightening his shoulders, he began to shift away.

"See you again sometime, Viscount. Ideally, next time we greet each other you won't threaten to drag me behind a horse halfway across the kingdom, hm?" Eric brushed past Fin as he spoke.

"Ideally, next time you will have changed for the better, Your Highness. I've missed my friend," Fin called to the prince's back.

Eric swung around, his eyes flashing. "It was you, wasn't it? You were the one who put it in my father's head that I should go to Troivack."

Fin let out a long breath before dropping his chin to his chest and giving it a shake.

"I was merely the messenger. It was actually Kraken's idea."

Eric's gaze flew down to the familiar in astonishment. He began to reconsider the seriousness with which he had learned Kraken's new title of "emperor."

Letting out a small grunt of displeasure, Eric turned and made his way toward the ship's gangplank where his own father stood waiting. He was forced to do his best not to curse around the members of the Daxarian court, who were huddled around their king and wishing their prince a safe journey, all overly eager and excited for him.

Fin hung back as he watched Eric's blond ponytail disappear into the crowd.

When he looked back down at his familiar, he noticed Kraken was once again fixated on the pigeons.

"You . . . You *were* kidding about the pigeons plotting a coup, right?"

Kraken chirped without looking at Fin. "*Of course, witch. The almost grown kitten may have been right; you need rest.*"

The viscount let out a sigh of relief and didn't bother responding to his familiar's concern before walking back to where his family stood waiting for him. Kraken should've known he made up at least a quarter of Fin's workload.

Meanwhile, the fluffy black cat turned his gaze to the two birds that had finally noticed him and were beginning to inch away.

"*Yes, you feather-brains wouldn't try something so foolish as a take over* again, *when you are oh so tasty, would you?*"

The pigeons glanced at each other, cooed a couple more times, and as a result, were caught off guard when Kraken launched himself at one of them and successfully caught it in his jaws.

What could he say? Asserting his dominance as emperor could sometimes be fun.

CHAPTER 10

BARBS OVER BEVERAGES

Night had fallen on their ship. Contrary to the earlier fair weather they enjoyed, the night brought with it a shift in the winds, making the decks rock more notably.

Katarina reached for her goblet while her gleaming eyes studied the ship's largest cabin warily.

"S-Sorry, my lady! The councils of both Daxaria and Troivack believed it'd be best to split the number of royals aboard each ship in case of attack," Thomas Julian explained as he shakily refilled Katarina's goblet. The poor lad was keenly aware of the foul mood between the prince and noblewoman.

"It isn't your fault, Mr. Julian; you don't need to apologize to her," Eric explained over the rim of his own drink that he subsequently downed in one go, then ineloquently ripped a dinner roll between his teeth.

Kat barely resisted snorting at his obvious abandonment of manners. At least it allowed her to neglect her own decorum. She propped her elbow on the table as she casually picked her way through dinner, even though the maid assigned to her sat in the corner and was fidgeting relentlessly as a result.

"I thought the captain of the ship would be joining us this evening," Kat mused idly, her expression unimpressed as she continued looking at everything except the prince.

"The change of weather means he is performing his duties. He doesn't have time to cater to noble frivolities," Eric chuckled scathingly, the look on his face indicating how childish he thought her.

At long last, Kat's gaze cut to the prince, and he would never admit that it sent a strange flush through him once it did.

"It's typical to receive notice of it though, and I didn't hear anything." Kat's eyes were narrowing as her opinion of Eric continued to plummet to new depths.

"The world doesn't revolve around you, Lady Katarina." He shrugged with a frosty smile as both his assistant and Kat's maid shared terrified glances.

The rage that surged through Kat had heat rolling off her, her eyes flashing, but her lips turned upward into a hungry smile.

Oh . . . she was going to make him suffer.

Eric was somewhat disturbed by the face she was making but feigned a cavalier expression.

"I'm well aware, Your Highness. After all, what kind of noble would inconvenience *an entire* group of people . . . or, say, *their leader* . . . with their whims?" Kat daintily sipped her goblet in delicious satisfaction while watching Eric's eyebrow twitch.

"I see what you mean. There even are some nobles who are selfish enough to cause trouble and stress all the time, to everyone around them—including their families—despite being raised in complete privilege."

"I'm amazed that someone as well traveled as yourself doesn't seem to know the meaning of the words 'selfish' and 'hypocrite,'" Kat replied with a sweet smile.

Eric was just about to open his mouth to expel another biting retort when the ship's cabin door opened and the captain of the vessel strode in with his first mate.

"Pardon my tardiness, Your Highness and Lady Katarina, the winds are starting to calm now, so I am comfortable leaving my first mate here, Frances, in charge."

Kat smiled genuinely at the old seadog. "I'm just happy everything is alright, Captain Alphonse."

The captain was a short, stout man in his mid-fifties with thinning wiry black hair that had gray touching his temples. He was clean-shaven with an impressive double chin and ruddy complexion, but he had a friendly shine in his dark brown eyes. Both Eric and Kat had been introduced upon boarding the ship, and given that neither of them were in fine spirits upon the meeting, the man had quickly impressed them both with his unflappable command.

"Yes, why don't you join us, captain?" Eric smiled warmly.

When she noticed that he could make such a kind expression, something in Kat felt . . . unpleasant. It was grating her nerves fiercely that he had saved so much awfulness just for her, and no one else seemed to realize he was a horrible, entitled arseho—

"It would be an honor, Your Highness. In fact, I brought a new beverage for dessert from one of the southern islands of Zinfera to celebrate the first night of our journey. It contains a cream of sorts that does not keep well, and the only reason I am able to share it with you both today is because I had the privilege of traveling with a water witch who kept the concoction frozen until this morning."

Both Kat and Eric perked up curiously.

With a single nod to his first mate, Frances turned to a crewmate that had waited in the dark galley and retrieved a small wooden chest with a gleaming brass lock.

The first mate proceeded forward and placed it on the long black dining table before the two nobles while the captain tugged his lapels and straightened his shoulders with a ceremonial air.

With a smile and twinkle in his eye, the captain reached into his coat and procured a small matching brass key from his pocket, which clicked open the chest to reveal three glass bottles containing a milky-looking beverage with a strange yellowish tint . . .

"On the island where I retrieved this, there is very little to recommend. It is filled with all sorts of fugitives and riffraff. Sailors who have upset their captains are left on this island as a punishment. There is nothing but fights, chaos, and the smell of sin in the air, but . . . there are some mad geniuses of pleasure there. They call this island—"

"Insodam," Eric finished with his eyes trained interestedly on the bottles, while a melancholy smile moved his mouth.

The captain's eyebrows shot upward before he let out a small chuckle.

"Yes, Your Highness. I'm surprised you've heard of it. Most don't like to mention it in fine company. It's one of the most diverse places on this earth, I reckon." The captain chuckled.

"The name once meant *indecent society*, but it has been changed and twisted in every Daxarian, Troivackian, Zinferan, and even Lobahlan mouth it has entered. Until now, where its title has firmly rested on Insodam."

Kat's interest sparkled in her eyes. The captain was a gifted storyteller, and even Eric smiled at her obvious captivation, momentarily forgetting that she was annoying beyond reason. Not that she noticed . . .

"From that hellish island, there has been but one sweet creation, and that is this here. The piña colada. Its name was decided upon by the Lobahlan, Troivackian, and Zinferan that teamed together to pass the time until their captains forgave them." Captain Alphonse gave a flourish of his wrist before lightly plucking up one of the bottles for dramatic effect.

"Sweet . . . tropical . . . and including the new brew from Zinfera that has graced the world these past ten years: rum."

Kat's smile was radiant. "Well, captain, I can safely say I am most curious to try it."

"It's been a small while since I was—since I've heard of Insodam." Eric drained the last vestiges of his wine before leaning back with a seasoned smile.

Captain Alphonse bowed. "I am happy you both are pleased with the ware. In the future, I hope to be a stakeholder in its mass production, and should it be as successful as I know it is capable of being, I feel confident it will be a bright investment should it receive Your Highness's approval."

Eric nodded, his expression courteous but not as warm as before. Talk of business was always a delicate matter, especially before sampling a product.

Knowing this, Captain Alphonse waved Katarina's maid forward, and the young girl hastily set three clean goblets before the captain, who poured the thick liquid carefully into each cup, He had her distribute the beverages to her mistress and Eric after taking a sip to ensure the drink wasn't poisoned.

Kat could tell from the pink in her maid's cheeks and barely suppressed smile that she was in for a real treat.

"A toast." Captain Alphonse raised his goblet, prompting Katarina and Eric to do the same while the first mate bowed and made his exit quietly. "To the health of our returned Daxarian prince. May your life be filled with clear skies and fair winds."

Eric's face faltered, and the air felt cold for the span of a breath.

With a renewed noble smile, the prince continued the toast, and the chill dissipated as quickly as it had come. "Also to Lady Katarina Ashowan, may she live her days devoid of senseless pettiness."

There was a beat of uncomfortable silence carried by the captain and Katarina—who was about to murder the prince—when Captain Alphonse turned to her swiftly. Despite his intention to smooth out the situation, he had to pause at the sight of the glowing orange and gold mixed aura around her.

The captain finally managed to speak, an affable smile cast toward the young woman that he had heard a good many rumors about. "My lady, I'm sure His Highness only meant that he wishes you to avoid misfortune."

For a moment, the smoldering magic around the young woman burned brighter, and Eric watched from his seat with passive interest.

Kat, meanwhile, gripped her hands together as she fought the all too familiar urge at such times . . . the urge to launch herself at the person being a complete and utter rotting turd and throttle them.

Despite choking on said violent urges, Kat recovered her voice with impressive speed. "It's . . . alright, Captain Alphonse. I'm sure the prince merely misspoke due to a cup too many of wine. He does tend to forget himself when drinking, you see. Why, did you not hear of his most recent incident where they found him in the pen of—"

"Lady Katarina, you forget yourself." Eric's voice was sharp and his gaze murderous.

Kat smiled, her ethereal eyes shining even more brightly, making everyone in the chamber feel incredibly wary, as though they were in the presence of a wild beast.

"Oh, Your Highness, I was merely trying to explain why you could be mistaken for saying something disrespectful. Especially given I am a single woman, alone on a ship with Daxaria's one and only prince. It could be seen as cold, callous, cowardly, immoral . . . oh my, listen to me prattle on. Can you think of any other adjectives, captain?" Kat asked while turning eagerly to the seasoned seaman, who had survived skirmishes less stressful.

"I-I'm afraid I cannot, Lady Katarina. However, you should take a sip, as this particular beverage doesn't take long to warm." The captain's previous control was slipping. He swallowed and once again tried to smile.

For a brief breath of silence, neither the prince nor Kat said a word as they glared at one another over the table. Their animosity was palpable.

Finally, with a wry grin, Eric reached out, lifted the goblet to his lips, and took a mouthful.

His eyes grew round, and his eyebrows shot upward in surprise.

"This is incredible, captain! I would gladly advocate for this dessert beverage. I believe this could make you a wealthy man."

The previous awkwardness forgotten, the captain's face lightened in delight. "Why, thank you, Your Highness! With your support, and Viscount Ashowan's backing, I now have no doubt that this will become a great success in Daxaria, perhaps even on the other continents as well."

Eric had been in the middle of taking another hefty gulp when he heard mention of Katarina's family.

Kat, meanwhile, watched his impressed expression fade to barely restrained bitterness.

"Of course the Ashowan's would fund something like this," Eric muttered darkly before draining the last of his drink and setting the goblet down roughly. "Pardon me, Captain Alphonse, I think I will retire for this evening. It has been a long day."

As Eric stormed out of the cabin, the captain was visibly confused and distressed over upsetting the crown prince, and as his attention was on the door swinging closed, he failed to notice Katarina Ashowan take her first sip of her own piña colada.

"Holy hell," she said breathily, drawing the captain and her maid's attention.

The two watched as Kat drained the remaining beverage in a single go, then promptly drop her cup onto the table with an invigorated smile.

"This is the best thing I've ever had in my life. Mind pouring me another, Captain Alphonse? Don't worry so much about the prince; I imagine he'll find some way to turn his mood around. He seems good at that."

The captain did not look convinced by the lady's words, but he proceeded to refill her cup nonetheless as he, too, drank eagerly.

Settling into enjoying her second serving of the refreshing drink, Katarina's mind turned over the events of her conversation with Eric.

He clearly had been to the depraved island of Insodam, meaning he had either gone there on purpose, or someone had left him there . . .

Then there was his reaction to the news that her family was offering financial investment in the best drink on the earth—at least, in Kat's opinion.

Why had Eric seemed so exasperated? Sure, her family owned most of the stakes of Troivackian moonshine in Daxaria, but it still didn't make complete sense.

With a sigh and a shake of her long gleaming red hair, Kat admonished that the prince was not only terribly annoying but also terribly mysterious. Sadly, it was the combination that was doing something dangerous to her thinly veiled penchant for mischief. Without much more inner turmoil, Kat began to think of new ways to torment Eric into revealing perhaps more about the many secrets he seemed to be hiding.

CHAPTER 11

CARD SHARK

The second day of the voyage to Troivack was bright and sunny without a cloud in sight. The brilliant blue sky settled along the horizon effortlessly as though one became the other when meeting at the ends of the earth.

The sailors off duty played cards on deck while the Daxarian staff either hid below or draped themselves over the ship's railings to relieve their stomachs. Not all of them were adapting well to life at sea.

Although Katarina was not afflicted by seasickness, she was, however, incredibly bored being one of the few people full of energy and entirely healthy. So, she set about finding something to occupy her time.

She gazed out over the endless waters, then looked to the captain, who was at the helm in serious discussion with his first mate. Off to the side of them, she noticed the prince leaning against the railing of the upper deck, his wavy blond hair once again pulled back in a small ponytail that was getting thoroughly tangled by the winds, his hands loosely clasped, and his hazel eyes staring out over the water lost to his thoughts.

After studying him for another moment, Kat turned her attention to the sailors huddled around their card game, and with a smile springing to her face, she strolled over to them, her target set.

Despite the players all being Troivackians, Kat addressed them easily. "Good day, everyone, what game are you all playing?"

The sailors all stiffened in their seats, their revelry deflated as they slowly and with great pains, turned to look up into the overly eager face of the noblewoman.

"Cards," the Troivackian sailor nearest to Kat grumbled before earning a sharp elbow to his side from his friend on the right. "M'lady."

Kat's mischievous smile didn't falter for a moment. "Right, I got that part down; what is your specific game? High or Low? King's Ransom?"

The men shifted awkwardly. "It . . . It isn't one a lady should play." The same Troivackian who had spoken before answered evasively.

Kat's eyes sparkled with delight. "Oh my, are you perhaps playing Bloody Four? Or . . . perhaps . . . Bullshit?"

The men all jerked back while wincing at the crude word leaving her mouth.

"Aha! Well, sirs, I'll have you know, I love both of those games. Do you mind if I join you?" As she spoke, Kat was already hefting up her amber-toned chiffon dress into her hands either to kneel or sit cross-legged around the makeshift table.

The men seized up as though paralyzed by a catastrophe unfolding in front of them.

"That isn't appropriate, Lady Katarina."

Kat's stomach lurched as she stiffened, then begrudgingly looked toward the voice, only to find herself facing the crown prince.

Eric stood with his arms folded across his chest casually, as the sailors behind Kat leapt to their feet and bowed to him hastily. He barely regarded them as he continued to stare at the redhead, who was pleased to note that she was at least half an inch taller than the prince.

"Lady Katarina, you must have forgotten, but it is considered inappropriate and wrong for a noblewoman in Troivack to partake in such pastimes." Eric's tone was bored, and behind Kat, he noticed the sailors exhale in relief.

Kat's eyebrows lifted. "How surprising—"

"It was most likely addressed in your lessons. Don't worry, I can remind you whenever you forget these things." Eric's voice had turned warm, but his expression never shifted. As a result, the subtle mocking was not lost on Katarina.

A fresh wave of heat burst from her, making the Troivackian sailors nearby look around in confusion as Kat proceeded to mirror the prince in folding her arms over her chest.

"What I was going to say before you *interrupted* me, Your Highness, is how surprising it is that Troivackian customs have extended to this *Daxarian* ship that is still in *Daxarian* waters. Laws, customs, and other unspoken rules are still under *our* kingdom's jurisdiction. At least that's what *I* learned in my lessons. Is this wrong, Your Highness?"

Eric's mouth turned upward into a dry smile. "Bloody Four and Bullshit aren't appropriate in Daxarian customs either."

Kat's eyes narrowed, her index finger tapping her arm restlessly. "I see. Well, you do know what *is* considered a polite custom in Daxaria for such a circumstance?"

Eric's smile drifted down into a flat line once more. He didn't like her new angle.

"A *lord* or respectable noble is to keep me company. Doing things like drinking tea and engaging in socially acceptable discussion. Meaning you and I will be forced to be by each other's sides every day for the next two weeks."

Eric frowned, and the Troivackian sailors witnessing the exchange watched spellbound. It was as though they were attending a private theater performance.

"There is also, of course, the matter of arranging documents for the princess's arrival in Troivack—"

"I finished that before boarding the ship." Kat smiled beatifically.

Eric straightened his shoulders. "I'm sure a *lady* such as yourself would have brought along some needlework."

"I sadly left my needles at home, though I must say, having something sharp in my hand does sound wonderful right about now." Kat's vehemence made a few of the Troivackian soldiers behind her smirk. They all appreciated a good lust for blood. Even if it was relatively strange for it to be doled out by a woman.

"So, Lady Katarina, you wish to spend all your waking hours at my side?" Eric asked with a scoff. He was going to call her bluff one way or another.

Kat straightened, her golden eyes growing crazed. "Well, of course I didn't want to be such a burden, which is why I was seeking these wonderful sailors' help in perhaps enjoying a few hours of harmless fun."

It was Eric's turn to smile as he stepped forward. "Now, now, my lady. We can't have me being the cause of you annoying others! Don't worry, I promise to keep you *most* entertained. In fact, if you could see about obtaining another barrel for yourself to perch upon, I'd enjoy your company a great deal while *I* join these fine Troivackians for a game or two of cards."

Kat wanted to kill him.

However, given the surplus of eyewitnesses, she knew she'd have to settle for subtle torture.

She gave a subtle bow of her head, though it pained her greatly. "Very well, Your Highness . . . I look forward to seeing how you play."

Eric, mistaking her concession and barely suppressed ire for a win in his favor, smiled genuinely and moved past her to join the men's card game.

It took the sailors several moments to shake themselves free of their trance after witnessing the heated exchange between the two nobles.

When Katarina returned, she was hefting the barrel herself and set it behind and to the right of the prince. She sat herself and crossed her legs.

Eric shot her one final smug half grin before plucking up the small pile of cards that had been dealt to him in the meantime.

"Alright men, what's the game, and what are the stakes?" Eric asked, eyeing the three other Troivackians around the table.

"Game is Bloody Four. We bet chores, Your Highness, until the last three days of the voyage when we bet coin or other assets." The same Troivackian who had first addressed Kat explained the rules, his dark eyes fixed on his own disappointing hand, earning a frown.

Eric replied, "Hm, a mite difficult in my case, but we could always make the winnings different based on the winners and losers. If I lose, I can bet my boots or belt. If you lose to me, you could perhaps bet your free time. For example, I may request a card game at night when you normally get an hour's sleep."

The men all perked up. It was a remarkably fair suggestion, and the idea of having a pair of fine leather boots was certainly intriguing.

"We agree to the terms, Your Highness." The Troivackian soldier on the prince's right spoke again, though he hesitated for a moment when he noticed Kat smirking. It made him feel as though she had rigged the game somehow . . . even though she wasn't playing . . .

Eric, however, failed to notice this as he arranged his four cards in his hands.

"Alright, I bet my belt," the prince announced, his face becoming passive. A sure sign of a seasoned gambler . . .

Eric's gaze cut over his hand to the faces of the men, who were suddenly smiling. When he glanced behind himself, Kat was sitting with a modest expression, her chin propped up in the palm of her hand.

For a moment he wondered if she would be the type to help the others cheat, but that would mean she knew how to play the game . . .

Would Finlay Ashowan allow his daughter to learn how to gamble?

Eric considered that option briefly before shaking his head.

No.

She was probably making faces at him behind his back like the child she still was.

Eric had won the first couple of rounds and collected a good amount of future entertainment from the men, but his luck had taken a turn when he lost the third hand, which included his belt, his trousers, and his vest. He assured the winners either he'd have the items sent to them by that evening or win them back. He wasn't worried. At least not yet.

"S'cuse me, Your Highness?" the Troivackian on Eric's right interrupted, his eyes darting to his own hand, then back to the prince.

"Yes?"

"Would you mind if we made the game a bit more interesting?"

Eric stared expectantly at the man.

"What if this round . . . if you lose . . . not only do we get your tunic, but also any Troivackian moonshine you have on board?"

Eric eyed each of the men carefully, all who were rather awkward, and two of them couldn't even meet his gaze.

He turned to stare at Kat again, who looked bored and lifted her eyebrows at him expectantly. She hadn't moved since the last time he'd checked on her, and considering how she seemed to have all kinds of restless tics, Eric narrowed his eyes briefly before turning back to the game.

"I will accept these terms if Lady Katarina goes and sits behind you." Eric nodded to the fellow seated on a pile of ropes directly across from him.

The men collectively hesitated, but Eric noticed at least one pair of eyes darted over his shoulder, then smiled in the direction of where Katarina Ashowan sat. It was this very man who replied, "As you wish, Your Highness."

Frowning, Eric waited as Kat sighed dramatically.

"Honestly, first you insist I keep you company and not play myself, and now I'm being sent wherever your whims take you." Standing with no small measure of indignation, Kat made a show of moving her barrel behind the Troivackian opposite the prince.

Eric didn't say anything as he watched her settle down, her legs crossed and her chin propped in her palm once more. He frowned again. He hadn't picked up his hand yet, but she didn't look all that bothered . . . But there *was* a strange glow to her eyes . . .

Just what in the world was going on?

Glancing at his cards, Eric noted he had a fair hand. Three kings and a two. If he could get a fourth king in his hand, he had a good chance of winning. Normally he would be confident in such a good dealing, but his prickling senses indicated not everything was as it seemed.

"One discard one pickup for all bets in?" Eric clarified, his eyes cutting to the men around the table to see if there were any tells on their faces.

The sailor on Eric's left cleared his throat, then nodded.

The one across from him nodded, his eyes not leaving his hand.

The Troivackian on his right also nodded to Eric, glancing at him only once.

"Then shall we?" Eric set down his two and plucked up . . . a king.

He almost smiled, but that was when a small movement caught his eye . . .

Katarina's index finger was tapping again. Her right hand was wrapped around her left arm that supported her chin. Her energy was restless again, but none of the men were looking at her. Lazily, her eyes drifted around the game, then met the prince's frowning stare. She smiled sweetly.

Oh, she had definitely been up to *something*.

Regardless, there was nothing Eric could do but wait for the other players to discard and pick up their final cards.

Eric set down his hand for everyone to see. "Four kings."

The Troivackian on his right dropped down two threes and two fours. He had a garbage hand.

The Troivackian across from him lay down a jack, a queen, a king, and an ace. A hand called the Royal Pardon that could have been helpful to the man had the game been longer than one hand, but one round with all bets in, its value still ranked beneath Eric's.

Finally, the Troivackian on Eric's left lay down his hand.

Three sixes and an ace.

The Bloody Four's highest ranking hand.

Eric had lost, and Katarina was smiling something fierce.

Leaning back in his seat, his arms folded, Eric nodded to the winning sailor. "You will have your winnings arrive by this evening. Now. Given that this is our first meeting, I won't be a sore loser about the cheating, but I will insist to learn just how you all did it."

The Troivackians burst into grins that matched Katarina's.

"Sorry, Highness, in Troivack, a good cheater is deemed every bit a winner as one who played honorably," the Troivackian on Eric's right explained while rising onto his feet with a stretch. "Well then, we best be getting back to work." With a nod to his fellow sailors, the men collected their cards and stood, meandering away with a certain measure of gaiety having earned their spoils.

Katarina stood as well, her hands clasped in front of her skirts as she took in a deep breath of sea air and let it out in triumph.

"So, how'd you do it?" Eric asked again, his tone flat.

Kat's gaze danced out over the water, her hand rising to shield her eyes as she looked to the horizon.

"I don't know what you're talking about, Your Highness. After all, as you said, it isn't proper for a Daxarian woman to play cards, so how could I have ever—"

Eric stood, cutting off her speech. "Lady Katarina, be careful how much you irritate me. I've been known to be rather vexing myself when I put my mind to it."

Kat turned to stare at him, her smile fading. "Interestingly enough, this wouldn't be the first time you've given such warnings, Your Highness, but in light of your terrible loss, I'm willing to be the bigger person. I'll tell you this much"—Kat rounded on him, her wolf's grin returning—"I have friends both in high and low places."

Eric opened his mouth to ask whether that was meant to be a threat, but a shout interrupted him.

"Oyy! Come check this out! Your Highness, Lady Kat!"

Eric's assistant, Mr. Julian was calling to them, and that was the perfect cue Katarina needed to leave the prince and avoid further questioning. Staring at Katarina's retreating back, the future king of Daxaria found himself with a renewed resolve not to let the infuriating Ashowan woman get the best of him ever again . . .

Though how realistic that goal was remained to be seen.

CHAPTER 12

THE BEST PIÑA COLADA

As Katarina made her way across the ship deck to where the prince's assistant had called out, she couldn't help but feel the pointed glare behind her from the inimitable Eric Reyes.

She knew rigging the card game would prick his pride, but he had started it by not letting her play herself! This way, she at least felt the satisfaction of winning in some manner. Plus, if the Troivackian sailors had any sense of gratitude for her assistance, she expected a cut of the winnings. A bottle of moonshine would certainly help make the journey a little more interesting for a night or two.

Upon reaching the assistant, Thomas Julian, Kat noted the boy's eyes were trained on something behind a coil of thick rope and between two crates.

"What is it, Mr. Julian?" Kat asked curiously as she heard Eric's boots on the deck, drawing nearer to them.

"Look, my lady! I noticed a dead seagull on the deck here, so I came to remove it, and that's when I heard them!"

Kat arched an eyebrow at the dead bird off to the assistant's left. It was odd for a gull to be so far from land . . . Perhaps it had died there yesterday . . . ?

A chorus of mews pulled Kat from her thoughts, directing her to peer more closely between the crates.

"Kittens!" she cried happily, dropping to her knees and reaching eagerly between the crates.

"My lady! Careful!" Mr. Julian seized her forearm. "If the mother cat is there, she could attack you!"

"The mother isn't there," she countered while gently easing her arm from his grasp.

"You cannot know that, my lady; it's too shadowed to properly—"

"Mr. Julian, I can see in there just fine. There are two kittens. No mother in sight." Kat resumed reaching behind the crates and plucked up the two creatures. One had a white belly with a smoky fur along his back, and the other was a soft-colored calico with only her nose remaining pink.

"It looks as though their mother left them here . . . They are old enough to survive on their own, so it happens," Kat announced after holding each close to herself and letting out a small sigh of disappointment. Neither kitten seemed to be her familiar.

"An expert on cheating at cards and kittens I see," Eric observed as Kat thrust the smoky boy kitten at him without another glance.

Kat rose with a sigh. Mr. Julian was eyeing the small, soft calico in her hands, so she wordlessly offered the little beasty to him, at which he couldn't resist breaking out into an excited smile.

"You missed one," Eric noted while crouching down and reaching behind the crate. "Looks like it hid."

Kat turned around, her expression still glum from the earlier disappointment.

Just then, the boy kitten she had handed to Eric began to squirm as the prince stood back up, and so he straightened abruptly to lean both animals against his torso.

Kat stared at the back of the new kitten's head, its face buried into Eric's shoulder.

Something was tingling in between her eyebrows, and it was making her feel . . . twitchy.

"Did you get fur in your eyes or something?" Eric asked with a small, dry laugh as he noticed Kat's face scrunching up.

"No, I just . . . Can I see that one, please?"

"It's clinging to my shirt; you'll have to grab it yourself," Eric managed as he shifted the animals in his hands awkwardly, the stubble on his face catching the sun's light and gleaming slightly.

Kat reached forward hastily and lifted the small kitten free of its hold, ignoring the fact that she had to brush Eric's hand and the subsequent rush it brought to her head. Then, as she looked down into their face, and they peered back, she felt her heart thud against her chest.

Heat surged through her body, and unbeknownst to her, an orange gold aura burst from her skin like flames.

"Gods! What is—" Mr. Julian yelped, leaping back with the kitten she had handed him still clutched to his shoulder protectively.

Eric's hand dropped to the dagger clipped to his belt on instinct as he, too, stepped back in surprise.

Katarina's golden eyes were shimmering brightly as she continued staring transfixed at the small kitten in her hands, completely unaware of the distress she was giving the two men in her company.

"Lady Katarina," Eric called out, wanting the strange glowing to cease.

When the young woman showed no sign she had heard him, he grew impatient. "Kat!"

At long last she blinked and looked up, still stunned for a moment. "I found them . . . I found . . . my familiar." Kat's words were choked as the small kitten in her hands allowed themselves to nestle against her comfortably.

Eric blinked in confusion, then turned his gaze down and noticed the kitten was another soft calico, with a white belly, paws, and snout, and on the very tip of her pink nose, was a freckle. He stared into the kitten's green gaze, then back at Katarina, who was grinning ear to ear with tears in her eyes.

"Congratulations, Lady Katarina, you have an adorable familiar," Eric responded casually. There wasn't any hostility in his tone, but there was a wariness about his manner after seeing her magic aura burn so wildly.

"I . . . I think I'm going to go try and find a new name for . . . her. A new name for my familiar!" Kat blushed happily after she checked under the small tail and discovered that the kitten was, in fact, female.

Without another word, Kat drifted away, her utter joy and excitement potent. She drew several of the sailors' eyes her way, though more than a couple of them had witnessed her magical flare earlier and were whispering intently amongst themselves.

Eric sighed, his previous anger and agitation toward the redhead dimming considerably. He knew it was an important day for witches when they bonded with their familiars.

"Th-That was a little scary," Mr. Julian confessed quietly while sidling closer to the prince.

"You don't have anything to worry about. After all, of the two of us, who do you think she'd be the first to attack if she went on a magical rampage?"

"That's true," Mr. Julian replied without realizing exactly what he was agreeing to as his attention turned back to the feline in his own arms.

Eric turned and shot the young lad a small, weary yet amused grin and decided not to give him too hard of a time over inadvertently confirming Lady Katarina Ashowan loathed him greatly.

"Are you going to keep that one?" Eric asked his assistant instead while gently scratching the kitten in his own hands around the scruff.

"I couldn't possibly, Your Highness. I have too many duties to properly mind a cat. Will you keep that one?" Mr. Julian responded importantly.

Eric glanced down at the downy fur in his hands and shook his head. "I have enough on my plate as is. Besides, it isn't a bad idea for there to be a couple ship cats. Keeps the rats at bay."

Mr. Julian nodded before turning toward the ship's stairs that would take him back down to the galley where their cabins were situated. "Doesn't hurt to have them around while we get a bit of work done either I think . . ."

Without another glance back, the assistant disappeared below deck, leaving the prince alone on deck once more.

With a sigh, Eric closed his eyes.

He had been able to distract himself for a couple of hours thanks to the card game with the sailors, and, annoyingly enough, Lady Katarina. However, the trip was going to be a boring one. Traveling as the prince when he had been absent for four years meant he didn't have any work waiting for him, as no one would have assigned him any routine tasks in his absence; they weren't going to trust him with any grand responsibilities just yet.

It also meant everyone was on ceremony with him. Honestly, if it weren't for Katarina's encounter with the Troivackians, they probably would have scattered upon his approach.

Instead, he now had a debt of time from the men, and he intended to use it to try and find . . . something. He'd make them play cards with him again *without* a meddlesome redhead, and hopefully he'd start figuring some things out.

Turning back toward the barrel where the men had been playing cards, Eric decided to wait and see if any of the other sailors would partake in another game or two. It didn't hurt to get to know everyone around him, or to rack up more debt from them. It'd make certain possibilities more available to him . . .

Kat held the adorable kitten in the crook of her arm as she lay stretched out on the cramped single bed she was to sleep on for the journey. Her maid's bed was across from hers, and only two trunks had managed to fit in the cabin, one between the two headboards, and the other at the foot of Katarina's bed. In fact, the room was so small that Katarina had made a point of spending as little time as possible in its confines. However, with Kat's newfound familiar fast asleep in her arms, her tiny, white paws occasionally twitching as she slept, there was nowhere else in the world she'd rather be.

"Thank you, Goddess . . . Thank you, thank you, thank you . . ." Katarina whispered over and over as she felt the magical connection between herself and the feline fill her with warmth and joy.

Kat couldn't wait to write to her father and tell him the good news. After that she would even write a letter to her brother, Tam, and brag for at least two pages. Perhaps she should even write a letter to Likon, her childhood friend turned Tam's assistant.

"So it's true." Katarina's eyes cracked open at the sound of her maid Poppy's excited whisper.

Grinning, the redhead nodded. "She's mine; there is no doubt whatsoever."

Poppy clapped her hands together softly and bounced where she stood, then thought better of the movement as a fresh wave of seasickness made her turn a new shade of green.

After swallowing uncertainly, the maid decided it was safe to speak. "Oh, my lady, I cannot believe it's finally happened! So, as a witch, what does this mean?"

"Well, it means I've found a place in my life, be it physically or situationally, that I am supposed to be in, as designed by the Gods. A place where I am supposed to flourish as a witch and contribute as a medium between nature and mankind."

Poppy's brown eyes were wide. "Oh."

"Not everyone has such a dramatic purpose, so no need to assume anything." Kat chuckled at the young maid's awestruck expression.

"But you're already dramatic as is, my lady."

Kat laughed while Poppy clapped her hand over her mouth briefly before adding, "Oh, I-I'm sorry, my lady, I-I didn't mean it in any kind of bad way! It's just you are . . . noticeable! You have a big personality! Why, the whole kingdom has heard of you!"

At this, the noblewoman's good-humored expression dimmed.

"Not all good things, mind you, but . . . you know what? Who cares! This may be my fresh start! I have my familiar now. It's time for me to be the best I can be! With this adorable little girl here. Though I still don't have a name." Kat sighed while reaching down and gently scratching the kitten's chin and watching her smile in her sleep, her whiskers twitching.

"Hm . . . well . . . what about Patches? She has lots of different soft colors in her fur," Poppy suggested while stepping forward and craning her neck to get a better glimpse of the kitten.

Kat wrinkled her nose and shook her head. "A bit too common a name. She's one of the best things to ever happen to me, and I want something special."

"What about calling her Princess?" Poppy mused, though she didn't look too set on it either.

Kat shook her head. "It could get confusing being around the Daxarian princess and my familiar at the same time. Even if Princess Alina is going to be the Troivackian queen soon."

"Wait! I got it!" Poppy snapped her fingers and stood up straighter in excitement. "What was something else you thought was the best thing recently?"

Kat frowned and racked her brain.

What was the best thing? If it wasn't the kitten in her arms, then whatever it was wasn't anywhere nearly as—

"That piña colada drink you had last night!" Poppy announced, pointing her finger excitedly to the kitten.

"Damn, that *was* incredible! Wait . . . So you're saying . . ." Kat dropped her golden gaze to the small kitten. "Her name should be Piña Colada?"

The kitten stirred from her slumber then, and with a yawn that revealed a thumbprint sized birthmark on the roof of her mouth, her sleepy eyes opened to regard the scene around her.

"Well, that settles it. This is Piña Colada. Pina for short!" Kat burst out, as she slightly changed the enunciation of the *n* for the nickname. Her cheeks ached from smiling so much.

Hastily dropping a kiss onto the kitten's forehead, Kat flopped back onto her pillow happily as Poppy beamed with pride over helping name her mistress's familiar.

What a spectacular omen for their time in Troivack.

. . . Or so they thought.

CHAPTER 13

DIPPING AND DIVING

On the seventh day of the journey, Katarina and her newly discovered familiar finally began reappearing on deck after having holed themselves up in their cabin and the dining galley. The witch often chattered to the feline she'd lovingly named Pina, short for Piña Colada.

When Kat stepped out, a blustery day greeted her, and the winds would have easily blown her long red hair into a web of snarls and tangles in no time if it hadn't been braided. The sails could be heard snapping in the gusts as shouts from the first mate beckoned the crew to harness the wind power. In the span of water surrounding them, frothy caps appeared, and the temperature had cooled greatly.

Placing her hands on her hips and letting out a long breath, Kat turned her cheek toward the small kitten perched on her shoulder.

"Well, Pina? Shall we go see what entertainment awaits us?" she asked with a grin.

The kitten's answer was to nuzzle her nose against Kat's ear and offer a loud purr.

Not needing any further inspiration, Katarina decided to speak with the captain, as many of the sailors performed their tasks hastily, their faces tensed, and she hadn't exactly been a great conversationalist during the dinners with the captain and prince since finding Pina. Often, she was in a hurry to return to her cabin either to feed her new familiar or introduce her to new nooks and crannies in the vessel.

As she mounted the steps to the upper deck, the captain was speaking to the helmsman.

"Good day, Captain Alphonse," Katarina greeted, her hand still resting on the polished railing.

"Ah, Lady Katarina, perhaps you should remain below deck in your cabin for today; a fierce storm is brewing over the waters." The captain responded without sparing her more than a cursory glance.

Kat glanced to the sky, and sure enough, the clouds were thickening, and off in the distance, they appeared black.

"Ah. Well, if you should need any help, captain, I would be more than happy to—" Kat began but was cut off by Alphonse.

"Niles, helm to me; go tell the men to tie their lines and latch all hatches. Pardon me, my lady, but I really must insist you go below deck now." The captain's voice was stern, but his eyes remained fixed on the horizon, his brow creased.

Shooting a glance over her shoulder to her maid, Poppy, who stood at the bottom of the stairs, Kat noticed the woman was beginning to look green yet again as the ship's rocking grew more dramatic.

Once she had touched down on the deck, Eric appeared, wearing worn, battered trousers and a tunic that probably had been white but currently was a yellowed gray. He swept past Kat, heading toward the captain himself.

"Get below deck; this is going to be rough," he cast over his shoulder without bothering to pause in his journey.

"Ah, Your Highness, if this storm takes us into the night, please remember I can see in the dark. If that could be of help, keep it in mind," Kat called out to his back, her tone rather breezy and easy-going.

Eric hesitated on the stairs then and looked at her with a frown. "You don't know the first thing about sailing, do you?"

"I don't know a lot, no, but even I know a good set of eyes is valuable." Kat shrugged.

Shaking his head, Eric turned to face her. "If someone who doesn't know what they're doing gets involved, it would be more harmful than good. Stay below deck." His order was made with a firm expression with no room for argument as he then turned and resumed his trek up to see the captain.

Kat sighed but could tell the stress in the air was high enough. It was true she didn't really know much about boats, she had gone sailing on her family's vessels before but hadn't really been involved in the actual work.

She shrugged.

A bit of a bumpy ride didn't bother her, though she couldn't say she looked forward to her cabin smelling like sick for hours on end, eyeing Poppy's olive green cheeks dubiously.

As she walked back to her cabin with Pina on her shoulder purring happily, Katarina tried to think of some possible games that could keep herself occupied. It seemed as though she'd have to entertain herself for the foreseeable future.

The storm raged well into the night, the deck pitching back and forth, up and down, relentlessly. After the first few hours, Poppy finally excused herself to stay in one of the storage cabins, as her ability to keep the contents in her stomach deteriorated, and Kat was growing nauseated from the smell.

Once her maid had gone, all Katarina could do was chuckle at her current game of hanging on for dear life to her bed frame, while Pina splayed herself across the blanket, her claws keeping her dangling body on the bed despite the rails of the boat turning precariously close to the water.

Giggling, Kat kicked her legs in the air as they hung freely, her grip on her headboard firm, as the ship tilted nearly ninety degrees.

"I must say, who would've thought storms could be this fun!" she called out gleefully, though her kitten familiar let out a particularly long mew that indicated the sentiment was not shared.

"I can't even tell if it's night or day out there! Isn't this exciting?" Kat called over the creaking wood and the shouts of the sailors heard over the thunderous waves and crackling lightning.

When the ship began to rock back to the point where Kat could lie on her belly safely, she turned toward the chest that had once been at the foot of her bed but had slid until it hit the door.

"Perhaps I get ready, just in case they need me, hm?" Kat remarked idly, her eyes sparkling with the delight of the thrill.

Pina didn't respond. She was still hanging onto the bed cover for dear life, clearly not willing to trust their temporary return to right-side up.

Kat proceeded to scramble over to the chest and quickly released its lock. She snatched her men's clothes just in time for a fresh wave to send her flying back toward her headboard.

Fortunately, she was able to seize her footboard at the last second before earning a bad bruise.

She then changed in the most inefficient manner possible while also dodging the open chest that had been sent careening toward the other end of the cabin. It would have most certainly broken a bone had she been in its path. However, this narrow miss of injury only served in adding to Kat's exuberance as she managed at long last to pull on the leather wrist cuffs she figured would be helpful in the event she had to grab any ropes.

"I'll just see if they need my eyes and be right back, Pina!" Kat called out to the kitten.

When she noticed the small familiar still clinging desperately to the bedding, the redhead hesitated. She needed to make sure Pina wasn't flung against a wall and hurt . . .

Picking up her discarded dress hastily, Kat snatched her familiar up, and despite earning a few scratches from her panic, she was able to fashion a sling out of the garment before then tying the dress's sleeves to her headboard.

Once in the confines of the makeshift pouch, Pina curled up gratefully, sensing this was a much safer option than merely attaching herself to anything she could get her claws on.

"Alright, I'll see you in a bit!" Kat darted to her cabin door just as the vessel pitched on its side again. As she began to close the door, she could see the chest once again sliding in her direction, and shortly after she slammed the door shut, heard it careen into the wood.

The smell of the sea filled Kat's nostrils as she leapt against the pull of gravity toward the stairs, her heart racing, and her smile blazing. She reached the soaked steps and began climbing them in time with the ship leveling itself out.

Despite this, she clutched the railing until on deck to keep herself steady as she surveyed her waterlogged surroundings. The wind was whipping the water every which way, the men were tying lines and calling out to one another as they attempted to hold the boom and mast in place.

Mountains of water rose and fell around them, flashes of lightning their only available light . . .

That is, until Kat realized she was already aglow in her familiar magical aura of flickering orange and gold. Her eyes, however, shone even brighter than her magical essence. She surveyed the scene, grateful that her hair was braided or else it would have become a great hindrance, and she looked for somewhere to help.

Eric was the first to notice Kat amongst the chaos as he braced his boots against the ship's side, clinging alongside four other sailors to the ropes that, if released, threatened to drop the mast onto the deck. He looked soaked, cold, and tired; it was clear he had spent most of the day and night helping the sailors keep the ship from sinking.

There was nothing but darkness and water. Over and over, the sea had submerged the ship and then cast it back out, making every man swallow more than their fair share of seawater, their eyes burning with the salt and strain of attempting to see even a foot before them.

"What the—" Eric had turned his head to hear another command from the captain, only he found his eyes resting on what appeared to be an ethereal being.

Her glow sent a surge of relief through his chest, as he finally could see in Katarina Ashowan's light that many of the men remained aboard and upright, though they looked equally exhausted and drenched.

So thankful was he for the light in the darkness, that it took Eric a moment to remember that Kat should still be below deck and nowhere near this hell of a storm.

"WHAT THE HELL ARE YOU DOING?!" Eric roared over the crash of thunder that threatened to break the sky. Another wave sent the boat's side almost horizontal into the water.

The men hung on for dear life as their feet lifted off the deck.

For a panicked moment, Eric couldn't look anywhere but his hands as he attempted to pull himself up, the rope around his waist tightening painfully. This was precisely when Eric realized that Kat wouldn't have had a line tied to her.

Cursing loudly and risking a glance over his shoulder toward the noblewoman, Eric found Kat's long limbs wrapped around the rail of the ship, and . . . she was laughing. She also appeared to be burning even brighter.

"IS SHE MAD?!" one of the sailors behind Eric bellowed into his ear as the deck finally raised back under their feet.

"COMPLETELY!" the prince replied as they quickly set to retying the stays yet again.

"GET HER BACK BELOW DECK!" was all the sailor managed to say before they scattered to help their colleagues. Eric was positive that if there was a second more of time, the man would've called Katarina a number of insulting names.

He knew because he was about to call her something colorful himself.

Clinging to the side of the ship, Eric slowly made his way over to the railing where Katarina was whooping as though she were having the time of her life.

"GET! BACK! BELOW! DECK!" the prince managed briefly before spitting out the sea and rainwater that filled his mouth.

Kat's golden eyes cut to him, her smile eerily peaceful.

"WHAT DO YOU NEED HELP WITH?" she called out gleefully as

she placed her feet back down on the creaking deck, her arms still wrapped around one of the pillars of the bannister.

"NOTHING! GET OUT OF HERE BEFORE YOU DROWN, IDIOT!" Eric shouted angrily while attempting to take another step toward her.

"WHAT IS WRONG UP HERE?" she asked instead, ignoring his order and his insult.

"EVERYTHING! INCLUDING YOU!"

"I WON'T LEAVE UNTIL YOU TELL ME WHAT'S HAPPENING!" Kat shouted back defiantly, her smile far too teasing despite the chaos around her.

"THE HEADSAIL HAS SNAPPED FREE. WE'RE TRYING TO SAVE THE MAST, AND WE HAVE NO IDEA WHAT DIRECTION WE ARE FACING! NOW, GET BELOW DECK!"

"THE HEADSAIL IS AT THE FRONT OF THE BOAT, RIGHT? I JUST HAVE TO TIE IT DOWN?" Kat released the banister and immediately darted around Eric with inhuman speed and agility before pouncing onto the railing on the opposite side of the deck Eric was tied to..

"KATARINA!" Eric tried to lunge for her, but instead his boots slipped on the wood and sent him careening into the side of the ship he had originated from, bruising his side painfully.

Once he was clutching the rail again and his feet were back under him, Eric looked up to see Katarina had already crossed the entire ship deck in a matter of seconds as though she were dancing and predicting every lurch of the planks beneath her feet. Before he could open his mouth to shout at someone else to seize the redheaded fool, he realized Kat was already climbing the ratlines closest to the bow with great speed and ease. When she was high enough that a fall could easily be fatal, she turned toward the rogue, deteriorating headsail.

In the light from her aura, Eric noticed the growing abyss of water in front of the bow.

"Oh Gods," he uttered, his heart sinking to his stomach as he beheld the tsunami-sized wave.

She was going to be killed.

"KATARINA!" Eric shouted just in time for his boot to catch on a loose rope, nearly causing him to fall overboard and bruising his other side.

When he was right side up again, wiping the water from his eyes best he could, he saw the magical burn that emulated from Katarina Ashowan high up on the ratlines like a Goddess . . . the wave had grown bigger . . .

Then, as though in slow motion, the boat lifted into the air as if it meant to challenge the might of the sea, and Eric watched horrified as the vessel's nose began to dive into the wave that consumed the sky.

Only the ship wasn't the only thing diving.

Katarina Ashowan, as bright as a star in the darkness, was diving for the loose headsail, its ropes whipping about in the air.

Eric's heart stopped in his chest. Through the darkness and over the roar of the storm, he heard the loud, laughing crow of the maddest woman he had ever met as she soared through the air toward certain death.

Before his yell was finished being torn from his lungs, the wall of black water consumed the vessel entirely.

CHAPTER 14

STUBBORN STORMS

Kat couldn't remember the last time she'd felt so . . . so . . .

She let out a pleased, intoxicated sigh, her limbs were blissfully heavy, and her head light and fluffy. For once she was . . . relaxed.

The air smelled great, and it was nice and cool outside . . .

"What do you mean she dove off to tie up the headsail?! I thought Kauchel had finally gotten it under control?"

"It wasn't me, captain."

"Oh Gods . . ."

"D-Do we turn around and search for her?! T-There's a chance she is still out there!"

Kat frowned at the voices. They were interfering with her dozing. Did they not know how difficult it was for her to completely deplete her reserves enough to reach such a state? Poppy sounded upset, but why would she be? The storm had tapered off an hour ago.

Oh, well. Kat was feeling weary enough that she could tune them out . . . perhaps she could go back to sleep again . . .

"I'm sorry to say this, but there is no way we'd be able to find her out there. The amount of damage we've taken from the storm is enough that we'll be lucky to make it to Troivack in one piece. We've also blown a few leagues off our initial course." The captain's voice was somber but resolute.

There was a lengthy silence, during which Katarina grinned to herself with her eyes still closed. She couldn't quite comprehend what was happening, but at least there was quiet.

It was perfect for a nice . . . long . . . nap . . .

"Who . . . Who will write to her family?" came the slow question from the first mate.

Another long pause.

"I will." Eric's voice penetrated through the haze of relaxation Kat was happily drifting through. His voice sounded hoarse and cold . . . Well, that was normal.

"I'll write her father and inform him what happened once we reach Troivack." Eric stopped talking abruptly, as though he were emotional . . .

I must be imagining things. Eric? Emotional? Pfft.

Kat continued lounging in . . . where exactly was she?

Not certain that she entirely cared where she was because it felt perfectly comfortable, Kat managed to crack open an eye and found herself staring into the unblinking carved wooden eyes of a mermaid. Her long hair covered her breasts, and her tail arched beautifully behind her torso, while a crown of laurels rested atop of her head.

"I don't know why you bother covering your breasts; you're part fish. Unless of course other mermaids raise a *clam-ity* about it!" Kat laughed to herself before once again closing her eyes. It was the best kind of day.

Little did the redhead realize, but the sound of her voice had made the people standing on the deck of the ship go silent.

Eric's bloodshot eyes snapped to the captain.

Had he imagined hearing Katarina Ashowan's voice? He *was* sleep deprived . . .

No, everyone was looking wildly about themselves as well.

"My lady?" Poppy called out tentatively, her eyes beginning to grow hopeful as her tightly gripped fists pressed into her chest.

"Lady Katarina?" Captain Alphonse called out, looking upward to the ratlines while shielding the sun from his eyes.

Eric continued peering around the deck before desperately shouting, "Kat!"

"Mmmmgaaarrrrd, sleeping! Sleeeep. Sleeping."

Everyone whirled around to face the bow of the ship, and when they still didn't see the noblewoman, Eric inched closer to the broken rail, leaned carefully over its edge, and peered down to see . . .

Katarina Ashowan.

Alive.

Unharmed.

Dressed as a man.

And . . .

Napping?

Eric blinked several more times, his eyes still burning from salt and exhaustion but it was real. Lady Katarina was sprawled out in the bow net that had dropped low. Apparently, the fully grown woman had decided to rest during the remainder of the storm there.

"Gods . . . Katarina Ashowan, so help me . . ." Eric didn't finish the thought as he turned and crumpled onto the ship deck, his back pressed against the railing, his final tendril of strength on the verge of snapping. He pinched the bridge of his nose, and relief flooded his body. He pressed his head back against the ship as the captain, first mate, and Poppy rushed over and took stock of Katarina Ashowan enjoying her new resting place.

"Good Gods! How did she survive that?! We all saw that dive for the bow, but . . . she roped off the headsail, and without being tied to the ship, survived *there*?!" Captain Alphonse was worn ragged himself, and so his grasp on his emotions was nonexistent.

"Yes, well . . . She's an Ashowan after all. Consider yourself now cursed with the blessing of making her acquaintance. I know I am." Eric slowly pushed himself into a standing position and, despite swaying on the spot, managed to nod respectfully to the captain and then head toward the galley, hoping to find a dry bed to collapse into.

"Your Highness! How do we get her up here! She doesn't seem to be able to wake up!" the captain called to Eric's back.

He hesitated a moment before answering over his shoulder, "Get her familiar on deck. What'd she name that beast? Peanut?"

"Piña Colada, Your Highness! Pina for short!" Poppy clarified while stepping forward eagerly.

"Right. Well, get the animal on deck. It'll most likely rouse her, and if not, well . . . you have yourself a new figurehead." Eric continued his mission to regain some of his lost sleep, but most of all, he wanted to shake loose the ire that resonated to his core that Katarina Ashowan should do something so reckless and scare him so soundly.

He didn't want to worry about her, or mind her, and most important of all, he *never* wanted to be the one who would have to tell her father that she had died.

Thankfully, the remainder of the journey to Troivack passed without any further catastrophes, save for one small development that put every passenger and crew member ill at ease . . .

The prince refused to speak to or dine with Lady Katarina Ashowan.

If she tried to goad him, he'd look on as though she weren't saying anything at all. If she sat down amongst the sailors and him as they'd play cards, he'd stand and leave.

At first Katarina had relished in being free from his presence and his barbs, but after a while, it began to irk her.

Why was he so angry with her? She had helped tie down the headsail, hadn't she? She was perfectly fine, too! The Troivackian sailors had even come to acknowledge and, to some degree, respect her for her bravery and assumed magical strength.

However, it was painfully clear the captain and first mate did not share these sentiments. There was a disapproving air about them that Kat was all too familiar with, and so she took to dining in her own cabin.

In truth, it was hard for her to care about how upset the three men were with her. They didn't understand how free she felt ever since using up so much of her magic during the storm. They didn't know what it was like to constantly be at war with yourself . . .

For the first time in nearly a year, she could sit still without her leg rattling the table. Her index finger didn't impatiently tap, and she wasn't prone to moody outbursts either. She felt calm. Happy.

She only wished she had a monstrous storm to burn her magic into on a more regular basis. If she were honest, when she let her magic overtake her like that, she wasn't always entirely sure what happened. Normally, it would terrify her to sink into the intoxicating magical pull of burning away . . . or toward . . . anything. But in the face of a storm with no one to hurt . . .

"My lady, there's the city of Norum! Oh, I do wonder if Her Highness Princess Alina has arrived. I pray their ship made it through the storm alright," Poppy announced worriedly as the two women sat on the ship's deck with cups of warm tea clutched in their hands.

It was a cool day, a sure sign the fall weather was going to be settling over the land in a span of a few weeks.

Staring over the turquoise water, Kat eyed the whitewashed walls in the distance and the roofs tiled in reds and blues, some even in copper. It was a colorful greeting to the foreign land, and Kat couldn't help but admit to herself that her stomach was doing somersaults.

A tickling purr in her ear reminded the redhead that Pina was once again on her shoulders.

"That kitten really doesn't like sitting on your lap, does she?" Poppy observed, pulling Kat's attention back to her.

"No, but that works for me; I can move around if need be," the noblewoman replied while reaching up and idly scratching the kitten's cheeks and sending a tuft of loose white fur into the breeze.

As Kat watched the hairs blow away, her eyes landed on the prince who was on the upper deck gazing out toward Troivack, his left hand restlessly thrumming against the battered railing.

Katarina tilted her head curiously. It was as though he were antsy about something.

Sensing someone's eyes on him, Eric's head turned, and his gaze cut to Kat—when their eyes locked, his expression turned icy before he quickly looked away.

"Pfft." Kat rolled her eyes as she, too, looked back to the city of Norum.

"He was terrified when we thought you were lost, you know," Poppy began with a feeble attempt at a casual tone.

Kat's expression turned wry as she leaned forward, put her elbow on her knee, and rested her chin in the palm of her hand. "No one wants to tell a parent their child is dead. It wasn't my intent to scare him; I just helped was all."

Poppy's expression grew strained. "My lady, it isn't your place to—"

"I'm a witch. It isn't *their* place to assume I can't do things. I'm tired of being undermined. I've asked people constantly if I might be of help to them, but they always say no. I never even get the chance to earn their trust or to show what I am capable of."

"My lady, they had the situation in hand. They were just trying to lower the risk of casualties," Poppy countered, though it was clear that arguing against her mistress was proving to be rather difficult for her.

"Well, there weren't any casualties." Standing swiftly, Kat could feel her anger rising.

She knew she had disobeyed their orders, but when would she ever get the chance to prove what she could do? If her magic was finally giving her peace of mind after her antics, wasn't that a sign she had done what she was meant to do? Risking situations too dangerous for normal people?

"The prince . . . he . . . he means well," Poppy attempted again.

Katarina turned her blank expression to her maid, her eyes must've shimmered, however, because the poor young girl recoiled ever so slightly. Not that Kat had much control over when her magic appeared in her stare . . .

"If he is angry with me, then it's up to him to say so and try to work this out. Not you. I'm sorry, Poppy, but this is a matter that I think best if we leave it be. Besides, now that we're in Troivack, I'm sure he will have too many duties to be around much. Not to mention I'm going to be busy helping Her Highness with the upcoming coronation plans."

Poppy cast her gaze down, sending a pang of guilt through Katarina's stomach.

She often felt as though she were being a good person and never meant to hurt people, yet it seemed to be all she was truly successful at . . .

As she stalked over to the railing and stared out at Norum, a small memory tickled the back of her mind.

Hadn't she said before that she wouldn't have to bother being around the prince because she was leaving for Troivack? That had turned out swimmingly hadn't it?

Kat chuckled bitterly to herself.

At least with the prince angry with me, it increases the likelihood we will have nothing to do with each other.

As Katarina sat uncomfortably at the dining table, she avoided eye contact with the captain and Eric as best she could. She wore a dark blue dress, kept her hair loose, and wore no finery. She didn't need to feel any more of a spectacle amongst the two men than necessary.

It was their final dinner before they reached Norum's shores, where then they would depart to Troivack's capital in the south, the city of Vessa. As a result, tradition and decorum dictated they dine together.

"After we dock, will you have time with your family, Captain Alphonse?" Katarina attempted to smile at the captain, whose shuttered expression remained intact while issuing a slight nod in her direction.

"I will spend three weeks with my lad at home, then will set sail once more for Daxaria. I plan on finishing the deal with your father regarding the piña colada."

At the sound of her name, the small kitten that had been set loose to roam the cabin mewed, drawing the captain's eye to her and making him smile.

"Aye, Pina, you should be my representative. I can tell you'll win the hearts of any man or woman." The captain reached down and gave her an affectionate scratch on the cheek.

If only I could charm people like that, Kat thought to herself bleakly while spearing a portion of her baked potato.

"Captain, might I persuade you to find a new investor for that beverage? Perhaps with the newly titled Duke Cowan. The lad could certainly use a promising business venture to take his mind off losing his father."

Katarina's eyes snapped to Eric, who was staring steadily at the captain.

To his credit, the captain didn't balk under the request, despite it being from a future king.

"Apologies, Your Highness; I've already begun the transaction with Viscount Ashowan. To back out now could ruin me."

"Oh, I'm certain I could lend a hand in dissolving things amicably." Eric smiled charmingly while raising his goblet to his lips.

"There is no reason to cancel the deal with my family. Other than your petty dislike of us." Kat had had enough passive-aggressiveness from him.

No. She was going to face him completely, and she was not going to let him reduce her to slinging insults yet again.

Eric's eyes cut to Kat, the hazel color darkening until nearly brown, and his tanned, weathered face regarded her with the same callous coldness it had for the past week.

"I'm merely suggesting business and wealth be evenly distributed throughout the kingdom," Eric countered innocently.

"Then find a new deal to encourage for Duke Cowan. To put Captain Alphonse in a tense situation is selfish of you."

At this, Eric set his fork down, plucked his white linen napkin up from his lap, wiped his mouth, and leaned back in his chair.

"You want to talk about selfishness?"

Kat's heart was hammering in her chest. "We've danced around the topic before. Why not get it out in the open? Best to air our dirty laundry before we bid farewell, wouldn't you say?"

Eric folded his hands over his belly and continued staring at her levelly.

Captain Alphonse, too weary from the journey and the constant tension that ran between the two nobles, decided for once that he would not play mediator.

"You, Lady Katarina, placed every man aboard this vessel in great peril and in a horrible position of responsibility had you died. You rushed into a situation against orders, put yourself in jeopardy, and added stress onto those around you." Eric's voice was calm and even, but there was fire in his eyes.

Katarina placed her cutlery down and leaned her forearms on the table. "I'm a witch. People seem to forget that, and you were being too stubborn to consider that I could have been of valuable help. Even before the storm arrived, you could have asked what I am capable of, but you didn't. You shoved me aside without gaining any insight into how much of an asset I could be. Now. On to the audacity you displayed of calling *me* selfish for adding stress to those around me . . ."

"You are not in a position to comment on my life or choices, Lady Katarina."

"You're within earshot—I'd say our positioning is perfect. Did you know that neither your father nor sister knew for sure if you were dead or alive for nearly two out of the four years you were missing? Without explaining a word, you threw them both under the carriage wheels to cover for you with the courtiers breathing down their necks."

"That's enough." Eric's voice turned sharp.

"Did you know your father would lose himself in his mourning for your mother for days? You left him and Alina alone to—"

Eric's hand slammed on the table as he stood, his expression foreboding. "That is enough, Lady Katarina."

Despite her hands beginning to tremble, Kat leaned back in her chair and stared directly back at him. "You don't owe me or any courtiers an explanation for where you were, but you sure as hell owe your sister and father one."

Something snapped in Eric, and both Katarina and the captain could see it.

For a moment it looked as though he were going to start shouting or throwing things . . .

Instead, the prince straightened and left the room altogether.

To go where or do what, neither the captain nor Katarina could tell.

CHAPTER 15

WINDS OF CHANGE

Eyes wide, Katarina took in the sea of Troivackians filling the docks and the shore. She had never been in a place where she wasn't one of the tallest people present. If it weren't for her fiery red hair and ethereal gold eyes, there was the sense that she fit right in.

As she stared at the unique, gauzy dresses in pale colors that fluttered by her and the shortened trousers on the men that revealed the beginning of their shin bones, Katarina quickly realized that just as many of them were studying *her* with equal interest.

She had worn a light, long cream dress, though it was horribly wrinkled from its time in her chest aboard the ship, but her hair had been piled atop her head in a twisted updo that made her rare hair color a beacon for curious gazes.

Women and men whispered to each other as they passed her, making Kat do her best to smile affably. She only remembered that showing such an expression disturbed the Troivackians further when one couple hurried away from her as a result.

Whoops . . . forgot about that . . .

"Poppy, how close is the keep we are meant to stay in?" Kat turned to her maid, having grown increasingly uncomfortable under the many stares. She was doing her best to act nonchalantly, but the attention was disconcerting . . . She was used to people being startled when they saw her, but their gawking like she was some kind of otherworldly creature was another matter entirely.

"I think it's the building there, my lady." Poppy clutched her white cap as it fluttered in the breeze and pointed to her left. In the distance, a large whitewashed tower pierced the sky with a pointed bronze roof that glinted in the sun. Its walls of windows were clear even from where Katarina stood. Attached to the tower was a stately structure that worked its way inland.

Frowning, Kat shielded her eyes against the sun and squinted. "Are there bars on those windows?"

"Pardon me, Lady Katarina?" a quiet voice interrupted the redhead's inspection of the building in which she was to soon be staying.

When Kat looked around, she didn't see anyone facing her—that is until she looked down and saw a surprisingly short Troivackian maid.

"Yes?" Kat raised an eyebrow, studying the girl. She had a notable beauty mark on the far left of her cheekbone and thick black eyebrows. However, her complexion was too pale to be entirely Troivackian, or perhaps she was one of the esteemed maids who only ever worked indoors.

"My name is Arianna. I am assigned to serve our future queen, and she has requested you to join her on her ship.

"The princess hasn't left the ship yet?" Katarina's concern ignited.

For all of Alina's wonderful, sweet attributes, the woman had been born and raised surrounded by comfort. She was not the type to lounge longer than necessary in a confined ship.

"No, my lady. Please follow me." The girl curtsied abruptly. Despite her short stature, something about the maturity of her voice indicated that she was older than Poppy—perhaps even older than Katarina.

Not wasting a moment, Kat set to following the small maid, while Poppy, still clutching her cap, struggled to keep up in the crowd.

"Are you serious?!" Katarina demanded, slamming her palms on the table in the cabin, making the servants present wince.

"Unfortunately, yes I am." Brendan Devark, the Troivackian king, stood behind his seated wife with his arms folded.

Alina was looking rather pale. It was clear sea life, as Katarina had predicted, had not boded well for the Daxarian princess.

"They haven't even *seen* Alina and they want her dead?!" Kat exclaimed angrily.

"That is what my informants have reported. It is rumored they have ambushes planned on our way to Vessa, which changes our own strategy," Brendan continued sternly. Despite his voice remaining calm, everyone could sense the gigantic man was barely restraining his ire over the news that his beloved wife was already being threatened.

"We now plan on taking a direct route to Vessa, but we are going to send two decoys as well. The first will go the original route as planned, the second will go along a route that is entirely off-road," Brendan explained while nodding to his brother, Prince Henry, who stood leaning against the cabin wall with his arms folded.

"My wife surprised me by traveling to meet me here in Norum, so she and I will take the off-road option, as she is the most familiar with that method of travel from her days as a nomadic performer. Not that I'm particularly fond of Kezia being in jeopardy, but try telling her not to do something and—"

Brendan cleared his throat, and Henry smiled apologetically.

"The more I hear about your wife, Your Highness, the more I think I'll really like her." Kat grinned at Henry over her shoulder before turning back to Brendan.

Her expression froze.

A realization about the couple being sent as decoys dawned on her and brought a feeling of sinking dread.

She stared at the Troivackian king desperately. He noticed she'd caught on.

"Gods . . . please . . . no."

"So I take it you and the Daxarian prince didn't bury the hatchet on your journey here?" Prince Henry asked wryly.

"Could someone *give* me a hatchet if you are going to ask me to spend another week with Prince Eric—"

"Two weeks," Henry interrupted.

Kat's jaw dropped. "*Two* Godsdamn weeks?!"

Brendan cleared his throat once more and frowned at her cursing, though he was distracted when Alina wearily raised her hand to her temple.

"Kat . . . my brother is not here for this discussion . . . for some reason . . . though we did summon him . . . But I'm sure at the very least you two can survive while in proximity if we allow you to travel in different carriages."

Brendan rested a comforting hand on Alina's shoulder as her eyes lifted weakly to look at Kat. The princess was struggling with her unfortunately poor constitution.

The redhead's concern for the princess momentarily shadowed her desire to board the next ship heading back to Daxaria. Her initial impulse to flee if it meant she didn't have to put up with Eric was replaced by the sincere knowledge that she couldn't abandon Alina. Especially with people threatening her life.

After her silent inner battle, Kat finally let out a loud groan.

"Separate carriages are a must. Besides, we won't be convincing pretending to be you two, as Eric looks nothing like a Troivackian."

"Which is why the curtains will be drawn on all of our carriages to avoid rumors," Brendan explained as Alina reached up and gently squeezed his hand that was still resting on her shoulder.

The sight of her friend's casual affection for her husband elicited a strange, unpleasant pang in Katarina's stomach. Was it sadness?

But why?

She herself wasn't particularly interested in getting married. It didn't make sense . . .

"Alright, I guess it's all been decided. When do we leave?" Kat asked, moving her gaze to Henry in hopes that her unwelcome feelings would pass.

"We will rest here in Norum at the Wisdeburg Keep for two nights instead of the three we had planned, and keep only the staff we brought with us. On the second morning we will depart."

Kat nodded and, with a long sigh, stood. Offering a begrudging curtsy to the royals, she exited the cabin.

Wordlessly, Alina turned her pale face up to Brendan and gave a small twitch of her mouth.

He nodded. "I'll go find out where your brother is and tell him the plan. A carriage should be outside momentarily to take you to the keep." The Troivackian king bent down and planted a kiss on the top of his wife's head, then left the cabin with his brother following behind.

As it turned out, by the time Katarina had carefully made her way down the gangplank to the deck due to her skirts threatening to trip her along the way, the Troivackian king wasn't far behind her. She suddenly stopped.

With a tilt of her head, Kat stared farther down the dock, making Brendan also pause and turn to look at what had caught her attention.

There was Eric Reyes, talking with some of the Troivackian sailors they had traveled with.

One of the men was a stranger, however, and Eric greeted him with a stony expression followed by a brief handshake.

Who did he know already in Troivack? Kat wondered.

"Pardon me, Lady Katarina, but I would like to get my wife a carriage while the day is still with us." Brendan's low voice interrupted Kat's thoughts, snapping her back into action as she resumed making her way to the dock.

As she passed through the crowd, she lost sight of the prince and instead found Poppy, who seemed all too eager to make their way to their new lodgings on dry land.

Brendan, however, could still easily see where Eric stood, bidding farewell to the sailors before turning on the dock toward the ships.

He appeared to be looking for someone, most likely his assistant, and therefore didn't notice the quiet approach of his new brother-in-law.

"See someone you know?" Brendan asked in a slight growl, making Eric stiffen and turn to face the significantly taller king.

"I was thanking the sailors who got us here safely and meeting a friend of theirs who mistook me for another crewmate for hire," Eric explained while turning to face Brendan, his right hand casually stowed in his pocket.

"You missed an important meeting. You were summoned, but no one could find you. Again." Brendan enunciated the word *again*, and he watched as the prince's expression grew guarded.

"Apologies for the inconvenience. I hadn't even seen Your Majesty or my sister yet so was unaware there were matters to meet about."

Brendan continued staring at Eric, his dark eyes boring into the prince's face unabashedly. "I hear there is some animosity between you and Lady Katarina. I don't know the details, as no one is being particularly forthcoming, but I gave an oath that she would be safe under my care. Should she be removed from your presence?" Brendan asked seriously.

Eric's eyebrows lifted in surprise before he started laughing. "You promised to keep that woman safe?" He laughed harder. "Here I was thinking you were so . . ." Fortunately Eric was unable to finish the thought as peals of amusement overtook him.

However, instead of irking the king into reacting, Brendan merely watched the prince. Unmoving.

"Your Majesty, like I said, we haven't had a chance to speak since docking, so let me give you a brief rundown of my time with Lady Katarina on the ship." Eric finally straightened, though a different, humorless smile began to pull at the corners of his mouth. "That woman dove from the ratlines to free up the headsail in that hellish storm we had, *without being tied to the Godsdamn ship*!"

Even Brendan was not immune to the shock of that report.

His eyes widened.

Yet he still managed not to speak.

"Then, when confronted with her carelessness, she announces that because she is a witch she knows her powers best, and she was capable of helping. She should've—"

"Was she glowing at the time? Could you still see her eyes?" Brendan interrupted, his shoulders relaxing but his gaze once again sharpening.

Eric frowned. "I could barely see anything in that storm, but yes, she was glowing. Surely you don't think just because she has *some* magic she can act so—"

"How was she afterward? Was she conscious?" Once again there was a keenness in the king's tone that was beginning to be a tad off-putting.

"She was taking a nap, but she was chatting to herself. She seemed drunk . . . Couldn't be bothered with anything until dinner time—when she nearly ate every crumb of food from the ship's stores."

Brendan nodded, his eyes becoming lost in thought.

"Your Majesty," Eric called out, drawing the king's attention back to him once more. "She is a mutated witch. Regardless of how mad or confident she is that she can—"

"I agree with Lady Katarina."

Eric stopped. Completely flummoxed by the announcement. "I can't have heard you right."

Brendan straightened his shoulders and looked down at Eric, once again his face a mask of indifference. "I have seen what Lady Katarina is capable of. She was right. You underestimated her. I understand your concern over her seeming lack of control, but don't worry. I have plans for her."

Without any further explanation, Brendan resumed his trek down the dock, leaving Eric not only speechless but feeling as though he were the only reasonable person in the conversation that had just ensued.

CHAPTER 16

ACHES OF ASSIMILATING

Wisdeburg Keep, as it turned out, *did* have bars on some of their windows.

The first- and second-floor windows.

Because it was Norum's prison.

Atop of it, on its third floor, were its wardens and magistrates, and on the fourth, were lavish rooms for esteemed nobles, such as their very own king and future queen.

It was meant to be symbolic that the king sits atop his people. His strength and position of responsibility superior to everyone in their kingdom.

Katarina was not handling the news well and voiced her opinions to her best friend over a private luncheon, while the king saw to the details of their revised travel plans.

"I know, it seems rather . . ." Alina started in response to the redhead broaching the topic.

"Disturbed," Kat supplied before taking a hearty drink from her goblet.

At least the wine was top-notch.

"It is a strange mind game to keep those in power on top," the princess admonished while taking a dainty bite out of a wedge of cheese.

Kat nodded before reaching for her fork to try some of the cold meats that had been laid before her. "I mean, I understand why the magistrates and offices are here, but . . . these quarters specifically for nobles who rank duke or higher? Seems like a waste of space. You just know some magistrates bring their mistresses up here when no one is using them."

Alina laughed dryly. "I was thinking something similar, but of course if I say that to Brendan, he'll defend them, saying it is an unwise tactical move to assume one's character without any knowledge of the people involved."

Kat rolled her eyes. "I'm not sure that I like how quickly you're learning to understand your husband."

This time Alina's laugh was genuine, and Kat couldn't help but smile. She really had missed her friend during the trip.

"Sorry again about you having to travel more with my brother. Honestly, I knew that people in Troivack would resist some of my ideas, but I admit I was surprised to hear that even my mere presence is unwelcome." Alina gave a weary sigh.

"Well, we knew there was a rebellion brewing, but I thought there had been talks of that even before your engagement," Katarina reminded while thoughtfully reaching for a bread roll.

"That's true, there was. However, I think that was with regards to those strange creatures being reported. Right now, the Aguas Coven here in Troivack isn't powerful at all . . . not since the war. After what Aidan Helmer did, there were many witches violently killed, but I'm hoping to reestablish them in light of the new creatures. Or at least, I *was* before learning I have to worry about being murdered on my honeymoon." Alina closed her eyes and gently rubbed her forehead.

"I'll take care of those pests, and because my last name is Ashowan, most people won't know about my relation to Aidan Helmer. So hopefully that doesn't hinder your plans to—"

"Oh, Gods, I was forgetting about that." Alina's eyes flew open. "We must make sure to keep your family name and relation to Aidan a secret. I had meant to discuss this further with Brendan, but with everything going on I—"

Kat waved her hand dismissively before smiling. "Don't worry. My mother said people in Troivack tend to overlook women a lot. I'll probably be forgotten about in no time."

Alina's flat stare followed by her silence made obvious her disagreement of her friend's ludicrous perception of herself.

"You're a smart woman, Kat . . . most of the time," Alina informed the redhead with a half jesting smile.

"Your Highness, I take offense to that!" Katarina fired back, her eyes flashing. "I am *never* a smart woman!"

Alina snorted.

"I am a brave woman, a loyal woman, a mad woman, but smart? Pffft. That's your job." Kat slumped back in her chair with a grin and once again lifted her goblet to her mouth.

"You *are* smart, Kat."

Katarina felt her cheeks ache as her face struggled to maintain a neutral expression. It meant a lot: her friend's quiet but serious compliment, which wasn't dampened by the familiar phrases of *You are smart, Kat, just reckless.* Or *You are smart, Kat, you just need discipline.*

Alina gave her the recognition free from the burden of her faults, and it was one of the many reasons Kat believed the princess would be an outstanding ruler.

When the redhead overcame her emotions and opened her mouth to continue their discussion, the doors to the solar banged open and in strode Brendan.

Then, all at once, Alina was no longer simply Kat's friend.

She was a wife . . . and the feeling that had been plaguing Kat whenever she'd seen her friend with her husband suddenly revealed its name.

Loss.

It was the feeling that her friend was drifting away to something wonderful, making her feel as though, bit by bit, over time . . . Kat would one day vanish from Alina's life completely.

Still feeling morose the following morning, Katarina barely ate anything at breakfast . . . however, that was by her own standards. In reality, her portion was still as much as two healthy men would consume in a sitting.

The upper dining hall of the keep had bright red-painted walls instead of the whitewash that ran through the hallways. Gold trimmed the entire dining room, and the furniture added to its drama, as it was heavy and painted black.

In fact, nearly every room for the nobility was painted the same way, save for the solar that overlooked Alcide Sea, which was painted a royal blue.

Given that Katarina had only been raised around natural stone, and whitewashed or wooden walls, the constant exposure to the colors was beginning to give her a headache on top of everything else.

Closing her eyes and rubbing her temples, she became vaguely aware that someone was sitting down beside her.

Half expecting Prince Henry to have resurfaced from his rooms with his wife, Kezia—whom she still hadn't gotten to meet—Kat opened her eyes and immediately felt her mood worsen upon finding Prince Eric Reyes sitting beside her.

"You look terrible," he greeted casually.

Kat resisted sticking her tongue out at him. Troivackian stewards were in the room, and she really did want to make a good first impression . . .

"Have you spoken with His Majesty about our . . . travel plans?" Kat asked instead. She pretended to be distracted by reaching for her water goblet when, in fact, she was only remembering that some of the stewards present may not be trustworthy and she shouldn't mention the details of their departure.

Eric shot Kat a brief side-glance with a raised eyebrow before a steward stepped forward with a plate of freshly cooked eggs for him. Meat and fruit had already been set on the table, as well as coffee.

Not giving the eggs a second look, Eric had the stewards prepare him a cup of the bitter bean brew.

"I haven't had a chance to speak with His Majesty or my sister yet, no. Some of the sailors wanted to take me out for a final drink and game of cards before we bid our farewells."

"You should visit with His Majesty and Her Highness soon. I'm sure you'll be as . . . *excited* as I was about the new arrangements." Kat began to stand, then noticed two out of the four stewards shift uncomfortably.

Oh. Right. Now that a man is present, I'm supposed to ask him to be excused. Gods, of course it had to be Eric to join me first. If I kill him right here in senseless violence, will that make me more respectable to the Troivackians or still just a criminal? This kingdom really does toe an interesting line when it comes to violence . . .

Eric looked at Kat when she was half risen out of her chair and hesitating.

He was momentarily puzzled until he realized the two stewards were glancing from him to her with small frowns.

Eric grinned. "Lady Katarina, is there something on the table perhaps you're trying to reach?"

Kat stiffly lowered herself back down onto the chair. "No, Your Highness. I was merely adjusting my seat."

Sipping his coffee, Eric suddenly felt in jaunty spirits. "Tell me, Lady Katarina, would you like to hear some worldly advice? As your elder, I of course have traveled and can offer you some helpful insights regarding the fair shores of Troivack."

Kat's left index finger was tapping dangerously close to her dining knife as her golden eyes sharpened.

It was rude in Troivack for a woman to tell a man to go to hell.

. . . Alright, it was also rude in Daxaria, but Kat wouldn't be shunned and outcast there at least.

"I'm afraid I have duties His Majesty has asked me to attend to once I'm finished dining—regarding the new travel plans you missed hearing about. Of course, while here in Troivack, I must obey His Majesty's orders."

Kat was lying through her teeth, but she couldn't let Eric have the satisfaction of maintaining the upper hand.

"Oh, I see, and what are these important orders?" The prince leaned back into his chair comfortably, then took a deep, satisfied whiff of the coffee in his cup.

Kat's thumb brushed the knife's gleaming handle.

Eric smiled charmingly.

"That is of a private nature, Your Highness," Kat managed, though she was starting to feel that irksome burst of heat that she hadn't been plagued by since the storm. Was her magic already rebuilding?

"I understand; of course I shouldn't pry. I'm sure His Majesty will understand, however, if you keep me company while I enjoy my coffee." Eric sipped from his cup leisurely.

Kat knew if she insisted otherwise things could go south quickly. The Troivackian king would either be roped in to validate her lie, or she would become known as a liar, and rude . . .

So, picking her evil, she gave a begrudging bow of the head in acquiescence.

Eric pulled two green grapes free from a nearby platter of fruit, then settled back down comfortably in his chair. "Would you like a cup of coffee yourself while we sit, Lady Katarina?"

"I don't drink coffee," Kat replied shortly, her eyes trained on the wall ahead of herself.

Just pretend he isn't here . . . he's just another arsehat prattling away. Yes . . . I'm currently practicing with knives, or out for a ride . . . far . . . far away from here . . .

"Surprising that you don't, given that it is yet another commodity your family holds a monopoly on. I would think you would know all about it given your interest in their investments."

"I don't drink coffee," she repeated, her expression relaxing as she noticeably tuned Eric out.

It took a few moments of silence, but the prince finally realized what she was doing.

So he reached over, plucked up her abandoned cup, and took a sniff.

"Chamomile, peppermint . . . lavender? Doesn't your father brew this as a sedative or sleep aid?" Eric asked with a chuckle, his eyes for a minute growing lost in a fond memory.

"I don't drink coffee."

When Kat parroted the same answer and the Troivackian stewards shared looks of confusion, Eric turned to face the stubborn redhead fully while taking another mouthful of his drink.

"I see this is a topic you aren't fond of discussing. So how about this one? I learned an interesting little trick regarding a card game. Bloody Four. Perhaps you've heard of it?"

Kat's slackened expression tightened.

"Last night, while I was enjoying a particularly grand time with the sailors who brought us here, they shared with me how some women of the night learned to help their clients cheat."

The Troivackian stewards shifted uncomfortably. Mentioning prostitutes was not an appropriate topic for a woman's ears in Troivack.

Noticing this at once, Kat wasted no time in seizing the new opportunity.

"Your Highness! I understand that you have been spending your time with uncouth characters for many years now, but please do remember, I am a *lady*." Katarina placed a hand on her heart, made her voice as breathtakingly naïve as possible, and turned her victorious gaze to Eric.

Her dramatic outburst stunned the prince, but he wasn't letting her off the hook so easily.

"You've mistaken my words, Lady Katarina. I merely wanted to commend you for being such a pillar of dignity in comparison to such characters. After all, it is well-known in Daxaria that *you* are always impeccably behaved! Always the upstanding moral figure for young maidens to look up to, and I'm sure *everyone* here will be watching you to see such a vision of purity for themselves."

Katarina's temperature spiked as Eric's smile cloyed at her nerves, making her want to smack the hand holding his cup and dump the scalding coffee all over his crotch.

In fact, the idea was so enticing, she was beginning to lose her inner restraint. Fortunately, the dining hall doors opened and in strolled Alina and Brendan.

The couple looked quite happy and at ease, but when they set foot into the dining room and took stock of Eric and Katarina at the table, then the stewards in the four corners, the couple halted in their tracks.

"Everyone but His Highness and Lady Katarina, please leave the room," Brendan rumbled, his usual dower expression sinking his previous lighthearted one.

The stewards bowed hastily and made their way out of the room.

Once the two sets of double doors were closed—one leading to the hallway and the rest of the keep and the other to the kitchens—Brendan strode forward with Alina on his arm, who was looking equally stern.

"If I had come into the aftermath of a bloody battle and the table flipped, this tension would make sense." Brendan announced, his dark eyes narrowed.

"Yes, and it doesn't help the room is sweltering . . . Good Gods, Kat, why didn't you get up and leave if you needed to burn off the magitch?!" Alina demanded while fanning herself.

When neither Eric nor Katarina supplied any commentary on the observations made, Alina's hand dropped, and she glared at her brother.

"What did you do?"

Eric sat up straight, his previous mask of composure replaced with one of annoyance.

"What do you mean, what did I do? Shouldn't you be asking her that? She could've left any time she wanted."

Alina turned to Kat, and despite the redhead not being entirely forthcoming with meeting her friend's gaze, enough was communicated that the princess understood the situation without needing to ask any further questions.

"Eric, don't hold her hostage. It is unkind when she is trying to make a good first impression. You know she doesn't like you and that it tampers with her free will if she has to grovel just to leave a dining table." Alina's cold voice made Eric no longer feel annoyed by the situation . . . No . . . Now he was angry.

"She could have asked to leave. No groveling would've been necessary. It is customary here in Troivack, and she's going to encounter it again with worse people. She simply didn't ask, so there's no need to assume I'm the villain." Eric's voice had dropped to match the same chill of his sister's.

The siblings glared.

"You aren't supposed to be like 'worse people,'" Kat interrupted with a sigh before standing. "That's what Alina wants to say, and honestly, it's something I could hear my da saying too, but you're right. This is a family matter between you two so I am going to excuse myself."

Katarina let out a sigh that was wise beyond her years, then glided around the table toward the doors. For a moment, everyone was mildly surprised at the redhead's calm, mature handling of the situation.

Brendan nodded his appreciation to Katarina, who turned and stared at the king expectantly.

"What're you doing? Can't you read the room? We have to get out so they can talk." Kat gestured to the open door with her thumb, then stared at the king in exasperation as she used her other hand to wave him forward like a dawdling child.

Brendan's arm flexed under Alina's hand, but when she squeezed his forearm and he looked down to see that she did indeed wish for a private word with her brother, he softened. Giving his wife a nod of assurance, he proceeded toward the exit without further complaint.

That is until he had to walk by Katarina.

"I don't much care for your tone this morning," Brendan quietly reprimanded.

"At least my 'tone' has variety. You just growl and bark at people," Kat fired back as they left the room, the door gently closing behind them.

In the silence, at last alone, Eric and Alina faced each other.

It was their first time talking since their last confrontation in Daxaria, and . . . something in the air indicated that it wasn't going to be any easier of a discussion.

CHAPTER 17

SUBPAR SINCERITY

Alina stared at her brother and he stared back for a long tense moment without a word being shared.

Taking another mouthful of coffee, Eric then gestured to the chair across from him, a move that was eerily like their father's. "Apparently you and I need to battle it out."

Alina's breath almost caught in her throat as anger quickened her heart.

"Is that really of any surprise to you?" she asked, her voice rasping.

Eric stared somberly in response.

"Are you really so . . . narcissistic that you have no idea what you put us all through?" Alina's voice was sharp, but the pain behind it was even sharper. "You reappear after four years, offer no explanation, and ask no questions about how we've been, what has happened in our kingdom . . . not thanking us or apologizing until nearly forced to. You constantly disappear as though you are desperately trying to escape, as though you couldn't be bothered with me—or anything for that matter."

His eyes never left his sister's face, but Eric still did not say a word.

"For some reason you torment my friend and continually make snide remarks about her family—a family that you owe everything to. I thought you were a good person, Eric. I remembered you as someone who could charm everyone and bring out the best in people. You never discriminated against rank, or gender . . . You were . . . You were one of my favorite people, and you left Father and I as though we were nothing. Suddenly, you're this . . . husk of a person. So I want to know why. I want to know why you are this way. You have no idea what I went through trying to keep *everything* together all while trying to find you."

By the end of her speech, Alina was crying.

She tried to dab away her tears and not allow her breaths to turn into shudders, but the droplets came faster than she could wipe, and her gentle cry evolved into sobs as she turned her body away from her brother toward the door. Her hand moved to her mouth to regain some of her strength to continue the conversation.

For several long, tear-filled moments, neither of them said anything.

It wasn't until Alina began drawing in deeper, slower breaths and her toes turned back to Eric that he proceeded to lean his forearms against the table between them.

"I'm not strong enough to face what I've done. That's the answer to your question why—why I didn't thank you or grovel at your feet when I first saw you. The detailed answers to your questions, good or bad, carry with them the burden of what they cost others, and I'm not strong enough to face that." Eric's voice was tight with emotion, but his eyes were distant as though even in that moment he couldn't be fully present.

"Why did you leave in the first place?"

"Father said it should have been him who died when he came to tell me Mom had passed. I was still sick with the fever, but I could see the truth was that I should have been the one to go. Not one of them. I initially left to distance myself from the guilt and lend help elsewhere." Eric reached for his coffee cup once more and took another sip, a slight tremor in his hand.

Alina faltered at that piece of information. "Then why didn't you come back when I begged you to?"

"I couldn't read your letters for about a year. They hurt too much, and by then I'd . . . started a new path that was so far removed from my old one that it made everything more manageable. When I did read one or two of the letters, it brought it all back, and I . . . well . . . traveled even farther to gain distance from it all." Eric's stare fell to the table, his expression growing hollower each time he spoke as though revisiting the tale took away what little else there was of him.

"So you wished you'd been the one to die. Then who would have taken over the kingdom? Who would have ruled? Me? At that time, I was confined to a chamber because I couldn't even be trusted to breathe in the same castle as a sick person," Alina reminded, her tone slightly less heated and more so anguished.

"To be honest? I talked with Finlay Ashowan about him taking over." Eric's tone grew bitter.

Alina's jaw dropped.

"I couldn't handle . . . father's pain, his grief . . . and our shared fear of losing you one day to your breathing troubles. I didn't think any of us had the strength to rule the kingdom without Mom." Eric's eyes grew misty before he again reached for his coffee cup and downed the chilled remains in one gulp.

"So you abandoned us to fall apart on your own?" Alina's voice turned hard. "You turned coward and ran?"

"Yes. Because I am a weak and horrible man. I didn't ask for forgiveness because I don't deserve it. I didn't tell you what I've been doing because it doesn't matter. And I didn't tell you why I did what I did because it's a disappointment."

Alina's anger bubbled back up to the surface as she reached forward and gripped the chair in front of her until her knuckles were white.

"So you hate the Ashowans for not taking on your responsibilities?"

"No. I dislike them because they don't always share the whole story, especially when it matters. On top of that, when Fin came to tell me I needed to return home the first time, he informed me I had better do so quickly because he wasn't going to remain as the viscount or help with any duties once his son took over. He relayed that I'd be on my own, and yet . . . he was the one who had always told me friends didn't leave when they were needed most."

"Neither should brothers," Alina reminded icily.

Letting out a long, labored sigh, Eric leaned back into his chair and crossed his arms, his head hung slightly lower. "Don't waste your anger or hope on me. You don't deserve that misfortune."

"Hard to do when you are to be king." Alina's reddened eyes filled with tears again, and so she turned to leave.

When she reached the door, she paused, her final words on her lips, but when she faced her brother, she couldn't help but hesitate at the sight of his soulless gaze staring idly at the wall opposite him.

Were the crushing grief of their father and burdening responsibility truly the causes for it all?

Alina turned her face to the floor, unable to keep looking at Eric. Even so . . . she had one final thing to say.

"Leave Katarina alone. She has done more for me than you could possibly imagine, and whether or not you like her is irrelevant. If you don't want to be dead to me, then don't antagonize my best friend from your grave."

After his sister had taken her leave, Eric sat in the quiet, his eyes remaining glued on the wall for several long moments before standing, the chair's slight creak the only sound in the room.

Turning to look out over the sea, the prince let out a small breath and allowed his shoulders to hunch before he pressed his right hand into his pocket and exited the room.

Once again, he was facing the simple, awful truth that he should have died and saved everyone a world of trouble.

Yawning, Katarina stretched her arms above her head as she strolled outside the Wisdeburg Keep, staring at the line of carriages.

A slash of pink broke the day's dark sky, and several servants were milling about.

Katarina and Eric's traveling party was to be the first to leave that day, followed a few hours later by Prince Henry and his wife, Kezia (who, strangely enough, Katarina *still* hadn't met), and finally, the king of Troivack with Alina.

All were set on separate roads to reach the capital of Vessa located in the south of Troivack.

It was to be a grueling two-week journey, and Katarina was incapable of lying to herself about just how grim it would be to ride in a hot carriage with the curtains closed for days on end.

But if it meant keeping Alina safe . . . she'd do it.

Swinging her arms back and forth breezily, Kat turned, looking for someone who could direct her to where her hell on wheels was located, but she didn't see anyone other than a few young serving boys, that is, until her eyes rested on a tall Troivackian soldier with a maroon cape attached to his armored shoulders.

"Ah, excuse me, might I ask which of these I'm supposed to board?" Kat called out to the man's back as she strolled forward leisurely.

When he didn't turn around, she tried again. "Excuse me? I'm supposed to be boarding one of these. Which one is—"

The man turned around so suddenly that she nearly leapt back in surprise.

The Troivackian was in his early sixties with two long scars running diagonally across his face. One stopped at the corner of his mouth and was nearly hidden by his short, trimmed salt-and-pepper beard. The other started at the beginning of his hairline and ran across the bridge of his nose until it ended at his left cheek. His short, curly hair matched his beard in color.

His nearly black eyes were sharp even before they narrowed upon landing on Katarina, and it was clear to her that he was not a friendly sort.

She grinned.

Big meathead, too serious for his own good?

Her favorite type of person to annoy!

Something in her smile must have tipped off the Troivackian about her mischievous intentions because he made a threatening growl in the back of his throat before facing her directly.

"You must be the Ashowan."

"*The* Ashowan? I quite like that title, sir! I will be sure to tell my family I am the one and only of our name now!" Kat put her hands on her hips and began bouncing up and down on the balls of her feet.

The Troivackian continued to glare at her in silence for several moments before extending his arm and pointing to an inconspicuous black carriage with its curtains drawn.

"You and His Highness will be riding in that carriage."

"Oh . . . no, no, I'm supposed to be in a separate one from him. You see, we might kill each other, and that might really put a damper on the overall mood of the trip for everyone." Kat's smile turned fragile.

It was the Troivackian's turn to look amused, albeit there was a touch of sadism to it . . .

"We aren't wasting valuable resources in an already dangerous situation with unplanned expenses because two grown members of nobility cannot be trusted to be civil. *That* is your carriage."

Kat's index finger began tapping against her hip. "I do hate it when I'm battled with logic . . . It's an old foe of mine, you see . . ."

The Troivackian knight began shifting away, uninterested in any further nonsense the redhead might spew.

"Out of curiosity, will you be traveling with us?" Kat's innocent question barely registered with the man.

"I will," came the terse reply before he stalked away without a second glance or proper introduction. That was most likely for the best . . . as Kat was already in significantly sunnier spirits.

She had some entertainment for her journey after all!

Humming to herself, Katarina turned toward the black carriage that sat second to last in the queue, then noticed a very nervous-looking assistant belonging to the one and only prince of Daxaria.

"Ah, Mr. Julian. I presume you've been told of the new plan? I'm to ride with His Highness." Kat greeted him with a smile. She rather liked the lad. There was a certain familiarity in his features, and his eager, pure aura made him easy company.

"Er, ah, um, well . . . Perhaps we can try to talk to the k-king about it and change it back . . ."

This poor child . . . We must have scared him while fighting so much on the boat.

Kat waved her hand in an air of resignation. "I understand where they are coming from. . . . It certainly would be a waste of resources, but given that Prince Eric and I have managed not to say a word to each other since arriving, who knows? We may make it to Vessa with minimal bloodshed!"

"Bloodshed?" The lad paled. "Y-You two haven't spoken only because the prince hasn't been to the Wisdeburg Keep since he and the princess sp-spoke . . ."

Katarina's good-natured expression faded away then.

Alina had told the redhead all about her confrontation with her brother, and Kat had been ready to throttle the prince until he gave his sister the apology and unyielding adoration she deserved.

Instead of trying to verbally bolster Mr. Julian's spirit again, Kat decided to settle with patting his shoulder.

"Are you here to tell us His Highness is late? Don't worry, I'm sure Prince Pain-in-the-Arse will be along shortly—"

"W-Wait!" Mr. Julian burst out as Kat's hand rested on the carriage handle. "Let me get you a steward to hand you into the carriage! I-It isn't proper that you enter without being properly handed in, a-and your maid . . . I'll go find her too!"

Katarina opened her mouth to object when the assistant dashed off desperately.

Blinking in surprise, she gave her head a shake. "That arsehat of a prince probably has tormented that poor child to his mental brink."

Tsking to herself, Kat turned to the carriage and opened the door, prepared to climb into its shadowy depths in wait for their departure, when she realized Eric was already inside.

His legs were stretched out, and his shoulder pressed against the far corner from the door, his head with its golden waves resting on the wall, eyes closed, and mouth slack.

"Ahh . . . that's why your assistant was so cagey. Have a few too many drinks?" Kat asked wryly as she climbed into the carriage while leaving the door open.

When Eric didn't answer, Kat seated herself as far as possible from him on the opposite black leather bench, then proceeded to study Eric's pale, slightly sweaty face.

"Hm." Kat's glowing eyes trailed over him, and she noted his unshaved stubble and rumpled, dirty clothes that could've been owned by any commoner. "You must have really—"

Kat then noticed the small leather pouch lying beside him.

Frowning, her gaze flitted to Eric once more. "Your Highness, I am going to look inside that bag unless you tell me not to right now. Ifyousaynothingyouaregivingpermission," Kat muttered quickly as she reached across and snatched the small bag.

Loosening its tie at the top, Kat raised an eyebrow as she gazed inside.

It was empty.

Sighing, she was about to toss it back onto the bench across from herself, when the smell of whatever had previously been in the bag wafted up to her . . .

A sweet scent that left a bitterness in the back of her throat.

Kat's heart thudded as her eyes snapped back to Eric.

The crown prince of Daxaria, future king, and brother to her best friend . . .

Kat's grip on the bag tightened, and her golden eyes glimmered even more brightly.

"I'm beginning to understand why my father said he'd abandon you, you selfish idiot."

CHAPTER 18

SILENT SUFFERING

A long time ago . . .

It means . . . erm . . . it . . . it means . . . that he has . . . four of a kind, but no faces or the winning Bloody Four!" Katarina burst out, sitting upright, her eyes flying to Likon's face as he smiled at her warmly.

"Exactly. See? I told you it was an easy method! Now, if you tell anyone that I was the one to teach you this, I will deny it no matter what, got it?" Reaching for the deck of cards between them, Likon casually flicked his sandy brown hair out of his face with a small jerk of his chin and set to cleaning up.

Kat sighed happily at her newly acquired skill and leaned back so that her back rested against the stone balcony before turning to look out at the setting sun over the water.

"I wish all my lessons were as interesting as this. Did I tell you Mum and Da are getting us *another* tutor?" Kat asked with a groan.

Likon ginned as he finished slipping his beloved playing cards into his leather satchel and turned his brown eyes up to stare at the young woman he had been growing up with since the age of seven.

"Remember, you didn't learn *anything* from me. Got it?" Likon emphasized carefully. "I don't need your parents coming to their senses about having gotten the short end of the stick when they agreed to take me in as a companion for you and your brother."

"Pfft. We were the lucky ones. Now, tell me about the houses! Da stopped letting me visit the prostitutes and madams with him two years ago, as you know," Kat began.

Likon nodded empathetically. "A very wise decision on his part. I'm just surprised he waited until you were thirteen . . ."

"Yeah well . . . I miss hearing stories from them. They have interesting things to say. All the girls my age are . . . different, and a lot of them are jerks to my brother." Kat looked down at her hands and noted two of her bruised knuckles. She had punched a certain lady who had announced Tam and Kat were half commoners and, therefore, dirtied blood.

"Ah, yes. The reason for tutor number . . . what is this? Six? Seven?"

"Nine," Kat admitted, finally dragging her eyes up to Likon's face. He was staring at her in that funny way again.

She had noticed it in the past year—he didn't look at other people the way he looked at her. There was an open fondness that he didn't exhibit to anyone else. Not even toward his sister and nephew who lived on the outskirts of Xava.

"I agree that Lady-What's-Her-Face deserved it. You and your brother are practically royalty here in Daxaria. Besides, if your father wasn't so adamant about not taking on the title of duke, she'd probably have to bow her head to you," Likon pointed out before leaning his cheek on his propped up fist.

"Da says if I want to do all the paperwork for him, he'd be happy to take on the title," Kat recited with a grin. "Besides, that means I'd have to take even more lessons on being proper, and that sounds awful . . ."

Likon laughed.

"So, is there anything else interesting happening in Austice? Come on! You're the only one my parents let out of the house on secret errands. You must have other news." Kat scooched forward eagerly, her eyes wide and pleading.

Likon's cheeks deepened in color at her sudden closeness, then swallowed with great difficulty.

"W-Well . . . nothing . . . that I *should* tell you." He was having a hard time thinking clearly as Katarina's eyes glimmered magically in the glow of the sunset, her wind-tousled hair ablaze in the light.

"I swear I won't tell anybody that you told me about it!" Kat placed her palm over her heart, her features stern.

The young man dropped his hand from his face and fidgeted, he was suddenly unable to meet her gaze.

"Likon?"

Slowly, he lifted his blushing face to stare at her eager expression that had . . . once again grown closer; his heart tripled in speed.

"Please?" Kat was taken aback by Likon's flushed face and desperate gaze on her, and she felt a strange awareness dawn in her mind, making her become hesitant.

"T-There's a new drug circulating in Daxaria. S-Some people think it came from Troivack, but no one is certain . . . It's called Witch's Brew. It has a-a sweet smell, but it becomes bitter in the back of the throat. They say . . . they say it makes you feel connected to nature unlike anything else, but . . . if used too often can lead to death. Depending on the dose, during the intoxication period, you either can talk but barely move, or you're almost comatose . . . If your lips turn blue it's too late. You're minutes from death," Likon explained, his voice warbling.

He had a powerful urge to kiss the young woman before him . . . the girl he had met when she was five years old, in the brothel his sister had worked . . . his savior. She had been the one to plead with her parents to take him into their household, and that led to him being considered the adopted son of the infamous house witch Finlay Ashowan.

What only a few people knew was it was the viscount's wife, formerly Annika Jenoure, who Likon ended up following.

While Lord Ashowan remained the wholesome face of the family, performing his viscount duties begrudgingly as he fought to make Daxaria a more civilized kingdom, his wife was one of the most fearsome members of the underworld, known to most only as the Dragon. Not even the viscountess's own children knew about her other identity.

She had approached Likon when he turned fourteen years old and made him an offer to learn from her. Become her pupil. After all, she was the sole survivor of the great spymaster Georgio Piereva, her grandfather.

The only issue . . .

He should have only one master, which he did, but . . . it wasn't Annika Ashowan, who had kindly taken him into her home and had Likon educated and exposed to wholesome filial love.

No . . .

His master was her redheaded daughter, who he had fallen hopelessly in love with.

Katarina Ashowan.

"Wow, so this drug . . . What does it look like?" Kat asked, snapping Likon from his spiraling thoughts.

His mind was too jumbled to clearly consider his actions, but Likon proceeded to enter back into his bedroom, then return with what looked like a moldy mushroom in his hand.

"See the blue spots?" he pointed out, his voice still hoarse, which resulted in him attempting to clear his throat.

Kat peered at the harmless little fungus in his hand interestedly. "It certainly doesn't look appealing . . . why do you have this?"

"Oh . . . Your parents wanted to show me just in case I saw anything like this during my . . . rounds," Likon finished lamely.

Kat peered at the little mushroom curiously, then tilted her head closer and gave it a sniff.

"You weren't kidding about the smell . . ." Kat reared back and gave a small cough and gag as the bitterness set in at the back of her tongue.

Likon chuckled as he carefully stowed the contraband safely away in the locked box once more.

"They are running tests on it to see how addictive it is and to see if there is an antidote for anyone who overdoses, but so far, there isn't," Likon concluded his explanation while still smiling at Kat, who was grinning delightedly at the secret information she had just obtained.

"Well, I most certainly will stay away from the Witch's Brew." Katarina placed her hands on her hips and gave a firm nod, making her look even more like her father than ever.

Letting out another quiet laugh, Likon noticed stray strands of her red hair clinging to the corners of her mouth, and without thinking, he reached up and freed them before tucking them behind her ears.

Kat blushed deeply and stood frozen for a moment.

Likon's eyes widened in realization over what he had done, and felt his heart skip several beats. "I . . . er . . . just thought you'd . . . want those . . . out of your way."

Kat remained motionless, but as soon as her mind whirred back to life, she dropped her hands to her sides and cast her gaze uncomfortably to the floor. At fifteen, she hadn't had an abundance of experience with men in such a way . . .

"I think I'll go back to my room and . . ."

"Yes, probably a good idea to . . . finish your homework . . ." Likon scratched his temple, feeling every bit as awkward as his seventeen years would allow. He had always believed himself to be more mature for his age, but it was most likely because he was surrounded by the less worldly noble peers. In moments such as these, he was painfully aware he was quite naïve in certain ways as well.

"Well, night!" Kat called over her shoulder as she walked expediently to Likon's chamber door without another look back. Her shoulders were hunched, and her voice had sounded more like a squeak, making the young man grit his teeth in regret.

As soon as his chamber door had closed, Likon dropped his face to his hands.

His small affliction of love was beginning to become impossible to hide.

Which could only lead to trouble . . . especially given that the lady he was in love with was none other than the most vexing young woman who had ever walked the earth.

Present day . . .

Eric awoke in a hot, sweaty, darkened carriage in motion, where the only light came from the occasional shift of a curtain that allowed in small, merciful streams of air.

His throat was parched, his stomach uneasy, and a dull pounding against his skull made him let out a small grunt as he shifted in his seat.

"Y-Your Highness, would you care for some water?"

The voice of his assistant, Mr. Julian, pierced Eric's head, making him wince.

The only response he was capable of managing was extending his hand and waiting for the flagon of water to be pressed into his sweaty palm.

"Did you have a good sleep, Your Highness?" Katarina Ashowan's voice was unusually loud, and it nearly succeeded in making Eric vomit as the pain wrenching through his mind nearly blinded him.

His hand flew to his forehead while doubled over as he waited for the threat of vomiting to pass.

When he was certain he wouldn't be sick over the floor of the carriage, he opened his mouth and risked a small sip of water.

"Why . . . are you in . . . my carriage?" Eric ground out before taking several rapid breaths.

"Well, if you'd perhaps been more present as of late, you'd know that they deemed us traveling in two separate carriages an unnecessary expense. Therefore, you and I are now stuck together for two and a half weeks with the company of my maid, Poppy (I believe you two have met), and your gracious assistant, Mr. Julian." Katarina explained everything while she leaned her head into her hand, her golden eyes studying him coolly.

Eric slumped back in his seat as he attempted to take in a breath of clear air but instead received the soupy humidity that brewed in their confined space.

"How long"—Eric paused and swallowed another mouthful of water, making sure his eyes remained closed—"until we stop?"

"We'll be stopping to change horses and rest this evening, so I'd imagine in the near future. You've been asleep the entirety of the day, Your Highness," Kat explained, once again, her voice increasing in volume.

Eric turned green. "Please . . . be . . . quieter."

Kat smiled humorlessly. "Oh, can you hear us all now? Forgive me, Your Highness, you have been nonresponsive most of the day. I thought I was being helpful." She hadn't lowered her voice at all.

Eric cracked open an eye, his hazel gaze unfocused. He was going to tell the redhead he wasn't in the mood for her games, when he saw the way she stared at him.

It was almost the same look as her father's . . . only there wasn't any sadness or pity in hers.

She had a knowing glint in her eyes, a cold seriousness, and despite her sweating as profusely as he was, a stillness that wasn't at all like her.

A horrible twist in his gut told Eric that Lady Katarina Ashowan had most likely discovered one of his most well-guarded secrets.

Closing his eyes once more, he let out a long sigh.

The Gods had a funny sense of humor.

Why was it always the Ashowans?

By the time the carriage stopped, dusk had settled over the arid land surrounding them, offering a blissful break from the heat.

The carriage had pulled to a stop under the cover of a stone inn with bright purple flowers climbing its walls. The establishment's sign simply read *Olgas*. It was one of only three buildings at the crossroads, and as a result, the area seemed to rest in a nearly constant quiet save for the occasional howl of a wild dog or the intermittent rapid fluttering of an unseen creature's wings.

As Katarina was handed out of the carriage by Mr. Julian, Eric slowly followed.

The threat of sickness had passed, and he was once again able to stand straight, though he still looked incredibly pale.

Everyone moved toward the building that had been completely emptied save for the staff of the establishment in the interest of protecting its alleged royal guests, but Eric stayed put as the carriage rolled away behind him.

"Lady Katarina, a word if you would, please."

Kat's back stiffened. She turned, her navy-blue chiffon dress fluttering in the night breeze. Her golden eyes were like two flames in the settling night.

Eric let out a long sigh as he watched her fold her arms expectantly, and both her maid and his assistant shared nervous glances before scurrying ahead of their mistress and master.

Stepping forward, Eric noticed the tightening in the corners of Katarina's eyes and his stomach once again lurched unpleasantly.

After a moment of standing silently toe-to-toe, the prince let out a short, resigned breath.

"Alright. Let me have it."

Katarina frowned at him in response.

"I can tell you know," Eric explained flatly.

Blinking in a brief flash of surprise, Kat dropped her arms to her side.

"This is why my father abandoned you?" she asked carefully instead of letting loose her judgment.

"Mostly," Eric replied, mildly surprised.

"How often are you taking Witch's Brew?"

Stunned that she even knew the drug's name, Eric's gaze fell to the ground, and he swallowed with great difficulty.

"Less than I was. Twice a year now. Though last night was . . . an exception."

"Is this why you hid from your family and duties?"

"Mostly," he answered evasively, his arms folding across his chest.

"Why?" Kat asked. Her eyes blazed much in the same way her father's had when he'd first stumbled across Eric in a place he never should have set foot in . . .

He didn't say anything.

Letting out a small snort, Kat shook her head, her eyes narrowing.

"You know, Your Highness . . . I never thought I'd come across someone my father cared for so deeply that I . . ." She trailed off, her anger for once outweighed by an even greater emotion.

Eric waited. Waited as he had the previous day for Alina to make whatever cutting insult she could muster. He was used to those and knew they were deserved.

Shaking her head, Kat turned from him, finishing her thought. "Someone who I could honestly say was worth the full weight of Finlay Ashowan's disappointment. More than ever, I now respect my father for protecting the king from knowing. I knew you'd made Alina and His Majesty suffer, but . . . I never realized how much pain you put my da through until now."

Eric felt the familiar stabbing guilt and bore it as he always did. In silence.

"I won't tell Alina, but I won't lie for you either," Katarina announced over her shoulder as she continued on toward the inn.

Eric didn't bother stopping her as he watched the redhead disappear into the building's welcoming light, leaving him alone in the darkness where he had been for many years.

He could have joined everyone inside for a good meal and much needed bath, but right then . . . he felt like an imposter who didn't deserve such luxuries, and so he instead went to find the barn. He would sleep in the hay as he had done many times before on nights such as these, when he was faced with his shortcomings.

CHAPTER 19

DEADLY DEVELOPMENTS

Katarina picked at the chicken, garlic, and sweet potato stew in front of her. Of course this *was* her fifth plate, but the fact that she was hesitating clearing it to make way for her sixth was telling.

How could Eric have done something so absurd as becoming intimate with one of the most potent drugs there was?! He even indicated it had been often that he had taken it . . . so . . . that meant . . . her father had probably found out years ago, and not wanting to expose the prince's poor behavior to the public, or even the king, he kept the secret safe.

Finlay Ashowan suffered everyone's scorn and his own grief over the loss of his friend, all without revealing a thing.

Katarina realized something as she set her wooden spoon down on the table, rested her elbows on its surface, and interlocked her fingers thoughtfully.

Her father would only threaten to abandon his position as viscount and diplomat in an effort to make Eric smarten up. If the prince had truly risen to the throne as troubled as he was, there was no way the infamous house witch would have backed down . . . It was a bluff . . . Surely Eric knew this . . .

Why was he so angry? Perhaps the drugs had rotted his brain? After all, Eric had to know it wasn't in Fin's nature to turn his back on not just a friend but an entire kingdom . . .

What *exactly* had happened between them?

"My lady," Poppy whispered to her mistress, breaking through Katarina's thoughts. "The serving staff is staring at you. I think they're wondering where the king is if you're the princess . . ."

The redhead raised an eyebrow, her mind slowly returning to the present.

It had been arranged that Katarina would seat herself with her back to the servants and keep her eyes cast down to the table in feigned modesty when her dinner was brought.

This had been strategized beforehand because one glimpse of her golden eyes, and it would have been all too obvious she was a witch and not the princess of Daxaria.

"Make sure to spread the rumor that my husband is hiding amongst the knights in an effort to find any assassin or spy. That'll keep them on their toes," Kat murmured, her index finger tapping on her hand.

"Yes, my lady." Poppy bowed her head before sidling out of the small corner bench with their empty plates.

The inn was small, cramped, and dark, but Katarina didn't mind. In fact, the low lighting helped her see expressions and movements that anyone with normal eyesight would've missed.

Of course she had to be discrete in her glances, else the magical glow of her eyes would be noticed immediately.

The knights collectively looked grim, their gazes darting about for any potential threats as they half lowered themselves to their meal on the table. The only one who remained seated with his back straight was Sir Cas.

The man stuck out like a sunflower in a bean field with his soft, clean-shaven jawline and bright, short blond hair.

Kat smiled to herself while reaching for her goblet of wine and taking a drink. Sir Cas's innocent, wide-eyes didn't indicate he'd noticed or minded being the odd man out, even though Katarina could clearly see the Troivackian innkeeper and his wife shooting him dirty looks.

"My lady." Poppy was trotting back to Katarina's table. "They have prepared a bath in your room. I casually mentioned what you said about the Troivackian king being hidden amongst the men. That gave them a good startle," the maid recanted with the quietest of giggles.

Kat grinned. "Good. Ready to guide me? If I can't look up, I'll probably bump into something."

Poppy curtsied dutifully as Katarina stood, and with her eyes trained on the black heels of her maid's boots, followed her across the room, making a number of knights and even the inn's staff bow in reverence.

Kat did her best to ignore the stifling silence that followed her up the stairs, however, she was grateful that the steps creaked as she climbed up.

The inn was humble, but there was no alternative given there was no other city for at least another day's journey in the carriage.

Retiring to her chamber, Kat couldn't help but notice the tension in the air. Unfortunately, because she was stuck being as discreet as possible for the entire trip, the chance to find out what felt so strange would be very difficult to discover indeed.

With a sigh, Katarina then noticed her familiar curled up on the four-poster bed, which succeeded in bringing a smile to her face once more.

At least she had Pina to help entertain her, and hopefully the kitten wasn't too mad about being placed in a slatted crate while traveling . . .

Eric was throwing an apple in the air and catching it, his back pressed against a sturdy wooden post in the barn. His only source of light was from a single lantern suspended above him on a simple wrought iron hook.

His casual handling of the fruit was earning a few interested whickers from the nearby horses. With a flick of his wrist, the apple was sent flying into the farthest stall before Eric reached into the sack filled with the rest of the bushel at his side and began tossing yet another.

"Your Highness."

Eric caught the apple and his shoulders stiffened, but otherwise he did not appear startled by the newcomer's voice.

"Hello, Leader Faucher," he greeted calmly without bothering to rise to greet the shadowy intruder.

"Call me Sir Faucher or just Faucher," came the blunt reply from the man as he stepped forward, his maroon cape swaying as he walked.

"What can I help you with, Faucher?" Eric returned his attention to the apple he was again tossing into the air.

"There has been an attempt on Lady Katarina's life."

The clap of the apple hitting Eric' palm matched in time with his head swiveling around to stare at Faucher. He was on his feet in an instant.

"She is fine, and in fact, unaware the attempt was made. The innkeepers had attempted to poison her wine, but it appears they failed. When that didn't work, they sent up a man hiding a weapon in the folded towels . . . We have disposed of him discreetly."

Eric let out a small breath of relief, his eyes closing for a moment before snapping open again and taking in the Troivackian before him.

"What kind of poison? Is it possible it will take time to affect her?"

"Nay, we found the remnants in the kitchen. They ground up rosie pea and put it in the bottle. Enough to be fatal."

"Gods . . ." Eric reached up and pinched the bridge of his nose. "I didn't think murder attempts would happen so quickly."

"Then you underestimate how unpopular our king's choice of bride is amongst some nobility. Princess Alina will not be warmly welcomed. We will have more than one powerful individual after her, and I foresee great potential for disaster ahead of us if caution is ignored," Faucher informed the prince darkly.

Eric felt his right hand clench into a fist.

"To your credit, Your Highness, casting yourself as an incompetent Daxarian steward has been the absolute best disguise. Though the innkeeper was heard saying—"

"I wasn't trying to disguise myself. I just am not comfortable in a proper bed yet."

Faucher paused. "Ah."

Eric stared flatly at the man.

Faucher didn't blink or bother apologizing for his insult. "Would you like us to inform Lady Katarina in the morning of the assassination attempts? It could serve as a reminder for her to be vigilant."

Eric began to shake his head . . . but then . . . her words from the ship about how he had undermined her . . . and then the Troivackian king's shared belief in her words, made him stop.

"It might be a good idea. Besides, it might even help curb some of her more rebellious tendencies . . ." Eric admonished wearily.

Faucher bowed. "I understand. Your Highness is wise to discuss it with her indeed."

"I didn't say *I'd* be the one explaining to her. Oy! Faucher! I'm not exactly her favorite person right now!" Eric was shouting at the Troivackian's head as he continued bowing, nonplussed by the prince's reaction. He turned to leave the barn as though Eric hadn't uttered a word.

The prince allowed his head to fall back in exasperation.

"Great. Hi, Katarina, forget for a moment I had abandoned my family and still take illegal intoxicants; let me tell you how people are trying to kill you. Great way to smooth things over," Eric muttered irritably to himself before plunking down onto the packed dirt floor strewn with hay.

"Of course I had to be made responsible for her. What a perfect method of revenge from the Gods . . ." Eric babbled on as he rubbed his eyes. "Someone tried to kill her . . . thinking she was my sister . . ."

His chest ached, and Eric felt an uncomfortable restlessness settle in his bones as he stared at the stables filled with the horses taking them to Troivack's capital. He turned to look out of the open barn doors through the dark, still night toward the inn, where Katarina Ashowan rested in her room unaware of such dangers for at least another night.

"I wonder what that woman will say when she finds out?"

* * *

Kat slowly blinked her eyes open as the early glow of dawn warmed her room. The buzz of unfamiliar bugs outside jarred her back to reality as she once again shook away the strangeness of awaking in an unfamiliar bed in a land with strange sounds and smells . . .

Standing and stretching, Kat yawned.

Perhaps it was still because of her burning away so much of her magic during the storm, but she had slept the entire night, which was entirely unlike her. Normally she could make do with an hour or three here and there. Her magic typically made it impossible to rest for long.

Strolling over to her trunk, she eyed Poppy's sleeping form on the small cot by the fire with an affectionate smile. She didn't need to wake her. She could hopefully make her way downstairs or call for a maid to bring her breakfast. She felt ready to eat a horse!

After quietly sorting through her trunk, Katarina found a pale blue dress the color of the dawn horizon that was light and felt like cool wisps trickling through her hands. It was made of material primarily found in Troivack, which her mother had ordered several of the dresses to be crafted from. This had been arranged for both Alina and her to better fit in and for them to be comfortable in the blistering heat of the day.

Slipping off her chemise and into the dress easily, Kat then found her gold bracelets and gold upper arm cuff, as was traditional for a noblewoman to wear.

Good. Ready to get some food!

Kat turned her excited gaze to Pina, who only gave a long yawn of her own, revealing the adorable dark birthmark on the roof of her mouth.

Kat resisted squealing over the cuteness and instead reached out and scratched the kitten's downy cheek before rounding toward her chamber door.

Carefully, she lifted the latch so as not to make a sound and opened the door a crack—or rather, that was what she had meant to do, but something rather heavy ended up pushing the door to swing open with great force, making Katarina leap back. Fortunately, she managed to catch the door before it struck the wall and woke Poppy, but then there was a tumble of something limp and dark onto her chamber floor that had her hopping back awkwardly yet again. This, in turn, made her slip on her skirt and fall onto all fours painfully.

Kat's golden eyes snapped up, her flickering orange aura already ignited over the incident, when her irritated gaze landed on just what had toppled into her room.

Or rather . . . *who.*

"Eric?" Kat breathed as the Daxarian prince sat up while rubbing the back of his head with a wince.

"Mm?" he managed with a sleepy grunt while he squinted in the still-darkened room.

"What the hell are you doing passed out against my door?" Kat hissed, then noticed that Eric had a sword in hand. Not a decorative sword, or a master's sword like he had been permitted to wield since the age of sixteen, but a worn down sword with the leather wrapped around its handle already fraying and falling off.

Kat straightened immediately. "Eric Reyes what is going on?"

The prince resumed rubbing his eyes and exhaled loudly.

Poppy stirred from her cot, a small moan escaping her own mouth before she could catch herself.

Eventually Eric turned to Kat, dark bags suspended beneath his eyes, as he regarded the redhead expressionlessly. He promptly flopped back onto the floor and once again closed his eyes.

"Nice dress. Mind going to get me a cup of coffee?"

CHAPTER 20

TRUST TROUBLES

Katarina sat with her arms and legs crossed. Irritated, she stared across the table at the prince of Daxaria, who was in the process of shoveling eggs and sausage into his mouth between gulps of coffee.

"So when are you going to tell me why one of the Troivackian knights is cooking for us? Where are the inn's staff members from last night? And oh . . . right . . . why in Satan's arse were you sleeping in front of my chamber last night?" Kat's voice was growing rather edgy as her stomach rumbled.

Despite being the first one to request her breakfast, the Troivackian knight-turned-cook had only delivered the first plate to Eric, as he was the noble of highest status present.

The prince himself looked too exhausted to bother thinking of decorum as he hunched over his breakfast and consumed it with great vigor.

"Well . . . you see . . . Gods, for a military man, Faucher can cook some good eggs," Eric managed between bites.

Kat's flattened stare inflated to one of annoyance. Not only was she hungry, but she wasn't getting any answers.

"I'm guessing the innkeepers were going to try and abduct or kill me? The Troivackian military leader . . . the one with the cape and some kind of pulsing vein . . ."

"I'm sorry, what's this about a vein?" Eric asked, suddenly attentive.

"Men with short tempers and no-nonsense attitudes usually produce bulging veins after I annoy them to a certain point . . . They could appear on their necks or foreheads. One or two even had one on their middle fingers," Kat explained with a small satisfied glimmer in her eyes while remembering her previous conquests.

"Huh. Which do I have?" Eric questioned with a good amount of egg stowed away in his left cheek.

"I think the neck. You tend to be the type to enjoy a good dramatic storm-off. Don't worry, I can do the same. Now, was my guess right?" Kat insisted, her index finger tapping her forearm impatiently.

Luckily, the Troivackian named Faucher dropped a heaping plate of food in front of the redhead, which succeeded in distracting her. The sunny yolks gleamed in the morning light, and the heap of sausages, ham, and a thick wedge of toasted buttered bread sat before her. While there hadn't been careful placement of the items, the smells had her stomach fighting off a groan of desperation.

"Thank you," she murmured while picking up her fork, her eyes hypnotized on the fare before her.

"Don't feel bad if a woman as slim as yourself can't finish it. I'm sure the dogs will take care of the rest," explained the burly Troivackian with the dual scars running down his face. He had already turned back to the kitchen to begin preparing the next meal.

"Will the dogs get something to eat even if I have seconds or thirds?" Kat called out to the man seriously as she laid her napkin in her lap.

Faucher turned with a grimace that could have possibly been a smile in an earlier year of his life.

"If you can eat three of those plates, I'll—"

Faucher quieted as he noted the lady was already eating with great gusto.

With her posture remaining perfect, the tower of food she managed to stack upon each forkful was noteworthy.

Faucher glanced at Eric, who gave an enigmatic partial shrug. He scowled. Giving his head a shake, the military man dismissed his remaining troublesome thoughts about how noblewomen should behave as he returned to the kitchen to continue preparing food for everyone else.

As Katarina tucked into her meal, it was as though she were entering into a meditative state. Eric finished his own breakfast and sat back with his arms crossed and watched her clear her plate in record time.

Once the dish had been mopped nearly back to a shine thanks to the bread Katarina had used to soak up any residual yolk, the redhead returned her attention to Eric.

"So, they tried to kill me, and you slept outside of my room because . . . ?"

Eric sighed.

Despite what some of the Daxarian knights had said about her not being the sharpest tool in the garden shed, he had always found her quite quick.

"Yes. They tried to poison you. No one in our entourage was hurt, thanks to Faucher, but"—Eric lowered his voice—"I'm not trusting anyone right now. They could have pretended that the inn staff made the attempt to get our guards down. So from now on, I'll be sleeping outside your door. We'll simply say that you are a needy, bratty noblewoman, who has a steward at her beck and call all hours of the day."

Kat frowned at the explanation, and before bothering to respond, turned toward the worn wooden bar where just beyond was the door to the kitchen. "FAUCHER! SECONDS!" she roared impressively.

Two greyhounds that were lying comfortably in front of the cold hearth on the other end of the room perked up.

Faucher's head popped through the door, glancing at Katarina's expectant face, then her empty plate; he rolled his eyes and disappeared back into the kitchen.

Returning her attention back to the prince, Kat rested her forearms against the table's surface.

"Do I get to *act* like a bratty noble?" she asked interestedly.

Eric narrowed his eyes. "I may not be someone you think highly of right now—"

"Correct."

"But . . . I think you do know that I won't try and kill you myself."

"Mm." Kat sounded unconvinced.

"Do you really think your father would've trusted you on a journey with me if he didn't at least hold me to the bare minimum of expectations?" Eric fired back darkly.

Kat's eyes rolled to the ceiling. "I suppose not . . . But do you really have to sleep right in front of the door? It's off-putting."

"So is being murdered in your sleep."

"Pffft, I'm usually awake all night."

"You didn't notice when I'd parked myself right in front of your door, did you? As soon as you opened it, you could've been shot with a crossbow or stabbed to death." Eric supplied the imagery, and his suddenly lifeless hazel eyes never wavered from her face.

Kat laughed indignantly. "Please, I only slept last night because I drank the poison!"

Then, realizing what she had blurted out, the redhead immediately pressed her lips together, her eyes widening.

"You . . . what?" Eric's voice turned rough as he slowly stood from his seat.

The room was so silent that a mouse's fart could've been heard.

Instead, Faucher burst into the room and plunked down Katarina's second helping of breakfast before eyeing Eric's intense stare at the young woman.

He decided the prince didn't look violent, however, and so he returned to the kitchen without another word.

Once they were alone again, Eric pressed his palms on the table and leaned toward Kat, who was finding it rather difficult to meet his gaze.

"Katarina Ashowan."

She squinted at the rafters. "Why, I think there may be a bird's nest up there."

"Kat, what do you mean you drank the poison? Are you alright? Do you need a physician?"

The tightness in Eric's voice finally succeeded in making Kat look at him.

"Oh, for—no. I'm fine. I just needed to sleep for the night. I didn't even know I'd been poisoned until you mentioned it. I didn't know why I had been able to sleep for six hours, but don't worry, it was rather pleasant really," Kat explained exasperatedly.

Eric half collapsed into his seat once more. "This is because of your magic? Can you taste poison? Or is it that you simply don't react? Or . . . or you *only* need sleep when exposed to something deadly?"

"If it's something that is meant to knock me out, I'll not feel a thing. If it's meant to kill, just sleep. The more potent, the more powerful. The longer I sleep. This one was . . . medium in strength?"

Eric paused in disbelief. "Did Fin feed you poisons to figure this out?"

"How bloody dare you!" Kat's hands curled into fists as she stood up, infuriated, her magic aura flickering around her.

"Then how do you know the effects?! Where would you have gotten poisons?!"

"I took them myself! My mother has an herb room that she uses to make sure the houses my family manages aren't offering any addictive or harmful drugs, so she tests them! I merely snuck in and . . . tried some to figure it out."

Eric rubbed his face, his heart pounding in his chest. "I feel like it's a Godsdamn miracle you haven't worried your parents into early graves."

"You sound like my mother," Kat muttered while seating herself back down and picking up her cutlery again.

"I have new sympathy for the viscountess, don't you worry," Eric replied dryly, his arms dropping to the table's edge.

Kat responded by sticking her tongue out at him before then loading her fork up to resume eating.

"Don't tell anyone else about your ability to consume and survive poison," Eric warned while crossing his arms over his chest.

Kat rolled her eyes but nodded as she continued eating.

After a moment of tentative silence, an expression of hesitancy shifted over Kat's features as she glanced to Eric almost shyly.

"Why is it . . . Why is it you began taking . . . the Brew?" she asked quietly while referencing Eric's drug of choice.

The prince stiffened, and his stomach churned as his gaze fell to the table. The brief light that had been behind his eyes once again dwindled to nothing.

"I wanted to go on a journey. Drink wasn't taking me far away enough, neither was mercenary work," he replied carefully.

"Oh, I thought you started mercenary work after your funds were cut off . . . Why were you doing it before the drugs?" Kat mused interestedly while her fork was in a perpetual cycle from her plate to her mouth.

Eric eyed her in a slightly disgruntled manner before clearing his throat. "Duke Iones recommended mercenary work to me. Said it would be good to see how the lowest of my future citizens live. The conditions, what they must do to survive . . . It was a good lesson."

"Except when they gave you drugs," Kat pointed out lightly.

Eric stared at her for a while before letting out a long sigh. "Except. When. They. Gave. Me. Drugs," he sounded out, his expression indicative of his deteriorating patience with Kat's matter-of-fact handling of things.

Only, this led to him developing a question of his own.

"Are you truly not scared of things?"

Kat paused, her mouth full and her movements stilled.

After a beat of being lost in memory, she blinked, finished chewing her food, and swallowed quickly.

"I've only ever really been scared twice in my life. The first was when my brother went missing. The second was when . . . well . . . That's a story for another time perhaps." Kat's hands shifted to her lap as she fiddled with her gold bracelets beneath the table.

Eric was about to try and pry for a little more of the story from her, when the rest of their traveling group could be heard rising and making their way down to the dining area.

The men all burst into the room, yawning and stretching, the majority of them looked as though they hadn't slept well, while the remaining minority looked markedly refreshed.

Katarina raised an eyebrow at this contrast, then Sir Cas strode in and caught her eye.

The knight waved, offering a sunny smile, and made his way over to the table where she and Eric sat.

"Good morning, Your Highness; Lady Katarina."

The fact that he greeted them using their proper titles meant that not a single soul from the inn's staff had survived the night.

A chilling fact that momentarily sobered Katarina before she forced a smile onto her face.

"Morning, Sir Cas. Would you like to join us?"

The blond knight grinned boyishly as he quickly joined her by sweeping his legs over the bench and settling down beside her.

The fact that he was seated right at Katarina's elbow made the corners of Eric's eyes twitch ever so slightly. However, when the knight smiled at him, he had his familiar mask of composure back in place.

"Sir Cas, do you happen to know why a good number of our knights look a little worse for wear?" Kat asked carefully as several Troivackian's shuffled by with their shoulders hunched and their expressions grim.

"Oh, they were up late playing cards. I went to bed early. Don't really like to gamble much myself! Every day you live life, it's a gamble, you know? You never know how the cards will be dealt, but if you're careful, you can make some educated guesses," Sir Cas explained happily while nodding to some of the Troivackian knights who passed by and visibly recoiled at his friendly expression.

Kat smiled.

Everyone was just beginning to settle down in their seats when Poppy finally descended the stairs from above. Evidentially, she had just finished packing up their things to continue their journey.

"Come, Poppy. It turns out our new friend named Faucher is quite the whiz in the kitchen!" Kat waved her over with a warm smile as Eric stood up and made his way toward the exit, quietly removing himself from the room without anyone's notice.

No one noticed except Katarina, that was, and when her eyes followed him, Sir Cas observed her doing so.

"Ah, don't worry, he probably just wants to go check on his assistant." The knight drew her attention back casually as Eric disappeared into the growing light of the day.

"Ah yes, I haven't seen Mr. Julian yet this morning. Is the lad doing alright?"

"Oh yes, incredibly sharp, that child is!" Sir Cas complimented brightly. "I'm sure he's just tending to the mage who arrived this morning to join us is aware of the traveling conditions."

Katarina's mouth had been open to welcome more food, but her jaw froze and remained open as her eyes widened.

Poppy squeaked, her eyes rounded, and she glanced back and forth between Sir Cas and her mistress worriedly before Kat dropped her fork with a clatter, then tilted her head back and let out a long groan.

"Son . . . of . . . a . . . *mage*!"

CHAPTER 21

HEAT OF HATRED

Katarina sat, avoiding eye contact with the mage who was perched across from her in the carriage.

The interloper of their journey was named Sebastian Vaulker.

He was a mage in his early thirties with round, black wire-rimmed glasses and long, straight brown-black hair that he wore tied in a high ponytail away from his dark brown eyes. It was clear that he was part Daxarian from his complexion, but even this interesting detail couldn't coax Katarina to ask him anything.

While she had actually enjoyed Mage Lee's company, his son, Keith Lee, made her perhaps a tiny bit excessive in her wariness.

Keith Lee had taken any chance he could to explain how things worked (even if she already knew), and while he was impressively well versed in many topics, common sense, humility, and social awareness were not among them.

Therefore, this new mage had only a fifty-fifty chance of being tolerable, and Kat was not in the mood to attempt civility when she was already restless in the hot confines of the jostling carriage.

Luckily, the Troivackian mage seemed to be just as happy not to engage in forced pleasantries.

It was only Poppy and Mr. Julian who were feeling the strain of the silence in the carriage, as Eric had decided to continue pretending to be a lowly Daxarian steward in the name of safety throughout the commoner towns they passed, and, therefore, he rode next to the driver in the front of the carriage, occasionally taking the reins when the man needed a rest.

Alas, this was yet another reason Kat was not in the best of moods. Her index finger and leg both remained in constant motion as heat continued to roll off her, making not only herself sweat but also everyone else sharing her confinement. She ached to be free of the vehicle and to move in any way possible . . .

Suffice it to say, by the time it was midday, the door to the carriage flew open the moment it rolled to a stop.

Kat had her skirts hiked in her hands as she leapt nimbly to the ground over the carriage step despite having traveled for hours of the day.

The Troivackian knights who were dismounting shared startled glances and shifted their eyes away awkwardly from Katarina's unladylike behavior. Meanwhile, Poppy and Mr. Julian half collapsed from the vehicle, their cheeks flushed and their clothes sweat stained.

Only the mage managed to exit the vehicle with an air of dignity.

Kat was fanning herself and taking big gulps of the hot, dry air with her eyes closed when Eric approached her.

"Water?" he offered, making Kat open her eyes and finally take stock of their location.

Surrounding her was a sea of desert that stretched to the horizon from every angle with only the occasional weedy plant springing from the sandy ground. However, the sky was a shade of blue so brilliant, it momentarily stunned Kat as she watched it span the world freely.

"This is . . . incredible . . ." she managed to say, unaware that Eric was watching her intently.

A gust of wind swept through then, bringing with it a small cloud of dust straight into Katarina's face. Wincing as the sand stung her eyes, Kat closed her watering gaze once more.

"Godsdamnit," she muttered.

"Here's your water; I'm going to go check on my assistant and your maid. They look like they're about to climb into death's carriage," Eric explained nonchalantly as he pressed the leather flagon into her one free hand and turned to leave her.

"Yeah, yeah . . . speaking of," Kat called Eric over as she successfully clawed out a satisfactory amount of grit from her eyelashes. "If I put on trousers, can I ride outside the carriage? I think at this rate I might cook us all alive."

Eric turned with a frown. "I thought you were roasting the carriage intentionally to annoy me. You mean you have zero control over the heat you emit?"

"No." Kat let out a long sigh. "I can't help how hot I am. It's one of the reasons I need to move around so much, it burns off the—"

"The magitch, right." Eric cut her off. "So you're saying we should ask Poppy to pretend to be the princess?"

"I mean, it isn't a terrible idea." Kat perked up when her suggestion wasn't immediately shot down.

"Pardon me, Your Highness; Lady Katarina."

Both Eric and Katarina turned to see that the mage had approached them, his hands behind his back, a leather cuff wrapped around his slim upper arm, revealing a sleeveless dull forest green tunic beneath his loose sleeveless gray robe. His mage crystal was small but dangled from his left earlobe, its jagged edges glinting in the daylight.

"With your permission, Prince Eric, I can control the temperature of the carriage and keep it at a more tolerable level."

Kat turned to face the mage while folding her arms. "You mean you could have done that this entire time?"

The mage didn't look in her direction or acknowledge her question, but instead he faced Eric and waited.

The prince raised an eyebrow. "I will repeat Lady Katarina's question: if you could have been doing that, why didn't you?"

Sebastian blinked once before replying, though his aloof expression did not change.

"Here in Troivack, we mages avoid interacting with witches as much as possible. It is their kind, after all, that has led to a great discordance amongst the public's image of magic. Not to mention Lady Katarina is a woman. Here in Troivack, we abide by the ruling of the highest ranking man in attendance. I believe this is well-known."

Katarina's jaw dropped, and even Eric looked properly stunned over the man's blatant yet calm explanation.

After a moment of digesting the mage's words, the prince drew up his shoulders and pressed his hand into his right pocket.

"Is it not a man's duty in Troivack to protect the women? As a part of their honor?" he asked, his voice taking on the faintest note of regality.

The mage tilted his head in response, his eyes slowly growing more focused on the prince's face. "I am a mage before I am a man."

"So your disdain of witches comes before decency?" Eric asked pointedly, his gaze effortlessly holding the mage's.

"That is correct." Sebastian nodded, his expression still unchanging.

The prince opened his mouth to say more when Katarina stepped forward.

"Your powers come from the Green Man, right?" The emotion in Kat's voice was hard to miss. It was obvious she wanted to inflict bodily harm on the mage in front of her and she was struggling with all her might not to.

Sebastian's lip twitched, but his eyes regarded her coldly. "They do."

"Does the Green Man bow to the Goddess or does the Goddess bow to him?"

Sebastian's eyes narrowed ever so slightly. "Neither bows; they treat each other with mutual respect."

"So, what arse-backward school did you attend that deluded you into your current beliefs?" Kat snapped, her golden eyes shimmering brightly for a moment, which in turn made the mage frown and the crystal by his ear glow.

"Troivack's school of mages, Ivorik, was burned down shortly after your grandfather led our kingdom to its loss."

Kat's heated expression froze in surprise. She had not been anticipating anyone remembering her kinship with Aidan Helmer, Troivack's former chief of military . . .

Eric shifted forward, partially blocking Katarina from the mage's sight. "The question still stands, Sebastian Vaulker. If you are aware of the nature of the Gods, then why do you look down on witches?"

"My attitude toward witches is common here in Troivack as well, and you would be best to be more mindful of that fact, Your Highness and Lady Katarina. As it stands now, you, Lady Katarina, have already disgruntled most of the men here with your lack of etiquette."

"What about witches?" Kat breathed.

Eric could feel the rising heat at his back that had nothing to do with the blindingly hot sun above them, and without looking, he knew Katarina Ashowan was already exuding a magical aura that had the mage's crystal glowing even brighter.

"Your kind is so arrogant to believe you are exempt from accountability. You've looked down on mages for decades and even have the power to curse, yet you've only hidden or done as you've pleased throughout history. Mages have always done everything they could to serve people," Sebastian retorted, his tone no longer cavalier.

"Given that mages were the ones helping hunt and kill witches until about seventy years ago, I'd say witches are within their rights to have some reservations! Furthermore, we *are* disciplined and educated! At least in Daxaria, we are! You're acting as though the first witch, child of the Gods, was her brother, the devil!" Kat shot back acidly.

Eric could feel the sweat rolling down the back of his neck from his efforts as a human shield between the mage and witch, and he was beginning to wonder if perhaps that was not the best of ideas . . .

"So why is it you can't control your own power?"

"Because my magic isn't like the others!" Katarina fired back, and Eric could sense she had stepped closer and was now standing shoulder to shoulder with him as she glared at Sebastian.

"So your coven lacks the resources to supply a refined education," the mage retorted.

"More like I'm unique. Witches are different on a case by case basis! Our magicks are complex and not easy to understand. You dislike me for something I can't help, but mages, on the other hand, choose to be arrogant arses, who—"

"Sirs and lady! Would you perhaps like to sample some wine! While we do also serve moonshine, my master's vineyards are incomparable!" A tall, lean man with shoulder-length layered black hair interjected.

All three sets of eyes swiveled over to stare at the distraction.

Despite the angry gazes that greeted him, the newcomer was not deterred.

"My name is Sam. I have some of the samples back in our tent over there!" He smiled charmingly, his white teeth flashing.

It was clear he, too, was half Troivackian and half Daxarian.

Katarina stared past the man over his shoulder, only then realizing the reason the group had chosen to stop in this exact location. On the other side of the carriage and horses was a smattering of tents that made up a small settlement at the crossroads.

Eric turned, forcing both Sebastian and Katarina to step back or else be pressed against his person.

"I know I would *love* a bottle or three of moonshine. What about you, my lady?" Eric bowed to Katarina, momentarily stunning her.

Regarding him dubiously, she wondered what the hell he was up to, until she finally recalled that he was pretending to be a Daxarian steward.

"I suppose I could use some libations."

Katarina moved forward, shooting a single dirty glare at the mage before leaving the two men. Eric bowed and gestured her by.

Once she had joined the seller named Sam, Eric lingered behind and waited until the redhead had moved out of earshot. He then faced the mage, his expression hardened.

"You will give her the respect she deserves as a *Daxarian* noblewoman," he warned icily. "Or I will rip that crystal out of your ear myself."

Sebastian had regained his composure during the interruption and responded to the prince's threat emotionlessly. "I will return the respect she bestows upon me . . . within reason."

"Make sure my assistant and her maid do not die due to overheating in the carriage," Eric added while rotating his toes away from the mage.

"She does not deserve so much of your consideration, Your Highness."

At this, Eric's head turned slowly and his stare turned black. "She is a citizen of my kingdom. I will protect her from any injustice. Are we clear?"

The reference to her as someone under his rule at long last seemed to persuade the mage to bend as Sebastian's eyes fluttered downward.

Accepting what he got, Eric then turned toward where the merchant and Katarina had wandered off, determined to buy every drop of alcohol in the ruddy place, even if it meant the redhead he had just fought to defend gave him one of her judgmental eyerolls that made his stomach turn uncomfortably. He knew it wouldn't mix well with the anxiety that was already bubbling forward, but he'd drank through worse conditions.

"What do you make of them?"

"She was . . . rather striking . . . interesting . . . a little unorthodox . . ." He chuckled before taking a drink from his goblet.

The two figures were alone in the darkened chamber, the cool stones a blissful reprieve from the earlier heat of the day. The one recanting his encounter with a certain noblewoman, had his tunic hanging loosely over his bare chest and his feet uncovered. The other remained standing with his hands clasped dutifully behind his back.

"Somehow, they caught wind of our plans to attack the Daxarian princess. Are you certain that of the three carriages they dispatched, this is the right one?"

"Oh, of course it isn't Princess Alina. No . . . this woman is a witch, and last I heard, our king's new bride was entirely human. The real princess and king must be traveling with one of the other two groups," the man explained before leisurely seating himself in his chair, a goblet filled with ruby red wine loosely clasped in his hand.

"Godsdamnit. With the princess's alleged weakness, I suppose it is more likely they would have kept closer to civilization than taken the scenic route. It'll be easier to hide our men amongst the citizens in the cities, but . . . it makes it tough to predict where they'll be staying on such short notice," the subordinate ruminated bitterly.

"No matter. If my current plan fails as well, we can continue our efforts to kill the decoys who passed through that settlement today. Perhaps even double our efforts in order to send a message. Who knows, the shock could bring about that young, naïve princess's death." The younger man clutching the goblet drank after making his statement. He almost sounded bored.

His companion looked mildly irritated by the fact but did his best to hide it.

"Very well. I'll arrange to increase the number of assassins and the reward amount. It'll be harder to kill the Daxarian princess once she reaches Vessa . . . but, then again, if we kill enough knights along with their decoys, it could be possible to slip more of our men into the castle in the wake of their losses."

The man who remained seated rested his goblet on the table and slowly pushed his hand through his ebony locks. "See if you might bring me the witch alive. She reminds me of someone I knew once . . . and I'd like to investigate more closely."

CHAPTER 22

GUT INSTINCTS

"What's wrong?" Eric barely glanced at Kat as he drained the last drops of his goblet and held out the cup to his poor assistant, who was eyeing the prince's increasing drunkenness warily.

"I thought I just felt a chill," Kat answered as she glanced over her shoulder into the darkness.

The group was seated amongst seven tables situated around their campfire, and Katarina had of course selected the seat farthest from the flames in order to not overheat yet again. The mage had thankfully chosen to sit on the opposite side of the setup.

"It does get drastically colder in these areas at night," Faucher growled while savagely tearing into the chunk of bread in his hand. "Sit closer to the fire if you're going to complain."

Kat's eyes narrowed. "I don't get cold. When I said I felt a chill, it's more akin to a bad feeling. A gut instinct, if you will."

"We don't need to hear about your womanly cycles," Faucher retorted tensely.

"Wh-What?" Kat half laughed in disbelief over the outrageous statement.

Eric had been in the middle of taking yet another drink but stopped and turned to the military leader. "Faucher, watch what you say to the lady. You lot aren't supposed to make me look decent by comparison."

"I thought she was the one bringing up the improper topics," Faucher snapped while dropping the crust of his bread and shifting his attention to the prince, who had proceeded to drain his moonshine once again.

When both Katarina and Eric stared at him in confusion, he rolled his eyes to the starry heavens.

"Women get gut feelings for their cycles!" Faucher continued.

Kat blinked in utter confusion at the man. "You've heard of having a bad gut feeling though . . . with regards to instincts, right? I know you have. I've heard the soldiers saying similar things, and even you, I'm sure—"

"Women get dreams for ominous warnings, not gut feelings."

Kat blinked, momentarily dumbfounded before snatching up her goblet, taking a tentative sniff, then doing the same to Faucher's. After accomplishing those maneuvers, she addressed Eric, who was watching her with mild curiosity.

"I don't think we've been poisoned, but he isn't making sense. Is it just me?" She turned to the prince on her left and then Sir Cas on her right, who had his cheek filled with food but was watching the entire scene play out while looking equally bewildered.

After a moment, Sir Cas remembered to chew the remainder of what was in his mouth, then swallowed before speaking. "It's not you, my lady. Sir Faucher, what do you mean women don't have gut instincts? Everyone has gut instincts. I know many Troivackians believe women to be inferior to men, but—"

"It is that we believe women have prophetic dreams and men to have instincts to survive in battle. They help one another. It is unheard of here in Troivack for a woman to announce she has a gut instinct unless it's about the topic of—"

Eric glanced sharply at Faucher, making the man stop and clear his throat instead of finishing his thought.

"Well, that's a bundle of nonsense if I've ever heard it. I have gut instincts all the time! For example, I am going to be one of the biggest irritations you will ever experience, Faucher. That is my *sincere* gut instinct." Kat pressed her hand to her chest and nodded her head adamantly.

Faucher glared. His jaw flexed, and he turned his face back down to his plate to continue eating.

"Temple," Kat whispered with a slightly deranged smile.

Eric snorted into his moonshine when he noticed the dark outline of an unmistakable pulsing vein on Faucher's temple.

Mr. Julian was quick to leap forward and began pounding on Eric's back.

Meanwhile, Katarina pretended to have nothing to do with his sudden inability to swallow his drink, and instead she turned her attention back to the knight on her other side, her expression once again woefully docile.

"Whereabouts are you from, Sir Cas?"

"Sorlia, Lady Katarina." He bobbed his head in response before loading up his fork with more of the roasted vegetables.

"Oh? How is it you became a knight? Was your father a knight?" Kat asked while reaching for the unopened bottle of wine on the table. Eric had the great fortune of being able to drink the Troivackian moonshine they'd purchased, whereas Kat, to continue acting as a proper Troivackian lady, could only drink the wine.

Once she wrestled the cork free and Poppy had stepped forward to pour the goblet, Kat turned back to the knight, who still had yet to answer her question as he continued shoveling food into his mouth.

"I became a knight . . . because of pure dumb luck," he finally managed between mouthfuls, though he became rather cagey about meeting her gaze.

Kat noticed this with a raised eyebrow. Faucher, however, fixed the younger man with a stern scowl.

"You're an elite knight. How is that only luck?"

"Well . . . you see . . . I . . . er . . . well . . . I admit I'm a bit gifted with the sword. I was one of the youngest people to ever reach the level of master, but my family . . . Well, I have five younger sisters, and I'm a commoner, so you can imagine they are a bit hard to care for." Sir Cas chuckled nervously, his cheeks deepening in color.

"A commoner reaching the level of elite knight with no connections? How . . . suspicious." Faucher's stare looked as though it were going to turn the poor young man to stone.

"In Daxaria, our king has set a great example about judging someone's worth by their skills and character," Kat interjected sharply.

"Yes, your cousin Antonio Faucher was in fact one of the driving forces of implementing my father's belief," Eric informed them with the hint of a slur.

Kat sat up, startled. "Antonio Faucher? *Captain* Antonio?! That's his cousin?" Katarina brandished her index finger in Faucher's direction, coaxing the vein in his temple to make an encore appearance.

"It's rude to point," Eric chided while once again drinking from his cup.

"Yes, your former captain was indeed my cousin," Faucher admonished, though it was clear it was not a fact he was proud of. "His father abandoned Troivack all for some batty woman, who—"

One warning look from Eric was all it took to stop Faucher from continuing.

No one risked a word for a beat, the silence only filled by the sounds of animals barking and brawling off in the distance.

Kat adjusted her attention back to Sir Cas. "I can't get over Faucher and Antonio being related! We were almost family!"

"What useless thing are you saying now?" Faucher demanded, his gaze becoming a little unhinged.

"Oyy! Faucher! We just talked about not making me look so damn good!" Eric interjected with a half moan.

Kat ignored the malice in the Troivackian's tone and instead smiled sweetly.

Faucher gritted his teeth.

"Didn't you know . . . ? Your cousin, dear, wonderful, Captain Antonio *Faucher* was betrothed to my grandmother right before her death. In fact, I still called him my grandfather when I was a child!" Kat's smile, as she explained, put the sun to shame.

And for every bit of her radiant amusement, Faucher rivaled it with his dark glower.

"Your jests border on insult, Lady Katarina. I suggest—"

"Oh, she isn't jesting. That was entirely true. He used to call her his little Spitfire if I recall correctly. I suppose because your family excommunicated Antonio's father, you weren't kept apprised of his life," Eric supplied while clumsily rubbing his forehead.

Faucher's mouth clamped shut, and Katarina's look of triumph succeeded in making the man return his attention to his plate.

Kat took the opportunity to resume her discussion with Sir Cas, who didn't look all that pleased with the conversation's development. "So, Sir Cas, what are the names of your sisters?"

"Lucy, Lily, Laura, Lynn, and little Liza," he recanted in a single breath, his face brightening.

"Do they all have your silvery blond hair and blue eyes? If so, I can foresee them being quite difficult to protect," Kat teased.

"Oh Gods, Lucy and Lily are already married, and let me tell you, I am beyond thrilled that time is over and done with. Laura wants to stay as an unmarried governess to one of our sister's families—or take care of our mother. Lynn wants to become a physician just like your grandmother was, Lady Katarina," Sir Cas explained happily. "Little Liza . . . well . . . All I can say is, at six years old, I can already tell whomever she marries will have his hands full."

"Stubborn?"

"When she has decided on something? The absolute worst. The funny thing is, she is normally so indecisive. It's just when she finally *does* decide—"

"You should inform her of the right decision early on and end her suffering," Faucher interjected without lifting his gaze.

It was the first time Kat had seen the angelic looking man called Sir Cas frown.

"Faucher, I respect my sisters and their minds. They are brilliant young women. To be honest, after hearing your thoughts and views, I'm surprised the Troivackian king placed you and Mage Vaulker with us and not Prince Henry given your nature."

"I'm the one who is supposed to ease you all, especially Lady Katarina, into Troivack. That's why he put me in charge of this group's protection," Faucher replied while sipping his own moonshine. "I've run into Vaulker a few times. He follows through on his promises and is a decent mage, so I scouted him."

"Oh Gods . . . he's saying he's the lesser evil." Kat breathed while her features morphed to express her dread.

"Troivack is no longer willing to bend for anyone or anything that is not of its own. Especially with our king's choice in bride." Faucher didn't bother directly addressing the redhead, and instead spoke to his plate.

"Explain this more to me then, He Who Knows All. What is so bad about him marrying Princess Alina? It creates a strong relationship and a good connection for resources with Daxaria," Kat queried with genuine interest.

"For one, we don't like change. For another, we have heard she has a weak constitution, and that is not what the queen of Troivack should be known for. Troivack's queen is meant to be a strong, silent support at her king's back. A model of demure grace and subtlety for Troivack's citizens. A Daxarian noble with their . . . eccentricities, loose morals, and lack of discipline is the antithesis. Not that I, myself, share that belief. Having met Princess Alina, I can say she is a well-mannered and intelligent woman, though I do not like how much our king turns to her to hear her thoughts, but I—"

Kat propped her elbows on the table and began rubbing her temples in slow, firm movements.

"Alina wasn't kidding . . . Making changes here is going to be a living hell . . ."

"Lady Katarina, *you*, on the other hand, are exactly what everyone is expecting a Daxarian woman to be. A fact that makes me wonder if my king has some sort of plan for you that I do not know of. Surely he does not tolerate your outspoken, rude nature and odd behavior any more than I do."

"I will have you know he has personally begged me to be the godmother to their children!"

"Kat, you can get charged for a lie like that," Eric warned lazily.

Hesitating for a moment, Kat rolled her eyes upward. "Alright, he hasn't begged me . . . yet. But he will! I have a gut instinct!"

Faucher shook his head and took another bite of food while Kat reached out and drank from her goblet, her eyes looking up to the heavens as she did so.

When she had finished taking a drink, her gaze remained fixated on the sky, and her face relaxed.

"I must admit . . . the greatest part of this journey has to be sleeping under the stars. It's the same sky as the one in Daxaria, and yet completely different."

Faucher snorted condescendingly at her words.

"Oh, I'm sorry, were you hoping I'd say it's your sparkling personality I'm so taken with?" Kat remarked dryly, her sarcastic expression returning once more as she leveled the Troivackian sitting across from her with her stare.

With a sigh mixed with a grunt, she chose to ignore Faucher's disgruntled reaction and instead reached for her goblet to take another sip. The military man seemed to have had enough of being pestered, however, and so he stood and stalked off with his maroon cape shifting about his ankles.

Once he had disappeared, Kat reached over and slid Eric's goblet away from him. "I was starting to forgive you today, but seeing you make an arse of yourself yet again has me rethinking that."

Eric didn't respond to her chiding tone as he waved Mr. Julian forward and took the entire bottle of moonshine from the lad. He was not so easily deterred.

Kat's hands suddenly flopped palm side down onto the table, and she let out a loud moan of exasperation.

"What now?" Eric asked dully while swaying in his seat.

Opening her eyes, her magic flickered outside of her body once more, making Sir Cas lean away from and stare at her in wonder.

"Godsdamnit, I've been poisoned again!"

CHAPTER 23

POSITIVELY POISONED

Eric was the first to respond to Katarina's outburst, as he slammed the bottle of moonshine down on the table and leapt to his feet only to trip and stumble back onto the bench. He began standing once more, but by this time, Sir Cas had recovered from the shock of the news and was also hastily rising to his feet.

"Gods, you need a physician!" Sir Cas breathed while his eyes scanned the crowd to send someone quickly to the nearest town.

Kat, however, was letting out a long sigh and waving her hand dismissively. "No, no. No need. I'm fine; I mean, I'll sleep for about five or six hours, and . . . Oh, would you look at that? They tried a different type of poison this time."

Looking down at her hand, Kat noted her magical glow flickering about her skin.

Eric had finally righted himself enough to clasp Katarina on her shoulder. "Are you certain you don't need a physician? Was it someone here who did it?"

Despite his speech slurring heavily, the prince seemed perfectly aware of the situation.

Meanwhile, poor Sir Cas was still reeling from her flippant attitude with regards to her attempted assassination.

"My bet is on the wine. Everyone else here is drinking moonshine, and it's typical the only people who wouldn't be permitted to partake would be the women," Kat pointed out, a sudden glint in her eyes appearing as she turned her chin upward.

"So . . . the simplest solution moving forward . . . would be for me to drink only moonshine with the rest of you."

"My lady, don't fret! You can always drink water instead," Sir Cas consoled while misunderstanding the redhead entirely.

Kat's hopeful gaze flattened. "How will that keep me warm at night?"

"You're always warm," Eric pointed out with a sigh before plunking himself back down clumsily. He then glanced over to where his assistant and Poppy stood out of earshot, confused about why the two men were showing sudden concern for the noblewoman.

"What is the big deal about women drinking moonshine anyway? My mother said they were permitted to do so here!" Kat grumbled irritably.

"When their husbands or father's permit them, yes. Most father's do make the allowance, unless the women are preparing for marriage," Eric explained, his eyes beginning to close sleepily.

"Well, I am not preparing for marriage, and I'm sure my father would have no problem with it given the amount my mother consumes," she retorted huffily.

"Your Highness, should we not alert the others that someone tried to kill Lady Katarina?" Sir Cas interrupted, his angelic, youthful face marred with a frown.

Kat jumped in before Eric could reply. "Ah, about that. We're trying to keep that private to figure out who is trying to do it. I mean, all the men present know I am not the princess, but that doesn't mean there isn't a weasel amongst us. So we are keeping my poison tolerance under wraps in case someone is reporting what's happening. Tomorrow, I'm guessing His Highness will announce that he heroically discovered the poison before I could drink it." Kat finished her explanation with a small jab of sarcasm at how Eric likely would handle the situation come the morning. She then grew fixated on her glowing hand, waving it back and forth rapidly as though trying to put out the light.

Sir Cas nodded along in understanding, until a sudden realization dawned upon him.

"Wait . . . you said you'd been poisoned *again*. You were poisoned before?!" Sir Cas was rising to his feet again until Kat yanked his sleeve and forced him to sit back down.

"I have, yes, and because of my magic, it doesn't affect me other than I actually need to sleep at night . . . And apparently now I'm glowing like a torch, but everyone here will just assume the prince annoyed me again," Kat reasoned, then noticed Eric's hand was still on her shoulder as he slept peacefully on the table. Kat slapped his hand off, then turned back to Sir Cas with an expression that indicated her point clearly was proved.

"M-My lady, shouldn't we be treating this more seriously?"

"Well . . . the way I think about it . . . that was a sealed bottle. Since purchasing it, the only one to handle it aside from me was Poppy, and I've been with her the entire time. This means that it was someone at the crossroads settlement we were at during the midday rest. By this point, they are already long gone. So our best bet is to wait until we get to Vessa and inform the king. He will be able to do a more thorough investigation. In the meantime . . . I just have to try and watch out for more assassination attempts!" Kat grinned.

Sir Cas recoiled. "Why are you happy about that?"

"Ah, well . . . to be honest, I've been a little bored on the trip. Having something to do or work on (other than annoying a certain mage) is a thrilling idea!"

The young knight grimaced. "My lady, this could place not only you, but others in danger as well, including the crown prince."

Kat shot a sardonic side-glance at Eric, who was beginning to drool on the table.

"He doesn't seem all that bothered by it, Sir Cas. Besides, these attempts so far have been pointed: both poison, both with my wine. The obvious solution is to drink no wine, just moonshine," she explained happily.

"My lady, I really do think we should be more wary about this. We should inform the men with us, about everything, and how close they've come—"

"No. Even Faucher only knew someone *attempted* to poison me at the inn, but he isn't aware of my . . . constitution," Kat explained delicately.

"Well, that explains the dead innkeepers." Sir Cas sighed with a frown.

"Wait. You weren't aware why we killed them?!" Kat turned on the knight in alarm.

"Not particularly. I just knew four of the Troivackian knights went out, there was a small scream, one cry, and then silence. By morning there was a suspiciously big hill five hundred yards from the back of the inn."

Kat gaped at the young man with wide eyes, her perception of him rapidly changing.

"Did you . . . not think to question that? Or . . . to be alarmed? I know I've been trying not to think about it!"

"My lady, on foreign land, a Daxarian knight has no right to interfere. My only right is to protect you, my lady—and the princess, but it's just you with us on this part of the trip. I figured if it was important, I would have been informed, and now that I know it pertained to your safety, I will make a point of addressing the situation with Faucher." Sir Cas nodded to himself before reaching for his goblet of moonshine. "I wondered if His Majesty the Troivackian king had ordered anyone who started rumors be put to death, so I didn't want to overreach my authority."

"What rumors?" Kat frowned.

"Ah . . . the innkeepers and the staff all had begun a rumor after we arrived that the Daxarian princess was in a scandalous affair with the inept Daxarian steward—pardon my saying so, Your Highness." Sir Cas nodded at Eric, who was still unconscious on the table.

"Rumors about . . . His Highness . . . and . . . oh Gods. Why in the world would they think that?" Kat groaned while slapping her hand to her forehead.

Sir Cas cleared his throat uncomfortably. "Erm . . . well . . . someone apparently saw you and His Highness talking alone outside, and . . . assumptions were made."

"That's all it took?! Gods, these people really are looking for any reason to destroy Alina's reputation . . ." Kat's gaze dropped to the table pensively.

"Pardon my saying so, my lady, but I believe it has been stated quite clearly what kind of social and political climate we are strolling into." Sir Cas looked sheepish.

Kat shot him a wry glance. "You're not what you seem, Sir Cas. For all your forward friendliness and filial fondness, you seem quite . . . *cavalier* about violence . . ."

For a moment, a look of somber weariness passed across the young man's features. A look that spoke of wisdom and gruesome times witnessed long ago.

"Not everyone is as they seem, my lady. It is a tough lesson I think that Troivack is more than willing to dish out," Sir Cas lamented with a humorless chuckle.

"I'm surprised you even bothered to speak up for your sisters," Kat muttered to herself as she shook her head.

"I protect my own."

Sir Cas's fierce reply made Katarina hesitate as she reached for her goblet. She then grasped its stem and brought it closer to her lips.

"M-My lady, that's poisoned. Why are you—"

"It's alright, I was just thinking it's about time for bed, and at the very least I may as well ensure I take enough to sleep through the night." Kat shrugged and tilted the goblet.

"But—" Sir Cas was cut off when a strong hand seized Katarina's arm, stopping her from drinking.

Startled, Kat sloshed some of the liquid onto the table and partially onto her skirts.

"What the—" she began furiously while turning her gaze to Eric, who still appeared asleep save for his hand encircling her arm.

"Stop drinking poison; go sleep," he mumbled, his grip on her arm gentling.

Kat frowned and opened her mouth to chastise him for trying to tell her what to do, when Poppy stepped forward.

"My lady, is everything alright?" she asked nervously while eyeing the prince and Sir Cas.

Glancing between the two men, Kat let out a sigh of defeat.

"No, Poppy, His Highness is just telling me to go to bed."

The maid clasped her hands in front of her skirts uncertainly, her eyes shifting to the prince's hand still gripping Katarina's arm.

Standing, the lady carefully freed herself from his hold, then gave a small nod to Sir Cas.

"Good night, Sir Cas. I shall see you in the morning."

The knight bobbed his head and half rose from his seat to give a proper bow, but Kat had already turned to retire for the night.

Once settled back into his seat, Sir Cas picked up Lady Katarina's goblet and tossed the remains into the sand behind him before giving the empty cup a sniff.

At first it smelled of regular wine . . . but then there was another scent . . . something that stung the back of his tongue . . .

Sir Cas frowned. If it was the poison he thought it might be . . . then one mouthful of the wine should have killed Lady Katarina instantly. She had had two . . . and yet she was perfectly fine.

Shaking his head in amazement, Sir Cas reached over and picked up the remaining bottle of poisoned wine with the intention of finding Faucher and informing him of the recent attempt.

He glanced at the prince who was fast asleep on the table and felt his expression harden.

All throughout his training as a knight, and even as far back as his boyhood, Sir Cas had heard of the prince of Daxaria's kind nature. He had heard how talented Eric Reyes was with a sword and how no one could leave a conversation with the man without liking him immensely.

However, Sir Cas only felt uneasiness around him ever since he had seen the prince visiting with the knights on the princess's wedding day.

With a small sigh, Sir Cas looked away from the noble and returned to his task of reporting the attempt to Faucher.

If he were honest with himself, the entire trip thus far had been one gut-twisting experience after another, making his instincts prickle multiple times. They were surrounded by danger, their allies were barely tolerating them, and the difference in ideals was alarming . . .

However, Lady Katarina's unrelenting spirit and positive (albeit mildly disturbing) outlook on the journey had somehow made everything seem alright. She'd simply make some flippant remark and have them all laughing or too distracted with her outrageous comments to recall being angry.

She was a hard woman to ignore, which made Sir Cas all the more resolved to protect her as she drew more and more eyes—especially knowing that with all that attention, there was a chance that the one and only daughter of the house witch would perhaps create a bit of magic and turn the world on its head for the better.

Sir Cas found himself grinning at no one in particular as he located Faucher on the other side of the fire, speaking with the mage.

Yes, of all the people in the world capable of breaking the norm and creating something new . . .

There was no one better to do so than Lady Katarina Ashowan.

CHAPTER 24

MINDING A MAGE

The bustling Troivackian town of Kimal drew Kat's ethereal gaze in every direction. The hot sun burned high above, and the layers of noise concocted from voices and carts clattering down the cobbled roads set the air thrumming with energy.

"My lady, please be sure not to wander off on your own. We are only changing the horses and eating our luncheon here," Mage Sebastian instructed, his tone a mixture of boredom and derision.

Kat didn't bother sparing the mage a glance as she continued peering with great interest at the various stalls along the lively street. "Mage Sebbie, please be sure not to be an arse of the highest order; we are only around each other because we have no choice," she recited back at him in an obvious attempt to mimic the mage.

Sebastian turned and glared at her, but Kat didn't bother acknowledging him as she made her way over to one of the nearby stalls. The vendor worked under a beige canopy covering a faded wooden booth loaded with various trinkets that gleamed in the daylight. The merchant, a bald man in his early fifties with a prominent mole near his temple, seemed to deal specifically in metal items.

The mage scoffed. "Women and shiny objects."

"Mages and their crap personalities," Kat retorted without missing a beat before stepping farther away from Sebastian, who visibly gritted his teeth in response.

Leaning over the wares that were splayed over a brilliant blue cloth, Kat perused the brass compasses, intricate incense burners, necklaces, and . . .

"Might I see that?" Kat pointed at the item that had caught her eye while turning her smiling face up to the merchant, who eyed her warily.

"My lady, that is a sextant. It is used for charting—"

"I know what it is," Kat interrupted the mage's spiel while she studied the instrument. She turned back to the seller, her smile gone, which brought the Troivackian visible comfort. "I will take this."

After paying for the gift, Poppy stepped forward to take it on Katarina's behalf before she turned back to the street.

"I was unaware you had a fascination for astrology and navigation." While still rude in cadence, the mage couldn't hide the note of curiosity in his voice.

"I'm not particularly. I enjoy the stars for being beautiful as much as anyone does, but the sextant is actually for my brother. He loves studying the constellations and the daily movement of the sky. When we were children, he would always tell me stories of the legends inspired from the constellations." A forlorn look crossed the young woman's face as her gaze grew distant.

For a moment, the mage was taken aback by the sudden shift in the foolish witch, but he quickly returned to his senses.

"I should have known it wouldn't have been of any interest to you." Sebastian gave a churlish laugh.

Kat rolled her eyes, her fond memories forgotten, as she was forced to be present in the street that was incredibly far away from her home and family.

"You're right, Sebbie, my interests have always encompassed weapons, or riding . . . You know—the usual feminine interests." Katarina's impish smile and childish nickname for him made the mage grumble without bothering to address her outlandish claim.

Raising her hand to shield the sun, Katarina stared through the sea of people, where there was more than one head that turned to stare at her interestedly. Her bright red hair, pale skin, and height made her a spark amongst the common scenery. The gawking, of course, was also increased by the fine quality of the plum-colored dress she wore, even though she had a gray shawl tied around her waist to protect her skirts from the clouds of dust rising from the hundreds of feet stirring the ground around them.

"You said the mage school had burned down shortly after the war, so how is it you learned magic?" Katarina asked as they picked their way down the road.

An elderly woman being guided by a younger one forced both lady and mage to the side temporarily as they passed.

"Mages here in Troivack have become nomadic since Ivorik burned down. We lend help in the form of small magicks that are hard to trace. For example, helping control a field burn, or negating greater damages from flooding."

Kat nodded slowly. "So how is it you fell under the employ of the king?"

Sebastian's usual calm composure didn't entirely succeed in masking his rush of self-consciousness.

"I . . . became friends with Faucher. He could have been the next captain of the Troivackian military, but of course as tradition dictates, when Captain Orion died in the war, the title fell to his next of kin. Faucher merely was a postwar placeholder until Orion's young son grew old enough to take over."

"Odd that they found a placeholder for the captain's position and not the king's given that His Majesty Brendan Devark was only a child himself when his father died," Kat mused aloud.

The mage hesitated in answering. "It had been discussed at the time, but the risk of a civil war as a result following our loss to Daxaria was too high."

Kat's face saddened, once again making the mage pause at her open show of compassion. The morose expression lasted briefly, however, before she once again brightened. "Well, at least he now has Alina—I mean, the princess! She is a force to be reckoned with in council meetings, let me tell you. She's small but mighty. I loathe meetings with a passion, but she had this way of making them—"

"The princess sat in on and contributed during council meetings? With her father, the king of Daxaria?" Sebastian interrupted with great alarm.

Kat laughed. "Of course! Everyone, including her fiancé, insisted upon it to help her prepare to be Troivack's queen."

Sebastian's thumb came up to rest on his lower lip, his eyes falling to the ground in intense thought.

"His Majesty . . . wants her involved in meetings . . . Gods . . . no wonder. If the duke knew of this . . . not to mention the others . . ."

"Duke? What duke?" Kat turned as a group of commoner children ran by hurriedly.

"Duke Seb—Icarus. Duke Icarus." The mage cleared his throat awkwardly.

Kat paused while lifting an eyebrow. "Duke Icarus, I seem to recall in my lessons . . . a man famous for his family's moonshine recipe. They were the main distributors until House Piereva entered the market. A poor relationship brewed between the two families—particularly after Duke Icarus claimed the former earl stole the recipe and cut off his expanding reach amongst merchants."

"You speak of your uncle Earl Phillip Piereva as though he bears no relation to you," the mage reminded curtly.

Katarina's gaze cut to the mage. "You know, I seem to recall that the duke's first name is Sebastian as well. Funny coincidence, especially given that you didn't want to mention that little detail, hm?"

The mage's lip curled as he rounded on the lady. "What are you insinuating?"

"Only that it was odd you froze when you almost repeated his first name." Kat's eyes were fixed on Sebastian, whose gaze turned dark.

"My personal relationships are not your business."

"So you admit it's a personal relationship. Interesting." Kat smiled triumphantly and watched Sebastian's brow furrow even more deeply.

Turning back to the street around them, Katarina was about to announce they should return to the carriage, when something else caught her eye.

While nimbly sidestepping a loaded wheat cart and a group of men in the middle of a dice game, Kat ducked under the canopy of a stall that was smaller than the others on the street. She didn't notice Sebastian had fallen behind.

Despite the space being shaded, it was stuffy enough to make Katarina begin sweating almost immediately. The entire stand was covered in weathered cloth that perhaps some time ago had been a lovely shade of lilac, but the sun had washed it of any vibrancy, and the windswept sand had worked its way into the fibers.

Hooks showcasing all manner of wares filled the stand's borders, and one table ladened with similar-looking items nearly took up the entire space.

There were pots and pans, a battered lyre, silken skirts with coins threaded on the hems . . . but the item that had caught Katarina's eye was a short sword.

Its leather sheath had a long, curved scratch marring it, and the brass along the tip and near the hilt were dulled from years of neglect.

However, it was the pommel in particular that had drawn Kat forward.

On it was a symbol . . . one that she had never seen before, but . . . every inch of her being hummed.

It was a witch's symbol.

She didn't understand how she knew this. A witch's symbol was unique unto themself, regardless of whether or not they were of the same element. Now of course there were similarities, but it always varied, typically in times of great magical exertion—or the day a witch first used their powers.

The symbol on this handle, however . . . It was something else. Something old . . . something powerful . . .

"My lady! You can't run off like that!" Sebastian huffed behind her with Poppy close on his heels.

Kat opened her mouth to reply, when a woman in her late forties rose from her inconspicuous seat in the corner of the tent.

While her head was covered in a worn beige cloth, her frizzy dark hair was streaked with gray and tied back in a braid that rested over her left shoulder, several hairs left fluttering in what little breeze entered the space. The woman had kind yet distant dark eyes, with a square jaw, and a corner of her thin lips quirked upward in what some could interpret as a friendly expression.

"Interested in something, lady?" she asked, her warm gaze roving over Katarina's striking appearance.

Kat couldn't move her eyes from the weapon that was partially covered by a broken lantern and a red collar with silver studding that must have been meant for taming a large beast.

"The sword there; might I see it?" the redhead asked while instinctively moving closer to the weapon.

"You have a good eye, lady. That there is a short sword made from the great blacksmith Theodore Phendor of Daxaria. One of his earlier pieces. It won't be as refined as his later work, but if the handle is repaired and the blade polished, I'm sure your husband would love it above his mantle." The woman smiled while bowing.

"This is most likely a fake," Sebastian muttered, casting a cold glance at the merchant, who lowered her gaze before him, whether from fear or guilt, it was not clear.

Ignoring his words, Kat reached forward and plucked the sword from the hook. A wave of magic pulsed through her once, and instantly, it felt as though the blade had been in her hand her entire life.

For a moment, Katarina wondered if the dull ring she heard was in her own head, but when the mage, Poppy, and the merchant all looked equally as stunned, she realized it had in fact sent out a resonant wave that had silenced some of the noise outside the stall.

"My lady! A sure sign it is of Theodore Phendor's work! He always said his blades sang once they found their true masters!" The woman clapped her hands, her dark eyes glittering with the pleasure of a sure sale.

Entranced, Kat gripped the sheath, intending to draw the weapon and gaze upon the blade, when Sebastian shook his head, his mage crystal jangling as he stepped forward.

"A sword is not a suitable purchase for a noblewoman. Unless you plan on gifting this to your brother or father as well," Sebastian interjected dismissively, though he kept his voice low.

Kat's thumb flicked the fine loose chain that used to be a part of the handle of the sword before she cast a slow smile over her shoulder at the mage.

"If you can outbid me on this sword, I'll leave it here."

"I don't have to buy it, just outbid you?" he asked indignantly.

"That's right. Assuming you have the coin on your person." Kat straightened her shoulders and turned toward the merchant woman with her bright smile. "I will pay three gold pieces for this sword."

The merchant woman frowned. She had been expecting at least five . . .

The mage scoffed. "I'll bid six."

Kat smiled cheerfully. "Wonderful. Now show me you have that money, and you win."

Sebastian glared and reached to his side for his pouch . . .

Then blinked in confusion.

"Oh dear . . . are you saying you can't prove you have the means to win the bet?" Kat smiled deviously.

"Devil woman!" Sebastian spat as he whirled on Kat, making her laugh. "What did you do with my money?"

"Nothing. Those children we passed by, however . . ."

Sebastian swore in the old Troivackian tongue, earning a look of confusion from the old merchant woman and a laugh from Katarina.

"Why didn't you say something?" the mage hissed.

"I'm a woman; why would I ever try to tell a man something that could embarrass him? Something such as *A small child lifted your pouch off your belt without even needing to break his stride* could be deemed too bold for a demure woman like me to say."

"I don't know why I'm surprised by such nefarious and underhanded dealings, but—"

"Sebastian," Katarina interrupted with a sly grin as she handed over her gold to the momentarily stunned merchant woman. "Did you forget? I'm half Troivackian, and in Troivack, a good cheat is still counted as a fair win."

CHAPTER 25

INFLUENTIAL INDIVIDUALS

Katarina strolled over to the group of knights where Eric mingled. The Daxarian prince seemed to have finally recovered enough from his hangover to not sway where he stood.

"Ah, my lady, are you ready to depart once more?" Sir Cas appeared from around the carriage, carrying several packages wrapped in crumpled brown paper.

"I am indeed!" Kat replied, her sunny smile bright enough to nearly cast an aura of its own. She had her hands clasped behind her back, and there was a skip to her step that drew several Troivackian knights' eyes. "Are those presents for your family?"

Sir Cas grinned back, oblivious, or at least pretending to be, of the overall disparaging group.

"Yes, they are! What has you in such good spirits, my lady?" the young knight queried merrily while setting the packages temporarily on the back of the carriage.

"So glad you asked! I happened upon a fantastic purchase today, didn't I, Mage Sebastian?" Kat looked over her shoulder and called everyone's attention to the mage, who was trudging up behind her at a notably slower pace.

When everyone took stock of the man, he somehow appeared shorter and significantly more drained of life than he had been only an hour or two earlier.

His shoulders hunched, lines had appeared under his eyes, and his sandaled feet barely left the ground.

"What's this now?" Sebastian asked with a grumble.

"Ahh, Sebbie, I was just telling them about my fantastic purchase today!" Kat explained while turning and placing her hands on her hips.

"Never call me that again," the mage uttered irritably, apparently having reached his limits of patience for the day, before bowing to Eric, who was watching the exchange while squinting. It was almost as though the prince were battling a terrible headache . . .

"Besides, I still have my doubts that that sword is Theodore Phendor's work. You got swindled."

"Better swindled than robbed," Kat pointed out a little too gleefully.

Sebastian made a growling sound from the back of his throat, then stalked up into the carriage and slammed the door behind himself.

After a beat of silence, Sir Cas turned back to Katarina.

"My lady, that's amazing! First you discover your familiar and now a sword by Theodore Phendor! It's like you're on a quest, and you're a fantastic hero from the old tales!" the knight exclaimed excitedly.

"It feels that way, doesn't it?!" Kat's own smile broadened. "Poppy is stowing it in the back of the carriage and—speaking of my familiar, I should go see how she's doing. Last I checked, she was drinking some water with Sir . . . what was his name again?" Kat linked arms with Sir Cas and strode away with him, leaving the rest of the knights and Eric standing alone to gape after them.

Once Katarina's chattering and Sir Cas's exuberant responses had faded away, the men all turned back to Eric, who already had his eyes closed and was carving circles into his temples with his knuckles.

"Your Highness, here." One of the men thrust a flask at the prince. "Takes the edge off the worst of it."

Eric accepted the offered goods and took a drink. While his headache initially did get worse when the burning alcohol touched his tongue, it dulled a moment or two later.

"What use could Lady Katarina have with a sword?" one of the knights asked, his arms folded over his chest.

"Most likely a gift for her father or brother," another knight volunteered.

Eric snorted as he took another swig of the moonshine, drawing everyone's attention to him. When he'd finished and was returning the flask, he addressed the questioning stares around him.

"Oh no, that sword is definitely for herself."

"A woman is never permitted to fight, so why . . ." one of the men began, alarmed.

Eric raised an eyebrow lazily. "What about witches?"

Everyone shifted uncomfortably. "Witches are what led to our loss in the war. It isn't illegal for them to fight, but it is . . . generally unwelcome. In my entire lifetime, I've met perhaps . . . one . . . now two witches, including Lady Katarina," one of the men explained.

"Good riddance!"

Everyone turned to the carriage to see Sebastian half hanging out of the carriage window, looking a little demented.

"Entitled, cocky, and they think they are above the law! They should live in the woods quietly if they are so set on being mediators of nature."

"I believe they are supposed to be mediators between nature and mankind. Bit hard to do alone in the woods," Eric pointed out, the alcohol making him feel more relaxed than he had been moments before.

The mage opened the carriage door with a bang and stomped down the step onto the ground to join the group of knights.

"What is it they have done to provide this mediation, hm? Beasts still attack, droughts still happen, homes still burn down, winds still sink ships. Witches are simply overpowered, self-serving—"

"Really? Because in my kingdom, when we partnered with them, they gave us their assistance in building roads, ensuring expedient and safe travel, providing education on plants and crops, reading the skies for storms . . . many things. How many witches have you met, and what was your experience with them?" Eric asked with a chuckle while he rested his shoulder against the carriage casually.

"I-I've met . . . three! All three were . . . weren't . . . they couldn't, or wouldn't—"

"Sebastian." Faucher appeared from around the carriage, his dark gaze homed in on the mage.

"You forget yourself."

His cheeks burning, the mage's gaze dropped to the ground, his jaw clenched.

"Apologies, Your Highness, I did not mean to speak out of turn."

"We were having a discussion. I was learning more about you. Are conversations considered rude?" Eric asked, holding up his hand toward Faucher, making the man cease moving forward.

"His tone was impertinent." Faucher's voice was cold as he once again turned to the mage.

"He was passionate about what he was talking about. Passion isn't bad unless it stops you from thinking clearly." Eric ambled forward and squared off with the large Troivackian military man.

"On that point we agree, Your Highness. However, he speaks without considering your words. Which is what I deem disrespectful."

Eric's eyebrows shot up before stepping back with a smile. "I concede. Apology accepted, Mage Sebastian."

"Thank you, Your Highness." The mage bowed, his shoulders sagging once more.

Eric waved dismissively. "No worries. Lady Katarina has a knack for aggravating people—a trait she inherited from her father—you'll get used to it."

The men around him shifted.

"Your Highness, the lady will be expected to curb her eccentricities once in Vessa. I'm sure this will not come as a surprise," Faucher interjected.

Eric shrugged. "I wouldn't be so sure about that, but no one other than your king can say otherwise, so why worry? Now, I'm going to find some lunch before we depart. Pardon me."

The prince turned and casually strode away, not bothering to dwell on the uneasy expressions on the ten men he left behind.

Mage Sebastian looked to Faucher, his calm composure fully returned. "He seems . . ."

"Disinterested," Faucher supplied quietly so that the knights who were disbanding wouldn't be able to hear.

"While clearly educated about our customs and laws, he doesn't seem all that invested in being a leader or representative of Daxaria in any capacity. Aside from ensuring we don't somehow insult Lady Katarina . . ." Sebastian continued speculatively.

Faucher made a guttural sound, but his agreement was clear. He added, "If I were a Daxarian, I would be worried for the kingdom's future."

Mage Sebastian nodded. "Their kingdom is going to a drunk who cares little for anything. Witnessing his current attitude makes it obvious to me why he was absent for so many years."

"And he is too old to change his ways, in my estimation." Faucher let out a short breath of disapproval. "Pity that the princess was born a woman. She would have been a far better ruler."

"Ah! Speaking of the Daxarian princess, I heard something rather strange from that witch." Sebastian turned fully to face Faucher, his expression serious. "She said that the princess has been sitting in on and participating at council meetings."

Faucher raised an eyebrow.

"Not only was the Daxarian king encouraging this, our own Troivackian king requested she learn such things as well!"

"Would Duke Icarus and the others be aware of this?" Faucher asked, his hand beginning to grip the handle of his sword.

"It's possible. If that is the case, there could be more than half of the council willing to side with him with regards to having the Daxarian princess . . . removed."

Faucher's brows knit together. "Pity. Our king seems to care for his bride, but it sounds as though she will not live past her first year."

Sebastian nodded with a long sigh. "Yes. We'll do our best to stop them, but with someone like Lady Katarina by her side and representing Daxaria so . . . *vividly*, paired with their agenda of changing the old ways, there isn't much hope."

Faucher nodded once and began to walk toward his steed that was being led over to him by a squire. "Our king has wonderful plans for change but has bitten more than he can chew if he thinks that he will be bringing the princess into the meetings. We will see if his sound judgment returns. I will encourage him to see reason once we are back within the castle walls."

Sebastian remained by the carriage but turned his toes toward its door. "Hopefully our king listens to you again. I have not yet met the princess, but if she has earned your approval, I trust she is a passable match for our king. If only she had enough wisdom to stay still."

"Sir Cas . . . you can see this, right? I mean . . . I did drink poison last night, so there could still be some lingering effects."

"No, my lady. I'm seeing it too."

"It's a little . . . unorthodox, isn't it?"

"More than a little."

Katarina and Sir Cas stood shoulder to shoulder, their gazes fixed on the knight that had been tasked with minding Katarina's familiar. The rough-looking Troivackian towered over his comrades and sported a shaven head, full beard, and a long, straight scar down his right cheek.

His terrifying image, however, was more or less destroyed by the money pouch that had been refashioned into a carrier slung around his broad chest, and where Katarina's kitten was now nestled. Pina's head poked out of the top, her eyes blinking open from a contented sleep.

"Erm . . . Sir Miller . . . is my familiar . . . bothering you at all?" Kat asked slowly while still reeling from the sight before her.

"Not at all," the Troivackian replied firmly before his head swiveled around, pure concern and worry welling up around his eyes. "Why? Does she look in pain? Does she seem distressed?"

Kat blinked in surprise before she glanced once more at Pina, who was sleeping again and somehow appeared to be smiling.

"Erm . . . no . . . she looks rather . . . comfy. Um . . . thank you for taking such good care of her," she managed to say as she watched the burly man let out a sigh of relief. He then reached up and affectionately scratched the kitten's cheek with the same measure of gentleness he would give stroking a butterfly's wing.

Leaning over to Sir Cas, Kat lowered her voice. "I suppose not all Troivackians are as rough as they look."

"My lady, he is infamous for being brutal on and off the battlefield. No one has seen him smile . . . ever . . . but—"

"You're so soft, princess."

Sir Miller's loving words, despite being whispered, still managed to interrupt Sir Cas and, once again, drew their perplexed stares.

The man didn't seem to notice or be bothered in any capacity by them, however, as he continued gushing over the kitten with a dreamy smile on his face.

"Do familiars have magic?" Sir Cas whispered, his tense features indicative of the sincere distress he was experiencing.

"They have higher intelligences, can share images of important places with their witches, and they can always find their witches when summoned, but otherwise, no. Gods . . . I know she's cute, but this is . . ."

"Maybe he is just overly fond of cats?" Sir Cas interjected again with a note of desperation.

"That has to be it," Kat whispered as she gradually turned away from the scene to return to the carriage.

"I hope so. I always felt a little uneasy about how no one in Daxaria seemed to be more concerned about the amount of influence Kraken, your father's familiar, had."

"You have great reason to be uneasy. That beast rules the kingdom, after all," Kat admonished with a slow breath out. Her eyes were wide as her mind flitted through old memories.

"I-I beg your pardon? What do you mean he—" The knight's face drained of color, and it was clear he was growing inordinately distressed.

"Ah, Sir Cas, I'm jesting!" Kat laughed hastily and patted his back.

"Oh good. That'd be absurd, after all. A cat ruling the kingdom . . . I know I'm gullible and prone to falling for tricks. Forgive me, my lady." Sir Cas smiled in relief.

Kat chuckled again and waved farewell as Sir Cas spotted a horse being led over to him, and so proceeded to briefly bow and leave the redhead's side.

Once the knight's back was to her, Kat winced. "Sorry for lying, Sir Cas. I don't think many people should know just how powerful Kraken really is . . ."

As she mounted the step to her carriage, Kat's mind then turned to the matter of her own familiar.

Sir Miller is probably just not as fearsome as everyone thinks. It doesn't mean Pina is magic or influencing him excessively . . . I'm not even anywhere near as powerful as my da, so she wouldn't need to be so effective anyway . . .

CHAPTER 26

FROSTY FEUDING

As the carriage jostled its occupants, desert clouds occasionally made their way through the carriage's closed black curtains, resulting in one or all of them having to scratch the grains of sand free from their eyes. It was not helping the journey feel any more pleasant, but at the very least the mage had proved to be slightly useful and had proceeded to make the interior pleasantly cool.

The mage crystal hanging below his ear glowed faintly, and his arms crossed as he stared blankly at the opposite wall of the vehicle. Meanwhile, Kat's foot continued wagging back and forth with great vigor, and her index finger tapped her carriage seat restlessly.

Poppy was attempting to stitch some embroidery, and Mr. Julian was nervously glancing back and forth from the mage to the lady while rubbing his knees with his hands.

"For Gods' sake, are you unable to sit still?" Sebastian snapped irritably. Mr. Julian froze fearfully until he realized the mage had been addressing the redhead.

"I'm bored," Kat replied, her tone exasperated.

"That is not everyone else's problem; amuse yourself and stop making the carriage rock even more with that infernal foot tapping." Sebastian scowled at the aforementioned limb.

"I can't help it. I don't like reading in carriages, or in general, and you have been a sullen maid ever since you let yourself get pickpocketed," Kat grumbled back.

When Sebastian said nothing and instead openly fumed, Kat let out a huffy sigh, then turned to face him more squarely.

"So, tell me, this Duke Icarus you mentioned . . . You made it sound as though he was the leader of the group of people who hold something against the princess. Who are the others?"

Sebastian continued staring daggers at her for a long moment before rolling his eyes and closing them with a disgruntled breath.

"Aside from Duke Icarus, there is Lord Ball, Lord Miller, Lord Vanier, Lord Daul, Sir Gorton, Sir Naumit—"

"Alright, alright, I get it. Is there anyone actually in support of Alina?"

Sebastian remained in thoughtful silence for a while. "At the very least you have . . . a respectable number of neutral members who are reserving judgment until they can meet and assess her."

"Wait, we have *no one* who sees their king marrying a foreign kingdom's princess as a good thing? Truly? With her dowry and the improved relationship with Daxaria, which opens up discussion for trades?!" Kat exhaled a breathy laugh of disbelief.

Sebastian raised a wry eyebrow in her direction. "You underestimate Troivackian pride. We have not forgotten the loss of the war. We do not wish for friendly terms. Things have improved by adhering to our own traditions and ingenuity. To avoid changing what is not broken is an understandably fair viewpoint."

"Even if it was the Daxarian King's agricultural and tax redistribution plan that set you all up for this success?" Kat asked with a smug half smile.

"Good luck trying to evoke any gratefulness or open-minded natures bringing that up," Sebastian countered evenly.

Kat folded her arms. "Well, I bet not all of you think that way, or His Majesty wouldn't have bothered going to Daxaria to court Princess Alina Reyes. It makes no sense if the overwhelming opinion of her is so negative. So, either you aren't close enough to the courts to know better, or you're lying to me to be an arse," Kat announced heatedly.

Sebastian regarded the redhead sternly, his cheeks tinged with red. "The members of nobility who are neutral were willing to acknowledge pros and cons of the match. To say they support the princess as their future queen would mean they have no reservations whatsoever—regardless of the fact they haven't met her to judge for themselves."

"So, you're saying Alina has to dazzle them to see if they will support her? Fine, fine . . . she'll be alright, then." Kat sighed and leaned her head back into the carriage seat.

The mage raised a haughty brow in her direction. "You seem incredibly confident about your princess."

"If you've seen how strong she has become and how quickly she has adapted over the course of a year, you would be too." Kat shrugged.

"Then what about you? Are you going to help her succeed, or will you be another obstacle for her to overcome?" Sebastian's gaze sharpened expectantly.

It was Katarina's turn to shoot the mage a humorless glance, then she slowly crossed her legs and leaned her elbow on her knee to support her chin. "I'll get by, but it's sweet of you to worry. Tell me, will I have the *joy* of your continued presence once we reach Vessa?"

The mage took in a slow, fortifying breath. "Yes, sadly. His Majesty intends to assign me to help guard the princess with Faucher's help. Though I will be busy setting up my quarters until the coronation. I have a great many research papers I've begun drafting that the likes of you wouldn't appreciate anyway."

Kat's expression grew pained. "How delightful."

"E-Excuse me?" Poppy interrupted nervously.

Both Kat and Sebastian looked to her at the same time, their gazes still intense, making Poppy shrink away. "I-Is Mr. Faucher a knight?"

Sebastian shot an appraising glance in the direction of the maid, which in turn made Katarina's finger start tapping, her murderous urges reflected in her golden eyes as she stared at the mage, hoping for his sake that he noted her warning to address her maid respectfully.

"He is more than a knight. He is a squadron leader of the first rank. Only three other men in his time have held such an honor."

"How did you and he meet?" Katarina queried with sudden interest.

Sebastian shifted in his seat uncomfortably and once again folded his arms over his chest. "That is of a personal nature."

Kat didn't miss a beat. "Is he your lover?"

Sebastian balked, his arms falling limply to his lap. "No. No. Absolutely not. No. Faucher is married."

"So, it's an unrequited love you have for him. I understand. My father has told me all about those . . ." Kat nodded sagely in understanding as she once again eased herself back against the wall of the carriage.

"Oh, for the—that man is nearly twice my age!" Sebastian snapped, the red in his cheeks spreading to the tips of his ears.

"I wasn't going to judge you for it, but if he's not your love interest, is he your father? Uncle? Cousin that you used to look up to and torment?" the redhead pestered, her eyes starting to sparkle with mischief.

"I have already said it is none of your business!" Sebastian barked, moving his gaze to the curtained window of the carriage in a futile effort to disengage from the conversation.

"Oh, oh, are you his brother-in-law? He's married, so perhaps you are his wife's younger brother, who was wildly jealous of the man who stole his sister away!" Kat volunteered enthusiastically.

When the mage refused to contribute to her musings, the carriage lagged into a moment of silence.

Which swiftly ended when Mr. Julian perked up. "What about best friends?"

"Oh, yes! Perhaps Mage Sebastian saved Faucher's life on the battlefield, and ever since then, they travel together on adventures!" Poppy leaned forward eagerly, enjoying this new possible direction of the story.

"They must have a trusty dog tagging along with them then," Mr. Julian added, smiling at Poppy, who blushed prettily in response.

"I agree! They named him . . . Bowzie. The Fiercest Barker. Then one day, Faucher meets a woman, and they fall in love. He and Sebastian have one final job to complete together before Faucher retires alone. However, during this job, Bowzie tragically dies, and poor Mage Sebastian is left all alone to wander on his adventures . . . though he reassures his best-est friend in the whole wide world that he truly will be fine on his own again, except . . ." Kat paused, allowing Poppy and Mr. Julian to shift forward on their seats like children on tenterhooks waiting for the next dramatic reveal in a bedtime story. She grinned.

"Except, Faucher is tasked with another adventure years later. Mage Sebastian, who was forced to dwell in darkness for years without a partner, receives a message. This new adventure involves escorting a group of Daxarians, and he needs his old comrade to help him."

Hearing the word *comrade* made Sebastian whirl back around, fire in his eyes, as he slammed his hand down on the carriage seat, releasing a small magical pulse of icy air.

"ENOUGH!" he roared.

"Goodness, of all the stories we were thinking, I thought that was a rather kind and beautiful one. No need to get your crystal twisted." Kat chortled while Mr. Julian and Poppy dropped their chastened faces toward the carriage floor.

Sebastian's breathing was ragged as his ire poured forth toward Katarina. "You, you and your games and your taunting. You think that you can—"

An arrow whizzed through the closed curtain, narrowly missing Sebastian's shoulder.

Shouts of alarm rang out around the carriage, and the sound of steel ringing as several swords being drawn were heard.

Sebastian's hand shot out to the wall of the carriage, and a crackle of ice began to spread from his hand. All the while, he uttered the ancient language only known to the mages. The others watched enthralled as the ice kept spreading in its spirals and beautiful patterns until it encased the entire interior of the carriage.

"What the—" Kat stared around in confusion, her eyes already aglow.

"This ice is two inches thick. It should stop or slow down any barrages, and they won't be able to open the door," Sebastian explained quickly, his hand remaining fixed to the wall of the carriage.

Katarina, Poppy, and Mr. Julian noticed then how muffled the shouts and battle cries had become courtesy of their new shield.

"We should go out and help them!" Kat insisted as she reached for her door handle only to find that it had been fully encased in the ice wall.

"Absolutely not. My job is to project you all. The biggest problem is that Prince Eric isn't in here as well!" Sebastian snapped while panting slightly from the sudden onset of stress.

Kat tried again. "We need to help them! You're the only one who can use magic! What if they have a mage, or worse yet, a witch?"

"If they have a mage, that would be a far greater worry, but they won't! There are only fifty mages at most in Troivack, and—"

The shouts grew louder, and a loud bang on the door immediately drew everyone's attention.

The four people waited tensely in the moment of silence, their breaths coming out in puffs, when another bang could be heard through the ice.

Then there was silence.

Kat looked at Poppy, who was shivering from the cold of the ice, and Mr. Julian, whose left hand was gripping a dagger he kept in his boot, but otherwise looking every bit the scared fifteen-year-old he was.

"We need to find out what's happening," Kat whispered urgently, her heart hammering in her chest, and her magical glow growing.

Sebastian's breathing had calmed, but when he looked at Katarina and noted the walls around her were beginning to melt, tensed once more.

"Gods, stop that! I am keeping you in here until I receive the signal from Faucher!"

"Stop what?! I'm doing nothing! You need to get out there! What if Faucher is dead?!" Kat demanded, her urgency rising.

"Faucher isn't that easy to kill." Sebastian let out a dry laugh, his eyes still fixed on the wall that was already starting to turn back to water around the redhead. His spell should still be holding steady despite the wretched woman's infuriating magic!

He turned his attention back to his hand and began to utter more spells to add another inch to the ice shield when the sound of a loud crunch snapped his eyes up.

He looked over to see Katarina with her skirts clutched high as she leaned to the side with her right knee curled under her, preparing to kick. She was raising her heel back yet again to kick the ice barrier, a large web already present from her initial blow.

"Are you mad?!" Sebastian demanded, unable to remove his hand from the carriage doorway or else his spell would nullify immediately.

"Where the hell have you been the past few days that you would even need to *ask*?" Kat breathed, her magical aura burning hotter as she delivered another ice-shattering kick to his wall.

"Stop that, you marsh-minded woman!" Sebastian shouted desperately, unsure of how the witch had the strength to break through two inches of ice so easily.

"Remember. My. Familiar. Is. Also. Out. THERE!" Kat shouted back as she continued kicking the ice away. At last, she delivered a final blow that cleared away enough ice for her to reach the handle.

"Finally." She exhaled, reaching out her hand with the intent of exiting the carriage.

"Lady Katarina! Cease this! You will only get in their way!" Sebastian was no longer shouting as loudly as before, as he now struggled to maintain a hold on his magic.

"Don't worry. If I die, that's my problem, but if they're all dead, that's yours! Deal?" Kat began to press the handle down, when suddenly she was thrown into the seat across from where she had been sitting only moments before. The carriage had jolted into motion, taking off at a breakneck speed, bouncing them around furiously and bruising them all soundly.

No one could find their footing or orient themselves as the vehicle commenced on a mad race. It was unclear whether someone was driving the carriage or the horses had turned tail to run during the fight. If it were indeed a person driving, there was also the uncertain matter of if they were friend or foe . . .

"When the carriage stops, we wait for the signal from Faucher or I'm building up this barrier and—Ouch!" Sebastian's head had careened into his own ice wall.

He didn't get the chance to finish his instructions either, for the wild carriage ride skidded to a halt.

"W-What do we do?" Poppy whispered, tears shining in her eyes as she looked from her mistress to the mage.

"Poppy, listen to me; it's going to be alright," Katarina consoled as her gaze fixed on the door. "Just promise me . . . whatever you see out there, you won't look at me differently."

Sebastian and Mr. Julian's heads turned to stare at the redhead. Mr. Julian looked fearful, while the mage's eyes were bulging and his teeth already gnashing.

"Lady Katarina, save whatever barbaric magic you are thinking of using. I will be the one to—"

The carriage door opened.

They could not see who was on the other side through the wall of ice. A hand slowly raised from the other side and knocked, making Poppy squeak as she succumbed to her tears.

"Don't worry, Poppy." Kat reached out and gripped her maid's hand, the heat pouring from her intensifying, and her aura brightening. "I promise I'm not going to die in a carriage with a Godsdamn mage. The Gods know better than to piss me off with an ending like that."

CHAPTER 27

RUNNING OUT OF TIME

The figure on the other side of the ice wall stood before the open carriage door as though waiting for something . . . The signal from Faucher was never given.

"Sebastian, what if you made that ice wall explode? It could disarm the man enough that perhaps we could make a getaway!" Kat breathed, turning to the mage, who was clearly trying to come up with a solution too.

"That could kill them *and* us. We don't even know *who* is out there . . . No. I need to preserve my magic."

"So we just sit here until it all melts?" Kat asked with an arched eyebrow.

"That is not what I said!" Sebastian countered hotly. "If we wait a bit longer, we may be able to hear more voices and get a sense of how many are out there. We can make a better decision after we have more information."

Kat sat back in her seat, her palms sweating and her aura growing. She hated that he was making a logical suggestion.

So she decided to attempt countering his point as similarly as possible . . . even if being reasonable and practical wasn't always her strong suit.

"Well, if it is one person, we blast the ice, if it is two or three, we blast the ice, and *then* we all fight the remaining men. If it's a group? There is nothing we can do but—"

"But wait in here until Faucher comes," Sebastian firmly finished for her.

"My Gods, your faith in him borders worship, you know that?" Kat lamented, her breath coming out in an icy plume.

Sebastian glared and did his best not to gape at the rising aura around the noblewoman.

"Do you think you could be quiet now so that we can listen?" he ground out after taking a moment to get his temper back under control.

Kat rolled her eyes to the roof of the carriage, her foot begging to vibrate once more as her magic continued to build within her. If she didn't get an outlet for it soon, she would be in trouble . . . She tried not to think about it too much . . .

The figure on the outside of the ice wall eventually moved away, heading in the direction of the driver's seat, and the carriage jostled slightly as whoever it was clearly had returned to the bench.

In the quiet, Kat turned to Sebastian with a frown. "It sounds like no one else is out there."

"It hasn't even been a minute; we will wait longer," the mage replied firmly.

Kat let out an angry huff.

Poppy and Mr. Julian shared nervous glances as they both experienced and acknowledged the rapidly rising temperature in the carriage that originated from the redhead.

After another lengthy moment passed, Sebastian was forced to squint due to the brightness of Katarina's aura, which was amplified by the ice around them reflecting it. Sparks of light appeared on the drops of water that were accumulating on the wall. Even Poppy and Mr. Julian were forced to avert their eyes to the floor.

"Gods, you're like a torch. Stop that!" the mage barked.

Katarina's eyes were closed, but there was a rigidness stretched across every inch of her being.

She swallowed with great difficulty and didn't dare shift a muscle.

"Sebbie, you're going to need to let me out of here. Now."

The mage turned to face her, exasperated, before once again having to avert his eyes from the brightness.

"I told you already, we should—"

"Sebastian . . ." Kat's voice had shifted to a hush, but there was something else that was strange . . . Her voice carried a reverberation, as though her own magic was choking her. "I'm not jesting. You all might get very, *very* seriously hurt."

The mage's concerned frown became tinged with apprehension. "Aren't you a weak, deficient witch? What could you possibly—"

"SEBASTIAN!" Kat shouted, her golden eyes snapping open to reveal their magic beginning to fill and even flicker in her eyes.

The mage jolted in shock, and as a result, a crack in their ice barrier appeared to Katarina's right, rivulets rapidly poured down around them.

Without waiting any longer, Kat stood, and with her heel, gave a single blow that decimated the ice wall and the unopened door on her side of the carriage. Outside, they saw dry, cracked earth and sparse vegetation dotting the nearby hills that were beginning to be cast in shadow by the setting sun, but they saw no attackers.

"W-What—" Sebastian spluttered but didn't get the chance to say more before Katarina took off running, her speed inhuman, as the glow around her flickered and spread as though she were aflame.

"My lady!" Poppy called out, darting from the carriage a few steps and stumbling as her legs immediately resisted the sudden activity after hours of sitting.

"What the hell happened?"

Poppy let out a small scream as she turned and saw none other than Prince Eric Reyes standing with his hand casually pressed in his pocket by the carriage's driver's seat.

"Your Highness!" Sebastian had been in the process of exiting the carriage, and once he realized that it was the Daxarian prince with them and not an enemy, let out a breath of relief.

"Yes, hello," Eric spoke over his shoulder to the mage as he leapt down from the driving bench and strode forward. His eyes were fixed on the shrinking figure of Katarina, who was still running. "Mind explaining why the human firefly is sprinting into the wilderness?"

"W-What happened to the attackers?" Mr. Julian asked instead of answering as he, too, lightened himself from the carriage.

"We were ambushed; Faucher told me to take off with you lot to play it safe. The knights will follow once they've finished handling things," Eric explained. Shielding his eyes from the sun, he struggled to see Katarina as she continued putting an impressive amount of distance between them all.

"So . . . once again I'll ask, what the hell happened to make Lady Katarina take off? Gods, she's fast. I think she could beat a horse . . . Must have to do with her magic . . ." Eric remarked in casual awe.

"Sh-She started glowing when we thought you were an attacker outside . . ." Poppy explained. "She kept trying to get out."

"Ah. I suppose I should go retrieve her. Mage Sebastian, are you alright to protect Poppy and my assistant?" Eric called over his shoulder as he returned to the two horses, then began to unhitch one.

"Of course, Your Highness."

Eric nodded his thanks, and in a matter of minutes, slid onto the bareback horse and set it to a moderate trot, leaving the group to watch his departure.

"Nothing ever seems to rattle our prince . . ." Poppy whispered, her hands clasped together near her mouth.

"I know what you mean. It's as though he's seen everything there is to see and nothing bothers him anymore," Mr. Julian agreed while staring after his employer with a strange mix of apprehension and awe.

Mage Sebastian said nothing and instead allowed himself to think a little more deeply on the strange magical power he had just witnessed from the Ashowan woman.

I've never seen anything like that in my life . . . I must mention this to Faucher when he returns . . .

By the time Eric located Kat, who was crouched into a ball behind a hill with her arms wrapped around her shins, night had settled overhead, the moon full and bright, with billions of stars swirling together on the canvas of deep blues and the occasional streak of purple.

As he approached, she didn't stir. Her forehead remained pressed into her knees, her face hidden. In the distance, an animal howled, yet Kat didn't move a muscle.

Eric pulled the horse to a stop and slid down with a slight grunt thanks to the stiffness of riding without any padding. Sighing with a mixture of weariness and relief, he worked the ache from his legs and back while ambling over to the redhead.

"Are you hurt?" he asked casually while twisting his torso back and forth in an attempt to crack his back.

Kat didn't say anything.

Stilling himself, the prince regarded her with a frown and crouched down until she would be eye level with him should she lift her face.

"Hey. Are you alright?" Eric repeated, his tone shifting to one of mild concern.

When Kat still didn't respond, the prince reached out and gently grasped her arms. His worry for her doubled when he noticed her skin was cool to the touch instead of borderline feverish, as was her norm. "Kat? If you're hurt, you need to tell me."

When she still didn't give any response, Eric moved two of his fingers to her neck.

At last Kat's head snapped up, her golden eyes open and in the darkness.

Her red hair was frizzy and windswept, her face pale. "W-What are you doing?" she croaked.

"I was checking your pulse," Eric explained with a small chuckle, his hand falling away.

"I'm obviously not dead."

"That's odd . . . because normally people who are still alive respond when someone asks them questions," he pointed out wryly.

Kat frowned and let out a small breath before dropping her forehead back to her knees.

Eric had never seen her so . . . dull. His eyes softened as he studied her strange state.

Reaching out, he then tickled her exposed underarms, making her snap back with a surprised shriek of laughter. As a result, she had half fallen back on her arse and was gasping slightly as she stared at him incredulously.

"Wh-What the hell was that?!" she managed while finally registering Eric's grinning face.

"Well look who's come out of her ball of solitude."

Kat blinked in astonishment. "That wasn't funny! I'm not a child you can—"

Eric reached out and tickled under her arm again, making her shriek with laughter, which in turn made Eric laugh.

"St-Stop!" Kat managed through peals of laughter as she wriggled helplessly away from him.

Eric obliged, his hand falling away as he continued smiling at her.

"That was wildly inappropriate!" Kat breathed, though she was still smiling helplessly.

"It's just us here, and you were being rather stubborn," Eric chided with a teasing tone as he slowly stood.

"Now that I see you aren't bleeding, nothing is broken, and you are conscious, how about we return to the carriage? The others are probably worried." He offered her his hand to help her stand.

The redhead stared at his proffered palm for a moment, her smile fading before, she sighed, accepted it, and rose.

"Mind telling me what happened?" Eric asked with a tilt of his head.

Kat dusted off her skirts that were caked in dirt and sand.

"It's fine." Kat's expression grew shuttered, and her previously lightened mood dissolved once more.

"Is it?" He tilted his head over his shoulder and shot her a look of disbelief.

"I just . . . needed to burn off some magic. I told you about the magitch. That's all." The redhead began walking quickly toward the horse.

"Kat . . . I've heard a lot of rumors about you. A lot. Honestly, I thought most were made up until I met you, but one rumor I never heard was that of you running faster than most beasts while blazing like a shooting star. So, this isn't the norm."

Her back turned rigid as she reached up and gripped the horse's rein. "Come on. As you said, they'll be worried."

"Kat." Eric stepped closer, his tone taking on a warning edge.

"It isn't your business!" Katarina snapped while turning her face away from his stare as he stepped to her side.

"I'm responsible for you on this trip; it most definitely is my business," Eric replied firmly.

"Pffft. Please. You're always drunk or on drugs. You can't even be responsible for yourself."

Eric froze at her harsh words and tone as though she had slapped him.

Kat stepped around to the side of the horse, increasing her distance from him.

After a moment of silent stillness, Eric blinked, and his darkened gaze fell to the ground.

Nodding to himself once, his expression still hardened, he walked around the horse to where Kat stood.

"Fine. If that's how you want things between us, so be it. But I would like to know one thing: what did I do to make you dislike me? You seemed fine with me when we were kissing during my sister's wedding reception."

Kat blushed and shifted her golden eyes away awkwardly before she swallowed and attempted to straighten her shoulders and meet his deadened stare head-on. "Well, your time with drugs and drinking are certainly—"

"No. That isn't it. You pulled that nasty prank with the pigpen after we had kissed but before anything else had transpired between us. Is this just how you are? Charming one minute and a conniving . . ." Eric trailed off and took a breath to calm himself before he blurted something a little too brash. "You know what I mean. So, is that it? Is this just your way?"

"No, it isn't!" Kat burst out vehemently.

"Really? Because I can think of no logical reason why you would pull something so petty. I thought at first your father had said something to encourage it, but when I spoke to him, he said he hadn't spoken to you about me at all. No, tell me. What was the *real* reason you decided to hate me?" Eric persisted, his tone soft, but his stare icy.

Kat was unable to look him in the eyes, as embarrassment and even some tears of distress began to rise. "It's just the way I am. I'm a horrible shrew. Are you happy now?"

"Haven't been for a long time. Regardless, I can tell now that that isn't the reason. Come on now. What was it? Did you feel I took advantage of you?" Eric's right hand found his pocket as he waited, the lack of expression on his face almost eerie.

"I . . . I . . ." Kat felt her emotions beginning to choke her, and so she let out a loud, angry breath before snapping her golden eyes to his lifeless hazel ones. "I went back that night. To the courtyard."

Eric raised an eyebrow. He failed to show any sign of understanding.

"I saw you with . . . the baroness," Kat finally finished, her hands gripping her skirts tightly. Despite being half an inch taller than the prince, she felt incredibly small in that moment.

Realization flooded Eric's features before they settled into an expression of disbelief. "Did we not agree it was a casual encounter we had? You are holding a grudge against me for that? How was what I did with the baroness any of *your* business?"

Kat blinked as tears escaped her eyes. She wasn't usually the type to succumb to them, but it had been a long day, and she was feeling more than a little pitiful . . .

"It isn't my business," she managed to say, her arm coming up and across her torso as her gaze remained fixed on the ground. "I'm sorry."

Eric let out an agitated sigh and turned away from her. Rubbing his face in exasperation, he took another moment to compose himself before looking at her again. "Great. Now I'm the arsehole. I guess we have no choice but to stay out of each other's business since we seem to bring out the worst in each other."

Kat didn't say anything as her hands continued gripping her skirts.

"When my magic charges up too much, I lose control, and I . . . I'm not entirely myself. That coyote over there?"

Eric frowned. He hadn't noticed any coyote . . . Then again, it was dark . . . but when he peered over to where Kat was looking, he saw the sandy-colored fur that lied motionless thirty paces away.

Warily, he stepped closer to the animal, and upon inspection, he realized it had several broken bones, and its neck . . . was snapped.

"I killed it."

Kat's whispered words made Eric's eyes leap to her face, his astonishment clear in the moonlight as he stared at the young woman, whose eyes glittered with tears while she beheld the lifeless animal on the ground. The only sound between them in that moment was the fluttering wings of nocturnal insects. The weight of what Katarina confessed rested between them and didn't seem to be in any hurry to lighten itself.

With a shuddering breath, she spoke again, her tears dripping down her cheek. "That's why I ran. When I lose control, I hurt whatever is around me, and there is a possibility that . . . that I could kill an innocent person."

Eric stared at Kat without moving a muscle for several long moments, then he looked back at the coyote.

"Why did you tell me?" he asked quietly.

"You said we bring out the worst in each other. You may as well know one of the worst things about me so you can confirm how right you are." She gave a humorless laugh before reaching up and wiping her running nose with her index finger while looking away from him. "Seems only fair since I know about your secret anyway . . ."

Eric walked over to her with hesitant thoughtful steps and watched her, his mouth firm and his expression stiff. "If you think it's going to happen again, you tell me. Understood?"

Kat jerked her chin down in agreement, and before she could get a handle on the bubble of emotion that burst in her chest, she let out a sob and clamped her hand over her mouth to stifle it.

An odd ache in Eric's chest bloomed as he watched her cry, and so his arms slowly lifted. He found himself drawing her into him and gently stroking her back, allowing her to soak his tunic with her tears. He had long forgotten how to console someone . . . but right then and there, Kat found a measure of solace she desperately needed in his embrace.

CHAPTER 28

CONFRONTATIONAL CANDOR

"I'll steer," Kat announced as she finished wiping the last of her tears from her face.

Eric blinked, his expression flat. "What?"

"I can see in the dark, it makes sense that I steer the horse back," she explained, finally able to look Eric in the eyes as she pulled away from him. His right hand lingered a little longer on her arm before dropping away.

"There's enough moonlight that it's like it's day. I'll be fine." Eric crouched down on the ground and interlocked his fingers to offer Kat an easy foothold for climbing onto the horse in her dress.

Despite his offer, she chose to mount the steed without his help, making Eric roll his eyes as he righted himself, then mounted the horse behind her.

The prince reached around her and grabbed the reins, filling Kat's stomach with a rush of tingles and causing her back and shoulders to straighten as a result.

"What's the matter with you? Relax." Eric's thighs squeezed the horse's sides and set it in motion.

Swallowing with great difficulty, Kat gave her head a small shake to try and scatter free the strange feelings she experienced, but the movement inadvertently made several of her hairs fly into the prince's eyes.

"Agh." Eric winced as he pulled back to free his vision from her assault.

"Ah, sorry about that." Kat cringed.

With an impatient grunt, Eric leaned forward again, then reached out and pulled Kat back into him with his left hand, her hair flattened between them.

Her heart tripled in speed, and a flush swept through her body as she felt his hard chest behind her and his strong arms around her.

"Are you sure you want to ride astride? It looks uncomfortable in that dress," Eric noted after a moment.

"I prefer this way regardless of what I'm wearing," Kat explained while still trying to grasp the funny reaction her body was having.

"Are you cold?"

"No. I told you, I don't get cold."

"Earlier you didn't feel as warm as usual. Even now, you don't seem anywhere near your normal temperature," Eric observed. He hadn't predicted his body would respond so swiftly to having Kat against him, and he was desperately trying to make conversation to take his mind off the fact . . .

Kat's stare turned to his profile. "I still don't *feel* cold. It's probably just because I used up so much magic that it isn't radiating off me. Besides, how do you know my usual temperature?"

"I've spent enough time near you to know. Not to mention we were rather close to each other in the courtyard that night we kissed," Eric recanted offhandedly.

Kat regarded him with a half smile. "You certainly are comfortable not only doing such things but also talking about them."

Eric raised an eyebrow and shot her a dry glance. "I'm a little old to be bashful."

"Mm. True. You are incredibly senile." She nodded wisely.

"By the way, that wasn't your first time kissing someone, was it? You claimed you had other experiences, but I wasn't sure if you were trying to appear more mature at the time," Eric pondered suddenly, a frown appearing on his face.

Kat smiled as she watched the way his eyes gleamed in the moonlight, his attention fixed on the ground ahead of the horse. "Would you feel wildly guilty and responsible for me if I said it was my first?"

"Not particularly. You're old enough to know better, and I have enough to feel guilty about for two lifetimes." He shrugged indifferently.

"Darn . . . it would have been fun to torment you."

"You already torment me. It's bloody annoying." Eric scoffed before giving a small sigh and shaking his head. "So, that was your first kiss?"

Kat's gaze fell to the horse's mane, and her fingers began to twine themselves amongst the coarse hair. "No. No, it wasn't."

Glancing at her with a mildly curious expression, Eric shrugged and moved his attention forward once more.

"I'm surprised you're not fat," Kat burst out in a desperate attempt to change the topic.

"What the—What?" Eric's voice had jumped an octave in obvious incredulousness, and he couldn't help but shoot her a flabbergasted look.

"Well, you drink a lot, and most drunks I know have a gut," she explained as though it were obvious.

"How many drunks do you know?" the prince asked, still attempting to overcome her baffling thought process.

"I saw a lot in Austice when I'd go with my parents to check their ships or to the brothels they owned."

"I still can't believe they took you and your brother there as children." Eric blinked several times as he relaxed again and shook his head in disbelief.

"Only around the Winter Solstice, or during the day when the only people around were drinking and not there for the women. My da thought it was good that we knew more about the world," Kat defended heartily.

"There are better ways. Going to help the homeless or the sick . . . But brothels? Ha," Eric said sarcastically.

"Hey, I'll have you know that's how we found Likon!" Kat retorted indignantly.

Eric paused as he cast his memory back, trying to recall who she was talking about. "Wait . . . that companion your parents took in? I thought he was an orphan they met on the streets."

"That's just what they tell the nobles so no one would say hurtful things to him."

Bitterly, Eric gave another short laugh. "Of course. *Of course* your family has more secrets."

"Every family has secrets. Look at yours. You're a—"

"Yes, yes. A drunk who dabbles with drugs and abandons his family for years at a time. You are a very lucky woman that I am not a tyrannical type of prince who executes people for besmirching his honor."

"You besmirched it yourself," Kat fired back matter-of-factly.

Eric's features turned stony when he looked at her. "That's enough. I've had more than an adequate amount of your condescension for one day."

Kat shifted uncomfortably at his chastisement and once again resumed combing her fingers through the horse's mane.

As the silence stretched on, the redhead found herself wanting to escape the awkwardness that had overcome them. Especially when she figured out that they wouldn't reach the carriage for at least another hour.

"For a long time, I thought Likon was going to be the one to take over as viscount for my father. My brother wasn't ever interested in it."

"I know. Your father used to talk about his concerns regarding Tam when he'd come for a visit." Eric's attitude remained complacent.

"Ah . . . well. Likon's a competent person. I think he started taking on more official duties by the time he was seventeen. He was even sending money to his sister and her family at one point," Kat continued as she thought back to her childhood friend and felt herself smile.

"Mm."

"He was supposed to keep me in line, but really he just helped me get away with more mischief. I remember one time we—"

"Sounds like a good friend," Eric interrupted tonelessly.

Kat frowned and turned on him. "You know, you were the one who started in on my family; I was just pointing out yours isn't all sunshine and peaches. You can stop being so sour."

Looking at her sharply, the intensity of his hazel eyes darkened, forcing the redhead to shrink back.

"You've been making barbs about my shortcomings since earlier, and while I am a pretty easygoing person, you're crossing some lines and you know it." Eric sounded uncharacteristically authoritative, and it was making it rather difficult for Kat to swallow.

She frowned. "Alright, I admit I've taken things a little far, but you've crossed some lines yourself with regards to my family."

Eric regarded her evenly, and after a moment of silent deliberation, finally spoke. "Fine. I'll leave it be."

Kat's frown shifted to a glower. "Just when I thought we were starting to get along . . ."

The prince didn't bother addressing her again.

They rode the rest of the way to the camp in tense silence.

Once Katarina and Eric found the carriage where they'd left it, they discovered the rest of their entourage huddled around a fire with dinner already being prepared.

"There you two are! Did you think it was a nice night for a romantic courting date?" Faucher barked angrily as he stormed over to them.

Eric didn't reply as he leapt from the horse and strode past the Troivackian without a second look. Kat managed to dismount on her own, though it was done gracelessly as she attempted to keep her skirts down. Poppy rushed to her mistress, tears already in her eyes as she began to fret over the state of the redhead's dress.

Kat, however, was too busy glaring at Eric's back as he seized a bottle of Troivackian moonshine from one of the men and proceeded to chug the alcohol for an impressive amount of time before stumbling off alone.

Faucher watched the scene unfold while scowling. He then rounded on the lady.

"Why the hell did you run off like that? Things are dangerous enough in case you haven't noticed."

Katarina stared at him, her frown deepening.

"It is my duty to keep you all safe, and you take off into the desert without any water or idea where you're going. I'm strongly considering chaining you to your carriage seat after this," Faucher continued loudly, making several Troivackian knights lift their weary stares to the scene.

Kat folded her arms quietly and continued staring at him, her magical aura beginning to rise and flicker around her body, though it was nowhere near as wild as it usually was.

He shook his head and let out a growl. "You are quite the spoiled brat."

"Faucher, that's enough." Sir Cas stood angrily from his spot by the fire.

Kat's eyes glowed brightly. "How much do you know about witches, Faucher?"

The military man frowned. "I know enough that—"

"You know shit all about them. I ran off because sometimes magic is difficult to control and can hurt people. Now, instead of making a scene to embarrass me, why don't you go take care of the prince, who you claim is the most important person here, before he chokes on his own vomit. If you try to bully me like this again, I may feel the need to write home telling my family about this. And let me tell you, if my parents become involved? You will discover that this spoiled brat isn't afraid of much for a good Godsdamn reason."

Kat's arms fell to her side, and she then shouldered past Faucher with enough strength that it knocked him back a step, her magic surging around her.

Striding over to her tent, the redhead disappeared inside, leaving the aftermath of her words to play out without her presence. Poppy timidly followed her mistress, unable to meet anyone's eyes.

Faucher stared after Kat, gritting his teeth before he turned to look in the direction the prince disappeared in. "These Godsdamn Daxarians are going to be the death of me . . ." he muttered darkly before stalking off.

The rest of the knights resumed their meals once Faucher had disappeared into the night, but the air of discomfort never left their company.

It seemed as though the remainder of the journey to Vessa was not going to be a peaceful one.

* * *

The morning after Katarina and Eric had returned was the first day the heat had abated enough that the group wasn't sweating as soon as they stepped out of their tents.

It was a welcome reprieve as everyone gathered around the fire where water was already being boiled to make the all-important first batch of coffee.

Kat sat amongst the troupe, already dressed with her hair piled atop her head, as she drank her tea while her maid worked on folding and packing her dirty clothes from the day before.

The knights present around the fire partook in the uneasy hush that stretched among them. Kat didn't bother looking at any of them, as her eyes remained fixed on the flames licking the bottom of the black kettle, her mind lost in her thoughts.

Shortly after the coffee had finished brewing, Faucher stomped over to them.

"We're going to alter our route to Vessa. There has been some sort of attack every day of this journey. It will add another two or three days until we reach Vessa, but— "

"No," Kat interrupted and stood to face him. "Let's just ride hard and arrive earlier than they expect."

Faucher straightened and looked daggers at her.

"That makes it more difficult to protect all of you. We will take the extra time and not take risks. This is not a discussion." Faucher emphasized that last bit before he turned and marched over to where the horses were resting.

Kat let out a small grunt of displeasure as she seated herself back down and took another mouthful of her tea.

"P-Pardon me, everyone?" Mr. Julian appeared from behind the tents that were being collapsed by some of the men in preparation for departure. The assistant was wringing his hands anxiously.

"What is it, lad?" One of the Troivackian knights stood and stared at the boy expectantly.

"I-It's His Highness, he erm . . . I don't think he's well."

Kat laughed scornfully. "I bet he isn't." She then proceeded to take another drink from her tea.

The Troivackian knight cast her a disapproving glance before stepping forward. "Let's go take a look."

The pair disappeared toward the prince's tent, and once gone, Poppy leaned forward. "My lady, I think you need to be more respectful. It's making the knights . . . rather on edge."

Kat sighed and placed her cup on the ground before turning to her maid. "You're right. I'll try to be a better behaved noblewoman. I'm still just rather peeved about last night when—"

"FAUCHER!" The knight who had disappeared with the prince's assistant was nearly jogging to his leader.

The two women watched as he reached Faucher and immediately started speaking in a hurry. Whatever was said had them both running back toward Eric's tent as though it were ablaze.

"My . . . My lady I think something is actually really wrong." Poppy breathed out her worries, but Kat had already risen and was walking quickly after the men, her stomach tying itself in knots.

As she neared the tent, she could hear shouts and other questionable noises that made her halt her progress; her heart pounded against her chest.

Something was definitely wrong.

CHAPTER 29

ALARMING ALTERCATIONS

Sir, I-I'm not sure what to—" the Troivackian knight spluttered to Faucher as they beheld the prince.

"Leave. Both of you. Now," Faucher growled to the knight who had first alerted him and to Mr. Julian. "Do not share the details with the others. Simply tell them that the prince is indisposed, and we will be leaving in another hour."

"Yes, sir." The knight darted out of the tent and headed toward the carriage and horses where most of the knights stood waiting. The prince's assistant was on his heels. Both were completely oblivious to a certain redheaded noblewoman standing and waiting to the side of the tent.

Once Kat made sure that the knight and Mr. Julian were occupied, she moved to the tent opening. Upon quietly stepping inside and laying eyes on the scene, she froze.

Eric stood shirtless with his long, unkempt hair curtaining his face, his arms braced against a small table, and a basin between his arms that was already filthy with his sick.

"Now, Your Highness, can you—"

"Dead . . . Dead . . . Dead . . . She's dead. Mother dead. Mother with the child, dead. In the hole they go . . . down in the hole they went," Eric muttered nonsensically to himself, making Faucher hesitate.

Rooted in the spot, Kat watched in shock. She noticed the scars that littered his bare torso, one near his heart, two along his right side amongst other smaller ones dashed here and there . . .

"Your Highness, you're in Troivack, do you understand?" Faucher began, his voice for once quiet and gentle.

Eric vomited, his arms trembling. "Dig . . . Have to dig," he managed to say when he'd finished as he slowly pressed himself back to standing straight.

"Your Highness." Faucher reached out and clasped Eric's shoulder to make him turn to face him.

Instead of complying, the prince rounded on him, grabbing the portion of Faucher's tunic that peeked through his armor, and with impressive strength, proceeded to headbutt him in the face. As he did so, he pulled Faucher's sword free from the scabbard and flipped it expertly in his hand.

While he had caught Faucher off guard at first, the military man already had grasped his knife, and his eyes were trained on his opponent despite blood flowing from his nose.

"Eric!" Kat called out.

Faucher's eyes darted to her only briefly before they returned to the prince, who showed no sign of having heard her.

"Lady Katarina, get out at once." Faucher spoke slowly and quietly, enunciating each of his word clearly.

Ignoring the Troivackian's order, Kat took another step into the tent. "Eric, do you know who I am?"

"Lady Katarina, I am not jesting. You need to lea—"

"In the holes. Have to go to the holes, I know," Eric interrupted with more ramblings as he turned slightly toward Kat's voice, the sword lowering perhaps an inch.

Kat took another step, her eyes remaining glued to his face. "You're in Troivack right now. You're traveling with me, Poppy, and . . . your friend Sir Vohn will be in Vessa when we arrive."

The prince frowned and blinked, confusion settling in his mind. Faucher tentatively began to reach for the sword in Eric's hand, but that only made the prince leap back and swing at the Troivackian. If Faucher had been a millisecond slower in dodging, he would have had his torso torn open.

"Eric! What did you get Alina for her birthday?" Kat called out again, this time a little more desperately, as she dared to move even closer to him.

Other than his breaths coming out rapidly, the prince didn't move a muscle.

"Lady Katarina, get out. He might attack you." Faucher carefully circled away from the prince, which meant Katarina was now the closest person to Eric. However, the prince's eyes followed Faucher, albeit blindly, as though he were staring at someone else entirely. Faucher was clearly trying to lure him farther away from her.

"Then I'll have something to really torment him about," Kat replied before moving forward yet again until she stood beside Eric.

"Lady Kat!"

Kat reached out and grasped Eric's face between her hands. "Hi," she greeted.

He went stiff and his eyes widened, unable to look away from the sudden golden gaze that filled his vision.

For a moment Eric stood motionless, his mind wading through its haze. It seemed he had relaxed by his next exhale, until he grabbed her by the front of her dress and slammed her down onto the table, the basin on the opposite end rattled from the impact. The sword in his hand had once again shifted so that the sharp edge of the blade was pressed to her throat.

"Lady Katarina!" Faucher shouted again and made to lunge forward, but when the prince's blade dug into her skin, the Troivackian halted his movements.

"Come in, my friend; sit down and grab yourself a pint," Kat began to sing softly, her voice trembling from shock, and her aura flickering to life again as her back throbbed. "The dice are fair, so grab a chair . . ."

Eric's heavy breathing turned halting as he blinked rapidly as though once again struggling with the fog.

"And . . . join . . . us . . . for a night," Kat continued the song while brushing her thumb along his cheek. Her gentle hold of his face had not once shifted. "Come on, my friend, deal in, and bet your coin away . . ."

Eric's grip on the front of her dress loosened.

"No use for gold, when you get old . . ." Kat continued softly even though her heart was hammering in her chest. There was no reason in his eyes, only wildness and shadows.

Her hands remained soothing and warm on his face. "So have fun, while you may."

Eric's hand gradually fell away from the front of her dress, and he slowly lowered the blade.

"Come now, my friend, perk up." As she continued singing, Eric's quiet voice joined hers, and together they softly sang the rest of the song as the prince backed away from Kat, his eyes beginning to close as his knees met with the seat of a chair by the table, prompting him to collapse. His eyes fluttered shut, and within a matter of moments, his bare chest rose and fell peacefully, indicating he'd fallen asleep.

Kat sat up from the table, her tranquil expression gone and instead replaced with one of grave concern as she studied Eric.

"That was foolish." Faucher moved forward and freed his sword from the prince's lax hand.

Kat didn't respond to his criticism and instead stood.

"Was he sleepwalking?"

Faucher turned so he stood shoulder to shoulder with Kat, both of them staring at Eric.

"I believe it was a mix of drink, sleepwalking, and—"

"A soldier's spell," Kat finished for the Troivackian, a somber knowingness filling both her voice and eyes.

Glancing at the redhead interestedly, Faucher's dark brows knit together. "How did you know to sing a song he was familiar with?"

Kat gave a brief, humorless laugh, her eyes falling to the ground. "I'm more than a little familiar with the soldier's spell."

Without adding any explanation, Katarina proceeded to turn and stride toward the mouth of the tent, only pausing before her toes reached the sands outside to address Faucher over her shoulder. "Don't tell him about what happened. I'm fine, and he doesn't need to apologize for something he can't control."

The Troivackian looked at her back, his hand resting on the hilt of his sword. "I thought you said you'd use it to torment him further."

"Truthfully, I said that more to make you stop talking. To use this against him would be torture, not torment."

Without another word, Katarina exited the tent, leaving the Troivackian leader alone with the prince as well as with his thoughts that dangerously began to tread toward the possibility that Katarina Ashowan was a far stronger and more honorable woman than he had first presumed her to be . . .

The carriage ride was bumpier than usual.

Also notably quieter.

By the time the sun was beginning to set in the sky, even Mage Sebastian was growing tense from the silence.

He glanced at the abnormally still Lady Katarina, her golden eyes half lowered demurely. Her posture was straight, both her feet flat on the ground, and even her index finger remained motionless.

"I see that you *do* know how to sit properly!" the mage exclaimed suddenly, startling both Mr. Julian and Poppy.

Kat gradually lifted her eyes to Sebastian, who was staring at her expectantly.

She said nothing.

"Was it Faucher's lecture that finally did you some good?" the mage asked condescendingly.

"Sebbie," Katarina started slowly. "Are you worried about me?"

The mage laughed, but there was a certain shiftiness in his eyes and body that indicated there was something to her question . . . as though there was the tiniest measure of truth to it . . .

"Why would I be worried about you? You are unharmed and here, aren't you? I merely was trying to find out how to implement this kind of behavior more often . . . though perhaps without the strange air of foreboding . . ."

"You can choose between my foreboding silence or my hopeful ramblings. Those are your two options," Kat replied flatly while once again lowering her gaze.

The truth was that she had burned away a large portion of her magic the night before, her back was aching fiercely from the prince's earlier attack, and the carriage's jostling was not helping.

Sebastian continued eyeing her with a slight frown, unaware of Mr. Julian's pale face and stressed expression.

"My lady, is it because you're concerned about the prince?" Poppy asked timidly while glancing at the assistant, then her mistress.

Both Katarina and Mr. Julian visibly tensed and exchanged glances.

"Why should I be worried about a hangover? He has them on the daily," Kat recanted while managing to smile fondly at Poppy.

"You and the prince seem to have an interesting connection," Sebastian noted with a small disapproving eyebrow lift.

Kat flitted her attention back to the mage, her smile fading. "He's been close with my father for a number of years."

"So, there are marriage talks between the two of you?" the mage asked calculatedly.

Kat cringed and leaned away before shaking her head.

"No. Nothing like that. Besides, I'm only the daughter of a viscount. I'm sure there are other more suitably ranked partners for him," she retorted, her voice becoming tight.

Sebastian gave a cool smile, sensing he was hitting a nerve. "Really? I heard that your father was in the works of accepting a dukedom from the king. It might not be so out of the question."

"Pfft. That has been in talks for a decade or more. My father says no every time. He hates the paperwork." Kat rolled her eyes while a small smile as she thought of her family.

A flash of anger appeared in the mage's eyes. "You mean to tell me he is insulting the privilege and generosity of your king because he is lazy?"

Kat's gaze sharpened. "My father has his own private reasons, and it is not your place to speak so disrespectfully of him."

Taken aback by the redhead's uncharacteristic authoritativeness, Sebastian took a moment to respond, though her eyes remained fixed on his face in such a way that was unnerving.

"I apologize for the insult, Lady Katarina." Sebastian briefly lowered his gaze, his features hardened. He clearly did not like having to humble himself to her.

Not bothering to respond, Kat's stare lingered on the mage to ensure he would not try to speak ill of her kin, then she dropped her attention to the carriage floor.

No one tried to spark another conversation until the carriage halted to rest for camp that evening, but there was the crackle of tension in the air that hinted at the possibility of a storm in their near future.

Sitting far from everyone else with her back to the travel party, Katarina stared out from her position at the top of the hill where they had chosen to make camp for that evening. Rich pinks and oranges rushed across the horizon as the sun descended, casting shadows amongst the small cottages and fields that lay below. A balmy breeze swept over the land. The redhead didn't eat or drink, but she did pet her familiar, who was cradled lovingly in her arms.

Most of the knights partook in their dinners quietly without sparing her a second look. However, Faucher would occasionally glance over to her, his expression unreadable, and that, in turn, made Mage Sebastian curious.

The prince was sitting hunched over while chewing a bit of bread, his complexion nearly gray. He didn't bother engaging in conversation with those around him, and even his assistant wasn't present to make idle chit-chat, as he was off to finish setting up their tent for the evening. The silence seemed to set everyone ill at ease, but of course, none of the knights said as much.

At long last, Faucher stood, put his plate down, and walked over to Eric.

"Might I have a private word, Your Highness?"

The prince paused, his lifeless gaze remaining blind to his surroundings for another moment before he slowly nodded and rose to his feet.

Faucher guided the prince away from the men until they were out of earshot and then turned to face him, his face for once . . . apprehensive.

"Your Highness, I believe it may be safest for you to abstain from drink for the remainder of our journey. It can cause a soldier's spell to occur more regularly."

Eric stared at Faucher blankly, then carefully widened his stance.

"I see. You said you weren't hurt from this morning, but I must have scared my assistant succinctly given how jumpy he is around me now," the prince speculated emotionlessly.

"Furthermore," Faucher began, then cleared his throat, his gaze shifting away in discomfort. Another odd display for the formidable military man . . .

"What is it?" Eric tilted his head expectantly.

"I . . . I believe . . ." Faucher let out a breath mixed with a grunt as though it were physically difficult to speak his next words. "If you show more amiability to Lady Katarina, the other knights may feel more at ease and inclined to be respectful of her."

Eric frowned. "Have they done or said something? Is that why she's been acting like a new widow all day? I thought she was simply angry about your confrontation last evening."

"None of my men would dare to speak or do anything excessive, but . . . It is there all the same."

Eric regarded Faucher carefully for a moment. "I heard Lady Katarina made some kind of threat to you. Are you saying this to me to try and work your way back into her good graces?"

The Troivackian frowned. "Pardon my saying so, but it would take more than a threat to move me."

Eric chuckled darkly. "You know, the perception of Lady Katarina might be aided better by your own attitude adjustment."

Faucher studied the prince for a moment without immediately responding. "To a point. Yes. However, it speaks even louder if a member of her own kingdom doesn't even look upon her favorably."

"I've been defending her a good amount, I'd say," Eric countered, his tone growing skeptical. "Faucher, did something happen I should know about?"

The Troivackian grunted, then moved his eyes over to where the noblewoman sat alone. "Did Lady Katarina ever . . . was her father ever abusive to her?"

Eric's astonishment made him straighten. "Gods no—He's a witch whose abilities center around the wholesomeness of the home. Faucher, why the hell are you asking that? I'm ordering you to tell me."

The Troivackian stiffened. "It was a passing curiosity. I will return to the fire now, Your Highness."

"Faucher, that wasn't a Godsdamn answer," Eric growled, stopping the man in his tracks. "You will tell me what makes you ask a question of that nature about Lady Katarina Ashowan."

Despite the ferocity of the prince's demand, Faucher's expression once again grew unreadable as he swallowed once, then turned back to face the young royal.

"I do not have a better answer for you at this time, Your Highness. Good evening."

Faucher stalked back to the fire without another glance over his shoulder, leaving Eric alone in the deepening dusk to wonder why anyone would think Katarina had anything but a carefree, sheltered existence.

CHAPTER 30

ASININE ALLEGATIONS

It was the second morning along their altered travel route when Kat found herself staring dumbfounded at none other than Eric Reyes, who stood outside the open carriage door.

"You want to . . . ride in the carriage with us all again?" she asked carefully, surveying the prince whose face had grown tan after sitting beside the driver for the past week.

Eric's bored expression shifted only slightly with a raise of his eyebrows. "Am I not allowed to?"

"Your Highness, of course you would be allowed to ride in some measure of comfort!" Mage Sebastian exclaimed, leaning forward in his seat eagerly.

"Y-Your Highness, if you'd like, I can sit beside Mr. Julian to give you and Lady Katarina the seat with the most room," Poppy suggested nervously while giving him a small bow.

"Poppy, you don't need to do that. I'm sure His Highness will—" Kat began while inching forward in her seat nervously.

"Why thank you, Poppy. Don't mind if I do," Eric interrupted while stepping up into the carriage swiftly.

The maid scurried to clear the spot for him and wedged herself close beside the assistant.

Once Eric had plunked himself down, he reached over and closed the carriage door, then folded his arms, shut his eyes, and slumped back.

Kat shot him an irritated side-glance before giving her head a small shake and moving her gaze elsewhere.

"Did you rest well last night, Your Highness?" the mage asked pleasantly.

Eric didn't open his eyes. "No, I did not. Sorry, Mage Sebastian, but I have a pretty terrible headache, so I'm going to try and sleep now."

"Of course! I did not mean to cause you discomfort."

Kat smirked to herself, though she kept her face turned away so that Sebastian couldn't see.

As the carriage jerked into motion, the occupants of the vehicle remained silent, though Mr. Julian was still eyeing his employer nervously as though waiting for him to have another episode again, and this was making Poppy, in turn, shift a curious eye to the future king.

By midday, no one had said a word, and Kat's foot tapping was beginning again, earning a scathing glare from the mage. Fortunately, the carriage rolled to a stop for a meal break and a change of horses before he was prompted to comment on the restless habit. The assistant and maid departed the carriage first, followed by the mage, who eyed the sleeping prince for a moment before making his exit.

Kat turned to face Eric and debated leaving him to sleep, but she didn't feel like dealing with a hungry grump for the rest of the day.

"Your Highness, we've stopped for lunch," Kat informed him flatly while starting to prepare to take her own leave.

When he still didn't stir, she sighed irritably and poked his temple. "Oyy. Wake up."

Frowning, Eric's eyelids lifted, albeit with visible effort.

"Honestly, if you're going to sleep off a hangover, why don't you do so back on the driver's bench so that we might have a bit more of an interesting time in the carriage instead of trying to be quiet for you," she muttered to herself while standing from her seat.

"I'm not hungover. I'm not drinking until we get to Vessa," Eric informed her with a grunt followed by a yawn as he slumped forward.

Kat sat back on the seat in surprise until she realized what had most likely happened. "Faucher is making you stay sober, isn't he?"

"Mm," Eric managed while rubbing his eyes.

"Well, best of luck then. Perhaps we can leave on time in the mornings now." Once again, Kat started to rise.

"Did you say or do something that would concern Faucher?" the prince asked abruptly, turning his lifeless gaze to the redhead.

Kat froze for a moment as though she were a deer caught by a hunter in the woods. She averted her eyes and gave a nervous laugh. "Of course not!"

Eric frowned. "He was asking if your father abused you."

Kat's look of alarm was genuine as she spluttered for a moment in light of the new information. "Of course not! Gods, he's a bloody house witch! You can't get any more wholesome than that."

"That was my initial reaction as well. I have my reservations about your family dealings, but I know Finlay would never lift a finger against you. Which begs the question, why does Faucher think you have some kind of trauma? Did you tell him about the coyote?" The prince lowered his voice and watched as all humor and brightness faded from Kat's face.

"No, I didn't. I'm sure Faucher was just caught off guard because I was more subdued yesterday. It was just because I'd burned away a lot of my magic, so no need to start making nasty assumptions about my family." Kat didn't allow herself to be stopped from leaving the carriage again after she spoke, and she set to taking in their new surroundings in hopes that the prince wouldn't pursue the matter further.

The temperature had thankfully failed to rise to the blistering height it had been when they first arrived in Troivack, and the occupants of the small town Kat found herself in seemed to be filled with renewed vigor as a result. While few people smiled, there was a lightness in their features as they passed one another in the street, exchanging greetings. Their houses were made of stone and clay, with rust-colored tile roofs. Many homes were covered in brightly colored flowers ranging from fuchsia pink to deep purples and blues climbing up their walls and doorframes. It made the village a charming sight after being stuck in a carriage with covered windows for days on end, only the barren land and desert to greet them. During her casual surveillance, Kat spotted a storefront that she had been hoping to find . . .

A blacksmith.

She knew there wasn't enough time to repair the handle of the sword she had purchased, but even if she could get it sharpened . . . The knights trained almost every evening, perhaps she could ask Sir Cas to show her some basic stances . . .

When she turned toward the back of the carriage to retrieve her sword, however, Eric Reyes was standing in her way, his arms folded.

"So, what are you hiding?"

Kat made a *tsk* sound before stepping around him to where their luggage was stored. Locating the sword easily enough, she plucked it out of the pile without disturbing one of the smaller chests in front of it.

"I'm not hiding anything; I'm going to get my sword sharpened. Now if you'll excuse me, I—"

"I will not."

Kat swung around, her eyes flashing dangerously. "Why are you being a beast again?" she demanded while gripping the sword's scabbard more tightly.

"You and your father have the same tells when you lie. You're lying about not saying or doing something that would make Faucher worried. I thought I made it clear that while you may not like me and I have my issues with you and your family, we are allies."

Kat didn't respond as she instead started walking again, ignoring the prince entirely.

He fell into an easy step beside her and pressed his right hand into his pocket.

"Now that you're sober, are you planning on being excessively overbearing with your unencumbered energy?" Kat snipped while letting out an aggravated breath.

"Just imagine how much more annoying I can be when I'm not allowed to have a good time," Eric mused lightly.

"So this is to entertain yourself?"

"It's to both entertain me and fulfill my duty to protect you. It's a fortunate mix of the two."

Kat shot him a dirty side-glance as she continued on her way, only to have Eric tug her into a small, shadowed alleyway mere feet from the sun-filled, bustling street.

"Do you like making people worry?" The prince no longer looked complacent as he regarded her seriously.

"Oh, for the love of—I swear, I didn't purposely make Faucher grow any mite of sympathy toward me. It isn't my style." Kat gave an indignant hair flip over her shoulder.

Studying her face for several more moments, Eric crossed his arms and tilted his head over her shoulder. "I'm going to find out what it is, no matter how hard the both of you try, so why don't we have a peaceful time of things and you just tell me now?"

Kat scoffed. "Your Highness, need I remind you, I am the most vexing woman on the planet, and I have earned that title. If you try to annoy me, I will be ten times worse in retaliation."

Eric smiled slowly, though it wasn't exactly a good-humored one . . . "We shall see about that, Lady Katarina. After all, I am your elder, and I may know a trick or two myself, as I've mentioned before. If you threatened Faucher in some significant way, or if you left him to assume something horrible, you will have to apologize for it."

Kat gave a sassy raise of her eyebrow but didn't say another word as she turned on her heel and marched out of the alleyway toward the blacksmith, leaving Eric alone in the shadows.

Shaking his head and letting out a world-weary sigh over the exasperating redhead, Eric resigned to himself that he may have a harder time foregoing drink than he may have thought. As he began stepping back toward the road, a sudden prickle at the back of his neck made him pause.

He felt someone watching him.

Turning to look around slowly, Eric saw that he still stood alone in the alley, but when he shifted his eyes upward and to the left, he noted there was a window on the second floor of the building with only one rust-colored shutter closed . . .

Frowning, he decided to investigate what establishment it belonged to . . . Something in his gut was giving off a warning signal, and he had long ago learned during his training and time as a mercenary to never ignore such instincts.

Especially when there had been assassination attempts on a near daily basis . . .

Katarina let out a long, exhilarated breath as she left the blacksmith's shop.

The man had not only sharpened the blade but also fixed the broken hardware on the scabbard for a decent price. She still had to wait until arriving in Vessa to finish repairing the handle, but she had accomplished more than she thought she would. The blacksmith had been the rare type of Troivackian who didn't ask questions or cast judgments about her managing a sword.

Feeling quite pleased with herself, Katarina continued on her way to find a bit of lunch and hopefully avoid a lecture about wandering off on her own again.

With Eric pestering her after leaving the carriage, she knew she hadn't given Poppy a chance to catch up, or Mage Sebastian, who had been tasked with protecting her.

As she strode forward in this moment of freedom, taking in the sights around her with a smile, she marveled at a merchant's display of intricately stitched fabrics.

A small tug on her skirts drew her eyes down.

"Excuse me?" a little girl, perhaps six years of age, asked. Her thick black hair was partially covered with a white kerchief as she peered up at the redhead in wide-eyed awe.

"Yes?" Kat asked with a bright grin.

"Are you the Daxarian princess?"

Kat chuckled and opened her mouth to reply, when an elderly woman scuffled forward and snatched up the child's arm.

"Shira! Come child, don't go touching strangers," the old woman chided, a note of fear in her voice.

Kat stepped forward with her hands raised. "No, no! It's perfectly alright!"

The older woman backed away several steps with the child pressed tightly to her shrunken body, which in turn drew attention from those passing by.

"She just asked me a question." Kat lowered herself down to crouch in front of the girl while the old woman continued to look fearfully at her.

"I thank you for the compliment, Shira. You think I look like a princess?" the redhead asked with a gentle voice.

The little girl, sensing her grandmother's trepidation, barely managed to give a shy nod.

"Well, if I'm perfectly honest, you look much more like a princess than I do. You have beautiful big brown eyes—you remind me of my mother, and bards used to write songs about her," Kat informed the child.

The little girl gave a small grin but quickly hid her face in her grandmother's skirts.

When Kat peered up to the grandmother, still smiling in hopes that she had proved she was harmless, the woman fell back yet another step.

"Demon . . . Y-Your eyes . . . like the devil, I've no doubt . . ."

Kat reared back in surprise, and it was a good thing, too, as the woman proceeded to spit three times on the ground before whisking away her granddaughter, leaving Katarina alone in a growing crowd of onlookers who didn't appear all that friendly . . .

"Erm . . . I'm not a demon though," she explained to the many faces turned toward her, sensing the heightened tension in the air.

Before she knew it, they all burst out in whispers.

"Her eyes . . ."

"Demon . . . has to be . . ."

"Not natural . . ."

"More like a witch!" one man shouted, wielding his finger in Katarina's direction.

"Well, you aren't wrong, but—" she began to say to the man, when a tomato was suddenly launched at Kat's head, making her quickly dodge.

It was then that the redhead realized she was center stage for most of the street's occupants, but right at that moment, she wasn't terribly fond of playing the lead role . . . at least not yet.

Then again . . . she on occasion was told she had a flair for the dramatic, thanks to her father . . .

Her only weakness in that department, unlike her paternal parent, was that when she made a scene, it didn't always end with everyone as friends.

CHAPTER 31

EAGER ENEMIES

Now . . . that was a terrible waste of a tomato! Your wife may have needed that for dinner!" the redhead defended, momentarily catching the waiting crowd off guard by responding so unpredictably.

"S-She didn't need it! Witch!" The man took a trembling step forward, still pointing accusatorily at the redhead.

"Well how do you know she doesn't need a tomat? What is she making for dinner?" Kat countered indignantly.

The crowd turned expectantly toward the man, everyone still too stunned by the shift of power in the conversation.

"How-How should I know?" he snapped defensively. "Maybe we should ask you, since you're a witch!"

"Why would I know what your wife is making for dinner if I'm a witch? Point is, you should buy her another tomato," Kat admonished, placing her hands on her hips.

"Ah, Arnie . . . your wife is going to be preparing shakshuka. She invited me for dinner; she will most definitely need the tomato . . ." A younger man stepped forward raising his hand in the air.

"Why would she invite *you* for dinner?" The original man who had lobbed the tomato at Katarina's head rounded on the interloper.

Kat turned, equally invested in the answer as the promise of a new drama began to unfold.

"Yeah, Mr. . . ?" she began, then paused.

"Mr. Blau," supplied the man whose wife was apparently in need of a new tomato. He hadn't taken his gaze off the other man.

"Yes, tell us why, Mr. Blau!" Kat burst out passionately, bringing even more attention around them.

"Arnie, she just asked me to help you retile your roof and wanted to thank me!" Mr. Blau replied exasperatedly, though his eyes were searching the crowd nervously.

"Pah! I can fix that roof myself!" Arnie bit back vehemently.

"Well . . . I don't know, Arnie . . . Last time you did break your leg . . ." another man in the crowd interjected hesitantly.

"Arnie, are you too proud to admit that maybe help is a good thing?" Kat asked while regarding the now blushing older man.

"I need no help! I am not carving my gravestone just yet, you know!"

"Age has nothing to do with getting help," Kat pointed out sagely, once again drawing Arnie's attention to her.

"What would a witch know?" he snapped angrily at her.

Kat sighed. "Well, for one, I know that your wife will be the one stuck taking care of you if you break your leg again, and I know she will also be the one having to change what she's making for dinner . . . both because of your pride."

"It is her duty!" Arnie huffed.

"To pay for your mistakes? I'm surprised you don't value her much more if she's expected to bear such a burden."

The crowd shifted then. The men tensed and recoiled, but the women who had previously shrunk and hidden themselves perked up . . .

"I'm just saying that you are doing something great by providing her a home and food," Kat started, once again holding up her hands and making the men relax . . . that is, until she spoke again. "But then again, so is she by protecting your pride and working to feed and please you."

Arnie glowered, then spit at Katarina's feet. "Godsdamn Daxarian women."

Kat raised an eyebrow and tilted her head, her eyes only momentarily darting to the crowd and back. "I know we're quite revolutionary but try to keep your fluids to yourself."

"You impudent—" The man named Arnie raised his hand to strike her, and Kat's magical aura flickered to life as she waited expectantly.

A sword rose between them, its steel glinting in the sun as its edge touched Arnie's unshaven throat.

"Stand back from the lady." Faucher's snarl made Arnie freeze.

The crowd backed away, and a child's cry could be heard amongst them.

Arnie slowly raised both hands in the air and moved back from Kat, who watched, unable to hide her disappointment.

"Be gone," Faucher snapped gruffly, flicking his blade away from the man's throat though he still glowered at him darkly.

Arnie carefully obeyed the battle-hardened Troivackian, and self-consciously adjusted his grasp around the cloth sack holding his foodstuffs over his shoulder. "That cape . . . Sir . . . are you Leader Faucher?"

"I am."

"Then . . . why do you lower yourself by guarding a witch?" Arnie asked, his gaze flitting to Katarina, and his eyes widening upon witnessing her burning aura.

"She is someone the king has commanded me to protect, therefore, I will obey our monarch. Even if it means cutting down a civilian. Am I clear?"

A heated murmur pulsed through the crowd.

"Oh. Now, now. I think that's slightly extreme. Arnie is just a bit emotional about his wife going behind his back to ask another man for a favor and then cooking him dinner— " Kat was interrupted by Faucher's threatening glare over his shoulder.

Then, before she could rally her wits, a tug at her elbow pulled her from the scene.

As she was pulled through the crowd that whispered and stared after her, Kat realized it was Eric who had come quietly behind her and was leading her away from the situation.

"You're just going to leave Faucher to fend for himself? I mean, don't get me wrong, he can be an arse, but irritating him is one of the few forms of entertainment I've found for this trip. We shouldn't leave him to be torn apart."

"You need to learn when to shut up," Eric informed her casually over his shoulder as they continued to make a breakneck pace toward the carriage.

"Pfft. If I'd have shut up when that all happened, I would've been pelted with more vegetables."

Shooting her a humorless glance, the prince picked up his speed once Mage Sebastian and the fellow knights appeared from the nearby tavern, where they must have just finished their luncheon. "It appears as though you are eager to be lynched by a mob. Pardon my intrusion on your efforts."

"Give me what's left of your moonshine for the trip, and I'll consider forgiving you."

Sighing, Eric thrust Kat toward her maid, who had appeared amongst the men, then turned back to the crowd to try and find Faucher again. There was no telling how much dangerous attention they had just attracted, and everyone present seemed to have a sense of this as they shared somber glances with one another.

There was a chance that a small rebellion would break out even before they reached the capital now that knowledge of a Daxarian witch under the king's care was out, and that meant they would be lucky to even step foot in Vessa alive.

Setting down the parchment, the young man raised his face to the mercenary known as Leo, a glint of amusement in his eyes.

"So you're saying the inept Daxarian steward, who is rumored to be the princess's paramour, is actually her brother, the crown prince, Eric Reyes, who had been missing for four years? And the witch I encountered before, who was traveling with him, is none other than Katarina Ashowan? Daughter of the Daxarian hero?" He laughed. Slowly with a few guffaws of disbelief at first but with growing ferocity.

"Yes, sir," Leo replied, his auburn head remaining bowed while he rested on his knees before his employer.

"Fantastic. This will drive a certain someone I know absolutely mad. It may even draw them out that much easier. Keep an eye on Katarina Ashowan. I'm no longer interested in taking her, at least not yet. The prince, on the other hand . . . Abducting him could make the princess more pliable, or at the very least, distracted." The young master stood and strode over to his window to gaze out over the cool night that had drifted down upon Troivack.

"If I may be so bold to say so, master . . . I worry about entangling ourselves with such a close relative of the house witch."

The raven-haired man tilted his head over his left shoulder and laughed again, though more softly.

"Really? You must realize . . . his familiar is by far the more fearsome adversary."

Leo, at long last, raised his face. "Master, what worries me is that quite frankly . . . the entire family is a deck of wild cards. We have yet to fully glean the reach Viscountess Ashowan has, or how much is due to her husband, the viscount. Not to mention his influence in Daxarian schools and the coven." Shaking his head with a frown, Leo continued. "They are a deeply rooted family, and we are discussing tormenting their daughter here in Troivack. Katarina Ashowan could have a separate agenda here on behalf of her family as well."

The black-haired man surveyed the Troivackian night sky from his window thoughtfully. After a few moments of rumination, he finally seemed to reach a conclusion. Turning around, he regarded the mercenary, who clearly had been staring at his back but quickly cast his eyes to the ground.

"Find out what abilities Katarina Ashowan possesses. Create a ruckus if you need to. Then take the prince and keep him hidden with you for at least six months . . . perhaps a year. That should be enough time to completely dismantle the Troivackian king's plans for bringing the princess into his courts. She will grow obsessed with finding her brother and won't be able to focus on implementing their changes. In turn, this will alienate her from the noblemen and the Troivackian women as she ignores her duties."

Leo lifted his gaze to his master. "What if the Ashowan girl is more powerful than we've heard? Or what if the prince escapes or is found early?"

The raven-haired man stepped forward, his smile eerie. "The prince is known to love his drink, and an informant of mine claims there is a chance he may even have an interest in Witch's Brew. Dose him as much as is safe to. It shouldn't be too difficult to keep him placated." He paused for a moment, his glittering eyes wandering to the ceiling before shaking his head as though trying to free an amusing thought. "If Katarina Ashowan proves to be more powerful than we've heard? I may intervene myself, albeit discreetly, but make sure to truly test her, Leo. I don't want any surprises."

Bowing his head even closer to the ground, the mercenary signaled his understanding. "I will do my best to not force you to become involved. With your permission, I will try my hand against Lady Katarina myself."

The master raised an eyebrow at his follower.

"If you show your face, that brings them closer to finding me, and we want to avoid such unnecessary risks as much as possible. We can't have *that* woman figuring out where I am, and with Katarina Ashowan—a wild card you called her family? We are going to play it safe. No. Send your three best and target her. One of them should be a mage. Use a witch if you have to. Make sure they wait for the battle to be underway before making their objectives known though."

"What about Faucher and the mage?"

"Faucher will try to protect the prince before he tries to protect a noblewoman. Overwhelm Faucher with numbers, and the mage will go running to him if he thinks he's in danger. That will be when Lady Katarina will be left vulnerable, and we can see what the scope of her power is."

"They'll be extra cautious after this attempt." Leo pointed out with a smile.

He did love a challenge . . .

"Extra cautious, but also in a hurry. Aim as close to Vessa as possible. That way, the princess will have hope of catching her brother and grow more panicked to act quickly." The leader, with his long, angular face and sculpted mouth that gave him both a regal appearance as well as an air of diffidence, issued his subordinate another slow nod as he explained his strategy.

"Now, get to it. With your oversight, I will not accept any more failures, Leo."

The lead mercenary's spine turned rigid and his face paled. "I understand, master. I will take my leave now so as to be at the target location long before them. I will ensure this is done right."

Pleased with his response, the raven-haired man waved Leo from the room.

The mercenary wasted no time. He had his orders, and they sounded refreshingly fun . . . the only dampener to the entire assignment being that in the slightest chance of his failure, he had a living hell waiting for him with open arms. And it was not an embrace from which he would ever be able to escape.

CHAPTER 32

DENTED DEFENSES

Kat glanced around at the men surrounding the fire, all with dark circles under their eyes, staring blindly around themselves. None of them seemed to have the energy to talk, as there was neither a word nor grunt shared. Instead, they ate their morning meal, swaying where they sat.

After Katarina's near persecution in the small town, they hadn't stopped aside from when changing horses, and they had instead ridden hard through the night to beat any rumors reaching their next destinations before they did. After traveling from midday yesterday through the night, they had at long last stopped for breakfast just outside yet another small village with the hope of stealing a few moments for sleep and a quick meal.

Kat felt perfectly fine, and if anything, the added physical demands of staying awake and traveling for even longer only helped keep her magitch under control and tolerable.

That being said, it also worked its way into her hunger, making her eat even more than usual.

"Gods, I hope your parents sent money to the Troivackian court to feed you," Mage Sebastian drawled wearily as he watched Kat finish her eighth sausage after also consuming an entire loaf of bread.

Kat's golden eyes fell to the mage, and with a slow antagonistic smile, she proceeded to bite into her last sausage while baring her teeth.

Mage Sebastian cringed and excused himself soon after.

A couple knights had also noticed and didn't have the energy to bother hiding their expressions of annoyance and disgust as they shook their heads at Kat's display of unladylike aggression.

As usual, she ignored this and instead allowed herself to finish her meal in peace.

When she had arrived in Troivack, she had every intention of making a good first impression, yet she had found that proper behavior made her invisible. Then she'd been condescended to and left out of discussions . . . It hadn't taken long for her to grow fed up.

So at least until they arrived in Vessa, she decided not to worry too much. She could always pretend she had acted out due to the constant stress of assassins being after her . . .

No one would know the truth about her true nature except Poppy, who wouldn't say anything, and Alina, who would be too busy to care as long as she behaved in court. So really that only left . . .

"Move." Eric nudged Kat's calf with the toe of his boot, his goblet and plate in hand as he waited for her to make space for him on the sun-bleached log they camped around.

Rolling her eyes, Kat abided and shifted down for him.

Once Eric had seated himself and began eating, Kat studied his profile out of the corner of her eye. He still looked pale and exhausted, somehow even more than everyone else, despite still riding in the carriage.

"So how many days until we reach Vessa? With all of these travel changes, I'm not sure what is happening." Kat put her question to the knights surrounding the fire.

All of them avoided meeting her gaze and instead continued eating.

Eric surveyed the reaction with his usual indifference until he caught Faucher's eye off in the distance while he conversed with the mage.

Clearing his throat, the men finally raised their eyes to him. "I have the same question. We had just adjusted the route to take three days longer, but after last night's progress, I'd guess we aren't too far from our original timeline."

Eric then proceeded to hunch his shoulders and eat.

"That would be correct, Your Highness. However, we are now avoiding any and all towns larger than fifty people. We will mostly travel by night now," one of the knights explained, sparing the prince a quick look and bow of his head before returning to his meal.

"Ah." Eric nodded, his right cheek full of food as he then returned his full efforts to his breakfast.

Gnawing on her tongue, Kat all but glared at the men who had ignored her.

Unsure if she'd be able to keep her thoughts to herself, she debated returning to wait in the carriage, when Sir Cas approached with his own meal and sat on the ground to her left.

"Are you looking forward to reaching Vessa, Lady Katarina?" the knight asked happily.

Despite being awake all night, Sir Cas seemed his usual sunny self.

His friendly nature considerably softened Kat's earlier irritation, and so she let out a small breath to release the tension building in her chest.

"I am. I'm especially excited to start my lessons," she replied, even managing a small smile as his bright blue eyes focused on her, indicating his undivided attention despite eating.

"Oh? What type of lessons will you be taking? Dancing? Or are you going to try learning some of the Troivackian embroidery styles?" Sir Cas asked, his engaging tone in no way demeaning, which allowed Kat to brush off his wildly incorrect assumptions.

"Oh, no. I have the permission of my father and two kings to finally begin learning swordsmanship!" she announced excitedly, her golden eyes sparkling as she leaned forward, eager to talk further on the subject.

Stunned, Sir Cas stared at her for a full minute before he managed to swallow the cheese he'd hastily bitten, and he broke into an excited smile. "Really? Swordsmanship? Both of the kings? How did that all come about?"

"I've been wanting to learn since I was a child, but my parents were more than a little wary of putting large weapons and me together . . . Though I did learn how to—" Kat stopped when she realized that Sir Cas wasn't her only audience.

Every knight present was staring at her.

Some looked on stonily, others looked angry.

"Oh sure, *now* you all hear me just fine." Kat didn't even try to hide her scowl when she registered their attention. "Do you have something to say?"

Her eyes began to glow a little brighter, making one or two of the men drop their gazes while shaking their heads disapprovingly.

"You can be charged with fraud and defamation for saying such a thing about our king." One of the knights sitting directly across from Kat leveled her with his stare that was filled with undisguised disgust and anger.

"Why in the world would I be charged with that? It was King Brendan Devark's idea in the first place!" Kat snapped, her magical aura flickering around her, which managed to draw Eric's attention up from his plate.

"Our king would *never* put forth such an absurd idea. You will apologize now." The knight set his plate down and locked his fingers in front of him sternly as he waited expectantly.

"How about we wait until we can ask him before wringing an apology out of me, hm?" Kat responded coolly while also setting down her own plate and folding her arms across her chest.

"You dare bring him into even more of your lies? You would slander and humiliate our king, who—"

"Aren't *you* being the disrespectful one by assuming what he would and would not decide?! You're doubting his judgment, aren't you?" Kat bit back as the knight's voice had begun to grow louder.

"It isn't his judgment, it is your words, your *integrity*, that I doubt."

Kat was on her feet instantly while both Sir Cas and Eric burst out with incomprehensible shouts.

Once Eric had finally swallowed his food, he stood. "Be careful what you are insinuating," he warned with narrowed eyes.

Sir Cas, meanwhile, had his jaw clenched, and his normally clear, angelic eyes darkened.

"What is happening here?" Faucher's sharp voice descended upon them as he appeared behind the knight who had been looking at Kat with cold, murderous intent.

"Leader Faucher," the knight began. "Lady Katarina here is slandering our king and insisting that he intends to train her in swordsmanship in Vessa. She even claims this was signed off by her father and Daxaria's king."

Kat's hands were balled into fists at her sides, her heart hammering against her chest.

Faucher frowned, his eyes lost in thought.

"I'm not lying! I even said he could ask His Majesty!" she burst out again.

Faucher's gaze snapped up to Kat's face as he observed her features carefully for signs of deception.

After a moment, he let out a sigh mixed with a grunt.

"Very well, this is what we shall do. For now, we will not question this far-fetched claim of Lady Katarina's, but she will be prohibited from bringing it up again."

The knight rounded on his leader, his fury palpable as he opened his mouth to argue, when Faucher shot him a warning look. He wasn't finished.

"However, if this claim of Lady Katarina's proves to be false, her crimes will be addressed in court before the king himself, and proper punishment will be decided then."

The knight's mouth clamped shut, and his eyebrows raised as he gave a small jerk of his chin, looking both pleased yet surprised at the same time.

Kat paused at the knight's reaction but figured she could ask more details about it later.

Besides, when she sat down and the knight gave her a smug smile, she returned her own wolfish one, which had the satisfying result of him getting bothered yet again.

Oh, how she looked forward to making him eat his words, even if it made her the most hated woman in all of Troivack.

As it turned out, Katarina found out rather quickly why the knight had looked so surprised and pleased at the same time . . .

"If you're lying about the king wanting you to learn swordsmanship, it will be a significantly bigger humiliation you will suffer as opposed to if Faucher had just made you apologize right then and there," Sebastian explained to Kat, shaking his head in exasperation.

"You will be subjected to not just the inner council for trial but the entire council. It could even be extended to the knights. If found guilty, you could be exiled or given lashings . . . Either way, you will be a shunned woman."

"You lot can shun a woman even worse than you already do? Oh wait . . . right. Yes . . . I remember from my lessons . . . Hair cutting, being thrown into the mud at the foot of the castle, no food or water for three days while kneeling in front of the castle. People will spit on me and scorn me . . . so on and so forth." Kat sighed and waved her hand tiredly despite Poppy's eyes widening and Mr. Julian looking aghast.

Eric, on the other hand, appeared mildly irritated before he once again closed his eyes and tried to return to sleep.

"You are that confident?" Sebastian asked, suddenly hesitant.

Kat's flippant expression morphed to one that was far more serious. "The king had several meetings with my father and King Norman Reyes about this. Furthermore, if King Brendan Devark rescinds this and attempts to have me shunned, there are several records proving otherwise, as the Daxarian king's lovely assistant, Mr. Howard, has taken detailed notes for each and every one of their meetings. His Majesty Brendan Devark will be in violation of several agreements if he tries to punish me on those grounds."

Sebastian grew pale. "Gods . . . if what you say is true, His Majesty Brendan Devark may not have wanted this shared. Do you realize you have now turned several people against this idea and, therefore, made it dangerous?"

"I didn't bloody announce it! That arsehole of a knight eavesdropped! He was the rude one to begin with! Ignoring me first, then jumping in on the conversation," Kat nearly shouted with rising exasperation.

Mage Sebastian pinched the bridge of his nose. "Lady Katarina, you . . . are quite adept at digging your own grave." Then with a sigh, he shrugged his shoulders. "Well, don't say we didn't warn you."

"Tell me, then. How should I have gone about this? Hm? I wasn't respected before and have had someone attempt to kill me just about every damn day here just by *existing*."

Sebastian shook his head dismissively. "It's a notion beyond you, but you shouldn't have tried to make them change to suit your ways and ideals so hastily. You won't alter an entire country by getting angry with everyone for not behaving like a Daxarian."

"I tried to be nice and act like a Troivackian woman; it did nothing."

"Firstly, I will say that your efforts had dissolved by the time we met, and you had only been in Troivack a matter of days. A few days is not enough time."

Kat barely resisted the urge to stick her tongue out at the man.

"Secondly," Sebastian continued, "the Troivackians you *did* meet while making an effort gave them a favorable first impression of you. Change has to be slow. Done carefully, and with great discipline," Sebastian countered, his dark brown eyes intent on her face.

At the word *discipline*, Kat clenched her teeth.

She didn't trust herself to say anything more, so instead she folded her arms and looked away.

A strange pang in her chest and twist in her gut appeared then as she thought about her home . . .

She thought about her brother, with his nose glued to a book and wandering around the keep, and his dry yet witty letters recanting interesting points of his travel as he trained to become viscount; her father greeting her from the kitchen where he worked and jested side by side with their family cook, Raymond; her mother poking her back to remind her to keep her shoulders straight before following up with a loving cheek caress and questions about her day; the smiling maids she knew all by name; the stableboys she'd play cards with . . . Likon . . .

Emotion bunched in Kat's throat, and she felt a tingling in her nose and behind her eyes. Blinking rapidly, she fought off the threat of tears.

She swallowed with difficulty as she tried with all her might to move her mind from the memories of warmth and comfort . . . of being loved unconditionally . . .

Her long fingers lightened around her arms as she continued to resist the tears, but she was forced to admit a simple truth to herself.

She was homesick, and there was no one she could tell.

So, she pulled her shoulders back and fixed her gaze on the carriage wall so intensely that she gave herself a headache, but she didn't dare look away. She couldn't let anyone see her moment of weakness. Instead, she tried to console and calm herself as she had done countless times before.

One more thing to hide won't kill me . . . It'll get better . . . eventually . . . probably . . .

CHAPTER 33

FLICKER OF A FLAME

Kat leaned her head back against the carriage wall, staring idly about herself, bored.

Night had once again descended on them, and across from her, Poppy had fallen asleep with her head on Mr. Julian's shoulder. Despite the young assistant's eyes being closed, there was a telling blush running across his cheeks and the bridge of his nose . . .

Kat gave a small smile at the sight, then her gaze moved to the mage, who had his mouth hanging open and a small amount of drool smeared across his cheek. She gave a halfhearted breathy laugh before finally moving her attention to Eric.

Who had his eyes open.

Jolting slightly from the shock, Kat quickly took a fortifying breath while closing her eyes.

"So . . . glowing in the dark . . . that's . . . a constant thing . . . ?" the prince asked slowly without hiding his mild annoyance.

In the darkness, Kat's magical aura continued to flicker. She began to roll her stare upward, then gave up halfway through and instead settled for rubbing her eyelids.

"Are you finally getting tired?" Eric asked, shifting in his seat to try and once again get comfortable.

"A little. I tried to not eat much after breakfast to force myself to sleep," she admitted with a long sigh.

"Ideally you marry someone who's scared of the dark . . . You'd be a match made by the Gods," Eric murmured, his eyes starting to close once again.

"And ideally you marry someone whose dowry includes at least four vineyards and large quantities of moonshine."

"Sounds like you're volunteering." Eric's eyes opened half way as he shot her a smirk.

"Ha-ha." Kat slumped into the opposite corner of the carriage, sarcasm dripping from her lips.

"So, how're you going to do the Ashowan thing?"

"What Ashowan thing?" Kat asked with a slight groan.

She was not in the mood to fight with him.

"The thing you all do to make everyone like you for no good reason."

"That's my father's thing," Kat retorted flatly.

"Your mother is quite beloved herself."

Kat's golden gaze cut to Eric, her poor mood written all over her face.

The prince gave a bored smile and shrugged without offering any other explanation.

"Tell you what, I'll do the Ashowan thing when you do the Reyes thing," she sniped acidly while once again folding her arms across her chest.

Eric's expression was beginning to drift to one more serious in nature. "Are you going to make a barb about me being an actual leader or something to that effect?"

"I was going to say 'likable,' but I'm willing to take suggestions."

The prince watched her for a long wordless while until Kat started squirming under his deadened stare.

"Are you angry because of the knight from earlier?" he asked at long last.

"Of course I'm angry. If I'm not painfully docile and well-behaved, I'm hated. Both options are awful."

"What do you want more; to be seen or to not cause trouble?"

"I don't even need to answer that."

"Exactly. So why are you angry? You succeeded in getting everyone's attention. So now you just need to figure out how to turn it around."

"Oh yeah? How?" she huffed indignantly.

"That's where your Ashowan abilities are supposed to kick in." Eric closed his eyes again, signifying the end of the conversation.

"Helpful," Kat retorted glibly before she, too, closed her eyes, hoping sleep wasn't far from her grasp.

"Talk to your familiar about it. Your dad was always talking to his cat. Other than the first few days with her, your kitten has mainly been with Sir Miller," Eric added with a yawn as an afterthought.

"I'll be honest, I think Sir Miller might kill me just so he can keep Pina for himself."

The prince snorted. "He *is* a little smitten with her."

"He hand-feeds her meat from his plate while cradling her in his arms."

Eric's snort evolved into an actual laugh, making a rare and handsome smile climb his face.

Kat's heart did a disconcerting flip at the sight, and she suddenly found herself forced to look away . . .

As her brain fumbled through other topics to try and end the feeling of warmth spreading to her face, the scream of a horse snapped her to attention.

Shouts of men could be heard, jarring awake Sebastian, Poppy, and Mr. Julian. Eric leaned forward in his seat and reached for the battered sword at his side.

"You three, stay in the carriage," he ordered before turning to the mage. "Use your ice shield if—"

Before he could finish his sentence, the entire carriage tipped over onto its side, pitching everyone in a heap. Poppy sustained the worst of the blow, with her head receiving a sharp crack against the carriage wall and both Mr. Julian and Mage Sebastian landing on top of her.

Kat's right arm was bruised horribly, and her head narrowly missed hitting the carriage wall and instead landed on the sand through the window cover, though Eric did land directly on top of her as well.

Before they could get themselves sorted, the carriage door blew off its hinges into the air, and Eric was suddenly jolted upward through the open door, already unsheathing his sword as he flew beyond their line of sight.

With the door gone, Kat could clearly hear the clanging of steel, the shouts, the cries . . .

Gods . . . please . . . Kat pleaded, slowly adjusting herself to standing while Mr. Julian and Sebastian began straightening themselves.

"I think I've dislocated my shoulder," Sebastian grunted while Mr. Julian winced over his bruised side, then immediately set to checking Poppy's pulse.

"She's alive, and I don't see blood . . ." he informed Kat, who was watching his inspection fretfully.

Giving the assistant a nod, she closed her eyes and took a long breath. Her aura began to grow brighter.

"Lady Katarina! Don't you dare do anything! Stay in here until—" Sebastian began but was cut off as he tried to move to stop her, but the shot of pain that ran through him from his shoulder made him double over before he could finish.

Kat ignored him, allowing her magitch to increase to a vibration through her body and then . . . it grew to a burning.

Her magical aura expanded . . . her vision started filling with golden nothingness . . .

Please don't let me hurt the wrong people . . .

The air witch who had grabbed Eric already had thrust him on a horse and into custody of a comrade. The knights battling their assailants were all strong and talented . . . but through a crowd of bodies, could only move so far.

Faucher saw Eric be taken and let out a shout that carried over everyone's heads, alerting them to shift their focus.

Three of the knights managed to break free and get on horses to chase after him, while the rest remained fighting.

Every knight battled for their lives, and as a result, all were too distracted to see what was happening behind the overturned carriage.

Esen, the air witch who had been the one responsible for blasting the carriage and magically hoisting the prince through the air, faced with mild interest the glowing redhead who had clambered out of the overturned carriage. She had two black dots under her right eye, her gaze was a pale blue, and her black hair was woven with white despite her only being in her late twenties.

At her side stood two large Troivackian men with their swords drawn and ready, though neither expected they'd need to bother using them.

"Nice to meet you, Lady Katarina," Esen greeted with a nod as she watched the young woman stroll forward, her eyes filled with magic.

She must already be burning close to her life magic if I'm seeing her aura this much . . . She's weaker than I expected, the air witch thought quietly as she let out a disappointed sigh. She had truly been curious to fight the daughter of Daxaria's hero.

"Oh well, I made a promise to test you thoroughly," she finished aloud. Esen waved her hand, intending to send Katarina flying back into the carriage with a concussive blast of air.

Only the redhead's aura flared brightly, consuming the wind entirely as she continued walking toward Esen without saying a word.

The air witch perked up. "Now that was a neat trick! Do it again!"

Esen raised both hands and sent a wind force that should have felt as though Kat had been hit by a galloping horse, but the aura around her once again surged and consumed the magic, all while seemingly . . . getting bigger.

"My Gods, you are far more delightful than I thought." Esen sighed dreamily before raising her index finger and twirling it in the air, intending for a tornado to sweep the redhead up in the air, then possibly fall to her death.

However, what happened instead was the hungry aura flared yet again, and with inhuman speed, Katarina moved in a blur until she was nose-to-nose with the air witch, whose eyes grew wide with shock.

Katarina's hand wrapped around her throat and hoisted her in the air with unnatural strength, choking the air witch and beginning to crush her throat beneath her hand.

Esen's eyes bulged as she tried to grab Kat's arm and wrench herself free, but it was as though the redhead's arm were made of steel. So Esen did the next best thing and tried to suck the air out of the redhead's lungs.

That was a bad idea—Esen heard a crack come from her body, then darkness consumed her.

"ESEN!" One of the men shouted while the other drew his sword.

"You Godsdamn witch! You absorb power and it makes you stronger? Let's see how you are against my sword!" The larger Troivackian man lunged forward expertly, only Katarina once again darted with incredible speed, and she was suddenly on his back, her arm wrapped around his throat.

Startled at the rate with which things were falling apart, the other soldier wasted no time in thrusting his sword into the redhead's exposed side.

Her glowing eyes turned to him, unaffected by the attack.

"Good Gods, you aren't human at all . . . demon . . ." the Troivackian man stumbled back as Katarina issued a blow to the back of her victim's head that had him crumpling to the ground.

She strode toward the remaining Troivackian, who felt his hands begin to tremble. The palm holding his sword grew sweaty as her overwhelming predatory power drew closer.

Four horses pounded around the carriage.

"Manuel! Let's go!" One of the riders called through the black kerchief tied around his face.

"Grab Esen—she's over there—and Rian is there!" Manuel shouted and pointed while gratefully running to the nearest steed and leaping atop.

Katarina stood perfectly still, her light-filled eyes watched them eerily.

The man on horseback frowned at the two crumpled bodies of his comrades, but a bright light beneath his tunic had them soaring in the air and into the saddles of two of their comrades.

Then, with a shout, the group began to retreat. There were at least a hundred men running or riding away from the scene like ants exploding from a crumbling hill as they raced into the desert.

Katarina's aura sank lower and lower, and then she was blinking with a frown, her golden eyes no longer bright or filled with magic. She turned her gaze to a dull pain in her side.

Her vision grew hazy as she rested her hand—that felt oddly cold—onto her ribs.

"Lady Katarina! Why in the world didn't you stay put?" Faucher roared, a small trickle of blood from the side of his head staining his face as he leapt down from the carriage to stand in front of her.

"You're lucky they didn't see you over here, and now we have to go and get His Highness back. We don't need your ridiculous, rebellious, selfish behavior! If we tell you to stay put, you stay put! I am chaining you to this carriage, and that is the end of it. Understood?"

Kat blinked up at Faucher blankly as Mage Sebastian finally clambered out of the carriage while clasping his dislocated shoulder. A handful of knights gathered to try and pull the unconscious maid out before setting the carriage right side up.

When the redhead said nothing but merely rocked gently side to side on her feet, Faucher stepped forward, his rage dark and all-encompassing.

"Nothing smart to say this time?"

Kat opened her mouth, and a small spurt of blood dribbled out.

Faucher reared back in shock. Then his eyes dropped to her hand clamped at her side.

"What happened—" Faucher began, but Kat collapsed forward, blood seeping through her fingers.

"SEBASTIAN, AIDE! WE NEED AIDE!" he shouted, catching Kat's limp body that was growing colder.

Kat stared dazedly up at him.

She finally felt sleepy . . .

Faucher was in the process of carefully laying her down on the ground while tearing his cape to tourniquet her wound when she reached her bloodied hand to touch his sweaty face.

"Don't worry . . . This isn't my first time . . . Do you . . . have . . . wheelchairs . . . ? They're great . . . fun."

"How can she still say mad things at a time like this?!" Sebastian exploded, though his face was wrought with concern as he crouched beside them with his bag filled with supplies.

Kat smiled, her teeth and lips bloody, but her eyes closed. "It's rather . . . easy . . . if I *am* mad . . ."

Then without further ado, Katarina Ashowan allowed herself to slip into the comforting darkness she seldom got to truly enjoy.

CHAPTER 34

AIMLESS ABANDONMENT

Eric stared at the bodies that littered the sands, his hazel eyes sinking back to their depths of emotionless weariness.

The three knights who had followed his pursuers had fought and died bravely . . .

And like a ruddy curse . . . Eric too had fought . . .

But he had won.

He had been magically thrust into the saddle of a horse by a Troivackian who had been all too eager to attempt to press a dosed rag to his face.

Unbeknownst to his assailants, however . . . the crown prince of Daxaria had had multiple prior kidnapping attempts made for him.

This combined with his recent sobriety and the fact that he had reached the esteemed level of sword master long ago meant . . .

He was a mite more difficult to overcome than they had originally estimated.

The struggle with the abductor aboard the racing horse had resulted in him being cast off the steed, killing him instantly upon impact against the cracked clay ground. Eric had slowed the horse and just slipped his feet in the vacant stirrups in time for more attackers to swarm him.

The odds were against him ten to one, and Faucher, with his men already out of sight, had the prince thinking his time to board death's carriage was imminent. That is, until three knights from his traveling party appeared, and together, they all cut down each and every one . . . until it left Eric battling the last man standing, but he, too, was bested by the prince.

Eric stared across the horizon, sweat dripping down his face as he regarded the blood-soaked sword in his hand, then his splattered tunic and trousers. Dropping the sword, he turned to the speckled horse that was frothing at the mouth. The animal needed water . . .

For several long moments, Eric deliberated.

He didn't need to rejoin the traveling party . . .

He could disappear again.

Alina had made it clear she didn't really need him, and he was only a liability to the traveling party.

Katarina was an Ashowan—she'd be fine one way or another . . .

Nodding idly to himself, Eric made his way to the steed, mounted him, and pressed his heels into its side without a second look at the carnage.

Before him lay all of Troivack, filled with five cities and innumerable small towns to explore and become lost in . . .

It was perfect.

Eric turned the horse south, recalling how he'd heard about the majestic mountains that bordered the kingdom. Perhaps he could traverse them for a year and eventually catch a ship back to Daxaria.

Yes, that was a good plan. It left lots of room for improvisation, and he could keep an ear out for Alina . . . though odds are she'd adjust swimmingly to her new life. She'd grown strong enough to not need her big brother's interference.

"How about we try and find you some water and me some moonshine, hm?" Eric asked the horse with a gentle pat of its neck.

The beast snorted but set himself to an easy lope, not seeming to mind his new master in the least.

Faucher kicked open the barn doors, Katarina unconscious in his arms.

The majority of the knights under his command had already disappeared into the nearest settlement to find a physician or someone with any surgical experience . . . anyone who could swiftly and discreetly mend the noblewoman's injuries and perhaps tend to theirs as well. They'd already lost at least two men during the fight, and the three that had been sent after the prince were still missing.

Finding a dusty table near an open window, Faucher set Katarina down, ignoring the blood smeared across his chest plate and hands that had previously belonged to her. His gaze then sought out Sebastian's.

"Can your magic do anything?" Faucher asked as the remaining knights escorting them to the safe enclosure left to begin securing the perimeter.

"I-It is generally frowned upon to dabble in magic that does not involve the elements. It can be seen as overstepping the magical gifts the Gods have—"

"Yes or no, Sebastian. If the Ashowan girl dies, there is no telling how severe the repercussions will be." The ferocity in Faucher's gaze made the mage's pale face begin to green.

"I-I-I've attempted small magicks, such as enhancing balms for bruises by bolstering the freshness of the ingredients, but nothing significant. If I try, I may make it worse."

"Godsdamnit," Faucher cursed, his gaze dropping down to the red-headed woman, who lay perfectly still on the table. She was a vision of tragic beauty, her light blue dress stained with blood, her face pale, and her brilliant red hair glowing in the daylight pouring in through the open barn window.

"Leader Faucher, we cannot find the prince. There were three of our knights slaughtered along with ten others belonging to the assailants, but His Highness's body was not amongst them. We found the sword he was carrying abandoned." One of the knights burst in through the barn door, sweat beading his brow.

A ferocious growl brewed in Faucher's chest.

"Sebastian, you are to remain here with Lady Katarina and protect her. I am going to find where the prince has been abducted and bring him back before dawn tomorrow. The longer we wait in retrieving him, the less likely it'll be that we find him at all," he barked over his shoulder.

Swallowing with great difficulty, Sebastian bowed forward, his gaze fell to Lady Katarina.

Her face suddenly screwed itself into a frown before her dull golden eyes slowly opened and her complexion sickened.

"Lady Katarina!" the mage burst out, instantly drawing Faucher's attention back to her.

Kat turned her head and spat blood onto the table before taking a wheezing breath.

"Sounds like they grazed her lung," Faucher informed Sebastian, his brow furrowed. "She can make a full recovery if treated swiftly and there wasn't any other damage."

"I . . . can hear you . . . you know." Kat's weak yet indignant tone succeeded in making a small flush of relief pass across Faucher's face.

"I wasn't speaking to you. Stay quiet and respectful during your treatment," Faucher ordered, though his dark eyes weren't as hard as they had been moments before.

"Belt," Katarina coughed, her pained gaze moving to Faucher's face with difficulty.

"What?" Faucher asked, his voice once again growing stern.

"Make sure . . . there's a belt for me to bite. And moonshine. Lots . . . of moonshine. There isn't . . . drafts like . . . last time . . . is there?" Her words were nonsensical.

"What do you mean by last time?" Sebastian asked, his voice irritated yet his face worried.

"You . . . ask . . . too many questions," Kat replied with a small groan.

Faucher gave a dry laugh before he glanced at the knight at his side, who was staring at the lady with obvious confusion and alarm.

"We'll have a belt ready, and we'll see about the moonshine. Sebastian, you're in charge until I return."

Once again Faucher turned to leave when a small tug on his cape drew his attention back to Katarina, her hand gently clasping the ripped fabric.

"They . . . talked . . . about testing me. The attackers . . . said they wanted . . . to see . . . what I could do," Kat explained with a frown, her eyelids beginning to flutter as she fought against unconsciousness yet again.

At this announcement, Faucher didn't say anything, only carefully freed his cape from her hold, gave her a stiff nod, and then took his leave with one of his knights at his side.

Once outside the barn, Faucher located the largest of their horses—one that could carry him the farthest and be strong enough to transport two riders in the event the prince was injured.

"Leader Faucher, why was the lady talking like she's been through this before?" the knight asked aloud, his curiosity getting the better of him.

"That is not our place to know, Sir Abaurus. You will go into the settlement just over the hill and see about getting her a physician. Sirs Miller and Herra will join me while I retrieve His Highness."

"Leader, what shall we do with our dead?" Sir Abaurus asked while pointedly refusing to glance in the direction of his five fallen comrades in the distance.

"Once we have had everyone treated and the prince is with us again, we will bury them and then we will head straight to Vessa. We are four days away, but we will try to make it in three. Relay this to the men."

The knight saluted before bowing to his superior.

Faucher then set off, summoning Sir Miller, who was tending to Lady Katarina's familiar while whispering soothing words to the kitten, and Sir Herra, who was already speaking with one of the men standing guard by the barn's side.

Things had spiraled out of control, but what Lady Katarina had told him was irritating the back of Faucher's mind to no end . . .

It seemed the princess wasn't the only one being targeted by rebellious groups, but why were they now so interested in Lady Katarina Ashowan? Was it because she was the daughter of Daxaria's hero?

Faucher's gut warned him that things were becoming complicated, and it made him all the more eager to reach Vessa where he could try and investigate the forces working against his well laid plans.

Hopefully His Majesty King Brendan Devark would have some insight . . .

Otherwise, it seemed unlikely that the Daxarians would last long in Troivack, and Faucher wasn't entirely sure if defending their foreign guests was a cause worth his life.

Katarina's visage suddenly appeared in his mind . . . The day she had told him not to tell the prince he had attacked her during a soldier's spell . . . The haunted knowingness in her eyes . . . The way she had grabbed his cloak like a weak child moments before to tell him important information despite the agony she was struggling against . . .

Faucher gave his head a shake.

Of all the traits she could have attempted to use to sway me . . . why did she have to reveal her honorable tendencies . . .

Eric sat smiling at the night sky, the Troivackian moonshine sang in his blood. The horse he had stolen drank from the trough of the inn he had paid to sleep in that night with the silver he'd found in the bottom of the saddle bags. He had even found a half filled glass bottle with moonshine.

Seated outside amongst other guests of the inn at a small table of his own, the only light of the night came from the torches of the buildings and small candles set at the center of each table. Street musicians played simple, enjoyable melodies quietly across the street so as not to disturb the residents nearby, while citizens and traveling merchants alike tossed coppers or even a spare silver into one of their open instrument cases.

It had been a long time since Eric had been alone and at peace. In Troivack, even the dried blood on his tunic wasn't minded much.

Letting out a long sigh, he closed his eyes and raised his cup to his lips, about to savor his next drink, when a sudden breeze and the smell of musk reached him.

With a frown, the prince opened his glassy gaze to find none other than Faucher seated across from him.

There was dark anger emanating from the man as he stared at Eric. It boiled from somewhere deep in his being, and it made the prince reluctantly set the goblet back down on the table while raising an expectant eyebrow. His usual emotionless expression returned to his features.

"Having a nice time?" Faucher's voice rasped with obvious restraint.

"It was a nice evening for a time, yes," Eric replied pleasantly.

"I foolishly believed you had been abducted when I found my own knights dead and your body absent."

"Sorry about that." Eric swayed slightly in his seat.

Faucher's expression turned murderous. "Have you no respect for our lives?"

"I have great respect for them. Which is why I left. If I am the one they are targeting given their most recent attempt, it'd be best if I lead them away from the others until you reach Vessa," Eric explained, his eyes already wandering around, looking for a barmaid to perhaps refill his cup. He had already drained the bottle he had originally arrived with.

"You did not bother checking on those who risked their lives for you." Faucher's voice dropped as the prince held up a finger to a woman who was clearing a nearby table. She nodded in understanding and turned back to the tavern below the inn.

"I saw the group fleeing from a distance and a few of them appeared to be carrying the injured. It looked like a retreat, meaning you would have won."

Faucher looked momentarily taken aback. He hadn't seen any injured parties picked up . . .

Setting that piece of information aside for another time and leaning forward, the Troivackian was about to speak, when the barmaid set out another bottle of moonshine and an extra cup for him.

Watching the prince refill his goblet and take another drink, Faucher didn't bother hiding his disgusted disbelief. "So you intend to run away from your duty?" His fist curled atop the table.

Eric eyed him wearily before setting his cup down once more. "It would make it far easier for you to travel to Vessa without needing to protect me, and at the same time harder for these attackers to find a single traveler. Seems a sound idea to me."

Faucher studied the prince's drunken, bloodshot eyes for a moment before letting out a small, humorless laugh. "Alright, and you will come to Vessa in your own time then?"

Eric gave a noncommittal shrug.

Shaking his head, his disappointment obvious, Faucher stood. "I pity your kingdom's future."

Eric raised his goblet in silent toast to him.

As the Troivackian turned his toes away to leave, he straightened a final time, staring at the prince uncertainly as though debating saying something.

"You know, you weren't the only one those men targeted," he began slowly.

As he lowered his cup, Eric grew stiff while also raising his questioning expression to Faucher.

"Lady Katarina was attacked."

Eric's stomach dropped as he stood before realizing what he was doing. "Faucher, what happened?"

"Glad to see you have some shred of care for someone other than yourself," the Troivackian observed coolly. "She was stabbed. It appears as though her lung was punctured. She has been in and out of consciousness. We're doing our best to find a physician, but that was hours ago. I do not know if she still lives or not, but I guess that isn't of any consequence to you with this new plan."

Eric's eyes widened, and his entire body felt as though it were doused in icy water.

Then, with his hands clumsy from drink, he pulled free two silver coins and tossed them on the table before taking a stumbling step forward.

"Let's go."

CHAPTER 35

REVEALING RESULTS

By the time Faucher, the knights he had taken with him, and Eric rejoined the rest of the party, dawn was beginning to crest over the horizon, dimming the skies in favor of a faint purple hue that swept itself over the sleepy world.

Striding toward the barn, Faucher surveyed the expression of Sir Abaurus, the knight who stood guard, and frowned.

"Have there been any changes?" he demanded as Sir Abaurus gave a swift bow toward Eric, then fixed his gaze on Faucher.

"We found a physician in the next town over—he only just arrived. Sir Cas and Mage Sebastian are inside holding Lady Katarina down. The physician refused to give her anything for the pain, he believes the moonshine could make the bleeding worse somehow . . ." the knight recanted nervously.

Faucher opened his mouth to ask another question, when a shriek pierced the air from within the barn that could only belong to one person.

Eric remained perfectly motionless, his right hand balled into a fist in his pocket as his eyes remained fixed on the door.

"Did she get a belt?" Faucher asked quietly when the scream subsided to fervid grunts.

"Yes, sir," Sir Abaurus confirmed with a nod.

Faucher said nothing else as he stared at the closed barn doors for a breath. After processing the information, he turned back to his subordinate. "How are the others injured?"

"Most of us just require a few stitches . . . Lady Katarina's maid is concussed, but otherwise fine. The physician popped the mage's shoulder back into place though he has a sling."

"How is he holding down the lady with one arm?" Faucher asked with a frown.

"Magic, sir."

"Right. For now, alert the others to go for an hour of sleep, then we will collect our dead and begin digging graves," Faucher ordered.

Another loud shout and colorful curse echoed from the barn.

The knight saluted, then took his leave.

Letting out a short breath through his nose, Faucher turned to the prince and regarded him with weary irritation.

"Will you go sleep, Your Highness?"

Eric swallowed, then turned his sobered gaze to Faucher. "I'll wait to hear how Lady Katarina's doing."

For once negating the bow that typical decorum dictated he perform, the military leader merely positioned himself as guard to the barn as the sounds of Katarina Ashowan being sewn up while awake without any form of pain relief carried on behind him.

Faucher's eyes stayed glued to a fixed point in front of him, his hand loosely gripping his sword's handle as he pointedly avoided thinking about anything to do with either of the Daxarians under his protection.

"She isn't human, Leo! I'm not facing off against that devil woman ever again!" Manuel roared at his superior's infuriatingly calm expression.

"Careful what you say to me. Remember you have brought me nothing but failure today." Leo's dark eyes shone dangerously in the dim firelight.

"Sir, you did not see her!" Manuel began again, though he paled notably and took a step backward. "She lifted Esen with a single hand and snapped her neck! The physician doesn't think she'll be able to move anything below her chin ever again! Rian, we don't even know the extent of his damage yet . . ."

Slowly, Leo stepped closer to his subordinate, his face a stony mask of indifference.

"What about the prince?"

"H-He fought off Wyatt, but we still would have had him, only by then some of the knights had caught up and—"

Leo drew his dagger from his belt, making Manuel back away until he hit the cold stone wall behind him.

"In an abduction that should have ended with minimal expenses, we have lost Rian—one of our best warriors—and an air witch no less. The sloppiness in the execution of this assignment is not to be tolerated. So"—Leo landed a firm punch to Manuel's gut, making him double over—"you and I are going to leave together, and we are going to take the prince regardless of whether or not he is in Vessa, or I will leave your head on your mother's doorstep, understood?"

"Yes, sir . . . What do we do if . . . *that* woman intervenes?" Manuel wheezed, his eyes watering.

Leo's lips curled into a cold smile. "Then you will wish I had killed you right here and now."

Manuel's breath stilled in his chest as he slowly straightened and managed to bow his head.

He knew the man who had come to be Leo's master was fearsome . . . and he also knew it was a blessing that he himself had not yet had to meet him.

Hopefully . . . it would stay that way . . .

It was midday when the barn doors opened.

Faucher and Eric remained silently rooted in their positions outside the barn. It seemed like they had been listening to Katarina's shouts and grunts for an eternity, but in reality it had only been a few hours.

At long last, the physician stepped out with Sir Cas, who looked grim, and Mage Sebastian, whose face was a delicate tint of green.

The physician was a small man in every sense of the word. His bald head and drooping upper lip made him resemble a tortoise, but his dark eyes were warm and kind.

He held a white cloth that he used to finish wiping blood off his fingers as he stared at Faucher and then Eric with a knowing half smile.

"The lady will be fine. She's a fighter. Never in my years as a physician have I seen a mage use magic to restrain a patient like that. Thank you for your assistance." The physician inclined himself to Sebastian, who was taken aback by the sentiment.

"It is my duty to aid the lady," the mage cleared his throat awkwardly.

Eric let out a long breath, his shoulders sagging in transparent relief.

"How long will her recovery take?" Faucher asked, turning to face the physician more squarely.

"Oh, she should be good as new in, say, a month and a half. If not sooner. She was incredibly fortunate that the lung was not fully punctured, or else she would've been dead long before I arrived. This little devil was quite helpful in stopping extensive damage." The physician reached into his pocket and withdrew a small dagger stained in blood.

"What is that?" Faucher asked, his brows lowered.

"A dagger the lady had strapped to her person under her dress. You can see by this dent here that it prevented the sword from fully meeting its mark." The physician pointed with his other hand to the unmistakable notch.

Faucher blinked, then nodded in understanding. "I see."

The physician smiled at the large military man, once again earning a look of wariness in return. "I recommend you travel to wherever you are heading swiftly. It'll be best if she can recover somewhere comfortable to keep her wound clean to stave off infection."

Again, Faucher nodded. Turning to Eric, the physician handed him the bloodied blade that belonged to Katarina. "She's still awake amazingly enough, if you'd like to check on her yourself. We've already covered her, so she is decent."

Visibly hesitating, Eric didn't say anything at first.

Then, with a small sigh of defeat, he slowly stepped around the physician to the open barn doors.

"Here is coin for your troubles." Faucher held out a small sack that jangled with gold to the physician, who was seeing to rolling his sleeves down.

He accepted the pouch with a small bow of thanks.

"There should be enough in there for you to also forget what you saw today." Faucher's voice had turned quiet as his stare shifted from appreciation to that of a warning.

A look of surprise crossed the physician's face before he shrugged and smiled. "No skin off my nose. She truly was a delight to treat. If only all my patients were so reasonable—though I suppose she had gone through this before, so it must have made it a little less frightening," the physician prattled as he tied the money pouch securely to his belt.

"What do you mean she went through this before?" Faucher moved forward, his eyes darkening.

"Ah, on her opposite side. She received a very similar wound some time ago . . . though that one looked to be more serious. Most likely she didn't have something there to block that attack as she did this time."

Faucher stilled. "You're certain it was a stab wound?"

The physician nodded while his eyes moved to the sky thoughtfully. "Indeed. That young woman is not like any other I've met. I hope you enjoy her company for the rest of your journey."

Without any other startling announcements, the physician bowed once more and began strolling away from the barn while whistling a pleasant tune.

Faucher turned to stare back at the barn, his thoughts growing even more troubled despite knowing Katarina Ashowan was alive and would make a full recovery. Primarily, the thought that was growing louder and louder until it nearly left his mouth was *Damnit, just why must you be so troublesome, and not at all like I had judged you to be . . . ?*

Eric walked into the barn, the dust dancing in the sunlight peacefully as his nails dug into his palm.

Kat lay on the table, her left hand idly scratching her familiar's head, which was curled peacefully at her side. Her golden gaze remained fixed on the ceiling, lost in thought.

The prince's eyes fell to her injured side that was covered with a peasant tunic.

Her bloody dress lay in a tattered heap on the opposite end of the table, and she was instead donning trousers . . .

Swallowing with great difficulty, he stepped closer.

"Do you think you could try not almost dying every week?"

Kat's head swiveled over to him, her face pale but her raised eyebrow and sarcastic expression the same as always. "Someone has to keep this trip interesting. Glad to see the kidnappers released you . . . Did they find out they'd have to guard their moonshine stash day and night and decide you weren't worth the hassle?"

Eric rolled his eyes and continued to move closer. "Your maid is fine by the way."

"I know. The physician told me after he had treated everyone," Kat informed him casually.

"He didn't treat you first?" Eric's eyes narrowed in a rare show of anger.

"When he determined that I wasn't on death's doorstep he went to check Poppy. Head wounds can be far more serious, and he needed to pop Sebastian's shoulder back into place so that he could focus on wielding enough magic to hold me down." Her easy explanation succeeded in making Eric slowly shake his head, dropping his chin to his chest.

"Why did you have a dagger hidden under your dress?" Eric asked after a moment.

"Ah, it was a gift from my mother. Self-defense in case of the worst case scenario," she explained while shifting her face to stare back at the ceiling.

Eric continued watching her silently for a while, making Kat eventually turn her head to lock eyes with him again.

"Are you going to lecture me too? Faucher already gave me an earful while carrying me here . . . though I understand . . . five men did die in total . . ." Her eyes drifted downward, sadness and remorse drawing themselves across her face.

"Kat, promise me you won't ever put yourself in harm's way like that again." Eric's quiet voice snapped Katarina's attention to him, the jolt from her shock making her wince against the throbbing in her side.

"I'm not going to promise you that! I wind up in all kinds of extraordinary circumstances, and I just never know—"

"Never again, Kat." Eric's deadened stare made the redhead hesitate briefly before she smiled.

"Pfft, now you sound like you were worried about me. You know I'll be fine. Weren't you the one saying I have the Ashowan talent? Well, there you go. I won't die easily; that is my skill set in the family."

Eric's eyes darkened with ire. He turned to stare at the barn wall for a moment as he tried to take a long breath to calm himself down.

Meanwhile, with shaking arms, Kat slowly and stiffly raised herself to her elbows, then eased her way to sitting. The effort brought a sheen of sweat to her face.

Turning to stare at her again, Eric was unable to hide his fury.

"I *am* worried, Kat. It's normal for people to worry about someone who gets stabbed. Why are you allowed to shun other people as though your feelings are the only ones that Godsdamn matter?"

Kat squinted at him, then took a long, shaky breath. "You know . . . I feel like . . . as the one who recently lost a battle with a pointy bit of steel, my feelings should count a bit . . ."

Eric rounded on her, his hazel eyes flashing. "A *sword* Kat. You got stabbed by a *sword*. Don't downplay this. I've just about made up my mind to have you turn around and tossed onto a ship back to Daxaria the second we get to Vessa. You're going to be killed within a month at this rate, and you simply don't give a damn about any of it! You think this is some kind of Godsdamn game!"

"Life is a lot more enjoyable if you choose to think about it in lighter terms, instead of what *some* people do when stuck in a hole of self-pity."

"There is having a positive disposition, and then there's being an idiot," Eric snapped, taking another step toward Kat who was now glaring at him.

"*I'm* the idiot? You reek of moonshine. You're the one drinking yourself into an early grave. Worry about yourself for a change and save others doing it for you," she shot back hotly.

"Is that what you think you're doing? Saving others from worrying about you by treating whenever you're hurt or afraid as though it's nothing?" Eric demanded, his gaze never leaving her face.

She shifted uncomfortably. For once, Kat couldn't think of anything to say in response. Her teeth remained clamped together, and she felt unable to meet his fierce stare.

"Why the hell do you think you are not worth worrying over?" While Eric's voice had become quiet, it still rasped, and for some reason it made tears rise to Kat's eyes.

She blamed the stab wound.

When he didn't say anything more and waited in silence for her reply, Kat felt her breaths growing shuddered, her hands gripping the table under her until her knuckles turned white.

Eric shook his head and turned to leave, when at long last, she answered.

"For a lot of reasons. For one . . . everyone was always worried about Tam. I didn't want to make it worse, and for another . . . if I admit when those things happen . . . I feel . . . weak. Like everything is too big for me, and I don't know if I can overcome my own problems. Lastly . . . because I . . . I want to be strong enough to take care of everyone."

"Why? Why is that *your* job?" Eric asked, his voice low, but intensity still burning in his eyes.

Katarina lifted her teary gaze to his, and a strange look of calm certainty filled her face.

"Because I know I can do it, and I know it's what I'm meant to do. Down to my soul. I know it."

Eric opened his mouth to argue, but Kat slowly extended her foot down to the ground, and with a grunt, she began to stand. A brief look of concern passed over the prince's face but was long gone by the time Kat was on her feet.

"Pina and I are going to go see about getting some food, and then we are going to attend the burial. Either get me a cane or Sir Cas to walk me out. I don't need you to worry about me, and I don't owe you any kind of promise."

Eric stepped closer and leaned forward so that his nose nearly touched hers, stealing Kat's breath from her for a moment as she blinked in surprise.

"You don't get to tell me who or what to worry about. If you're set on ignoring the concern others have for you, you're going to keep putting them at a distance until you're entirely alone with no one to take care of but yourself. And yes. I do speak from experience."

Eric turned and stalked out of the barn, leaving Katarina by herself, her heart racing fast enough to make her dizzy and forced to lean against the table, where her familiar remained curled up peacefully. Pina's bright green eyes slowly shut as a low purr rumbled in her belly, though Katarina was too distracted to notice.

Faucher watched as Lady Katarina climbed into the carriage with the help of Sir Cas, followed by Mr. Julian, who handed in Poppy. They had rested for half a day before deciding they were going to head directly to Vessa.

It would be a strenuous ride for them all, especially Katarina and her maid, who were still recovering, but Faucher had insisted they couldn't risk another encounter. He had even sent a missive to the castle for additional knights to meet them partway there for extra protection.

With a short breath that bordered on a grunt, Faucher looked at the cloudless blue sky.

He was eager to be rid of the Daxarians. A drunkard prince whom he had to drag along, a wild child witch woman who also happened to be nobility, and constant attacks and assassination attempts . . . He felt as though he had been on a journey for several months as opposed to a week and a half. *No wonder His Majesty gave me a pay raise recently . . .*

Giving his head a shake, Faucher turned to his horse and noticed the prince was once again on the driver's seat of the carriage.

Faucher barely managed to hide his hostility as he turned rigidly back to his previous task of mounting his steed.

As if he hadn't had enough to think about, the previous evening, Lady Katarina had requested that he not report her injury . . .

When he had told her that the event was impossible to omit from the Troivackian king, she instead requested that *only* the king know so as not to give the Daxarian princess more worries.

Giving his head a shake, Faucher was forced to admit he had grown to have a begrudging respect for the noblewoman. Even if she was annoying.

Holding up his fist, he signaled the group to begin moving as he squeezed his horse's sides into movement.

Ah well, soon I'll be free of the Daxarian nobles once and for all.

Unfortunately, what Faucher didn't know, however, was that he wouldn't be free of them quite as soon as he had hoped . . .

CHAPTER 36

A LUKEWARM WELCOME

"My lady, look!" Poppy was nearly bouncing in her seat as she peeked outside the black window covering.

"Ah, is Vessa at long last in our sights?" Sebastian asked with a breath of relief.

Kat managed a weak smile at her maid before once again closing her eyes.

She had seriously underestimated how painful it would be traveling while recovering from a sword wound.

"Oh my—it looks rather beautiful!" Poppy chattered happily before settling back into her seat.

Mr. Julian grinned at her before leaning over and looking himself.

"The air is much cooler now. Is it because of it being the beginning of autumn? Or is it because we are near the mountains?" the young assistant asked the mage, who had perked up considerably with the news of reaching their destination.

"The autumn weather most likely. In another month or so, the winds will grow stronger," Sebastian explained, a shadow of a smile touching his face.

"Did you grow up in Vessa?" Kat asked while cracking open an eye.

Sebastian's good-humored expression dimmed slightly, but he regarded the noblewoman without his former animosity. In fact, ever since Katarina had been wounded, the man had been downright reasonable. Then again, she wasn't all that energetic or talkative since then either . . .

"No, I grew up in the north. Though I spent the past five years here in Vessa, and I wish to never live anywhere else."

Kat nodded and once again shut her eyes, focusing on willing away the pain to the best of her ability.

"I-I'm sure it'll help your recovery, getting to sleep in a proper bed." Poppy turned to her mistress sheepishly after realizing that Katarina couldn't move easily to marvel at the view.

"Of course. Don't worry, Poppy, I'll make you chase after me again in no time. Remember what we all promised though?" Kat's eyes flew open as she regarded each of them seriously. "The princess is going to be burdened enough with the news of the attack and assassination attempts. Don't tell her a thing about my little . . . incident."

Sebastian rolled his eyes toward the roof of the carriage. "Using the future queen as an excuse to avoid getting lectured again . . . Unbelievable."

Kat stuck her tongue out at the mage, who scoffed indignantly in response.

"It was kind of the prince to ride the rest of the way on the driver's bench. It gave you much more room." Poppy changed the subject while clasping her hands together.

No one responded, as everyone but the poor maid were all too aware that the prince and lady had not bothered to talk with each other after he visited her in the barn.

"Well, I suppose I better try and behave myself again . . ." the redhead sighed.

"I'm excited to see that," Sebastian interjected candidly.

"Try to contain yourself," Kat retorted while feeling uncharacteristically weary.

"I, for one, am most curious to see how your time with Troivack's former queen will affect you," Sebastian added with a rueful smile.

Kat raised an eyebrow. "Why?"

"Our former queen . . ." the mage trailed off as pride shone in his eyes. "Was the epitome of a great Troivackian woman. Strong. Regimented. They say her only folly is that her youngest son turned out the way he did."

"Prince Henry is a wonderful person," Kat said with a frown. "A real shame the rest of Troivack fails to see that."

Sebastian didn't bother arguing his point, as the clatter of the carriage wheels along cobblestones rumbled loudly beneath them.

"Ah . . . we've officially arrived in Vessa." The mage smiled, and given that no one had seen him do such a thing, it had the unfortunate result of making everyone wary.

The carriage stopped.

"Now you've done it. You smiled. Straight to the dungeon you go." Kat pointed dramatically at Sebastian, who scowled in response before turning his questioning gaze to the window.

A moment later the carriage door opened, and before they could do anything, Eric had stepped in and closed the door behind himself and sat on the opposite end of Kat's bench, forcing her to shift her feet away from him.

"Ah . . . I suppose it would be strange if Your Highness wasn't riding in the carriage," Mr. Julian noted once they all had adjusted to Eric's sudden appearance.

The prince didn't say anything and instead pounded the roof of the carriage twice, signaling the driver to begin their journey once more.

For some reason, Eric looked rather pale and unsettled . . .

"Is this your first time in Vessa, Your Highness?" Sebastian asked while eyeing the prince as he wiped his palms on his trousers and slumped against the black leather seat of the vehicle.

"No. I visited here about ten years ago with our diplomats."

Everyone exchanged uneasy glances as Eric proceeded to fold his arms and take a long breath, the heel of his boot tapping restlessly.

Kat stared at him, then his bouncing knee, and turned to Sebastian. "Alright, I apologize. You're right. That *is* annoying."

The mage was torn between being aghast at Kat's rudeness and being smug over her admission.

Eric shot her a brief no-nonsense look but stopped the restless bouncing of his heel.

"Is there some particular reason you are—" Kat began drolly.

"No. And I'm handing you out of the carriage when we get to the castle. Don't be a chit about it," the prince snapped.

"Sheesh. I thought you'd be happy to be finished with this bloody trip . . ." Kat muttered while once again closing her eyes.

"Don't fool yourself. The trip was the easy part," Eric countered, his gaze fixed on the covered window where the muffled sounds from the bustling city street trickled into the carriage.

"Speak for yourself." Kat gave a humorless, breathy laugh that made her wince in pain.

Eric didn't bother contradicting her further, and instead they waited in the mounting tension as the carriage jostled onward to the castle.

After what felt like another hour, they finally pulled to a halt.

Eric blinked slowly and swallowed. He looked like a man about to walk the gallows. No one dared move in the tense silence that stifled the air.

"Presenting His Highness Crown Prince Eric Reyes of Daxaria and Lady Katarina Ashowan of Viscount House Jenoure."

The imperial tone that echoed outside startled Kat. The carriage door opened with a creak, allowing daylight to spill in, which was pale thanks to the clouds that gathered in gray puffs above them, blocking the sun.

Stepping out of the carriage, Eric surveyed the large, silent crowd, then the three rows of servants lined up before them, creating an aisle toward the front of the castle doors.

There was an eerie quiet in the courtyard with the only sound emanating from the two grand braziers on either side of Eric, marking the beginning of the aisle, their flames flickering in the cool breeze that drifted across the stone magnificence before him.

The entire castle was built to be the picture of imposing. Long stone steps that rose to the expansive landing before the great doors that could have been built for giants remained as unchanged as when Eric had last laid eyes on them.

Despite the rather bleak exterior, inlays of marble along the front doorway arches and in the massive pillars hinted at the magnificence that lay behind the castle's wrought iron doors.

Standing at the top of the stairs at the head of such imposing majesty was Brendan Devark, and at his side, looking every bit as the queen she would soon be, was Alina, Eric's sister. Her dirty blond hair and pale face were a respite from the otherwise looming and dark surroundings . . .

The royal couple awaited their guests, their faces matching in their deference.

Even though his heart was pounding fiercely, Eric didn't permit his expression to change as he turned and offered his assistance to Katarina.

Slowly, the redhead allowed herself to be handed down from the carriage before straightening herself to her full height as she, too, peered around at her new surroundings.

When her gaze brushed past the nobility, she noticed several people flinch away from her golden eyes, but she didn't show any reaction to them; she was already used to such responses.

As Katarina took a wary step forward, her wound screamed at her, though somehow she kept her expression cool and dignified.

Except when she tried to release Eric's hand, he clasped her fingers tighter, then pulled her hand around his arm.

"Bear with it; I'm doing you a favor," he managed quietly while barely moving his lips as they strode forward side by side.

"What favor? Other than making me look a lot better groomed by comparison," Kat murmured while briefly flicking her gaze to Eric's ponytail and travel-worn clothes that made him look like a poor mercenary.

"It'll be harder for people to look down on you if they think I'm willing to escort you myself. It means you're well connected in the Daxarian court," Eric explained with a note of irritation.

"I am already well connected to the court."

"It helps having a personal reference here."

Kat would've said more, but when they passed by the servants, they were met with synchronized bows and curtsies.

The gesture was received by the noble Daxarians as a mix of being off-putting and impressive as Kat began to climb the stairs and immediately grew winded.

"Shit." She breathed, unconsciously gripping onto Eric's sleeve a little tighter.

Sensing that she was struggling, the prince subtly lingered on each step.

"If you faint here, I'm not going to lie about your wound for you," Eric informed her under his breath.

Kat's magical aura flickered slightly making several knights who were positioned on either end of the stairs reach for the hilt of their swords, until they noticed Brendan's dark gaze warning them to halt.

Regaining some of her strength thanks to her magic, Kat made it to the top of the stairs and proceeded to dip into a curtsy that made her dizzy and would've caused her to stumble if she weren't still holding onto the prince's arm.

Eric executed his bow smoothly and straightened, his arm tensing as he felt Katarina's unsteadiness.

"The castle remains as impressive as it was ten years ago, Your Majesty," Eric greeted the king quickly, who bowed his head in acknowledgment.

Kat's golden eyes moved to Alina, and she very nearly broke her commitment to proper Troivackian manners by smiling at her friend.

She had missed her dearly.

Alina regarded Kat with a nod and indifferent expression that in turn made Kat uneasy . . . even though she knew her best friend was acting for the sake of her future citizens . . .

"I see the carriage needs a great deal of repair," Brendan noted while nodding toward the vehicle that had been sleek and black upon leaving Norum but now sat dusted, scratched, and with its two mended doors no longer able to hang perfectly straight.

"It served us well on the journey," Eric returned calmly.

"Yes, I heard that there was some trouble along the way. It is fortunate you arrived safely," the king's dark eyes were intent on the prince's face.

"Leader Faucher escorted us skillfully. We owe him our appreciation." Eric continued giving the perfect responses for the occasion, leading Brendan to nod approvingly again.

"Come, a feast is being prepared to celebrate your arrival. Your rooms are ready with fresh clothes and baths."

"Your generosity is a blessing." Eric bowed again, reminding Katarina that she, too, needed to curtsy.

She did so and almost pitched forward onto her face from the pain, but Eric's arm circled her shoulders and helped her straighten, making everyone present momentarily taken aback at the show of such casual touch.

Thinking quickly, Eric pivoted and dropped his arm while gesturing with his other.

"Did I not tell you of Vessa's majesty, Lady Katarina?" He turned toward the castle wall where just over its gate a few peaks of other buildings could be seen.

Catching on quickly, Kat nodded. "You did, Your Highness. Thank you . . . for . . . that."

Clearing his throat, Brendan shot Eric a final glance with a raised, questioning eyebrow before turning with Alina's hand on his arm to guide them into the castle.

The prince reluctantly offered Kat his arm again.

When they were walking through the spacious front hall and out of earshot from anyone else, he spoke again.

"Godsdamnit."

"I couldn't help it," Kat murmured defensively.

"If you just let them know about what happened, I—"

"I'm keeping quiet about *your* . . . issues. You keep quiet about mine," she shot back while once again gripping his sleeve tightly.

"You do realize most of these nobles will now assume there is something between us, right?"

"They'll figure out otherwise eventually. Besides, this is all because of you wanting to do me a 'favor,' so really, this is your fault," Kat said while fixing her gaze ahead on Alina's straight back, where her dirty blond waves had been brushed to a glow.

Eric addressed her directly, his voice a little louder, "You ungrateful little—"

"Lady Katarina, I will escort you to your chamber myself." Alina turned, her hazel eyes already warmer than when she had first greeted her brother and best friend.

Kat grinned, then quickly schooled her expression when she remembered the knights who had followed them in from the front entrance were only a little way behind her.

"Thank you, Your Highness, it is a great honor." Kat released the prince's arm, and without a moment's hesitation walked happily to her friend's side.

When the two women disappeared, Brendan faced Eric, his expression stony and his gaze sharp.

"Leader Faucher will be imminently joining me in my office to debrief the details of your journey, though rumors have already been spreading through Troivack like rapid fire."

Eric kept his expression neutral. "I take it you'd like my participation in this meeting?"

The king turned and wordlessly gestured in a different direction than Alina and Katarina had gone, and Eric supposed Brendan's office was in a different wing than the promised hot bath.

So with a small sigh of resignation, he kept pace alongside his brother-in-law and braced himself for the storm that was to come, yet again wishing he could have avoided coming to Troivack in the first place . . .

CHAPTER 37

DRESSING DOWN

Eric stood, his eyes fixed to the back wall of the king's study.

It was a spacious room, decorated with a plush burgundy carpet in front of the hearth and chairs with matching cushions facing the fire. A single peaked window remained open, revealing the view of Vessa's many roofs that pressed proudly against the cloudy sky. Their colors ranged from rust to black to brilliant blue. A wondrous sight to behold in different circumstances . . .

"Is that everything, Faucher?" Brendan Devark asked, his voice coming out as a foreboding rumble.

"Yes, Your Majesty."

"You are dismissed."

Faucher bowed to the king and turned to leave, his ripped maroon cloak billowing behind him as he left the room.

Brendan stared daggers at Eric.

"You attempted to run again. My men died to save you, and you ran."

The Daxarian prince didn't say anything for several breaths before his gaze finally drifted down to the king though he failed to make direct eye contact.

"When it appeared as though my presence would place others in—"

Brendan's palm slammed down against his desk with enough force that it was a miracle it didn't crumble to the floor.

"You ran, and Lady Katarina is lying to my wife—despite her pain—to protect her mental well-being. How is it that despite being her brother, it is only her friend who cares enough to go through such lengths?"

Eric said nothing in response.

Brendan seethed. "I'm in awe that the most selfish man I've ever met is not only related to Alina but is also meant to run a kingdom one day."

Eric's eyes finally locked with the king's.

Brendan stood, his size and glare intimidating. "If you try to flee again, I will cripple you myself. You will not put Alina through any more pain than you already have. Am I clear?"

The prince gave a single nod, though his lack of emotion only pricked Brendan's fury even worse.

"I will not tell Alina what you did, but if you feel an ounce of guilt, I recommend you tell her yourself and apologize."

Eric didn't argue or defend his actions . . . but he didn't apologize either.

"Furthermore, unless you have sincere intentions toward Lady Katarina, distance yourself. Immediately. The rumors around my kingdom are that the Daxarian princess is in a heated love affair with a homely, idiot Daxarian steward. Then when they found out it was Lady Katarina, many nobles assumed that you and the viscount's daughter were already betrothed."

At this, Eric winced. Given that this was the prince's first reaction to anything Brendan had said, His Majesty stepped closer, his expression growing dangerously wary.

"Nothing happened that could be damaging to Lady Katarina, correct?" the king asked, a flicker of concern entering his tone.

Eric frowned. "No. She was stabbed, not bedded."

Brendan studied the prince carefully before nodding and letting out a tense breath.

He turned back to his desk and slowly lowered himself down behind messy stacks of paper.

How he could work amongst such a disastrous state, no one ever knew.

"I don't care what you drink or how much, but do it alone in your chamber. Alina needs to establish herself here without you bringing shame to her," Brendan added while picking up his quill and turning his attention back to his work.

Eric looked to the ceiling for another moment as though praying to the Gods, then bowed to the king, and took his leave without another word.

Brendan stared after him, wondering if Lady Katarina was not going to be his biggest headache for the next year after all . . .

"I heard you were nearly poisoned!" Alina burst out as soon as they were alone in Katarina's chamber.

The redhead grinned easily at her friend while sinking gratefully into the cushions of the sofa before the cold fireplace.

She had had a hell of a time pretending to be fine while climbing up to the third floor of the castle. Fortunately, she had been able to grip onto Alina and make it seem as though she were simply excited to see her friend.

"Yes, yes. Actually, I drank it both times, but you know with my abilities, it isn't as effective," Kat reminded while slumping even farther back into the couch and pressing her head to her fingertips in what she hoped was a casual manner.

Alina sighed and shook her head. "Thank Gods you're alright. Of course, we didn't hear about anything until we got here two days ago. I've been up pacing every night worried about you . . . Then of course those silly rumors about you and a steward . . ."

Kat snorted. "Ah. That rumor ended up circulating? I heard that one shortly after arriving in Troivack. I think it annoys your brother more than he lets on that he had had no intention of appearing inept while posing as a steward . . ."

Alina laughed. "I suppose you and my brother have come to an understanding of sorts? You two seemed chatty when you entered—plus the fact that he escorted you speaks well of your standing in Daxaria, which is good."

"Your brother and I . . . well. Let's just say I'm looking forward to spending time with the better Reyes child." Kat reached out and grabbed Alina's hand, squeezing it affectionately.

"Oh come now, no one's here; I can hug you!" Alina threw her arms out toward her friend with a smile.

Kat's eyes went round as saucers as the threat of her wound being squeezed nearly made her feign a faint, when the Gods smiled upon her, offering a knock on the chamber door, which heralded the arrival of the maids and the tub and hot water for the redhead.

Dropping her arms and straightening her posture as the serving staff entered, Alina lowered her voice.

"So, did you learn more about my brother's absence?"

"He's an arse. That's all you need to know," Kat informed her quietly as the maids worked behind them. She was still recovering from the panic of her best friend unknowingly subjecting her to torture.

Sighing, Alina shook her head. "Things are stressful enough . . . Hopefully he stays out of trouble."

"Just lock your ale cellars," Kat muttered under her breath.

"What was that?" Alina asked, a little louder while leaning forward with a frown.

"Ah, nothing. So how is your mother-in-law?"

At this question Alina's expression grew tense. "Ah . . . you've heard about her already, have you?"

Kat raised a curious eyebrow.

Alina's gaze briefly darted to the maids before she leaned forward. "She's just so . . . formidable. Like a wall. I can't tell if she hates my guts or likes me."

"Who could hate you? Hating you is like saying you hate kittens—which reminds me!"

Kat couldn't hide her smile as her face lit up excitedly.

Alina straightened in excitement. "Wait . . . your familiar?! I still haven't met her!"

"I wanted to introduce you when we first arrived in Norum, but you were a little . . . occupied." Kat's smile turned teasing as Alina blushed.

"Well, you know . . . being . . . married . . . means . . . those things are involved . . ."

Kat inched closer to her friend, momentarily forgetting about her wound and nearly flinching from the pain as a consequence. When she'd recovered from her small jolt, she dropped her voice to the barest of whispers.

"So . . . how is *it*?"

Alina turned the color of a tomato as she dropped her face to her hands, hiding her smile.

"Ooh." Kat smirked. "Too bad I'll never get married; I guess that means I just get to tease you about it until you're a grandmother."

"I'll kill you by then," Alina managed to say through her hands.

"Pfft. Even when we're old crones I'll still beat you in a fight, no problem."

The princess let out a long breath as she once again regained her composure, though she failed to remove the smile on her face.

"So, is there anyone else I need to be wary of?" Kat asked instead as she once again eased back into the couch.

"Everyone, Kat. Remember your mother's lessons?"

Rolling her eyes, Kat sighed. "Okay, but anyone that's been an arsehat to you already?"

Alina's good-humored mood did fade then as her own gaze drifted downward. "A few . . . but I'll work them over in time."

The petite woman gave a brave look to her friend, who nodded.

"Of course you will, and once I learn how to stab people more efficiently, I'll—"

"No killing my new citizens."

"Why not? It'd make life so much easier for us . . . Then again I could always just go around smiling at the lot of them until they agitate themselves to death . . ."

At this Alina released a small snort. "Prince Henry has already broken them in—speaking of, his wife is lovely! A little strange, but . . . I'm sure you two will get along swimmingly. She's incredibly beautiful. In fact, she's going to be another handmaiden for me, at least until she gives birth. A lot of courtiers are upset about that because she was a nomad before . . . but blast them. Another noblewoman from the north is coming to help as well. A widow . . . No one is telling me about her, which is making me nervous. And then of course I have Lady Sarah."

Kat turned, her eyebrows arched in curiosity.

Alina's expression had fallen flat at the last handmaiden's name.

"Lady Sarah is . . . well . . . whatever you do, Kat, you are not allowed to hurt her. Believe me, I have to remind myself regularly, and it's only been two days."

Kat opened her mouth to ask more about the Troivackian noblewoman who clearly had to be a very trying person to be able to irk Alina so thoroughly, when she was interrupted by one of the maids.

"Pardon us, Lady Katarina. We have prepared your bath."

"Wonderful! I can handle things from here, thank you." Kat stood while using every ounce of control she possessed to not double over in agony and nodded to the women, who collectively hesitated before filing out.

"You know they're supposed to assist you while you bathe," Alina pointed out wryly.

"I'd like to get to know them a little better before exposing myself to them is all." Kat shrugged while clasping her hands in front of her skirts and offering the Gods a silent prayer that Alina wouldn't needle her any further on the matter.

"Since when do you think about being modest?" The princess eyed her friend suspiciously.

"After the third or fourth assassination attempt, I've realized I can't say I'm fond of the idea of being found dead naked in a tub," Kat explained breezily.

Alina's face shifted to remorse as she stared at Kat more seriously.

"I'm so sorry you had to go through that because of me . . . I . . . Kat, I'm so happy you're here . . . This is all so terrifying . . ."

Kat grinned and poked Alina's forehead. "Stop that. You know I love adventure. This just gives me good stories. It helps that your husband has to be nice to me now, so I'm beyond thrilled."

Alina laughed again, threw her arms around Kat, and squeezed her tightly. "Gods, am I lucky to have you as my friend."

Katarina patted Alina's back. "The feeling is mutual. Now, that tub looks rather incredible, so pardon me while I try and smell a little less ripe."

Alina pulled away from her friend, noting how pale Katarina suddenly appeared. "I can tell even you are tired from all that traveling. So take your time, and someone will come for you when it's time for the banquet."

Kat managed to smile. "Sounds wonderful. By the way, would you please ask the maids outside to send me Poppy? She's fantastic with doing my hair now, and I'm sure it'll save the maids here in Troivack from having to learn their way around it."

Alina hesitated as she stared at Kat's face for another moment, then nodded and took her leave.

As soon as the door closed, Katarina proceeded to sink onto her knees while grasping her side where she was certain one or two of her stitches had popped because of Alina's embrace.

"Gods . . . damnit . . ." she cursed, her breaths ragged.

When the pain finally subsided enough that it was manageable, Kat carefully removed her dress, and sure enough, found specks of blood dotting her bandaging.

With a sigh, she looked to the heavens.

"Did you have to make my mother right about Troivack being a little too prone to violence? At this rate, even *I* might have to wave the white flag."

CHAPTER 38

DISMAYING DAWNS

Kat sat at the long table amongst the Troivackian nobles, wearing a forest green dress made in the Troivackian style, a gold necklace, bracelets, and matching earrings. Overhead, ornate silver chandeliers lit the exquisite room despite the ceiling arching high enough to cast shadows. Below Katarina's feet, marbled floors that bore dark, swirling inlays stretched across the room and were polished to a shine. Behind where the redhead sat were four twelve-foot glass doors, which stood open to reveal the gardens and courtyard. Gauzy white curtains fluttered in the night breeze and helped cool the room despite it being filled with nobles and servants.

The entire room, like the rest of the castle, was opulent and imposing.

Though Katarina couldn't take her time to enjoy its splendor, as all around her were unfamiliar faces save for Alina's, the king's, Eric's, and Faucher's. The military leader, who had ensured she'd arrived alive to Vessa, sat rather far away on the other end of table, drinking and eating without engaging either of the noblemen seated at his sides. To Kat, this felt both odd and also true to his character as she'd come to know it.

She resisted the urge to sigh.

It was Kat's first true test, but the dinner was already pushing her limits.

At formal banquets, it was Troivackian custom that the women did not speak unless spoken to, and so most sat silently beside their husbands. Eating gracefully, their eyes modestly cast down to their meals before them.

On Kat's left sat an elderly man, whom she had to watch for long periods of time to ensure he was in fact breathing. The man on her right was perhaps two or three years younger than Katarina, and he was far more interested in the discussion happening with the man on his other side to bother with the Daxarian noblewoman.

Across from Katarina sat none other than Rebecca Devark. Former queen of Troivack, and Brendan and Henry mother.

Rebecca was tall and dressed head to toe in black. Even her hair was swept under a twisted black cloth of sorts.

Kat eyed her curiously. Her bold mouth, her square jaw, her almond-shaped eyes . . . She certainly had a domineering look . . .

Sensing the attention, Rebecca's dark eyes flitted upward, locking with Kat's, which in turn gave her a small startle.

Blinking back at the woman, unable to say anything, Kat watched as the former queen gradually lowered her gaze back to her plate without so much as a flicker of emotion.

Shooting a quick glance at Alina, she was relieved to see that her friend had seen the whole exchange, and in return shot her a knowing look.

Kat was about to take another bite of her food, when someone spoke to her at long last.

"So, Lady Katarina, you're a witch?"

She turned and stared at the Troivackian man with short, straight black hair only a few inches long and clean-shaven cheeks. He appeared to be in his late twenties and must have been a noble of sorts since he was seated next to the former queen. The redhead blinked at his bluntness, then straightened herself.

"Yes, I am."

The man gave a half laugh as he continued chewing his meal. "What was glowing around you earlier?"

Kat set her fork down to face him without a chance of distraction, sensing that the man was going to demand every ounce of willpower she possessed. She was unaware that Brendan, Alina, Eric, and even Faucher on the opposite end of the table were watching the exchange while completely frozen. All of them shared the keen sense of how delicate the situation before them had become.

"Witches sometimes emit a magical aura. I was unable to contain it out of gladness for seeing His Majesty and Her Highness safe." To the untrained eye, Katarina bowed her head prettily, and her golden eyes glowed in contentment at sharing details about her abilities. She had even managed to sound respectful!

To those who *did* know better, they shared the visage of a large, hungry cat prowling closer to a blind mole that had decided to present itself to the hunter while slathered in gravy.

Alina was dangerously close to laughing, and so she quickly reached for her goblet and took a drink.

"So, it doesn't do anything? The glowing thing?" the man asked while revealing the half masticated meal in his gaping mouth.

"I've been told it makes me rather useful in the dark."

The man gave another derisive guffaw while continuing to eat.

"Mr. . . ?" Kat asked, blinking innocently.

The entire table shifted uncomfortably as she spoke without being first addressed.

However, he merely turned a haughty look to her in response. "I am *Lord* Ball."

"Lord Balls?" Katarina frowned as she feigned being hard of hearing, making Eric swiftly take another mouthful of his drink as he, too, struggled not to laugh.

"*Ball*," the lord repeated, irritably.

"Ah, Lord Ball. Wonderful to make your acquaintance." She bowed her head.

He eyed her darkly for another moment before turning back to his meal.

Katarina picked up her cup to take a drink herself, when the young man on her right decided to try speaking with her in a show of vague social awareness that things were becoming a little tense.

"I am Lord Edium. I hear you are only in Troivack a year, Lady Katarina?"

Kat almost grinned when the young man made a point of introducing himself first but caught herself just in time.

"Yes, that is correct."

"Unless you marry here, of course."

Brendan, Alina, Eric, and Faucher all stilled yet again as though stuck moving from tableau to tableau, their gazes still fixed on Kat, which in turn drew more attention to her.

"I have no designs to marry any time soon, Lord Edium." She gave an appropriate bob of her head.

Brendan glanced at his wife, who openly expressed her shared trepidation that the young man would make the grave error of prolonging the topic.

"Well, surely your father has a match in mind for you," Lord Edium continued, unaware that he was causing great distress to many esteemed nobles around him. He reached for his goblet and took a sip.

"Quite the opposite, in my estimation. He'd rather I stay at home as long as possible." At this, Kat couldn't help but give a small smile. She did her best to dismantle the expression, but it had the unfortunate effect of bringing forth *everyone's* attention.

"So you . . . will remain unmarried? Your family *planned* such a thing?" Lord Edium was struggling to grasp the notion.

Sadistically, Katarina was all too willing to help make it clear for him. "Not precisely planned. I suppose if I ever changed my mind about the whole thing, they would—"

"*Your* mind? So you are saying your father leaves such an important matter for *you* to decide?" Lord Ball cut in condescendingly.

Brendan looked as though he were about to rise from his chair and usher Katarina out of the room as quickly as possible, knowing there was a distinct chance the redhead was dangerously close to openly cussing out Lord Ball in many colorful ways.

Kat gave an enigmatic smile to the lord, which further agitated several members of the monarchy.

"Of course it is my decision. I'd be the one living with whomever it is. Surely you've heard that many of Daxaria's noble families allow their daughters to have the final say regarding their marriages."

Lord Ball stared at her with a mixture of disbelief and scorn, but Katarina wasn't finished.

"Why, Princess Alina for example *chose* your king. Was that not a *fantastic* decision she made?" The redhead's eyes sparkled as Lord Ball began to glower.

"I suppose I cannot wrap my mind around such an *inefficient* way of going about things," Lord Ball muttered when he noticed Brendan's warning gaze.

"Depends what you find inefficient. Marrying someone who you think about throttling for the rest of your days seems a wildly inefficient way to spend your life, in my opinion." Kat continued to stare at Lord Ball, who had rested his forearms against the table, meeting her willful stare head-on.

"For a woman to talk about throttling her husband—is that another Daxarian custom?" he asked, his eyes flashing.

"Is chewing with your mouth open a Troivackian one?" Kat shot back flatly.

Brendan stood so quickly that it startled the entire room. "Lords and ladies, I wish to offer a toast to our esteemed guests from Daxaria's shores."

With that, everyone shifted their focus back to their king, and when he finished his brief speech, he made sure to dominate the conversation with

Lord Ball and a few other nobles around Katarina, forcing an end to the feud that had already begun between his guest and vassal.

Suffice it to say, Lady Katarina Ashowan had made a strong first impression at her Troivackian court debut. Though in years to come, Brendan would be forced to admit she had lasted far longer during the dinner than he had originally estimated.

Katarina awoke early the next morning with a groan.

Her side was still smarting fiercely from where Poppy had restitched her wound.

The poor maid had been trembling and crying and had required a good amount of consoling from Katarina both before and after, but once finished, she'd been gifted extra coin and the remainder of the evening off to rest.

"I should try and find some moonshine to filch and take the edge off this pain," she mused aloud while slowly easing herself up from her bed and over to the water basin.

"I'll annoy Eric into giving me some once I figure out where his room is."

After selecting her gown for the day and brushing her hair, she glanced outside to where dawn had only just begun to lighten the dark sky.

"Even while injured I can't sleep right." She sighed and made her way out of her chamber, thinking she may as well explore the castle while waiting for the rest of its occupants to awaken.

However, Kat had forgotten that exploring meant an excessive amount of stair-climbing, so she settled for remaining on the first floor after nearly fainting from the exertion of getting there.

As she wandered, she managed to find the servants' dining hall, the kitchens where breakfast was already being prepared, and then she eventually made her way to the west wing of the castle.

The entire castle was spacious with excessively high, smooth ceilings and majestic pillars set flush against the walls. She discovered tapestries depicting hunting or equestrian scenes, and a few portraits of former Troivackian royals . . . Then Katarina found herself standing in the doorway leading to what must have been the training grounds for the knights. Wooden crosses with straw men stretched across them stood ready to be torn apart, while a barrel filled with broken weapons across the massive, cobbled courtyard stood under the eaves of a two-story stone building separate from the castle . . . perhaps the barracks . . . or weapons storage. Its small, narrow windows and black roof looked rather dreary . . .

Stepping down onto the cobbled ground, Kat began to draw closer to the barrel of broken weapons curiously. The three walls that enclosed the training ring had a covered walkway wrapping around it that allowed observers to view the knights at work. Tall, peaked windows looked down from the second floor. However, at that time of day, they remained dark, and the only source of light aside from Katarina's eyes was the lit wall sconces and the four massive braziers around the courtyard. It was perfectly still and silent.

Turning her attention back to the mysterious detached building, Kat noted its arched door was propped open, yet it only revealed a shadowy interior. She drifted closer to it, her steps falling quietly on the stones as she made her way across the courtyard, her curiosity pulling her toward the unknown like a moth drawn to a flame. She reached out her hand, intending to reveal just what exactly the purpose of the building was, when . . .

"Are you lost?"

Kat let out a small shriek, her aura flaring as she jumped and swung around, her injury sending a blast of pain that had her hand grasping her side.

When she finally registered who she was staring at, she let out an unladylike groan.

"What the hell are you doing here?"

Eric regarded her blankly as he took another drink from the water flagon in his hand.

Damp with sweat, a white towel was draped around his neck and a sword was in his hand. He raised an eyebrow. "Planting petunias," came the sarcastic retort.

"I'm surprised you're not passed out in your chamber." Kat breathed while straightening slowly.

Eric shot her an unamused expression as he turned to one of the straw men and hung his flagon around its neck. "Were you looking for me?"

"Well, not exactly, though I was going to later. You need to give me some moonshine."

Eric stared at her for a moment with wry astonishment. "You have some audacity asking me for that."

"It's for the pain. Alina hugged me yesterday and I had to get restitched." Kat groaned while allowing herself to lean against the weapons barrel.

"Sounds painful. It's almost as though *not* telling her you're injured is a horrible idea."

Eric then proceeded to flip the sword in his hand and strike two expert blows on the straw man.

Kat watched, momentarily entranced, before giving her head a quick shake.

"Please, Eric?"

Giving her another unimpressed glance, the prince shook his head and proceeded to attack the dummy.

"You need to avoid me, remember? I'm in enough trouble as is without risking giving you moonshine."

"You're in trouble? More of it? I thought I was the only one who mucked up the dinner . . ."

Eric stopped his attacks and cracked a small smile that he kept directed at the straw man. "I still can't believe you called that lord *Balls*."

Kat couldn't help it; she gave a small laugh. "He's a massive arse. Where do you think his bulging vein is?"

Eric's smile widened. "I think I started to see it on his neck."

"I'll certainly try and find out more next time." Kat laughed.

"Gods . . . I think you're going to be the death of my brother-in-law. The king was about to have a heart attack when the poor idiot started in on you." Eric resumed his strikes against the dummy while carefully avoiding his flagon.

"So why are you in trouble again?" Katarina persisted as she continued to watch Eric train.

"Remember when you were stabbed?"

"Vaguely."

"Well, after I got away from the attackers, I left," Eric replied before performing another impressive combination of attacks on the dummy all while his flagon remained untouched.

"What do you mean you left?" Kat asked with a raised eyebrow.

"I took one of the abductors' horses and went to a town a few hours' ride away. Planned on staying gone and eventually going back to Daxaria."

"Oh." Kat took a moment to absorb his confession. "So men died, and you took off, and Faucher is rightfully pissed about it . . . and I'm guessing he told the king, who probably lectured you. Maybe even threatened bodily harm for cowardice."

Eric glanced at her, then tapped his nose in confirmation before returning to attacking the dummy.

"Did Faucher drag you back kicking and screaming?"

"No. He told me you got injured, and I came back on my own."

Kat began to smile with a hint of smugness. "You went off on me about staying safe when you'd literally just returned from having run away?"

"Had to make the trip back worthwhile," Eric confirmed, his breathing growing harder as dawn began to brighten their surroundings. "Kat, you really do need to go somewhere else. We have enough rumors going around."

"Not until you agree to give me moonshine. Look, I'm not going to drink it to get drunk! I'm just going to try and avoid fainting from pain every time I'm faced with the stairs."

"You should keep in mind if new rumors get bad enough about the two of us, the nobles may expect me to marry you to take responsibility."

Kat cringed.

"And unfortunately for you, I don't plan on getting married. Even if your reputation goes to the dogs," Eric explained while adjusting his footing.

"Aren't you supposed to be a king? How can you not marry when you're supposed to produce an heir?"

"I can adopt. Preferably a seventeen-year-old with whom I can have a few drinks and then pass the kingdom over to."

"You really are hell-bent on getting out of responsibility," Kat spluttered in astonishment.

"I think it has been said by three different people in the span of the past week how I am not fit to rule. I agree with them, and I'm taking responsibility for that fact in my own way."

"Gods." Kat gave a laugh of disbelief over his frank admission. "What happened to you to make you like this? I've heard so many rumors about how talented you were. How people who had met you admired your wit and insight. How you were a natural leader. Then you disappeared. So . . . what changed?"

Eric sliced the dummy all the way down to its wooden post, and with a grunt, wrenched his sword back, for once falling back in a small stumble.

Panting heavily, sweat dripping down his face, he turned to face her, the familiar shadows in his hazel eyes appearing once more. "I've already said to you and my sister—"

"No, no, no. Not that hack of an answer about traveling around. An actual answer. You know almost all my secrets, so it's only fair."

Eric rolled his eyes and began using the towel around his neck to wipe his forehead dry.

When he didn't respond, Kat decided there was no use waiting around to get in trouble, and so she stood with a grunt and began to step toward the castle entrance.

"Do you remember the fever that killed my mother?"

Kat turned back around to face him, unable to fully mask her surprise that he was answering her.

"Yes."

"That fever . . . *ravaged* the kingdom, but it was far worse in Rollom than anywhere else . . ." Eric began, his eyes fixed on the ground. "My father deliberated on banning travel to and from the city, but when my mother died, he delayed that decision by a day. *One* day. Do you know how many people died in that *one* day?"

Eric's gaze rose to Kat's at long last. "Seven hundred and sixteen. And those are just the deaths we know about."

She blinked in astonishment.

"Two towns were wiped out. When I recovered from the fever myself, I went to help with the various secluded camps that had segregated the sick from the healthy. The bodies were piled in heaps . . . Children screamed day and night, and there weren't enough physicians. I could do nothing but—"

"You dug the graves," Kat interrupted, a strange knowingness filling her features.

Eric straightened and frowned. "Yes. How did you . . ."

Kat shook her head. "It makes the most sense is all. Go on."

Eric eyed her carefully for a moment before he continued, now pacing, the flat of his sword pressed against his shoulder.

"After spending months burying the dead, I ended up traveling to the various towns to offer my grave-digging services, and eventually I just stopped being a prince. I stared at the faces of the people we failed to save and instead put them in the ground. Sometimes animals had already gotten to the villages before I did, and I had to search for the remains." Eric halted his movement as horrors from those days flashed in front of his eyes, and Katarina momentarily worried he would fall under another soldier's spell.

"Then I met my first mercenary group. I suppose I started drinking more with them. We got along fine; they had been paid to bury the dead and assumed I was like them. We traveled together, taking on odd jobs for three months or so . . . When I decided to return to Duke Iones's keep in Sorlia, I finally confessed to the mercenaries my true identity."

A bitter note entered Eric's voice as he began pacing again. "They turned on me immediately. Held me at knifepoint and made me write a letter requesting ransom."

Kat stiffened in surprise.

"I killed them. All four of them. I buried them too. Then I decided I didn't have to return just yet. I met up with Sir Vohn a few times to make sure someone other than your father knew I was alive. I traveled around Zinfera. Joined different mercenary groups . . . got kidnapped once or twice more. Killed more people than I care to count . . . and at the end of it all, I suppose I'm tired of the amount of death being a prince or a king forces upon me. I'd rather live without owing anyone anything, in peace."

"So . . ." Kat began, her throat suddenly feeling incredibly dry. "Get rid of your inheritance as Daxaria's king as soon as possible . . ."

"Yes."

"No wife. No children of your own."

"Correct."

"What about the drugs?"

"Won't matter if I take them or not once I'm alone, will it?"

"What about your father and sister?"

"Alina will adapt here and probably won't be home much once she has her own children. I'll do my best to check in on my father until he passes . . ." Eric shrugged. His entire past and future described and concluded tidily.

"Are you going to be happy with all that?" Kat asked quietly.

Eric took in a deep breath, then exhaled before fixing her with a firm stare, his eyes dark, and his face weary. "I don't really deserve to be happy, Kat. Now go away. I've told you before, I have enough to feel guilty about."

CHAPTER 39

TENSE TEACHINGS

Katarina sat in the solar debating how she could discreetly . . . and deftly . . . stab Lady Sarah in the eye with her needle.

"Lady Katarina, your stitches are too broad. Tighter stitching like so," the Troivackian noblewoman called over for the tenth time that hour. Each time, she held up her own embroidery pattern of the mountain view from the castle walls.

Kat was beginning to develop a twitch under her right eye as she thrust the needle through the cloth and bit her tongue.

"Lady Sarah," Rebecca Devark called out softly, making the younger Troivackian woman turn expectantly. "I seem to be running out of the red thread. Could you please go to my chamber and fetch it for me?"

"Of course, ma'am." Standing swiftly and giving a militaristic curtsy, the handmaiden exited the solar, leaving Alina, Katarina, and Rebecca alone for the first time that morning.

"Lady Sarah is . . . a permanent handmaiden to you, Your Highness?" Katarina asked tightly.

Alina turned to her friend, her lips pursed. "Until she finds a husband, yes."

"Is Lord Balls single?"

"It is Lord *Ball*, Lady Katarina," the king's mother interjected coolly.

"Ah, yes, that's . . . what I meant to say . . . Is Lord Ball single? I'm sure they would make a lovely couple."

"He is married, actually," Alina informed Kat with a barely contained laugh.

Kat didn't bother hiding her surprise at the news.

"What's his wife like?"

"Hard to say. She's rather quiet, but then again, most Troivackian women seem to be more reserved when meeting someone new. Much like how your mother said they'd be," Alina noted thoughtfully.

"Your mother tutored both of you?" Rebecca asked Kat, her eyebrow rising, but her expression otherwise remaining unreadable.

"She did, yes. My mother is Troivackian, actually—"

"From the Piereva family here in Troivack. Yes, I remember her."

"Did you meet my mother while she was here, ma'am?" Katarina looked at the woman interestedly.

"I did. She was briefly thought of as a candidate for King Matthias. However, the fact that her mother was Daxarian eliminated her as a possibility outright," the former queen informed them calmly.

"I never knew she was considered for a marriage here in Troivack!" Kat announced with a smile, which in turn earned an extended look of judgment from Rebecca.

"So, tell me, was Brendan always so serious as a child?" Alina interrupted, drawing her mother-in-law's attention back to herself.

"Yes."

"Ah." Alina nodded and glanced at Katarina awkwardly in the silence before fixing her attention back to her stitching.

"Was it you who hired Lady Sarah for Her Highness?" Katarina asked suddenly, a strong suspicion brewing in her gut.

"I did," came the toneless reply.

Alina looked up from her embroidery, wide-eyed.

Before more could be said, however, Lady Sarah returned with more thread for Rebecca, and so they settled in for another hour of stitching with Lady Sarah's grating interruptions and criticisms eating away at their patience.

"Yep. She hates you," Kat announced while collapsing onto the sofa in her room with Alina at her side.

"Completely," her friend agreed glumly.

"The former queen definitely seems like someone who would also hate kittens. Oh! Maybe I should bring Pina with me this afternoon!" Kat looked at the sunny patch on her bed where her familiar was prone to sleeping on, only to see that the kitten had moved elsewhere.

"Don't antagonize my mother-in-law! I need that woman to like me! Gods, Kat . . . what am I going to do in a year when you have to leave me here?" Alina turned to her friend, sighing, her stress lining her face.

"You already trashed my escape plan for you at your wedding; now you expect a new one?! You ungrateful wench," Kat grumbled.

Alina laughed. "This afternoon we will be starting to prepare for my coronation next month. Maybe things will be a little better once we all settle in."

"I hope so. There are two people I'm already wanting to smother in their sleep . . ." Kat rubbed her eyes wearily. "Not to mention that aside from you and your brother, I have to be on my best behavior around everyone . . ."

"I thought you and Eric don't get along?" Alina queried interestedly.

"We do and we don't. We despise each other, but we also can show each other our worst sides because of it. It's rather cathartic."

Alina sighed, her eyes growing lost in her thoughts. "I haven't been able to talk to him since we arrived in Norum. Am I a coward for avoiding him?"

"A little, but I think you also have more important things to do, so it isn't like you can focus a lot of your attention on it either."

"Kat, finding my brother was important enough that I risked both our lives and got us kidnapped. Now he's here in the same place as me, and I can't even be bothered to have tea with him."

"Then have tea with him. I know you told him you'd treat him like he was dead to you, but I've told him off in twenty worse ways and he still talks to me, though usually it takes a few days for him to cool off . . ." The redhead idly twisted the gold bracelet around her wrist, making Alina reach out and grab her hand, her own bracelets jangling against them.

"Could you be there with me when I meet with him? At least for the first cup of tea?"

Kat narrowed her eyes at her friend's innocent and pleading expression. "What do I get in exchange?"

Alina gently stroked Kat's hand. "I can have a bottle of moonshine secretly sent to your chamber."

Katarina's skeptical expression shifted to one of pure exuberance. "I would *love* to have tea with you and your brother, you brilliant woman! How could I say no?" Kat gushed enthusiastically, once again making Alina laugh.

Unbeknownst to the two friends as they continued to enjoy each other's company, the Troivackian king was having an interesting meeting of his own . . .

"A soldier's spell?" Brendan frowned as he regarded Faucher, who sat beside him in front of the hearth in his office, wearing a black tunic and burgundy vest.

"Yes. I think a combination of the drink, sleepwalking, and a soldier's spell made him especially volatile. I couldn't mention this to you in his presence, as there is a detail even the prince is unaware of, which has been bothering me."

Brendan nodded encouragingly to him.

"When I was trying to snap him out of it, Lady Katarina came in, and despite me ordering her to leave, she didn't."

Brendan waved his hand in understanding, indicating to Faucher that the king was most definitely familiar with Lady Katarina's nature.

"She then proceeded to intervene. He got a little rough with her—she probably was bruised or at the very least sore for a day, but she sang to him, and it did calm him down. He has no recollection of this happening, and she asked that I not share it with him."

Brendan had gone still as he listened.

"What bothers me is how familiar she was with the soldier's spell and the fact that she always hides injuries and pain . . . Then the physician told me she has an old stab wound . . . It all makes me wonder . . ."

After long moments of deliberation, Brendan let out a breath, then leaned forward so that his elbows rested on his knees. "Faucher . . . what I am about to tell you is never to be repeated. I had not planned on sharing this information with anyone else, but in light of your . . . experiences with Lady Katarina, as well as another detail I need to share with you, I feel it best you become aware."

Faucher straightened, his brow furrowing as he waited to finally have the curtain of mystery pertaining to the redheaded witch lifted.

"Last year, while I was visiting Daxaria . . . the princess and Lady Katarina were abducted."

Faucher stilled.

"I have kept this information from our court for the obvious reason that they may try to spread horrible rumors and lies regarding their virtues. Even in Daxaria, efforts were made to dampen the excitement given the nature of the events." Brendan paused as though second-guessing whether to share this information. "Lady Katarina is responsible for having saved Alina. She escaped, alerted us where they were, and then she went *back*."

At this Faucher blinked, dumbfounded.

"I watched her beat one of her abductors to death with her bare hands, and during that time, she was stabbed. After everything they endured, Alina started experiencing the soldier's spells. I was present the first time it happened, but it would occur a few times a month before I left, and Lady Katarina quickly became rather adept at helping her through them. I am beyond grateful and indebted to Lady Katarina Ashowan, for everything. She saved

Alina and has been my wife's salvation and rock for the past year while we prepared for the wedding."

Faucher was unable to speak as he processed the information. At long last he asked, "Does Prince Eric know about any of this?"

"Prince Eric doesn't even know about Lady Katarina helping him during his own spell. I am not a gambling man as you know, but I would wager a decent sum he hasn't any idea that he, too, owes Lady Katarina this same debt." At mentioning the prince, Brendan's voice took on an edge.

Faucher let out a weighty breath as he raised a hand to his brow and rubbed it thoughtfully.

Everything certainly made sense now, the only problem was . . . even Faucher could feel his own shame over thinking ill of the Daxarian noblewoman as a result.

"You tell no one this. Not even Sebastian. Understood?" Brendan warned, his voice turning imperial.

Faucher nodded wordlessly.

"Now . . . the reason I chose to tell you this . . ." Brendan settled back in his chair, his eyes drifting to the ceiling as though he were suddenly uncomfortable. "It has been decided that Lady Katarina is going to learn swordsmanship while here in Troivack."

Rounding on the king with great alarm, Faucher spluttered, "She wasn't lying?! That truly is going to happen?!"

At this Brendan smiled slowly. "It is, and *you*, old friend, are going to teach her."

Faucher's mouth opened and closed several times before finally managing to find the words. "Dear Gods, no. Not me. No. No. No. No. No, Your Majesty. Absolutely not."

"Faucher, it's integral to my plans. You will teach her, and when she is ready, she is going to fight against Captain Orion's best pupils that recently joined our ranks, and win."

"Your Majesty, she may be a witch, but she is still a woman! I admit a better one than I wanted to give her credit for, but she cannot beat Orion's best!"

Brendan smiled, and it made the short hairs on the back of Faucher's head prickle.

"You haven't seen the extent of what Lady Katarina can do; I can tell."

"I know about her ability to stay warm and see in the dark, but swordsmanship? Why don't you just hang targets on her front and back? It'll yield the same results!"

"Faucher, push her. Don't go easy on her. Push her like your men, and she will surprise you," Brendan soothed patiently.

"She's still recovering from being stabbed! Like hell I'm teaching her." Faucher sprang to his feet and began to pace rapidly.

"Lady Katarina will be recovered in a month, though you're reminding me I need to arrange for a physician to see her discreetly," Brendan concluded thoughtfully before turning his attention back to one of his closest advisors and friends. "Faucher, if you train her, and she beats Orion's men, do you know what that will do?"

"Buy Lady Katarina and me tickets aboard death's carriage?"

"I'm not used to you being so theatrical, Faucher. No. It will prove beyond a shadow of a doubt you should be captain in my court. It is grounds to make people realize certain positions should be designated by skill and capability rather than bloodline. Furthermore, it will help my wife's cause of proving that she is capable of ruling as my partner rather than from the shadows."

"Gods, what did they do to you in Daxaria that you've started scheming this amount of madness?" Faucher growled.

Brendan rose slowly. "They showed me a happy kingdom. One that is making advancements left, right, and center. While we are now in a time of peace here in Troivack, and we are faring well thanks to our booming trades, we still need to change some of these dated laws. Laws that you yourself told me you'd support being updated."

"There's changing role assessment and assignment and then there's giving that woman a sword and throwing her at the mercy of Troivackian knights! You're banking all of our carefully laid plans on a woman who I have personally witnessed hiding cat shit in the shoes of the knight who annoyed her!"

Brendan paused at that piece of information. "Did you take the shit out of his shoes?"

"I did, and Godsdamn you, Your Majesty, because now that I know she was telling the truth about sword fighting, he bloody well deserved to step in that shit!" Faucher closed his eyes and rubbed his brow more intensely than before as he attempted to calm himself.

"I can tell she has tried your patience," Brendan began quietly.

"*Tried* my patience?! *Tried my—*"

Clasping a hand on Faucher's shoulder, Brendan stalled what was sure to be a glorious tirade.

"You are the only one who can teach her. You are the best."

"Nothing you say will convince me," Faucher rumbled, his fiery gaze indomitable.

"If you don't agree to teach her, I understand. Though I will instead assign you as her personal guard and full-time escort for the entire year. Any and all of her blunders will be yours to answer for, and you will not be permitted to teach anyone else during your time at that post."

Faucher's intensity melted from his face. "Threats won't work on me, Your Majesty."

Brendan's smile faded as he released his friend's shoulder. "Threats? Faucher that was not a threat. A threat would be reminding you that you have an unwed daughter, who I could arrange to be married to a Daxarian. In fact, Lady Ashowan has a twin brother who is unwed."

Faucher's face went ghostly pale.

Brendan waited a moment before turning back to his desk and settling down behind it. "Let me know when you've reached a decision."

Faucher didn't move an inch.

"Is it really so important . . . that you would bring Dana into this?"

Brendan raised his gaze, his dark eyes intense.

"Yes, Faucher. It is. This is far bigger and more important than you realize."

For a long moment, Faucher stared at the king, whom he had trained, taught . . . and befriended . . . and in a way . . . loved.

At long last, he let out a defeated sigh, and his face shifted to one of pained apprehension.

"Where am I going to even train her?"

CHAPTER 40

MOTHER-IN-LAW, OH MY

Kat gaped at the sight before her, unable to find the words that would best fit what she was thinking at that moment.

"It's rather . . . imposing . . ." Alina began while clearing her throat.

"I have never seen a 'room' this . . ." Katarina attempted to finish her sentence, but like her friend, was unable to.

"Yeah," Alina cut her off, her casual speech highly indicative of just how deeply shocked she was, especially given that her mother-in-law was standing to her left, staring out across the throne room with deep reverence.

"So this entire room . . . will be filled with people?" Katarina asked slowly before turning to face the former queen.

"It will, yes."

"And we . . . have to decorate and plan for them all to eat and dance here?" Kat continued carefully. At long last, she tore her eyes from the room that made her feel as though she were as insignificant as a fleck of dust in a field.

"That is the custom for coronations, Lady Katarina," Rebecca Devark replied while gracefully picking her way down the marble steps until her foot touched on the ground beneath them. The two younger women remained standing atop of the landing that overlooked the splendor.

The throne room where Alina was to be crowned queen was massive, the marble pillars and ceilings that were impossibly high . . . the heavy navy drapes that framed the three-story glass doors, which opened to an elevated stone and gold-veined marble balcony . . . It was radiant, cavernous, and wildly intimidating . . .

"This room will be filled with nobility, our elite knights as guards and a select few knights from each family's house. After your ceremony, you typically wouldn't be required to make a speech. However . . ." Rebecca eyed Alina for a moment before continuing, her emotions masked, but her stare appraising. "His Majesty has determined that this will be the first time you will address your people. Therefore, you can make no mistakes, and you must be seen as strong as the king himself to avoid their condemnation." Rebecca peered up at her petite daughter-in-law, who was in the process of taking slow, deep breaths.

Kat watched the stress form in the corner of her friend's eyes.

She knew exactly what was troubling her.

It wasn't that she had to speak in front of so many people, and it wasn't that her mother-in-law was informing her that nothing less than perfection would be permitted . . .

It was that Alina knew she would never be able to shout loud enough to be heard in the back of the room. She'd have a breathing episode before she'd get halfway.

A thought occurred to Kat then that had her brightening excitedly.

"Oh . . . I just had a perfect idea . . ." she burst out before turning to her friend, her eyes sparkling.

Katarina noted Rebecca Devark's tensed expression at her words but ignored it and trapped Alina's hands in her own.

"Remember what Keith Lee does during our festivals? With the bowls?"

Alina blinked in confusion for a moment, until her eyes widened with the realization of her friend's idea.

"Gods, Kat, that *is* perfect!"

"We could line them on either side of the aisle as you come down, and for dramatic effect light them up like they do at Winter Solstice!" Kat explained hurriedly, her excitement getting the better of her.

"Need I remind you both, that a coronation is for some people a once-in-a-lifetime event. It is not to be compared to a Winter Solstice celebration," Rebecca Devark warned, her dark eyes hardening, and her hands folding in front of her skirts.

"We aren't comparing the two; it's just a method used back in Daxaria that will make things very effective—" Kat began, but the former queen held up her hand, silencing the redhead.

"Lady Katarina, Lady Sarah is here now with our afternoon refreshments."

Sure enough, the handmaiden appeared in front of a line of maids and stewards who were carrying in tables with cups for cool water and various fruits and meat.

As both Alina and Kat began to descend the stairs to join the former queen, already whispering intently back and forth with each other about Kat's plan, Rebecca Devark stepped forward.

"Lady Katarina, a word."

Kat paused, glancing at Alina, who looked equally confused, but who nodded and released the redhead's hands as she turned to the table that was in the process of being set.

Kat tentatively followed Rebecca while doing her best to straighten her shoulders. She appreciated that she was two inches taller than the woman, but she couldn't deny there was a far superior strength and wisdom surrounding the former queen that made her feel small all the same.

The two stepped so that they were on the opposite side of the long stairs, and despite the massive hall being prone to echoes, Rebecca's words didn't spread far.

"You are a poor influence on Princess Alina."

Kat blinked at the woman, who made the statement in a calm manner without any inflection or passion.

"I was impressed with her in the two days I witnessed her etiquette and respect of our customs, but as soon as you arrived—"

"She smiles more and is excited about things?" Kat cut in, her tone growing a little too accusatory.

"She shows her emotions and acts like a foolish young maiden," Rebecca countered firmly.

"No, she just has someone with her she is free to show how brilliant she is! Do you think His Majesty fell in love with her while she was on her best Troivackian behavior?" Kat snapped, her anger rising steadily.

"That is not the point. She needs to remember she is here in Troivack, where there are enemies lurking around every corner, watching her every move. If she shows them these weaknesses—"

"Her being open to ideas outside of tradition isn't weakness." Kat's words had an edge, and her eyes flashed.

"Whether you believe it or not, Lady Katarina, I am merely trying to help her survive here in Troivack," Rebecca replied, her face stern.

"You're trying to get her to survive. She and I are plotting on her succeeding." A rush of golden magic ran around Kat's eyes as her breaths deepened in an effort to calm down.

Rebecca dropped her voice, though that made her sound all the more severe. "If she wishes to change our kingdom for the better and be heard? If she wishes to be respected and be revered? She will fail if she is seen gossiping with her friend and making plans in whispered giggles; she will doom herself before the coronation."

"We weren't giggling, we were discussing—"

"Do you know why I brought in Lady Sarah?" Rebecca questioned, her tone imperious.

Kat raised her eyebrow coldly. "To show how much you dislike your Daxarian daughter-in-law?"

Rebecca's eyes turned steely. "You would accuse someone so carelessly? A member of royalty far outranking yourself. Do you not see your folly even in *this* moment? Lady Katarina, you are going to be the death of your friend if you are not careful."

"Why did you pose it as a question if you didn't want my honest answer?" The redhead practically growled.

"To make you think!" Rebecca burst out, which in turn made her stop before saying more. She exhaled with closed eyes before once again lifting her gaze and leveling Kat with it. "You two need to show more caution in how you conduct yourselves in front of others."

"And you need to not assume every Daxarian trait and idea is going to be a matter of life or death." Kat managed to keep her voice quiet, but her defensive tone and angry stare were unrestrained.

"Consider who is around you, consider how it could be seen. Remember to hold your true thoughts and intentions to yourself, or else they will be used against you," Rebecca admonished while beginning to stride away, intent on ending the conversation.

"I wonder why Troivackians grow more bitter with their own lives when faced with happiness." Kat's volume had risen, and so a small echo rang out from her as the former queen halted in her tracks and slowly turned.

Rebecca didn't retort, didn't lecture, but her stare . . . her glinting stare made of pure strength . . . of disapproval, of warning . . .

Katarina felt her magical aura appear, flickering before the woman, who eyed it with a small eyebrow lift, then turned to rejoin Alina and Lady Sarah by the refreshments.

The redhead, on the other hand, moved toward the door that led to the room behind the throne where the king and queen would ready and wait for official events and hearings.

Concluding she couldn't be trusted to be close to Rebecca, Kat decided to take a lengthier exit. And so she stormed off through the door in hopes of getting rid of the magitch that was beginning to crawl along her skin. She prayed she wouldn't need too much time to calm down.

* * *

Rebecca Devark marched toward the kitchens to issue the menu for the following day, her head held high as a number of maids and stewards bowed and curtsied to her. Dusk was settling over the castle, and with it a chill that for the first time since the beginning of summer had multiple hearths lit in the noble chambers to keep their inhabitants warm.

Rebecca eyed a chestnut tree that stood outside the window and noted its leaves beginning to yellow.

Fall was descending upon them . . . She would need to begin preparing for the harvest feasts soon . . .

As Rebecca turned around the final corner toward the kitchens, she noticed a flicker of light out of the corner of her eye, drawing her attention.

The door to the cellar was opened a crack . . . A wall sconce had been lit.

Odd, dinner had long been over . . .

As she neared the door, her hand outstretched, she was given a start when it suddenly swept back fully open with great vigor to reveal . . .

The Daxarian prince.

Eric Reyes.

Freezing in place, Rebecca noted in the split second her startle worked its way through her mind that his eyes were cast down, and his wavy blond hair was untied and in a disorderly fashion. He had a cork wedged between his teeth, two bottles pressed to his body, and a single cup clasped in his hand as he proceeded to exit the cellar and close the door behind him.

He took a step and nodded in her direction, revealing that he had sensed her presence there the entire time, but when his eyes registered her identity in passing, he stopped and turned to face Rebecca directly, removing the cork from his teeth.

"Ma'am, good evening." He bowed to her.

"Good evening, Your Highness. Was there something in particular you were searching for?" Rebecca greeted while pretending not to be recovering from the shock.

"Ah, no. Pardon me for startling you." Eric bowed again, and as a result missed Rebecca's subtle expression. He had barely looked at her, and yet he had known he'd caught her off guard . . .

"Your Highness," Rebecca heard herself say the words. There was a strange fluttering in her throat as she said them . . . It was untoward of her to prolong the conversation . . . She knew this . . . and yet . . .

"Might I discuss a couple matters with you? Briefly?" she inquired with a regal bob of her head.

Eric stiffened, his stony gaze disconcerted as he studied her. Then a look of realization dawned over his features, which was shortly followed by relief . . .

"You want to talk about Lady Katarina, don't you?"

The former queen hesitated before she managed to give a single slow nod.

Then, the prince did something she hadn't quite expected . . .

He smiled.

The shadows in those hazel eyes danced, but in that moment of flashing his smile, it felt as though some sort of peace also appeared, albeit fleeting, as though the topic of Lady Katarina was one he was comfortable, in any capacity, in partaking.

"I understand Lady Katarina has a rather . . . strong flavor," Eric managed, his smile fading, though his eyes still crinkled in their corners.

"I fear for her influence over the princess. Lady Katarina could alienate the Troivackian courtiers and as a result destroy the both of them," Rebecca reasoned while inclining her head slightly and eyeing the quiet doors nearby.

Eric turned toward the nearest window ledge and set down the bottles and cup. He selected the bottle he had uncorked and poured from it.

"Honestly, what you don't know is that this is the best behaved anyone has seen Lady Katarina in ages. I haven't been in court for a few years, and when I returned, found that I could not pass a single corner of the castle without hearing some sort of rumor or story about her."

Rebecca's brow furrowed at the information as Eric drained his cup in a single mouthful, then poured another one.

"Forgive me asking, Your Highness, but then why was she permitted to come to Troivack with the princess? What you have said just now only deepens my worries."

At this, Eric turned to regard the former queen with all former levity on his face replaced with weariness.

"That, I am afraid, I cannot answer, ma'am. It was a decision reached by my father and His Majesty King Brendan. I will ask, however, that you're patient with her. I understand this is not an easy request." Eric's tone turned somber, and his eyes inexplicably shifted into darkness yet again as he picked the bottles back up to take his leave.

Rebecca studied the man, who was a year older than her own eldest son yet somehow seemed even more mature . . . the weight of the world bending and breaking him.

"Your eyes are your father's—"

"Ah yes. I'm told I take a great deal after him," Eric cut her off while beginning to place a polite countenance around his features.

"I was going to say your eyes and forehead are your father's, but from the bridge of your nose down to your smile and jaw, is your mother. Her Majesty Ainsley Reyes was a gracious woman. She had a strength I never could fathom."

At this, the prince turned rigid, then with a sad smile, he bowed.

"She was indeed remarkable. I thank you for the compliment, ma'am. I hope you sleep well." Without waiting to hear her response, Eric departed without another look over his shoulder.

The former queen Rebecca Devark was left to stare speculatively at his retreating back.

Interesting . . . I never would've thought I'd see such a thing in his eyes . . . I suppose with his favor behind her, I will need to try and be a little more patient with Lady Katarina. For now.

CHAPTER 41

AN INVITED INTRUSION

It had been two weeks since arriving in Vessa, and Katarina was stir-crazy being stuck within the castle walls with nothing to do but plan for the coronation and constantly mind her manners.

Though after her first dinner where she and Lord Ball had fought a battle of wills, she was mostly ignored during mealtimes, which was both a blessing and a curse. It was far easier to stay out of trouble, but also magnificently dull.

Alina did her best to bolster her friend's spirits, but of course she was busy working on taking over her duties, placating her mother-in-law, actively ignoring Lady Sarah, and also still enjoying the throes of newlywed bliss.

All of this left Kat spending a decent amount of time idly chatting to her familiar, Pina, in the night. At the very least, her stab wound was feeling significantly better, and according to the physician who King Brendan Devark had sent to examine her, she would be fully healed before the coronation!

Yes, it was excellent news, and Kat was desperately hoping that then she would hear more from the king about training with the sword.

A knock on Katarina's chamber door snapped her from her thoughts as she paced back and forth swiftly in the early morning, hoping that she could burn off enough energy so that her skin wouldn't be itching by lunchtime . . .

"Yes?" she called out while eyeing Pina, who was stretched out and asleep comfortably on her windowsill.

"Lady Katarina, His Highness Prince Eric Reyes and Her Highness Princess Alina Reyes are awaiting you in the garden for tea," the voice of a maid rang out from the other side of the closed door.

"Shit, right . . . !" Kat scurried over to pick up the shoes she had kicked off after breakfast. One was in front of the fireplace while the other rested beside her bed.

Hastily, she dove for the door and wrenched it open while panting slightly. "Completely forgot, thank you for the reminder."

The maid eyed her coldly, but proceeded to bow her head.

Katarina wasn't sure what had prompted it, but sometime around the end of her first week in the castle, the serving staff had started to treat her rather disdainfully . . .

Doing her best to ignore the servant's visible disrespect, the redhead proceeded to follow the maid out of her room and down the corridor. She eyed the dim day outside with a small sigh.

Apparently fall weather in Troivack involved mostly cloudy days as its normally scorching earth gradually cooled. While some people had already begun to wear warmer clothes, Katarina remained perfectly comfortable in a short sleeve dark green dress with a V neckline and a thin golden belt, which rested on her hips—a nod to the Daxarian style. Her dress remained light and fluttery as she yet again was unaffected by the cold, and while some noblewomen had opted to forgo wearing large amounts of metal that could grow cold against their skin, Katarina's wrists were still adorned as always with her golden bracelets.

Descending the grand stone staircase, then winding down and around to the north side of the castle, Katarina exited to the expansive gardens that were filled with gravel paths and flourishing fall blooms of yellow and deep purples.

Near the center were four wrought iron arches that positioned themselves around a cobbled center where a temporary canopy had been constructed, and under it, was a black iron table with matching chairs. Tea along with fruit and biscuits had been laid out between the two people already present . . .

Eric and Alina.

The Daxarian prince wore his usual off-white peasant-quality tunic and leather vest. Though instead of faded, worn black trousers, he wore ones of cream color with fine brown boots . . . This indicated a small amount of effort had gone into his appearance. Across from him, in a burnt orange dress with gold edging, her long wavy blond hair partially swept back, sat his sister.

The siblings were clearly partaking in a thick serving of uncomfortable silence. Alina's gaze drifted idly from her steaming tea to the flowers, and Eric appeared to be observing either the castle or the sky in his usual nonchalant manner.

Letting out a small, determined yet disapproving sigh, Katarina straightened her shoulders and flipped her red hair back.

"Well, good day, Your Highnesses!" she called out loudly, making the maid escorting her shoot her another withering stare over her shoulder.

This was a fact that Alina missed, but Eric noted with a casual glance of disapproval in the maid's direction, motivating the woman to flinch and bow.

Kat noticed none of this as she descended upon the Reyes siblings gracelessly and plunked herself down in the chair to Alina's right.

"Hi, Kat." Alina breathed, gratitude filling her smile.

Eric grunted while lifting his cup to his mouth and taking a gulp.

"Sorry I'm late; completely lost track of time!" Kat gushed easily as a steward stepped forward and poured her a cup of tea that had her nodding her thanks. "So, what were you two discussing?"

"Nothing of consequence," Alina replied mildly, though her eyes were sharp on her brother's features, glinting more amber than green that day.

Eric remained unaffected by the stare as he continued allowing his attention to drift around the gardens.

"Ah . . . so . . . Eric, what is it you've been doing as of late? I hear you haven't attended any council meetings," Kat began conversationally, though as a result, Alina stiffened.

Shit, I should've brought Pina with me to help—wait. She's my familiar! I can summon her!

Kat closed her eyes and reached out to her connection with her familiar. It was hard to find at first. It was such a gentle thread . . . soft even . . . much like Pina's fur . . . She had never summoned her before . . . but . . . Eric and Alina needed all the help they could get. That much was obvious.

Pina . . . please come . . . I need your assistance in the garden . . .

"Are you falling asleep?" Eric's dry tone interrupted Kat's thoughts as she cracked open an eye and scowled at him.

"I'm summoning my familiar, if you must know," the redhead responded before leaning back and crossing her leg while her right arm draped itself around the back of the chair. "You didn't answer my question."

Something flickered through Eric's dull eyes . . . a strange emotion that Kat didn't understand . . . because it seemed something like relief . . .

Oh . . .

It was the first time she had spoken to him since that early morning in the courtyard when he'd confessed more of his haunted past to her.

It wasn't that Katarina had avoided Eric on purpose! It was that there truly hadn't been the opportunity to be around each other . . .

"I've been working with the Troivackian knights to try and figure out where the assassins originated and where they might be hiding now," Eric explained while reaching forward and plucking a small bunch of grapes that he leaned back in his chair with.

"Have you found anything?" Alina asked seriously, as she couldn't help but shift a little closer to her brother.

"There are holdings that exist in remote locations that could act as a base of sorts for two of the attacks. One belonging to a baron, the other a marquess. We will be riding out to investigate in a week's time. We should be returning before your coronation, and hopefully that will be the end of the threats, and you won't have to worry anymore." Eric's head bowed toward his sister, his eyes unable to meet hers as his shoulders hunched ever so slightly.

Alina took a deep breath that only Katarina saw, and it was then the two women locked eyes and shared a silent conversation.

"You're going with them, are you? His Majesty permitted that?" Alina asked tightly.

"Captain Orion is asking for my inclusion this afternoon at the council meeting," Eric replied as he dropped the grapes back onto his plate.

"I see." Alina's attention lowered to her teacup, her expression stony as she proceeded to take a dainty sip of her beverage.

Kat winced, then attempted again to save the conversation. "Well . . . I mean . . . it's good news that hopefully the death threats will stop. Was there any mention of Duke Icarus?"

Both Alina and Eric's eyes snapped up to her.

"Where did you hear about Duke Icarus?" Alina blurted, her gaze sharp on her friend's face.

Katarina blinked in surprise. "Sebbie told me about him. He was trying to scare me into behaving. You know how he is . . . I hear he's been privately tutoring you." Kat nodded slowly to the princess. Then she slid her questioning stare to Eric, who was rolling his eyes briefly before closing and rubbing them in exasperation. "What's wrong . . . ?"

"Kat . . . don't throw around his name so easily. That man has the possibility to be a kingmaker if we don't tread carefully. Also, *Mage* Sebastian most likely told you that information to caution you. Duke Icarus is not to be taken lightly," Alina warned, a chastising note entering her voice.

Kat faltered.

Alina's disapproving and even borderline mothering tone . . . Eric's condescending head shake . . .

The redheaded witch glared.

"Sebbie chucked the duke's name at me casually enough. He didn't add a ton of import to the man, so I was unaware," she informed them coldly.

"He is *Mage* Sebastian, Kat. He's going to become the royal court mage once His Majesty finishes persuading the council members. We're hoping shortly after the coronation we can make it so. You know magic has been frowned upon since—"

"Ah yes, since my grandfather," Kat interjected breezily, though her golden gaze shone a little brighter.

Alina's eyes widened in alarm, and Eric gave the slightest of grimaces.

"Kat, quiet! You know that Aidan Helmer changed the entire kingdom's view of magic. Don't tie yourself to him! Especially because—"

"Especially because of *what*?" Kat interrupted Alina, a small glow appearing around herself.

"You know you've already made a terrible first impression," Eric volunteered, his tone indicative of the obvious point he made.

"W-What?! Truly?! I've barely done anything aside from that first dinner!"

"You made the former queen raise her voice. She's *never* been heard doing such a thing," Alina explained patiently.

"You've also become known to show your facial expressions as easily as the sun is seen on a cloudless day," Eric continued before reaching for his tea and taking a hearty gulp.

Kat stared first at Eric, then Alina, in open betrayal.

"I come here to help, because you two cowards can't be left alone to figure things out, and yet all you two do as a family is throw me under the carriage! What a fine thanks this is." Kat huffed before reaching for an apple and biting into it while eyeing her company with open irritation.

Eric raised an eyebrow and shook his head with a humorless laugh, but Alina turned to face her friend more squarely. "I mean it, Kat. I really can't do much to help you at this point."

"So how am I supposed to fix it then?" the redhead asked while leaning back in her chair and crossing her right arm over her middle, her shoulders tensed as a particularly biting gust of wind passed through.

"Hide your expressions more . . . be a little quieter . . . You really should join me for my lessons with Mage Sebastian." Alina fidgeted with her thumb. A sure sign she was feeling uncomfortable.

Kat grinned. "Ask Sebbie how he feels about that."

Alina raised an eyebrow. "Kat, I know Mage Keith Lee wasn't your favorite person in the world, but you did like his father. Don't tell me you're biased against Sebastian just because he is a mage."

"Pfft. No, no. It's because he's a sexist, arrogant arse. Though I'd like to say we bonded a little by the end of the trip."

"That's because you actually slept most of the last few days of the journey. Not to mention I imagine he was a little worried about you—" Eric jumped in while slowly crossing his arms.

"You? Sleeping? Why was Mage Sebastian worried about you?" Alina frowned while regarding Kat, who was in the middle of making a slicing motion with her hand across her neck while staring at Eric.

"Erm. Well, you see . . . It wasn't for any specific reason . . . I-I-Oh, there's Pina! Thank Gods . . ." Kat muttered the last part hastily as she stood and watched as the maids and stewards shift in confusion and ill-hidden excitement as the small kitten trotted over to them.

Even the maid who had been rude to Kat couldn't help but lean over to the steward nearest her and whisper, "She's so cute!"

Stepping around the table and scooping up her familiar, Kat proceeded to pepper one of her soft cheeks with kisses while scratching the other cheek lovingly, which in turn earned some hearty purrs.

"Why did you summon your familiar here?" Eric asked while watching with the faintest of amused smiles.

"Well . . . Alina, you're still annoyed with your brother, right?" Kat asked bluntly without lifting her gaze from Pina's face.

"Wh-What?" Alina blushed and was unable to look at the prince, whose lightened expression faded.

"Don't worry. It'll be easier to stare at him when I do this."

Kat proceeded to place Pina on Eric's shoulder, where she perched tenuously for a moment. Her tiny paws shifting uncertainly.

"Wh-What are you—" Eric began but was cut off with a wince of pain as Pina's back paw slipped, making one of her claws pierce through the prince's shirt. "I don't think she likes this; take her off."

No sooner had Eric said the words than Pina leaned in toward his cheek, her small round eyes crossing as she stared at him closely, while her freckled pink nose twitched with interest.

"Gods . . . that *is* adorable . . ." Alina said breathily, unable to stop a bright smile appearing on her lips.

Eric turned, not fully understanding the appeal of what the kitten was doing, when he locked eyes with the feline staring up at him.

His lips twitched.

She leaned forward and rubbed her cheek against his.

"Aw!"

Kat turned around and noticed the sentiment had been uttered by one of the guards watching, who didn't seem at all bothered that he was . . . in fact . . . *smiling*.

Though . . . everyone . . . was . . . smiling . . .

Kat looked back to her familiar, stunned as the realization of Pina's effect on everyone sunk in.

However, before she could begin to think through the implications, the kitten proceeded to nibble the very tip of Eric's nose, and suddenly . . . everyone was gushing and exclaiming all at once . . . even Kat, her alarm all at once forgotten at the new adorable feat Pina had just performed for her unworthy audience.

CHAPTER 42

MAIDENLY MEETINGS

Kat was sitting and reading in the solar while Alina, Lady Sarah, and the former Troivackian queen worked on their embroidery.

It was quiet, and the dinner hour was nearing, which Kat was more than thrilled about, as her beastly appetite was returning alongside her improving health.

A knock on the chamber door, however, interrupted the ladies from their tentative peace.

After calling out permission for the steward to enter, they were apprised of the cause of his visit.

"Your Highness, Lady Kezia Devark has returned with Lady Wynonna Vesey."

Rebecca Devark's face stiffened as Alina fought a smile at the news.

"Wonderful. I take it they are bathing and preparing for dinner?" the princess replied smoothly while rising.

"Yes, Your Highness."

"Thank you for the message. If you could please tell the ladies to join us here after they've washed, I'd like to take the time to introduce Lady Katarina to them before we sup." Alina nodded to Kat, a happy shine in her eyes that made Kat smile fondly despite Rebecca Devark's cold stare.

Lady Sarah eyed the sunny expression with a raised eyebrow but said nothing.

When Kat finally noticed the Troivackians' reactions, she couldn't help but become defensive. "I'm trying. I swear. Imagine if you came to Daxaria and were expected to smile, would you be able to change immediately?"

Lady Sarah frowned, while the former queen's face remained smooth.

"You had a year to prepare, Lady Katarina," Rebecca reminded calmly.

"It's not like I went around not smiling that entire year either. If I did that . . . Gods . . ." Kat shook her head, unwilling to imagine the ludicrous things her father or even her other beloved household members might do to draw out her good mood. Raymond would have picked her up and shaken her to loose a smile or laugh from her, or he would constantly press peach rum pies in her face . . . Her father might have taken her on a sky ride or made some elaborate dessert that resembled something silly. Once he had made a sausage look like a dog by using thin skewers to create the dog's legs and head out of other bits of sausage and some olives. Tam, her brother, maybe would have gone along with one of her wilder impulses. Her mother . . . her mother would have taught her a nifty new knife trick . . .

As she thought about her family and the warmth of her home, a pang reverberated through Katarina's chest, making her adjust the mustard-colored pillows surrounding her on the bench to hide her expression. She often situated herself under one of the three windows when the women convened in the solar, the spot being one that placed her at the farthest distance from Lady Sarah and the Troivackian queen while also getting a spectacular outside view.

No one said anything more, though the air was heavy following Kat's outburst . . .

Another hour passed in the quiet, and then a knock rang out.

"Your Highness, Ladies Kezia Devark and Wynonna Vesey have arrived," the steward announced behind the closed door.

Alina didn't even attempt to hide her eagerness as she rose from her seat, her embroidery tossed immediately to the side.

"Enter!"

Kat eyed her friend's eagerness with a faint, good-humored chuckle, before turning her attention to the final two handmaidens.

Lady Kezia Devark, her middle rounded with her first child, was divinely beautiful.

Her eyes were an electrifying blue with the occasional dark streaks that contrasted ethereally. She had olive skin, raven hair that fell in thick, sculpted waves midway down her back, and she wore a black ribbon around her throat that bore an oval silver locket. Her dress, a royal blue with a black belt wrapped under her bosom, made her pregnant bump almost come as a surprise.

Lady Wynonna Vesey, however, was incredibly different . . .

She wore a dark wrapping that hid her hair, much like Rebecca Devark, though she also wore a veil that draped down her back. Her face was pale, her eyebrows titian, and her eyes . . . green . . . or blue . . . or gray . . . remained downcast. Unlike Lady Kezia, who stood nearly six feet, the other newcomer stood several inches shorter with hunched shoulders.

Katarina gaped at Lady Kezia's beauty, her thoughts melting to a pile of mush, barely noting Lady Wynonna.

"Lady Kezia! At last!" Alina crossed the room eagerly while reaching out to grab her sister-in-law's hands.

Kezia then did something strange.

She smiled.

As a result, Katarina began to question whether she could possibly be attracted to women as well as men . . .

"Ah, sister, it is wonderful to see you in good health." Kezia's voice was every bit as beautiful as the rest of her. It was lyrical and clear, though there was an airy quality that made her seem all the more untouchable.

"Yes, I am doing wonderfully. Lady Wynonna, it is a pleasure to have you join us. I thank you for your service," Alina addressed the meek noblewoman, who gave a small curtsy, though she looked a little unsteady on her feet.

"Lady Kezia, this here is Lady Sarah Miller." Alina turned to Sarah, who was watching the two newcomers with disapproval aglow in her dark eyes.

"Ah, yes. We have been acquainted," Kezia nodded her chin casually to the woman, which in turn made Sarah frown.

"Lady Wynonna Vesey, I do not believe I've had the opportunity to meet," Lady Sarah stepped forward, her stare sharp and condescending on the turned face of the woman, who despite obviously being Daxarian, was a Troivackian noble . . .

Lady Wynonna curtsied again, bowed her head, but didn't say a word.

Alina eyed the widow with a small, perplexed frown.

Sensing the growing unease in the room, Kezia's attention drifted over to Katarina.

"Oh, my! You must be Viscount Ashowan's daughter, Lady Katarina!" She moved forward, her smile warming.

"H-Hi!" Kat returned, still flummoxed from the beauty before her. "Y-You're . . . uh . . . wow."

Kezia laughed, and Kat nearly fainted.

"You're just as incredible as Princess Alina described! Those golden eyes . . . You have a great life planned for you, I can tell," Kezia announced sincerely, with her voice tinkling. She then reached out and gently clasped Kat's hands in her own.

The redhead's face flushed as she struggled to find the words to respond.

"Lady K-Kezia, how . . . is it . . . we have not met sooner?" Kat finally managed, though she was still unable to meet Kezia's eyes.

"Ah, well . . . in Norum, Henry was rather surprised with my sudden appearance, and so we left to return here quickly. After a brief recovery here in Vessa, we received word that Lady Wynonna was having difficulties organizing her departure to come serve Her Highness, so I went to assist her. Though given that I am growing a little more rotund, I imagine I should stay close to my husband from now on," she explained, her brilliant blue eyes amiable as they studied Kat's features.

"Y-You're not rotund, you're . . . stunning," Kat blurted awkwardly while Alina couldn't help but grin at her normally unflappable friend's clumsy reaction to her sister-in-law's beauty.

"I thank you for your kind words, Lady Katarina. However, if you speak too many of them, I fear you may make my dear husband a bit jealous. So would you mind if we state here and now that we are to be wonderful friends?"

"Of . . . of course . . . Lady Kezia." Katarina finally met the noblewoman's eyes and smile, though her cheeks deepened in color yet again.

"Ladies, you must be famished from your travels. Shall we retire for dinner?" Rebecca called out, her chin raised high, and her imperious voice easily bringing everyone's attention to her.

"Of course, ma'am, you are quite correct." Alina's smile faded as her mother-in-law cast an appraising eye at her. When she faced her new handmaidens once more, Alina gestured to the exit with a slight incline of her head.

Kezia gave Katarina a wink, then turned to the door and took her leave, followed by the former Troivackian queen, then Alina, who glanced at the widow Lady Wynonna Vesey with a small tilt of her head before sending a brief glance in Kat's direction.

It was all that was needed for the redhead to understand what her friend was asking of her.

Noting Lady Wynonna's gently clasped pale hands and bowed face, Kat ignored all Troivackian decorum and gave the woman a friendly smile.

"Hi there, I bet it's a little intimidating seeing us all at once. As you probably heard, I'm Lady Katarina Ashowan. I see you're Daxarian! Have you been in Troivack long?"

At long last, Lady Wynonna lifted her face to stare at Kat, revealing her age to be in her early thirties.

Her eyes were wide as she peered up into Kat's striking face, and then, without further ado, she opened her mouth, and burped.

Kat let out a laugh of surprise, until she realized she smelled . . .

Moonshine.

The widow was drunk!

Grinning, she reached out and clasped the lady's hand. Her face had already turned a fantastic shade of fuchsia.

"I can tell we'll get along just fine." Kat pulled Lady Wynonna's hand through the crook of her arm and turned toward the door, suddenly in wonderful spirits. "Now, stick by my side, and no one will know a thing! Though, I must inquire . . . do you have any . . . *libations* you might be willing to share with a new friend?"

The widow gave a small, nervous smile and leaned in close. "Most of my luggage is actually just moonshine."

Kat's eyes sparkled in delight. "Splendid!"

Officially, the entourage to the future queen of Troivack had gathered, and the group of misfits were set to ensure Alina Reyes would find nothing but success!

This was assuming, of course, they could manage the rest of the Troivackian courtiers . . . a feat they hadn't even deigned to think about tackling just yet . . .

With the arrival of the new handmaidens, the seating arrangement at the lone, long rectangular table had shifted, and as a result, Katarina found herself with Lady Wynonna on her left, Prince Eric on her right, and Kezia across from her.

While Lady Wynonna did a smashing job of downing at least half a bottle's worth of red wine, Eric was rather stiff.

It had been a while since Katarina had been so close to him, and he had forgotten the heat that she exuded. It must have been the odd sensation that was making his heart thrum a little more noticeably in his chest . . .

"Is my sister's new handmaiden inebriated by chance?" Eric asked quietly as he reached forward and sipped his own goblet without alerting anyone that he was addressing the redhead.

"She is indeed. Poor woman must've been nervous coming to court as a Daxarian," Kat answered breezily.

"I've heard rumors that she wasn't taking the death of her husband well," Eric continued while cutting into his pheasant.

"That could put a damper on one's spirits, I imagine."

"Depends on the wife," he managed to say before taking a bite of his food.

"Or the husband," Kat interjected helpfully before she, too, reached for her wine goblet. When he didn't pick up the conversation again, she leaned in a little closer. Unbeknownst to her, Eric froze as a result of the tingling rush that swept through him. "By the way, you aren't really going to investigate the potential hiding spots of the assassins yourself, are you? Not after you *just* attempted to run away."

"I rather like my legs intact, and if I did try to run, they would not remain so. His Majesty is still considering it," Eric replied calmly.

It was beginning to dawn on the prince that he wasn't entirely certain when talking about his demons and follies with Katarina Ashowan had become so comfortable . . . He hadn't ever intended to share with anyone as much as he had with her, but there was something appealing about the way she didn't pity him, or weep for him, or offer sweet condolences. Instead, she often responded in a matter-of-fact way that let him feel like he still had a grasp on some tendril of normalcy—when she wasn't insulting him, of course . . .

"Word to the wise, Alina will be furious if you do go to investigate with the knights," Kat interrupted his thoughts, her tone careful as she reached for her cutlery and speared a roasted carrot.

"I don't understand why. I barely see her as is."

"And whose fault is that? You know her main pass time is embroidering these days, right?"

"She could be the one to arrange the time between us then," Eric pointed out, finally risking a glance at Kat and immediately regretting it, as a magnetic pull toward her golden eyes had him faltering yet again.

It took him a moment longer than he had intended to look away, and then it took another breath longer to once again seem casual.

Three people had then taken notice of the exchange as a result . . .

"Or *you* could be the one to arrange the meetings. She wrote to you endlessly for four years . . . It seems only fair that you take some of the initiative." Kat's tone, while teasing, carried with it a note of sincerity.

Eric let out a long sigh, unable to stop the smallest of smiles before he shot her another good-humored side-glance while she feigned sipping her goblet and looking to the ceiling innocently.

"Will you stop tormenting me if I acquiesce?"

"Your Highness, I can't believe you would suggest such a thing," Katarina exclaimed indignantly while revealing the full might of her wolfish smile and glancing at Eric playfully in return.

"You're right. I don't think there is anything in this world that could make you give up your favorite hobby."

Kat couldn't help but let out a small snort and took in a breath to issue another witty retort, but he cut her off before she could.

"By the way, that dress?"

Kat stopped, blinked in confusion, then looked down at the fluttering lavender gown. "What about it?"

"It makes you look like a pastry topping. It doesn't suit you. Darker colors are better for you." Eric reached for his goblet while Kat poked her tongue into her cheek and pursed lips as she stared at him with a raised eyebrow, her eyes dancing. The urge to smack his shoulder was fierce, but even she knew that would garner all kinds of disapproval around the table.

"Well, your ponytail looks like a dirty pup's snipped tail."

He grinned back at her. "I've figured out why you never dance at balls."

Kat stilled, her eyes fixed on his face, breathless for a moment.

"If your foot and finger tapping are any indication, you can't keep tempo to save your life."

She let out a breathy laugh, all at once delighted at the banter, when a small throat clearing drew their attention.

The pair found themselves staring at Prince Henry, who was giving them a strained smile while his wife was doing her best to hide her grin behind the rim of her goblet. Eric caught the gaze of the Troivackian king, then Alina's.

Both looked far less amused and a great deal more ominous . . .

His smile fading, Eric returned his attention to his plate. An uncomfortable wave of self-consciousness washed over him, and he didn't dare address Kat again.

He couldn't help but have a bleak premonition that he was going to be having yet another unpleasant conversation with the Troivackian king . . . and he didn't need great wisdom to know what it would be about.

CHAPTER 43

THE DEALINGS OF THE DEVARKS

Katarina was nearly skipping out of the dining hall after her evening meal, her spirits high and the promise of consuming her long awaited Troivackian moonshine guaranteed, thanks to the newest handmaiden for the princess, Lady Wynonna Vesey.

The redhead had made it all the way up to her chamber and was even able to ignore the whisperings from the maids that trailed behind her as though they were attached to the skirts she wore, when she realized Prince Henry and his wife, Lady Kezia, stood in front of her chambers.

There was a tension between them as they faced each other. The couple shared an obvious attraction as they gazed upon each other, but with Kezia's arms folded across her middle and Prince Henry's look of exasperation, it was evident they were in a disagreement about something . . .

Given that they are standing in front of my chamber, I'm guessing this has something to do with me. Katarina resisted slumping her shoulders forward.

She'd been having such a lovely evening . . .

"Ah, Lady Katarina," Prince Henry greeted, clearly forcing a note of cheeriness into his voice while Lady Kezia breezily waved away the two maids behind the redhead.

"Yes, hello, Your Highness. Lady Kezia . . ." Kat greeted as she glanced over her shoulder and noted the two servants silently disappearing back down the corridor.

"Lady Katarina, we were hoping for a quick word with you," Prince Henry began while his wife shot him a sidelong, sardonic glance before shifting her attention to the redhead.

Once again, Katarina was floored by Kezia's beauty; her fierce expression made Kat weak at the knees.

"We-Well, sure . . . what can I . . . How can I help you?" she managed while barely tearing her dazed stare from Kezia to Henry.

"We need to speak with you about Prince Eric."

At this, Katarina's expression grew guarded. "What about him?"

Henry briefly looked at his wife before casting an uncharacteristically somber expression toward Kat.

"Your interaction with His Highness at dinner this evening was . . ." he trailed off, unable to find the words.

Katarina turned to Kezia, who gave a small, adorable huff before fixing her electrifying gaze on the redheaded noblewoman.

"You and the prince displayed the camaraderie of lovers. Everyone noted it at dinner. The rumors had just begun to quiet down, and now they are aflame once more. Are you certain there are no marriage talks between your father and the Daxarian king?"

Kat felt as though her brain had been doused in sudsy water, her mind fizzling in confusion and wholly unable to fathom just what was happening.

"You mean . . . when I insulted him?"

"Was that what you were doing? Because from everyone else's viewpoint, he looked quite enamored with whatever you were saying," Kezia informed Kat, her voice soft and alluring as she stepped closer.

Henry meanwhile looked pained as he rubbed his mouth worriedly before attempting to speak again. "You chucked him in pig slop. I had thought he irritated you in some way, but after tonight . . . Lady Katarina, I have to ask . . . what is the nature of your relationship?"

Kat felt a strange cocktail of emotions brew in her gut. Irritation, defensiveness, vulnerability and . . . vulnerability? Bashfulness?

Why on earth would that be happening?

"Wait, What is this about pig slop?" Kezia turned to her husband with a befuddled frown, which in turn helped to snap Kat out of her strange thoughts.

"His Highness and I enjoy insulting each other without political recourse. Or so we did before your observations," she explained at last with a vaguely annoyed sigh.

Kezia continued studying the redhead silently before the corners of her lips quirked upward and a strange knowingness filled her effervescent gaze.

"Then why did you two look—" Henry started, but his wife lay a patient hand on his arm stopping him.

"My dear, I think I have grasped the situation. Perhaps we leave things be for tonight. I am quite tired from traveling today." She turned the full power of her blue eyes to her husband, and all at once, his attention was completely absorbed as he gently clasped her upper arms.

"Of course, my dear. How thoughtless of me. Good evening, Lady Katarina." Henry didn't even glance at the redhead as he carefully guided his wife back up the corridor while whispering questions about whether she ate well on their trip and whether she had felt any of the babe's movements.

Katarina found herself smiling at their backs, an ache appearing in her chest.

While she was no stranger to witnessing couples deeply in love—after all her parents were one of the most notorious matches in Daxaria—something about their obvious adoration filled her with an emotion she couldn't place.

Turning toward her chamber with a shake of her head, Kat's mind shifted to the questions they had asked about her and Eric's relationship.

Had it really been so strange? Hadn't they ever teased their friends?

With an irritated grunt, Kat clasped the door handle to her room and decided that the Troivackians were the ones overreacting.

Besides, she should be happy! She had made a new ally who enjoyed Troivackian moonshine, and who was willing to share! And given that Alina still had yet to send her the bottle she had promised in exchange for attending the tea meeting earlier that day, she couldn't be more pleased with this new development.

Eric stared at the king and his sister flatly. While Brendan Devark sat in his office chair glowering at him, Alina stood, her arms folded and her gaze unimpressed.

The king's desk was even messier than the first time Eric had visited, and he had already removed his fine black coat and rolled up his sleeves following the dinner.

"What is it?" Eric broke the tense silence, wanting to hurry the process along.

"Do you remember how I asked you and Lady Katarina to avoid each other due to the rumors in order to protect Lady Katarina's reputation?" Brendan began, his voice a low rumble.

"Right, and of course I was the one to draw up the seating plan." The prince's glib response made Alina's eyes narrow.

"I had asked you before if you were going to officially court her, and you made it clear that it was not your intention. Is it that you care so little for her that you would irresponsibly cause a scandal?" Brendan continued, his dark stare flashing ominously.

Eric took a slow breath in, his hazel eyes growing darker as he looked at the floor.

He knew that the king's concern wasn't entirely unreasonable.

Some part of him knew he was being drawn to Katarina more and more, and it was a slippery slope with an ending he couldn't quite make out . . . which made it all the more important to avoid her . . . It was just harder than he had realized it'd be.

"Eric, are you flirting with her for fun? Or do you actually *care* about Kat?" Alina asked quietly, her face softening as she regarded her brother's serious expression. For once, he didn't look as though he were being evasive or defensive . . .

The prince lifted his tired face to his sister, a small half smile tilting his mouth upward.

"I believe I'm being careless, just as your husband said. Katarina is familiar to me because of her father, but His Majesty is right in that it is all the more reason to be mindful. There is no ill-intent between the lady and me." Eric bowed, his gaze shuttered, which succeeded in making both Alina and Brendan wary.

"Alina, may I have a word alone with your brother?" Brendan's attention remained fixed on Eric's bowed head, but he still reached out and gently squeezed Alina's hands.

For a moment, she took exception to being dismissed, but there was a strange understanding in the king's eyes that prompted her not to argue with him. And so she planted a kiss on Brendan's temple, making him smile before she swept from the room, leaving the two alone.

For several moments, the fire crackling in the hearth was the only sound in the chamber as Brendan leaned back in his chair and folded his hands over his flat belly. Eric had already straightened and was staring at the king calmly in wait for whatever lecture he was about to receive.

"You don't simply care for the lady. You're attracted to her like a moth to a flame, aren't you?"

Eric frowned and opened his mouth to object.

"You don't want to hurt her," Brendan continued, his voice casual, but his eyes piercing. Eric met it head-on, but there was a strange rising panic in his chest . . .

"I also can see that you know that if things were to proceed, you aren't strong enough to bear the responsibility it'd entail. I respect your wishes, but you must first admit to yourself that there is something to everyone's suspicions. Once you do that, it should be motivating enough for you to take avoiding interacting with Lady Katarina more seriously."

Eric didn't say anything, although he couldn't deny an uncomfortable rush in his stomach that was shortly followed by an unpleasant grip on his heart.

After another beat of forcing his deadened stare to remain locked with the king's, he gave another small bow and left the room.

Brendan sat in the quiet of his office, his eyes staring down blindly at the work on his desk, lost in thought.

He believed he understood what the prince of Daxaria was feeling . . . but he also recognized that Eric Reyes did not have any sort of mental capacity to overcome what he would need in order to pursue a relationship with Lady Katarina.

With a sigh, he closed his eyes and shook his head.

Ah well.

As if there wasn't enough on his plate . . .

"Ma'am, a word," Alina called out in the shadowed corridor after she finally found her mother-in-law.

Rebecca Devark was talking to two maids who Alina couldn't identify from where she stood, but she didn't pay that any mind as she stepped closer and gave a quick bow of her head that the former queen returned.

"Yes, Your Highness?" Rebecca asked serenely.

Alina glanced at the retreating backs of the two maids, ensuring they were out of earshot before turning to face her mother-in-law, her gaze calculating.

"I found the seating arrangement tonight . . . odd. I recognize that these duties typically fall to the queen of the castle, and you have been generous in insisting to carry on these tasks while I adjust here," Alina began as she stared boldly into Rebecca's eyes.

The former queen said nothing.

"Why did you place His Highness and Lady Katarina beside each other when it is well-known that we are trying to douse the rumors?" Alina asked directly, her gaze never wavering from the queen's dark eyes that strongly resembled her husband's.

Rebecca's eyebrows raised as she slowly clasped her fingers in front of her ivory skirts.

"If there is nothing to the rumors, then there is nothing to hide."

Alina's features hardened. "Rumors come from excitable minds, not critical reasoning, and I know you are not foolish enough to think otherwise."

Rebecca's gaze narrowed ever so slightly, and she tilted her head regally.

"Very well. I did so to gauge the true nature of their relationship."

Alina smiled.

Though it wasn't the type of smile that would get her in trouble for being foolish . . . It was cold—a warning traced itself along her face as a result. "Ah. You are trying to discover just how much power and favor Lady Katarina has in Daxaria by observing how close she is with my brother."

Rebecca looked pleased by her daughter-in-law's keen observation as she straightened her shoulders and continued observing her.

Alina didn't care.

"Ma'am, regardless of how you tested your vassals in the past, I do not approve of your methods. If you attempt to wield power over those in my charge, I will not let it be. I will issue you one piece of cautionary advice regarding Lady Katarina Ashowan." She stepped forward, her eyes suddenly every bit as dark as her brother's . . . "If you cross or defame her in any manner, you will bring the wrath of not only her family, but my own. Am I clear?"

Rebecca regarded Alina studiously for a moment. The former queen was irritatingly unmoved as she straightened and let out a long breath. "She is dear to you. Don't allow your fondness to blind you. She could be not only your undoing but your brother's as well, from what I've seen."

Alina let out a humorless laugh.

"You know, ma'am, if I didn't know better, I would say Lady Katarina scares you."

At long last, Rebecca looked irked.

"I have survived far worse than the likes of Lady Katarina, and I will continue to do so. My concern stems for my son, Your Highness. I will not allow him to be placed in more jeopardy than necessary for the sake of a viscount's daughter."

Alina stared at her mother-in-law for a long moment. She debated how much more to say but in the end settled on, "Your son is old enough to make his own decisions. I have said my piece; take heed of it."

Without giving a proper bow or nod of farewell, Alina departed, her back straight and her footsteps silent, leaving the former queen in the darkened hall.

Staring after the small blond woman, Rebecca took a quiet fortifying breath.

She is strong. That is good. As long as she is capable of following through on her threats, she will survive here . . . Now I just need to figure out why my son has brought Lady Katarina to Troivack and what to do about the obvious affection the Daxarian prince has for her . . .

CHAPTER 44

AUGMENTING ATTENTION

"Your Highness!"

Eric didn't hear Captain Orion calling him as he struck the straw dummy over and over, his mind lost in a maze of thoughts. Sweat poured from his brow as he repeatedly dealt powerful, expert blows that had more than one Troivackian knight stopping their own training to watch in interest.

"Your Highness!" the captain tried again, this time stepping into the prince's line of sight.

Eric's dark hazel eyes at long last snapped up. Without a second thought, he finished his set of blows rapidly, then sheathed his sword, earning even more murmurs of admiration from those around him.

"I received His Majesty's final decision regarding you joining us in our investigation," the captain began as he bowed to Eric.

Panting, the prince placed his hands on his hips and nodded permission for him to speak again.

The captain was seven years younger than Eric, and the young man, while bold in voice, still had an uncertain air in the way he carried himself. His black hair was straight and a few inches in length. His sideburns were trimmed close to his face and ran down to his jawline. He was tall and broad-shouldered, but he hadn't yet built the hulking muscles most of the military men surrounding him had due to his youth.

"You are to remain here in the castle and help Leader Faucher train the new knights who were hired recently," Captain Orion informed the prince once he had straightened. He barely managed to meet Eric's eyes. The leader of Troivack's military would never admit that the Daxarian prince's haunted gaze chilled him.

"I see," Eric replied, his voice tight.

After the previous night's discussion with his brother-in-law, he had to confess he was rather surprised that he *wasn't* being sent away . . .

"In fact, five of the new knights have arrived just now. Would you be able to greet them, Your Highness?" Captain Orion asked. His right hand rested on the hilt of his sword, and he gingerly rubbed his thumb along the grip.

Eric let out a slower breath as he turned and snagged his towel off the dummy's shoulder and wiped the sweat from his face and back of his neck.

"Very well," he agreed. He was still clutching the worn leather scabbard in his hand while he set himself to fastening the attached belt around his hips.

As Eric moved amongst the men who all towered over him, he tried to bring his thoughts to the present, though it was proving difficult, as his gut brewed warily.

Katarina Ashowan . . . She was impossible to ignore. He enjoyed being around her. He didn't believe he wanted more than her friendship . . . though he couldn't deny he was attracted to her . . . What man wouldn't be? She looked as though she belonged to another world with her golden eyes and brilliant hair . . .

"Your Highness, this here is Mr. Broghan Miller, Lord Miller's youngest son."

The captain's voice once again interrupted the prince's thoughts as he gestured to the first of five men who stood before the stone building that was detached from the castle where the captain's office door stood open.

The men stood at attention, their feet all braced apart, their hands clasped behind their backs, and their eyes fixed forward.

Eric's gaze swept over the first young man, no older than nineteen, his face clean-shaven, and his curling black hair cropped close to his head. His eyes were full of innocence and determination . . .

The prince nodded and moved his attention to the next man in line.

"This here is Mr. Ezra Manuel."

The man was sweating profusely, his eyes wide and wild as though he were a stag that had been chased by the hunter to the ends of the earth . . . He was older, perhaps in his mid-twenties, and he was clearly well trained. He had a forgettable face save for a small, crossed scar on his left cheek just above his neatly trimmed black beard.

Eric eyed him suspiciously but said nothing as he continued on.

"This here is Mr. Joshua Ball, Lord Ball's younger half brother."

Eric stopped and squared off with the man, an interested glint in his eyes that had the young man straightening his shoulders.

Joshua Ball looked like his older brother . . . He had a long face and thick brows . . . but whereas his brother's gaze was filled with arrogance, his hid his true feelings. He was no older than twenty-one.

"I've been acquainted with your brother, Mr. Ball. Is he aware of you entering the castle to be trained as a royal knight?" Eric asked while tilting his head over his shoulder casually.

The young man stiffened.

His answer revealed despite being wordless.

"I see."

Eric stepped on to the next man. He was tall, muscular, and sported a shaved head with a thick, ropey scar curving around his ear.

"This here is Sir Herra's younger brother, Caleb Herra. He was a squire here three years ago but needed time to heal his wound." Captain Orion nodded at the scar on the man's head.

Staring at him more closely then, Eric realized that despite the man's fierce appearance, he was in fact only in his mid-twenties . . . He looked far more terrifying than his brother, that much was certain . . .

"And lastly, here is our most promising candidate. This is Mr. Leo Konrad."

Eric turned to the final candidate who appeared to be of mixed parentage. His dark eyes were Troivackian, but his skin pale and his auburn hair appeared to be fading to a chestnut hue thanks to the recent arrival of autumn.

"We are considering him to replace one of Princess Alina's guards, who was sadly killed during the journey here from Norum," Captain Orion announced.

Eric's gaze lingered on Leo Konrad's face. There was something arrogant about him that he didn't like. He was strong, lean . . . had a small silver hoop earring in his left ear, a ponytail, a scar dashing his right eyebrow, and his posture was a little too lax.

"What was your occupation before being hired here?" Eric asked evenly, his true suspicion masked.

"A mercenary, Your Highness."

"What was the nature of your last job?" the prince's calculated stare made the young captain at his side shift uncomfortably.

"That is confidential, Your Highness."

Eric said nothing for a moment.

Then his sword was drawn and angled against the man's throat in a flash, the ringing of steel seemed to reach everyone's ears long after it happened.

"You dare touch a weapon?" Eric said coldly.

For a moment no one knew what the prince referred to, until knights standing on Leo Konrad's periphery startled at the realization that the new candidate was clutching a blade that had been stowed behind his back.

"Old habits, Your Highness. My apologies." Leo managed to lower his eyes, but his tone was far from contrite. Even after he spoke, his hand lingered on the handle of the dagger behind him.

When it finally fell away, Captain Orion stepped forward and seized the blade from the recruit, his brow worried into a frown.

"I don't believe you are fit to serve His Majesty King Brendan Devark or my sister, Princess Alina Devark. Please see yourself off the castle grounds." Eric removed his sword from the man's neck, noting that he had left the barest of scratches on his clean-shaven neck.

Leo bowed. "I beg of you, be merciful, Your Highness. I left my old position in order to—"

"Your Highness, perhaps you should see him fight," Captain Orion interjected hurriedly. "I recognize he has been disrespectful, but you know how mercenaries are. They are all rough around the edges until we train them otherwise. You need to see his potential for yourself."

Eric's disinterested countenance changed immediately, his expression foreboding, when he glanced briefly to the captain and then back to Leo.

"As you say, Captain Orion, I am familiar with mercenaries. I have seen mercenaries capable of being trained to be men of honor, but that is not the case here." Eric stepped closer to Leo, whose eyes seemed to be laughing down at him.

"Here in Troivack, a man caught putting a hand on his blade toward his superior does not apologize or give an excuse. He drops to his knees and offers his life for his disobedience. Mr. Konrad's reaction here, however, is indicative of a man who prizes his own survival and pride before anything else."

Leo cocked an eyebrow, then slowly knelt, first onto one, then two knees. "If my life will serve as a suitable penance, then so be it, Your Highness."

Eric stared down at him dispassionately. "Be gone." Without another glance back, he moved away to resume his training.

Captain Orion fidgeted where he stood, wishing to intervene but knowing he couldn't . . . Instead, he turned to Leo quickly.

"I will address this with a few other Troivackian nobles. Stay in Vessa for now, and I will be in touch."

Leo rose to his feet and bowed wordlessly. The captain set his feet toward the castle, already determined to keep the new talent he had found.

As the men surrounding the scene gradually moved back to their sparring practices in light of the captain's departure, one of the other newcomers sidled over to Leo nervously, though he pretended to be watching the other men's swordplay.

"What now?" Manuel whispered to his boss.

"Be calm. I planned to be kicked out. I saw enough. I now know the layouts of the training grounds and barracks. Watch the prince train and tell me his habits. Find out when he drinks, when he rests, and the weaknesses in his swordsmanship. We'll try to take him before that woman learns of our presence."

"W-What if she *does* see us? *He* will kill us." Manuel's breath shuddered in his chest.

"Oh, our master will do far worse than kill us should we draw *that* woman's attention, Manuel. So make sure you do your job well." Leo's threat was followed by him making his way casually toward the exit, his movements smooth and powerful like a panther's.

The entire exchange had been observed by Eric, who was beyond earshot but couldn't help feeing the familiar prickling on the back of his neck as he watched the mercenary leave.

Sensing the attention, Leo shot the prince a languid sidelong glance and flashed him a sly smile before he mounted the steps to the castle and disappeared in its shadows.

Without any semblance of proof, Eric had an undeniable sense that the man he had just faced was far more than he had pretended to be. Despite being dismissed from the castle grounds, Leo's presence lingered, causing unease to build in the prince's gut.

He would report his suspicions to his brother-in-law, but something told him that even that might not be enough . . .

There was nothing more he could do in that moment, however, and so he continued his previous task of venting his frustrations on the straw dummy that was already ripped to shreds from the previous efforts of his blade.

Brendan stared at the notes with a frown, then glanced up with a disgruntled sigh at Mage Sebastian and Faucher.

"More sightings close to Norum?" he asked while leaning his forearms on the edge of his desk.

"Yes, Your Majesty. My former teacher claims there was a tribe of the stone golems—he guessed around fifteen. He also suggested there were smaller creatures on their shoulders. They appeared to be winged, but we aren't sure if they are in fact the fey that the legends describe or not," Sebastian explained, his round spectacles glinting in the pale autumn sunlight.

"It is confirmed then that they are stone golems? From the mountains?"

"Yes, of that there is no doubt. The only problem is . . . somehow, whenever we go to engage with them to find out if they are friend or foe, they . . . well . . ." Sebastian cleared his throat.

"Anyone who has gone to approach them becomes disoriented and winds up hundreds of yards away from the place they last remember," Faucher finished for the mage bluntly.

"Were there any humans spotted with them, and through which territories did they pass?"

"They bordered Lord Vanier's lands most recently. As for humans traveling with them, there haven't been any sightings, but the growing numbers of mercenaries under Leo Zephin and his rebellion have been reported all over the south as well."

"I recall Lord Vanier being one of the more vocal noblemen who was against my choice of bride," Brendan began, his hands gently clasping atop his desk.

"Correct, Your Majesty. He will be in attendance for Her Highness's coronation." Faucher volunteered the information with a raised eyebrow.

"Yes, as far as I'm given to understand, the planning is going well for my wife to finally take her place as queen."

At this, Sebastian grew uncomfortable. "Your Majesty, if I may be so bold to offer another observation . . . ?"

"Speak," Brendan ordered, though it was obvious by his distracted stare that he was still lost in thought about Alina's ascension to the throne.

"The unrest regarding the princess's presence has been overshadowed by talk of Lady Katarina Ashowan."

At last Brendan's gaze jumped upward, a ruthless smile touching his face, which made both Sebastian and Faucher feel equally taken aback.

"Oh? Do tell."

"W-Well, there is the fact that she smiles and expresses herself openly. It also has become well-known that she has the ear of the princess, and now . . . especially after last night . . . word of her possibly becoming the next queen of Daxaria has caused a great amount of . . . *uncertainty* around her."

Brendan proceeded to shake the two composed men to their core as he released a boom of laughter.

"Oh, don't worry, I guarantee there will be far more interesting things to talk about after the coronation. Faucher, I hear that of the five new hires, three of them are to be your new students to help hone their swordsmanship."

"Yes, though Captain Orion said the other two men they hired were skilled enough for a more elevated position, but His Highness Prince Eric dismissed one of them abruptly."

This piece of news succeeded in surprising Brendan.

"Prince Eric Reyes dismissed someone?"

"Yes, Your Majesty. He also has been making an impression on the knights."

Brendan raised an eyebrow and waited for his friend to find the words that he was being very careful in formulating.

"They say he is incredibly talented with a sword, but he insists on using a low-ranking knight's quality of blade. Some of our men are wondering if this is some kind of specialized training method and have begun asking for their own crude weapons to practice with . . ."

The king stilled, then nodded thoughtfully. "I see . . . do me a favor, Faucher."

"Yes, Your Majesty?"

"Send a formal invitation to the prince. I'd like to have a proper sparring match with him tomorrow morning. I think I should see for myself what skill my brother-in-law possesses. I've been far too busy to truly gauge this, and perhaps it will offer more illumination to his character."

"As you wish, Your Majesty." Faucher bowed his head, but his hesitancy was poorly hidden.

He knew the prince still drank in excess at night, though he had done well in keeping his habits hidden from most of the castle's occupants. However, Faucher was also acutely aware that when Eric Reyes trained first thing in the morning, he was still drunk from the night before, and he wouldn't be sober until evening . . .

Faucher decided he would rush to Eric's chambers to warn him about the appointment with the Troivackian king . . . though even with warning, it wasn't a guarantee that the prince could abstain from his tendencies.

It didn't help that Brendan Devark was incredibly perceptive, especially when it came to judging a man. A duel may result in even more stress for the Troivackian king once he gleaned more insight into the depth of Eric's depraved state of being.

"Faucher, are you well?" Sebastian's voice broke through the military man's thoughts, jerking him back to the present, where Brendan Devark watched him expectantly.

"It has been a long day. Permission to be dismissed?" he asked gruffly. He couldn't afford to waste any more time waiting to warn the prince about avoiding the drink for a night.

Brendan raised an eyebrow, and something in his gaze seemed to carry some sort of awareness of exactly what his former mentor would be going to do. "Very well, Faucher. I shall see you in the morning."

Standing with a bow and not bothering to look to Sebastian, Faucher exited the study in haste, his mind once again turning to the prince.

Recently, Eric Reyes had seemed to have more days where he appeared clear in the eyes . . . but it still was not often enough to bet upon.

Perhaps what made the whole ordeal even more problematic, if Faucher were honest with himself, was that the only time the future Daxarian king seemed more than a mere shell of a soulless soldier was when he was interacting with Katarina Ashowan . . .

Faucher understood the root of the rumors about the viscount's daughter and Eric Reyes, and he knew they weren't entirely outlandish.

Yet he also knew that a man as lost as the Daxarian prince would drag loved ones, or worse yet, an entire kingdom into their darkness unless they themselves found the will to climb out of his pain.

Faucher subconsciously braced himself for the king's reaction after facing the prince. He begrudgingly admitted to himself that he shouldn't have discouraged Brendan from sending Eric away on the rebel investigation assignment . . .

Climbing the stairs to the third floor where the prince's chambers were located, Faucher barely registered the stewards and maids who passed by him.

Part of him wished to let the stones fall where they may and allow the prince to suffer the consequences . . . but . . . the memory of Eric's wild soldier's spell wouldn't let him. A broken soldier was never to be abandoned. It was one of the principles Faucher lived by, and even if he wasn't particularly fond of the Daxarians in his company, it didn't matter. Those broken by worldly violence and loss did not deserve to be shunned when they struggled to rise once more.

Of course, the burning question remained . . . Would Eric Reyes have the strength to stand tall ever again?

CHAPTER 45

SPARRING SPARINGLY

Katarina lounged on the sofa in her quiet chamber, her face and fingers tingling delightfully. The two empty bottles of Troivackian moonshine were hidden in the bottom of one of her chests filled with summer dresses. She could dispose of them later. Her attending maids kept trying to force her to wear warmer clothes anyway, so they were unlikely to find them.

Given that the former Troivackian queen had suddenly felt unwell with a headache, and both Lady Kezia and Lady Wynonna were still recovering from their trip, Alina decided that they all could spend the rest of their mornings independent of one another.

Though Kat knew another reason for that decision was that Alina was itching to go over notes and documents the king had been smuggling to her. The couple had made such an arrangement to keep Alina apprised of situations being discussed in the council meetings. After all, once Alina was crowned, it wouldn't be long before the pair started making waves by having Alina take part in the meetings. This was a fact that the princess was incredibly excited about, and Kat couldn't help but feel proud of her friend.

She sighed happily. Everything was finally coming together, and with it, at long last, peace.

All that was left to do for Alina and Kat's secret coronation plans (which Rebecca Devark had no idea about), was to convince Mage Sebastian to help them a little. Katarina wasn't too worried about that . . . She had a hunch she could bother him into acquiescing to their request relatively easily.

As the redhead continued allowing her slowed thoughts to pass by lazily, Pina saw to jumping up and settling down in the crook of Kat's crossed legs.

Her faint purr rumbled against her witch's thighs, and Katarina couldn't help but feel her luck was beginning to turn around.

A knock on her chamber door interrupted the quiet. Startled, Pina leapt back out of her lap and waited to see if she needed to hide elsewhere in the room as Kat made her way across her chamber to her door without bothering to ask who it was seeking her company.

When she opened the door, however, she found herself wishing that she had inquired, as the sight before her startled her into speechlessness.

Sir Miller, the massive knight who had been Pina's guard while they all journeyed to Vessa, stood in the corridor, his jaw set, his eyes steely . . . There was a guard at his side who looked uneasy, which didn't help Kat feel any better about the abrupt visit.

"Good day, Lady Katarina," Sir Miller greeted stiffly, his voice its usual rumble.

Kat gawked at his shaven head and full beard, with the long, straight scar running down his face that made him all the more terrifying.

Despite the Troivackian castle being made for giants, the massive size of the knight before her still tested its confines.

"Hello, Sir Miller . . . Have you been well?" Kat asked while noting the guard continued looking as hopelessly confused as she felt.

"Well enough. How is Pina?"

Blinking slowly, the redhead's hand slipped from the door handle.

"She is doing fine . . . thank you for asking . . ." she trailed off uncertainly. Had the knight come with another topic in mind?

"She likes to be scratched along her cheeks, and she enjoys watching the sunrise." Sir Miller's heavy brows were permanently settled in a thick line over his eyes, but there was a flicker of some other pained emotion in the dark recesses of his gaze.

"Erm . . . I knew about her cheek scratching, but the sunrise information is new . . . Thank you."

Sir Miller let out a small huff.

"Did you . . . want to see . . . Pina?" Katarina asked carefully while once again eyeing the Troivackian guard, who grew even more flummoxed.

"I . . . don't want to bother her, but if she doesn't mind, I would be . . . honored." The barely restrained excitement and hopefulness emanating from the knight was met with her silence.

Katarina openly gaped at the man for several moments before she turned back to her chamber, where Pina still lurked in wait to see if she should hide or not.

"Pina, Sir Miller . . . the one who you traveled with? He would like to visit with you."

"Only if it's alright with her!" the knight insisted hastily, his voice desperate.

". . . Right. Only if you feel up to it." Kat didn't even turn around to look at her familiar when she added the last part, as she couldn't help but watch the hardened warrior place a hand to his chest and take a steadying breath as though he were nervous.

Slowly, the small kitten stepped quietly over to the doorway, her freckled nose twitching as she peered up at the mass of muscles.

Sir Miller's eyes shone down at her.

"Thank Gods. I worried you would forget me." He crouched down and held out his enormous, calloused hand to her to daintily sniff.

As Pina did so, she proceeded to move forward interestedly, until at last she seemed to recognize the knight. She happily pressed her cheek to his hand as he instantly saw to scratching it properly. Purring, she leapt nimbly onto his shoulder, further rubbing her small nose against his beard.

The burly, muscular knight, known to be fearsome and bloodthirsty on and off the battlefield, smiled. His blissful expression made both Katarina and the guard present gawk in open disturbance.

"S-Sir Miller, shouldn't y-you be practicing this morning?" the guard asked once Pina had settled herself lovingly around the knight's toughened neck.

"We were given the morning off while His Majesty and Prince Eric are sparring," Sir Miller recanted idly. He looked joyful while watching Pina close her eyes and offer what appeared to be a grin.

"I'm sorry, Eric and the king are sparring? Right now?" Kat asked while standing a little straighter.

"Mm-hmm," Sir Miller managed to respond as he began nuzzling the side of Pina's face, making her purrs grow louder.

Distracted by the news, Katarina stepped from her chamber and closed the door behind her.

"Mind watching Pina for me for a bit? I'd like to go witness the sparring."

The knight was too entranced to register what she was saying, while the guard was too fixated on watching Sir Miller's state of ecstasy that he didn't show any sign of hearing her either.

Kat didn't mind their unresponsiveness. With a small smile, she hiked up her skirts and took off toward the training ring.

She jogged by several servants, who gasped and whispered as she passed by, but she couldn't be bothered to care that a Troivackian noblewoman wasn't supposed to run through the corridors. She had to see the sparring.

Prince Eric Reyes had been known as an incredibly skilled sword master, but so was the Troivackian king. Not to mention Brendan Devark was six or so inches taller . . .

At the sudden recollection of their height difference, Kat found her smile fading to strained concern. Her brows tensed, as she moved expediently through the Troivackian castle's halls.

When she arrived at the training courtyard, her heart was beating loudly in her ears. She pushed through the two rows of onlookers that wrapped around the grounds under the covered arches, and she arrived at the forefront.

Eric stood sweaty and panting, a cut over his left eyebrow dribbling blood slowly down the side of his face. Brendan Devark wasn't entirely unscathed either; a dash of blood marked the underside of his chin, and he was equally sweaty, though his eyes were alight with more fun than Eric's.

The prince's gaze was dark as always, but there was a grim surrender in them . . .

The two opponents were breaking on the sidelines to take water from their flagons, clearly already having fought at least a round or two.

Kat's hands drifted to the stone ledge of the arch she watched from, unaware of the multiple eyes interested in her pointed reaction as she beheld the prince.

Eric drained the last of his water, and his eyes closed briefly while regaining more of his breath. Brendan Devark had been going easy on him, that he knew . . . And if he weren't hungover, perhaps would have studied the monarch's movements with a little more interest.

Oh well. Doesn't really matter.

As though he sensed someone's particular gaze upon him, Eric's head snapped around to stare directly at Kat.

A jolt ran through her, but she decided that must have been more to do with the moonshine affecting her senses . . . even though she couldn't tear herself away from his eyes.

They were dark and mossy, and that morning there was more shadow than man in their depths, but when she held them, a strange light from within herself flickered.

Perhaps it was because of the drinks she had consumed, but she called out unabashedly, "KICK HIS ARSE!"

A deathly silence settled over the training ring, and both Eric's and the king's gazes were fixed on her playful, mischievous smile. She was completely unaware that the men who had been standing beside her were already inching away in discomfort.

While Brendan shook his head and took a deep, patient breath, Eric let out a small chuckle of disbelief as he wiped his face and tried to ignore her presence.

Unfortunately, as soon as he'd seen her, a wash of tingling awareness and that troubling pull began to flow between them.

He swallowed with difficulty, the smile on his face disappearing.

Why was his Godsdamn reaction to her getting stronger?

Eric wiped his brow using the crook of his elbow and proceeded to crack his neck, then knuckles before once again striding back to the middle of the training space. He already could see Brendan surveying him and Kat sharply.

Once the two men stood facing each other again and were out of earshot of others, they raised their swords for the beginner's stance.

"Don't talk or look in her direction. I have no idea what she thinks she is doing making a scene here. There aren't any other women in attendance," Brendan rumbled under his breath.

Eric didn't give any reaction on his face, but he replied with, "That's just Kat being herself. I'll leave through the barracks after to avoid any further risk of contact."

Brendan gave a grunt of approval before he swung his sword down upon Eric powerfully. The prince deflected the blow expertly and in-stepped to give a sharp jab with his elbow to the king's breastbone.

Brendan's features hardened.

Before Katarina Ashowan's arrival, Eric had given textbook standard strikes and deflections. All skillfully delivered, but they were moves one could carry out without much creativity or forethought. To Brendan, it had felt as though the prince were rising and falling through comfortable stances and combinations like a revision of the tried and true basics. He hadn't minded—in fact, he found his brother-in-law's methods rather enjoyable, almost like rereading a beloved story.

However, the jab to his torso had broken that pattern.

Katarina's presence had changed Eric's fighting.

Brendan drew his second short sword with the pommel pointed to the sky so as to attack with his left in upward motions while continuing to rain down assaults with his broadsword in his right hand.

Eric dodged the broadsword and focused his defenses on the short sword, minimizing having to meet Brendan's brute strength with his own. It was a good strategic move given their size differences.

Though the prince wasn't attacking, his gaze was different, and as a result, the king didn't let his guard down as he kept trying to knock his brother-in-law's weapon out of his hand.

There was no longer the muted emotions suggesting a morbid acceptance of possible injury or death in Eric's face, but rather . . . a flicker of something harder . . . something that spoke of a seasoned fighter with the barest desire to win.

Brendan switched his footwork and began pressing the prince back closer to the opposite wall, coincidentally bringing them closer to where Lady Katarina stood, as though testing Eric's resolve to stay away from the noblewoman.

Sensing this, the prince's eyebrows twitched in annoyance. He knocked down the king's short sword in two small but controlled blows, which in turn gave him an opening to step around Brendan and redirect their movements away from Katarina. Out of the corner of his eye, he could see her magical aura flickering about her . . .

Brendan noticed it as well, which in turn made him frown as he flipped his two swords and switched their movements. His broadsword couldn't make the same precise attacks as his short sword, but it did mean more power had to go into Eric's defense, and it also meant the prince would have to be quicker about dodging the faster short sword even though he was already tired.

Noticing this change in tactic, Eric felt himself ebb closer to conceding for the day. He'd put on enough of a show to satisfy everyone.

"FIGHT DIRTIER!" Katarina Ashowan's shout startled everyone within earshot as they all were mesmerized by the sparring taking place between the two talented swordsmen.

"She is making a spectacle of herself," Brendan ground out angrily.

"It's normal in Daxaria . . . for there to be more of a commotion . . . on the sidelines," Eric managed to reply, though it did cost him a millisecond of movement, which was when a sharp sting on his right forearm told him he hadn't been fast enough in avoiding the short sword.

Brendan didn't bother saying anything more as his attacks became brutal.

He wanted to end the sparring so that he could deal with Katarina Ashowan.

Little did he know that this subconscious switch in his fighting style would have a very different effect than what he had anticipated.

He had sensed Eric was nearing his limit of caring about the match. He'd known the man had little to give in terms of effort or presence from the very beginning of their sparring due to the prince's bloodshot eyes and lingering smell of moonshine.

So when Eric suddenly threw all his weight into casting off the short sword with his own weapon, and a dagger that Brendan had forgotten Eric had under his tunic appeared in his hand, the king was unprepared.

The prince had spun in close after deflecting the short sword, and he used his body to throw Brendan's forearm responsible for swiping his broadsword out wide. Eric's shoulder was under the king's arm, stopping him from moving the broadsword again, but even if Brendan had managed to regain movement from either arm, the point of Eric's dagger foretold the results of the spar.

He'd lost.

The blade was angled upward, and had the prince not stopped himself, would have begun to gut Brendan, killing him in a matter of moments.

No one breathed.

The courtyard was silent.

Brendan Devark stared down into his brother-in-law's eyes in that moment of stillness.

Sweat and blood poured from Eric's face, but there was something else . . . A haze in his eyes, and beneath that, a coldness.

It was then the Troivackian king realized that Eric Reyes had been far closer to killing him than the onlookers would have known.

Eric's mind was slipping into a nightmare or worse yet, a memory that he was barely resisting.

Brendan carefully, and slowly, disengaged. Eric was about to slip into a soldier's spell, and so the king began thinking how he could get him somewhere private as quickly as possible.

When lo and behold, Katarina Ashowan, with her magical aura dancing around her as though she were set aflame, appeared at their sides.

"Gods, that was brilliant! Water?" She offered a flagon to the men, her cheeks flushed and her golden eyes sparkling.

Brendan's intense stare turned to her, a roar building in his throat as the Troivackian knights all around the ring began to murmur in disapproval and judgment of the noblewoman.

Kat turned to Eric.

"For a moment there I thought you fainted into His Majesty! Was it Antonio who taught you to fight with a dagger at the end? Or was that

Lord Harris? How long ago was that?" Her pointed questions about times long ago with old friends and the way her eyes were fixed on the prince quenched Brendan's building chastisement. He watched dumbfounded as Eric blinked . . . then frowned . . . as though struggling to hear Lady Katarina over the loud noises blaring in his mind . . .

Giving his head a shake, Eric closed his eyes and pinched the bridge of his nose. He looked as though he were plagued with a nasty headache. When Eric finally managed to look at Katarina again, he appeared incredibly weary.

Brendan noted that the redhead had casually stepped closer while Eric struggled with his mind. She stood before him in such a way that she filled the prince's sight . . . slowly pulling him back from the threat of the soldier's spell . . .

The smallest of smiles touched Brendan's face before Eric spoke and shattered his momentary appreciation of Katarina Ashowan.

"Godsdamnit, woman, are you drunk?"

CHAPTER 46

THORNS AND FLOWERS

Katarina froze after hearing Eric's exasperated accusation of whether or not she were drunk. She placed her hands on her hips and let out a small sniff of indignation.

"I'll have you know, *Your Highness*, I am perfectly fine! Now, if you aren't going to tell me the secret of who taught you the knife trick, I shall make myself scarce! Good day to you—ah, and to you, Your Majesty." Kat bobbed her head quickly toward Brendan, unable to meet his flat stare.

The king could tell that while she may not be drunk . . . her cheeks were too rosy.

Deciding he had enough to clean up with regards to the scene she had simultaneously created and saved, Brendan turned to Eric and clapped a hand on his shoulder, forcing his eyes away from the retreating back of the redhead to meet his own gaze.

"A fine swordsman will take the throne of Daxaria. I am pleased my wife comes from such ilk. Shall we share a drink in my study, Your Highness?" Brendan's voice easily carried around the courtyard, and many of the knights around the ring began to disband, both rejuvenated and intrigued with the sparring match that Lady Katarina had managed to make even more dramatic.

The redhead, however, was doing her best to speedily make her way back to her chamber without giving people enough time to whisper loudly about her as she passed by.

Alas, she was intercepted.

"Have. You. Lost. Your. Mind?!" Mage Sebastian had appeared from the crowd and joined her at her side with a low hiss.

"Sebbieee! So nice to see you again! Listen, would love to have a cup of tea and chat, but I—"

"You'll get lashings for that! Do you have any idea the embarrassment you've brought onto Her Highness?"

Kat gingerly slowed as she mounted the steps toward her chamber, observing a pair of maids already shooting her dirty looks. Sebastian remained by her side as she moved.

"Ah . . . lashings . . . Only had those a couple times before . . . pity." While Kat's voice sounded nonplussed, the mage noted that she looked stressed.

"So, why did you do it? You clearly know better!" he asked desperately, while subconsciously shielding her face from view by angling his shoulders slightly.

"Eric—the prince, I mean . . . He was going to let the king win."

Sebastian almost froze on the stairs in confusion but forced himself to continue keeping up with the redhead.

"So what if he let him win?!"

"Eric—His Highness—is a wet rag."

". . . Come again?" Sebastian countered while finally stopping to catch his breath on the third floor.

Realizing there was no one in earshot, Kat halted her harried movements. Her aura was once again beginning to flicker around her body. Despite the moonshine that she had partaken in, she was already sobering up, and she was beginning to regain her magitch . . .

"Lady Katarina, on top of everything today, are you really going to disparage His Highness—"

Kat let out a moan mixed with a sigh and closed her eyes.

"He wasn't going to try. He doesn't try or care about a whole hell of a lot either, and I just figured a little Daxarian encouragement could maybe do him some good."

Sebastian fell quiet over her explanation.

So she had noticed the prince's fighting was lackluster as well . . . She's a little more insightful than I realized.

"If I get lashings for making him actually put in effort in his sparring? It was worth it. Besides . . . isn't how the court sees Eric going to affect how they treat me as well?" Kat pointed out with a wave of her hand.

Sebastian's eyes widened. "Gods, you *are* capable of thinking ahead!"

Kat rolled her eyes and resumed her journey to her chamber. "As I said, I *am* trying here."

Sebastian watched her part from his company without another word as he infuriatingly realized that there might be a method to Katarina Ashowan's madness after all . . .

Alina looked at her friend suspiciously over their table set for lunch. The maids were whispering and glancing at the redhead, who was doing a splendid job of ignoring them as she tucked into her heaping plate.

Lady Kezia noticed the same thing with a slight frown.

And Lady Wynonna . . . The woman appeared to barely be awake and was swaying in her seat.

Lady Sarah kept glaring at the obviously drunk noblewoman and shaking her head disapprovingly.

"Oh, Your Highness! I had a spectacular idea just now! Since the council meetings started late today due to the sparring match taking longer than expected, I wondered about us maybe redecorating some of the castle." Katarina's slightly louder voice succeeded in both startling everyone present and also breaking the tense silence.

It appeared that no one had told Alina about her little escapade at the training ring yet, so Kat decided to prolong her carefree existence.

"Oh?" Alina asked while daintily placing her teacup down.

"Have you noticed how the castle colors are basically gray, black, and white save for some rugs and coverlets in our chambers?" Kat asked brightly.

"Yes?" Alina asked hesitantly, then she, too, suddenly perked up. "Oh! I know! I actually have been thinking about adding some flowers around here . . . We passed by so many quaint villages that had beautiful blooms climbing all over the walls. Some were blue, some purple, some pink—"

"Those are all the same flower." Lady Sarah sniffed as she raised her teacup to her lips. "Morning glory. They change color throughout the day."

"I see. Well, they are very beautiful!"

"What if we had a waterfall of flowers all the way down the two turrets at the front of the castle? Wouldn't that be incredible?" Kat asked excitedly, her eyes sparkling.

"It absolutely would be," Lady Kezia agreed with a warm smile. "Though growth to that extent isn't possible unless—"

"Unless we get Mage Sebastian to help!" Katarina jumped in all too quickly.

Lady Kezia glanced at Alina, her own ambition rising. "What do you say, Your Highness? I think it could be a beautiful way to add a welcoming touch to the castle."

"Lady Kezia, you are a woman after my own heart." Kat sighed dreamily while gazing at the Troivackian beauty.

Lady Wynonna didn't say anything, but she did let out a small hiccup and giggle.

"Well . . . why not! Shall we, ladies?" Alina couldn't help but begin to join in on her two handmaidens' excitement.

"*I* think we should wait for Lady Rebecca Devark to confirm this change before we go and—" Sarah began sharply, her posture stiffening.

"It's flowers. We aren't painting the entire castle yellow," Kat argued with a chuckle before trailing off. "Though a yellow castle could be quite striking in its own right . . ."

Lady Sarah grew pale.

Kezia stood and smiled down at them while extending her hand to Lady Katarina. "Shall we go find Mage Sebastian for the princess to make the request?"

"Lady Kezia, you could ask me to bathe in dirty dishwater and I'd still say yes." Kat rose with a grin, and as a result, Lady Sarah grew more alarmed.

"No! Absolutely not, we should wait for the former queen to recover from her headache and—"

"Well the future queen is right here, and given that she seems on board and will be living with these changes, I think I'm going along with it," Kat interrupted breezily before turning toward the chamber door and offering her arm like a lord would to Lady Kezia, making the woman laugh.

Lady Sarah blushed in irritation and glowered at the two women.

Meanwhile, Lady Wynonna folded her arms on the table before her and proceeded to rest her head, falling fast asleep in a matter of moments.

Alina gave a guilty shoulder shrug to her least popular handmaiden before reaching out and refilling her teacup.

"Don't worry, Lady Sarah, I think flowers are an appropriate change to make. I hope we didn't make you uncomfortable."

Lady Sarah didn't answer, and instead she crossed her legs as well as her arms and leaned back into her chair.

Alina didn't have to be a mind reader to know the woman was already resolute on going to Rebecca Devark and complaining.

With a sigh and a small shake of her head, the princess decided she didn't care.

She was in far too splendid a mood to let her mother-in-law hamper her day.

* * *

"This . . . looks . . . amazing!" Kat exclaimed excitedly as Mage Sebastian stood off to the side of the castle wall looking a strange mixture of pleased by the flattery and annoyed by the task.

"I agree! Look at all the people down by the entrance staring! I think I even see a few of them smiling," Lady Kezia noted while Alina also leaned over the massive swell of blooms to stare down at the growing crowd. Everyone peered up in wonder at the brilliant blue and purple swaths that ran down the two stone towers at the front of the castle.

The three women laughed happily, all feeling more than a little proud and excited at bringing color to the otherwise drab building.

"Sebbie, you said they will last until the first frost?" Kat asked over her shoulder, though she couldn't bring herself to look away. It seemed like a long time since she'd seen something so cheery.

"Yes. Which is partly what makes this pointless. The first frost is mere weeks away."

"We could always change the vines to something more colorful for the colder months—Oh! What if we had holly replace these for the Winter Solstice!" Kat burst out, practically bouncing on the spot.

"That would look absolutely magical!" Alina began to gush when her attention suddenly snapped over to a figure that was approaching them swiftly. His black cloak billowed about him in the fall chill and his mother was at his side, her face pale with rage . . .

"Your Majesty!" Sebastian spluttered in astonishment and obvious trepidation while folding himself in half to bow.

When Brendan halted in front of the three women, there was a hardness in his face that made even Alina raise an eyebrow.

"Your Highness, ladies, please follow me to my study. I believe a conversation is due." The king's greeting to his wife had Alina's previously exuberant expression mellow to one of chilly regality.

Rebecca Devark, with her head held high and her appearance as immaculate as ever, shot Katarina a blackened sidelong glare that had the redhead's aura warm itself back to life.

She had already paced around her chamber after Eric's sparring match to try and burn off more of the magitch, but Alina's mother-in-law had a knack for being irritating.

The troupe made their way to the nearest room of the castle, which looked like an office that had been abandoned for years . . .

The room contained a small circular window, four marble pillars set flush against each corner of the room, and an overturned desk and three chairs pressed into one of said corners gathering dust. Black-and-white marble tile beneath their shoes patterned itself into a circular mosaic, but it, too, had a coating of grime.

Upon entering, Brendan stood with his back to the window and faced the women . . . and Mage Sebastian, who had followed before realizing what he was doing.

"Lady Katarina, after this morning's display, I would have thought you would have known to behave yourself until I got the chance to speak to you about your punishment. However, altering the castle's appearance with this display—"

Alina stepped forward, interrupting Brendan as she calmly stared up at him, earning a startled expression followed by a frown from her mother-in-law.

"I haven't heard anything about any issues with Lady Katarina."

Brendan let out an almost imperceptible steadying breath.

"She attended my sparring match with His Highness Prince Eric and proceeded to make a scene by loudly cheering for him. I planned on being lenient given the other details of the situation, however, this further act of rebellion with the flowers—"

"I'm the one who suggested the flowers. What's the issue?" Alina's voice was hard, and the king was immediately rendered speechless.

Rebecca Devark moved closer to her daughter-in-law. "It is not your place to make changes to the castle without confirming with His Majesty or me."

"That isn't what I was told upon entering this castle," Alina countered evenly while eyeing her mother-in-law frostily. "His Majesty said I was welcome to make changes where I saw fit as it pertained to the castle decor. Am I incorrect in my recollection, Your Majesty?" She turned to face Brendan, who looked like a bear that had realized how deep of a pit he had just fallen into.

"You are correct in your recollection . . . however," Brendan proceeded with extreme caution, sensing his mother's displeasure. "Lady Katarina will need to be punished for her behavior this morning."

"As the highest ranking woman of the Troivackian court, this duty falls to me." Rebecca Devark stepped past Alina, her head held high as she regarded Katarina almost eagerly, her dark eyes angry and triumphant.

Kezia subconsciously began to put herself in front of the redhead, but Kat gently touched her shoulder to stop her from interfering. "It's alright you magnificent creature, I made the bed, so I best lie in it."

The whispered exchange that was heard by everyone in the room only made the former Troivackian queen's ire visibly intensify.

"Now, hold on a moment here." Alina turned to face her mother-in-law's back, but the woman held up a hand as though commanding the princess to be silent.

"You are not queen yet, Your Highness, and until then, matters of the Troivackian court— "

"Ah, but that's the thing now, isn't it?" Alina strode past Rebecca and rounded on the woman, her expression still. Regardless of their height difference, the threatening aura emitting from the short blond was rather startling.

"As you say, you may be the highest ranking woman amongst the Troivackian courtiers, but Lady Katarina Ashowan isn't a Troivackian courtier, is she? She is a *Daxarian* guest, and as you *kindly* pointed out just now, I am still very much so the *Daxarian* princess. Meaning she is *my* responsibility."

A glimmer of respect mixed with displeasure filled Rebecca's eyes as she stared at her daughter-in-law's formidable face.

Silence stretched the tension of the room to a near breaking point, which had the predictable result of prompting Lady Katarina to make the unwise decision to open her mouth.

"Gods, I've had people fight because of me, but never *over* me! I'm beginning to feel special . . ."

"Shush!" Sebastian whispered desperately, sounding like he was being strangled from the oppressive quiet. He slowly reached out as though intending to put his hand over the redhead's mouth.

Regardless of his efforts, the redhead had effectively broken everyone's emotional trance, and so Rebecca turned to her son.

"What say you, Your Majesty? Her Highness and I can debate until night settles, but you are the uppermost authority. Who shall be in charge of Lady Katarina's punishment?"

Brendan straightened his shoulders with the shift of attention, and he held his mother's gaze for a long moment. Emotions that no one save for Alina could see passed through his dark, fathomless eyes.

"I believe . . . my wife is correct, ma'am. She will be the one to decide Lady Katarina's punishment, though I will be a part of the process."

With Rebecca's back to the rest of the occupants in the room, her son was the only one who saw the brief flutter of her eyelids, making his heart twist painfully in his chest.

"Very well then. I shall resume resting in my chambers until the dining hour if I am no longer needed here." Rebecca turned abruptly, her moment of hurt gone behind her mask of marbled perfection as she took her leave, her champagne chiffon dress fluttering behind her as she moved.

When Alina saw the look on Brendan's face, she intuitively knew everything she needed to do in that moment to best tend to her husband.

"Lady Kezia, Katarina, and Mage Sebastian, please leave His Majesty and me. We need to have a private discussion."

The trio behind the princess carefully shuffled toward the door. None of them wanted to linger, but at the same time all had the sense that one wrong move could result in a rather violent outcome . . .

As Sebastian closed the door behind them, however, Katarina Ashowan's voice carried through for one final untimely outburst.

"Holy shit! That was so much more intense than the sparring earlier!"

CHAPTER 47

GIRL TALK

Alina stared at her husband, his jaw flexing, causing his cheek to develop a small tremor.

"I know that must have been hard for you. Your mother has been by your side advising you since you were a child."

Brendan's shoulders turned rigid. "We don't need to speak of it."

Slowly moving closer to her husband, Alina kept her expression as neutral as possible. He needed to experience his own emotions without hers interfering just then.

"I do want to say thank you," she began quietly while folding her hands gently in front of her skirts. "I am very happy that you did agree with me. It is intimidating here, and I'd be more than a little afraid without your support."

Brendan's eyes settled intently on his wife as he raised an eyebrow. "It seemed to me you were perfectly fine standing up to my mother."

Alina's face turned innocent as she took yet another step toward her husband. "Katarina is my responsibility, and as you know, I'm not one to shirk those."

Brendan couldn't help himself. Seeing her wide hazel eyes peering up at him with a small playful smile curving her lips made his own mouth twitch for a moment before remembering the look of hurt on his mother's face moments before.

"I take it my mother is not a fan of Katarina Ashowan."

"In my opinion? Katarina is to your mother what Viscount Ashowan is to the king's assistant, Mr. Howard."

"A one-sided attraction?" Brendan asked with a furrowed brow.

Alina snorted and succumbed to peals of laughter as she imagined what her father's beloved assistant would have said if he had heard their conversation.

When she rightened herself, she reached out and clasped Brendan's calloused hand before moving nearer to him yet again. She had to fully drop her head back to stare up into his face.

"*Annoying* was the word I was going to use . . ."

Brendan nodded. "Lady Katarina does have a strong skill set in that area."

Alina smiled warmly before her gaze dropped to his chest and her cheeks grew oddly pink . . .

"By the way, I . . . wanted to tell you later . . . in our chamber, but since I got to see you sooner, I don't think I can wait."

Brendan stood patiently while his wife became more adorable as her embarrassment rose due to whatever charming thought she had traipsed upon. She always looked uncomfortable and sweet whenever she wanted to express her sincere feelings or thought of a new idea for an activity they could do together as a couple . . .

"I'm pregnant."

Alina watched as the indomitable king of Troivack, the infamous mountain of a man, who was always calm and collected, never caught unaware, grew pale. His unblinking eyes widened and flew upward and fixed on the wall over her head, his entire being rigid.

"Are you alright?" she asked with a quiet chuckle.

"Of course I am, I . . . I just . . ."

Between his uncharacteristic stammer and Brendan's complexion shifting to green, Alina became concerned, especially when he started swaying.

"Oh dear, oh no—maybe you should sit!" she burst out when she realized that her husband was on the brink of fainting.

Half stumbling back against the nearest wall, Brendan clumsily leaned himself back and slid down carefully until he was comfortably seated on the floor. Alina followed him, one hand placed on his forearm and the other on his shoulder.

"Deep breaths," she murmured while kneeling beside him.

"I'm fine," Brendan attempted to say in his usual gruff manner, but his voice warbled slightly. Closing his eyes, he attempted clearing his throat and sitting a little straighter, which fortunately succeeded in returning some color to his face.

"When are you expected to deliver?" he asked, his eyes opening and fixing once more on the wall and not his wife as he struggled to contain his emotions.

Alina wasn't having any of it, however, and so she gently reached out and, with her palm caressing his cheek, turned his face to her own smiling one.

"Early summer."

Brendan stared into his wife's peaceful face and felt his gut twist.

Without a word needing to be said, Alina frowned and grasped her husband's muscular arms firmly. "It doesn't mean I'm going to die."

Brendan couldn't speak, his throat closing as he struggled to hold his wife's gaze while a suspicious warmth in his eyes threatened to betray him . . .

"We won't tell anyone yet. I won't even tell Kat. We will wait until absolutely necessary to share the news, just in case." Alina tried to soothe her husband, but his anguish on behalf of her safety was beginning to bring tears to even her own eyes.

Unable to say just how terribly happy and just as equally petrified he was, Brendan pulled Alina into his embrace, pressing her firmly against his chest where his heart's rapid beats felt weak. He clutched her tightly but try as he might to not think how she may not live past their first year of marriage, the mere shadow of such a dark thought broke him.

He held her, his face pressed into her dirty blond hair that had grown blonder in the Troivackian sun. Despite smelling the familiar faint aroma of the oils the other noblewomen used in his court . . . he could still find the lilies and jasmine he had always been able to smell on her.

Unbidden tears warmed his cheeks and soaked her hair as he silently clung to her.

If the Gods had a drop of mercy in their beings . . . they wouldn't tear her from him.

Kat paced her chamber, her hands on her hips while Pina watched nonplussed from the bed. Her paws folded daintily under her small body as she occasionally allowed her eyes to slowly blink shut.

"Sebastian mentioned lashings, but would they really go that far? I also know that being publicly shamed is a common punishment here . . . I don't do well with facing the public . . . or shame . . . I tend to have a bit too much fun with both . . ." she muttered to herself while her hand drifted up and she began to chew her thumbnail.

After a moment more of frenzied thought, she threw her hands in the air in exasperation.

"As if I don't have enough on my plate . . . Alina's mother-in-law is out for my blood, the king hasn't said anything about my swordsmanship training, and I'm supposed to be distant from Eric but that mess impersonating a noble shouldn't be left alone. Not to mention Sir Miller having a weird obsession with my familiar . . ." Kat's face stilled, her golden eyes became lost and dimmed in the pale light from her window. "I'm trying not to let my magic get the best of me where I end up killing people . . ." Kat stopped all her movement as her family's faces flashed before her eyes.

"I wonder if Tam gets homesick when he's traveling in Daxaria . . ." she pondered, her chest aching as she recalled her brother's pale face, turned downward, his dark gaze observant yet fearful at the same time. She gave her head a shake.

A small knock on her chamber door snapped her from her frantic thoughts.

With her shoulders slumping forward, Kat crossed the room, the soles of her feet dragging across the stones as she opened the door.

Lady Kezia stood with Lady Wynonna beside her.

"We heard that you're waiting to hear about your punishment." Lady Kezia smiled sympathetically. "I wondered if you'd like some company while you wait."

Katarina wanted to hug the woman, but out of respect for Lady Wynonna, who still had barely said more than twenty words since meeting everyone, kept to herself.

As the two visitors settled onto the couch and Katarina the armchair, she proceeded to let out a rush of wind.

"The waiting is the worst, in my opinion," she confessed while raking her hand through her hair.

"A-Are you not afraid of being flogged?" Lady Wynonna asked quietly. "Do your powers mean you don't feel pain?"

Katarina raised an eyebrow and smiled at the normally quiet woman. "Oh no, I do, though usually it's delayed. When I get scared or in danger, my magic kind of . . . postpones things."

"The shame may be the worst of it if they have it take place in the court," Kezia reminded seriously, her beautiful dark brows slanted into a small frown.

"Yeah, I don't know that Alina—sorry, Her Highness—will do that . . . She knows the odds are too high I'd do or say something to make it worse," Kat explained without looking all too guilty.

"That might make your punishment more severe," Wynonna pointed out. She reached a finger under the black wrap that she wore over her hair and gave her scalp a quick scratch.

"I notice you and the queen both wear those coverings, but no one else does. Why is that?" Kat asked, suddenly interested in the hunched woman.

"Oh . . . well . . . it used to be the custom in Troivack for a widow to wear this type of head wrap for a year. My husband hasn't been gone quite a year yet, and I worried that my staff would turn on me or leave me once he was gone. So I tried to be as traditionally Troivackian as possible to appear favorably in their eyes. I can't speak for the former queen though," Lady Wynonna explained while fiddling with the corner of the veil that ran down her back.

"Where in Daxaria are you from?" Kat asked interestedly.

"Outskirts of Xava. My father was a wealthy merchant, but I wasn't a noble. I was just lucky that my husband took a liking to me and didn't mind marrying someone without a title," Wynonna explained with a tight-lipped smile, her eyes growing lost amongst her memories.

"Do you want to return to Daxaria?" Kezia faced Wynonna curiously. The woman had been unbelievably shy until then, and it was nice to finally get to know more about her.

"Not for a while I don't think . . . Especially not now that I get to serve Her Highness. I would've never imagined that I would go from a simple merchant's daughter to closely serving the queen of Troivack; it's an amazing opportunity! Plus, I've heard my brother is here in Troivack now, and I'm desperate to see him again."

"Oh? Were you and your brother close?" Katarina asked while once again remembering her own annoying yet wonderful sibling.

"We were, but . . . we had an awful fight before I went to Troivack, and since then we've avoided each other. After losing my husband though, I realize how we never know how long we are in this world. I don't want things to carry on like this . . ." Determination filled Wynonna's eyes, and Kezia couldn't help but reach out and clasp her hand.

"I'm sure your paths will cross again, and you two will be close once more."

Wynonna swallowed with apparent difficulty as she slowly removed her hand from Kezia's grasp, as though the action made her emotions too difficult to handle.

"Thank you . . . What about you, Lady Kezia? Are you close with your family?"

"Of course!" Kezia smiled, which enchanted Katarina into giving her her full attention. "We were nomadic, and so my two sisters, three brothers, and I were thick as thieves as we traversed all of Troivack with our parents."

"How is it you even met Prince Henry?" Wynonna asked intently.

"Ah. We were in the northeastern city of Biern, purchasing a new horse to pull our caravan when we met. The horse we bought was startled by something and was rearing up. Henry was with His Majesty and the two were about to intervene, but when they saw me calm the beast down, I suppose I caught Henry's attention. Of course I didn't know who he was, and when he eventually told me after we had spent a few weeks together, I . . . panicked a little. Especially when I realized his brother, who was never particularly fond of me, was the king of Troivack . . . So I ran away." Kezia winced at the recollection.

"What made you come back?" Wynonna wondered, clearly spellbound by the story.

Kezia's smile grew as she turned to face Kat. "After His Majesty fell in love with Princess Alina, he encouraged his brother with his blessing to track me down. Six weeks after the king and Henry returned from Daxaria, we were wed. It hasn't all been easy with my humble origins, but we're happy."

Katarina couldn't hide her astonished expression, and even Wynonna looked disquieted.

"His Majesty, the big, grunty Devark brother? *He* was the one to encourage Henry?" Katarina finally managed without caring that she was being far too casual.

Kezia laughed and leaned back into the sofa, her hand casually resting on her swollen stomach.

"Yes. That one. In fact, he was the one to find me before Henry and convince me. He scared the moonshine from my family when he rode up, but here we are. As for becoming a handmaiden . . . seeing the changes in my brother-in-law made me determined to meet and help our future queen, even if Rebecca Devark actively fought against it."

Kat leaned forward eagerly. "Yes, I heard she was the one in charge of hiring the handmaidens aside from myself. I'm a little puzzled over her selection, if I'm honest—no offense, Lady Wynonna," the redhead nodded apologetically to the woman, who shrugged indifferently.

"Ah, you haven't figured it out yet?" Kezia raised an eyebrow in surprise. "To be honest, Lady Katarina, I would have thought you would've been more observant of these things since you grew up as a noble."

Blinking in obvious confusion, Katarina searched her memory but failed to find any hint of an explanation.

"Lady Rebecca Devark did not choose you or me for clear reasons, but she sent the offer for Baroness Wynonna Vesey with the purpose of helping Her Highness adjust as a Daxarian here in Troivack. Lady Wynonna has made no waves since arriving, and thus she is deemed a success here in Troivack despite Daxarian spouses not being popular choices. Lady Sarah is Lord Miller's daughter, and while he is a gentle man, his daughter is not like him. She holds Troivackian customs and traditions as pillars to her life regardless of how dated or harsh they are. She is also one of the highest-ranking women in the court. If Princess Alina impresses her, Lady Sarah will ensure the other noblewomen near Princess Alina's age will be more accepting. However, Lady Sarah is a double-edged sword in a sense, for she can just as easily tarnish Her Highness's odds of success here."

Kat's mouth hung open. "That sneaky wench."

Wynonna coughed.

Kezia laughed. "Perhaps don't speak about the former queen like that. While she and I are not fond of each other, she is due a great deal of respect."

"Hard to respect a woman who's a bit too eager to have me whipped," Kat muttered darkly.

Kezia opened her mouth to say more but was interrupted by a loud knock at the door.

"Lady Katarina, His Majesty has summoned you to his council room." A steward's rich baritone voice rang through the heavy door.

Glancing at the ladies, her expression grim, Kat let out a long sigh while rising to her feet.

"Well, I guess my time has come. Ladies, it has been a pleasure spending my final moments with you." Kat curtsied, her head hanging while her fellow handmaidens rose.

"Come now, you are an Ashowan. You shall bear this with the dignity your magnificent family boasts," Kezia encouraged gently while stepping over to the redhead and resting her hands on her shoulders.

Katarina looked into the former nomad's shimmering blue eyes and allowed herself to bask in their loveliness briefly before responding.

"As touching as that compliment is, you've not met my family. *Dignity* is a bit of a . . . *bold* word choice."

Kezia linked arms with Kat as they began to stroll toward the door, leaving Wynonna to fall into step alongside Kezia.

"Well, either way, we'll be waiting for you on the other side once we are permitted to rejoin you. So, do your best."

Katarina nodded and began to open the door when Lady Wynonna leaned forward, her voice dropping to a whisper in case the steward would overhear, and said, "I'll send you more moonshine, don't worry."

Reaching over and grasping her hand, Katarina's golden eyes looked suspiciously damp. She replied just as quietly, "You are one of the best women I know."

With a final look of sympathy from Kezia, Katarina took her leave to receive the punishment that had been decided for her, her heart in her throat and her palms sweaty.

Gods . . . I really hope it's something I can handle . . .

CHAPTER 48

WHIPPED UP

Eric continued attacking the straw dummy with his sword. His mind was blank as he tried to ignore the lingering stares from the knights who were still in awe of him beating their king. As a result, his swipes and stabs began to grow clumsy and halfhearted as he refused to rest and give them a chance to approach him.

He had been hounded with questions any time he didn't have a sword in his hand, and he was beginning to look forward to the evening when he could drink alone in peace.

Captain Orion approached him.

Eric halted his attacks and exchanged a brief nod with the man before Captain Orion held up his fist, which in turn made all the knights cease their training and give their superior their attention.

"Everyone, fall in!" Orion called across the yard while pointing to the stairs leading to the castle entrance.

The men sheathed their swords and carefully formed three lines.

"What's happening?" Eric stepped forward while also stowing away his own sword and snagging his white towel from the straw dummy's shoulder to wipe the sweat from his temples.

"Lady Katarina's punishment for her behavior this morning." Orion didn't look at Eric as he explained, but rather nodded toward the castle doorway, where His Majesty Brendan Devark appeared with Alina at his side. Behind them, Katarina Ashowan trudged, her eyes dulled as she stared warily around the training courtyard.

"What did they decide?" Eric asked tightly as his stomach clenched unpleasantly, though his expression remained neutral.

"Twenty lashings on the back of her legs and an apology to the knights."

Startled, Eric turned to the man. "*Twenty* lashings? Most I've ever heard being given to a noblewoman was ten."

"Given that no one other than the knights are to bear witness, and they are banned from speaking of the event, this was a lenient punishment. Her Highness will be the one to give the lashings, and I'm certain she will not deal the same damage to Lady Katarina as our former queen would."

Alina has to whip Kat? Eric frowned in alarm as he watched his sister's cool expression surveying the men before her. Her eyes met her brother's briefly but shifted away quickly as though she hadn't seen him.

Meanwhile, Katarina stepped forward before her audience, her forest green dress with gold embroidery fluttering in the chilly fall breeze. The redhead didn't show any signs of being cold despite the drop in temperature and her arms nearly being entirely exposed save for her golden bracelets and upper arm cuff.

Her gaze swept over the men, her hands loosely clasped in front of her skirts.

"I would like to issue . . . an apology . . . for . . ." Katarina trailed off. While the knights presumed it was out of nervousness, Eric could tell it was because her words were insincere. "For disrupting the sparring earlier this morning. In Daxaria, it is a custom to cheer on the duelers, but I suppose that could be seen as . . . 'improper' here. Though if anything, it makes more sense to get used to fighting with distractions going on—"

Brendan cleared his throat loudly behind Katarina, who barely resisted the urge of rolling her eyes.

"Right. So. Apologies and thank you for your time."

The knights all glanced at each other, uncertain of how to take her half-hearted words, that is until she picked up her skirts and made her way to the bottom of the stairs.

Taking a painstakingly slow, dramatic breath, Kat lowered herself to her knees before them and fixed her gaze ahead of herself while sliding the back of her skirts forward, revealing the backs of her pale calves.

Alina turned partially to the steward who had appeared with a pillow in his hands. On its velvet surface lay the black leather whip.

Eric looked on, transfixed. His insides had turned to stone as he watched Alina descend the stairs with her back ramrod straight, her attention never shifting from the back of her friend's head.

Once positioned beside Katarina's legs, Alina cast one final glance at the redhead, then drew back her arm and brought the whip down on the back of Katarina's calves.

The redhead blinked, and her eyebrow raised. It was as though she were still waiting for it to begin . . .

Alina, on the other hand, despite clearly struggling to remain calm and collected, lifted her arm back yet again and brought down the whip. Then again and again.

It was around the tenth blow that Katarina's expression no longer appeared at ease. Her features had grown tense, and her aura flickered to life.

Alina's face drained of what little color it still had as she rested her arm for a moment and stared at Kat unhappily.

It was apparent she loathed having to carry out the task, and as a result, the last half of the blows seemed to only occasionally fully meet their mark, while the rest of the time the leather strands merely slapped the stones.

When the task was done, Alina's lips were pursed as she turned and rigidly strode up the stairs to place the whip back on the pillow, then return to her husband's side, a little unsteady on her feet.

Behind his cloak, Brendan's hand gripped into a fist as he fought the urge to hold Alina's hand to offer comfort in that moment. Instead, he stepped forward to address the knights when a sudden movement drew his eye.

Eric Reyes was striding through the crowd toward where Katarina remained kneeling, his eyes foreboding as they peered up at the Troivackian king.

Brendan gave a small, almost imperceptible shake of his head in an attempt to warn Eric away.

But the prince didn't adhere to the signal as he pressed through the lines until he stood in front of the redheaded noblewoman, who stared at him wide-eyed before glancing at the knights behind him with a small cringe.

Eric offered her his hand.

After a moment of staring at his hand, then back at his emotionless face, Katarina pressed her sweltering palm into his and allowed him to draw her up to her feet.

Releasing her hand, Eric then moved in front of her and addressed Brendan.

"It is indeed Daxaria's custom to cheer for the duelers. While I understand Lady Katarina should have abided by Troivackian customs, I hope everyone present can appreciate that it was a *minor* oversight."

Brendan regarded the prince silently, his expression enigmatic as he stared down at Eric.

As always, the prince showed very little intimidation despite most of the knights growing uncomfortable by their king's stillness.

Brendan nodded to Eric after a moment before lifting his gaze back up to his knights.

"His Highness is right. Lady Katarina's offense this morning was not born out of disrespect to our ways, and I am glad that she has accepted the reprimanding with grace. We will not speak of this again, and your discretion is appreciated."

The men let out a single 'Hoh!' in perfect unison, startling Kat and making her jolt before placing a hand on her chest and staring around at them all, as though they were the strange ones.

Eric glanced back at her, his composure slipping for a moment as he shot her a single look of exasperation. She responded by sticking only the tip of her tongue out at him so that only he could see.

Sighing, the prince then gave her a slight incline of his head and strolled back amongst the knights, leaving Katarina to pick her skirts back up and retreat into the castle under more than fifty pairs of eyes.

Once the redhead had passed by the royal couple, and Alina and Brendan took their leave as well, the knights resumed their training.

Everyone had become all the more confused about what they should think about Lady Katarina Ashowan, as she was apparently close with the Daxarian prince, but also . . . eccentric.

Typically, individuals who did not follow tradition in Troivack were not looked upon favorably. However, after seeing her bear the lashings without so much as flinching, the knights did collectively agree on one thing: Katarina Ashowan was at the very least, a strong woman . . . and strength in Troivack was *always* revered.

Faucher stared at the three new recruits he was to train alongside Katarina Ashowan after the coronation and felt his mood sour.

Lord Miller's and Lord Ball's younger sons were going to do well. They wouldn't surpass their elder brothers, but at the very least they should prove to be swift and capable learners.

Sir Herra's younger brother, Faucher could already tell, would take exception to learning alongside a woman, and he was not looking forward to trying to mediate the endless conflicts they were inevitably going to have . . .

"Alright men, today we are going to start building your strength. I trust you have received the basic training that your families saw to providing. You will run twenty laps around these grounds, and afterward, do twenty push-ups. Any questions?"

Lord Ball's son raised his hand tentatively as he eyed the field behind Faucher.

"Yes, Ball?"

"Why is there a figure eight pattern in the field?"

"That is for when you begin sparring with one another. We will not be doing any matches for the first few weeks at least."

The young man kept his pale brown eyes fixated on the field before swallowing slowly.

"Is something wrong?" Faucher asked irritably, his voice beginning to shift from concise and stern to a low rumble.

"It's just . . . the numbers eight and nine are unlucky to me, sir."

Faucher stared blankly at the youth.

Was he jesting?

If he was making a poor joke, why wasn't he laughing?

Stepping closer, the military man scowled at Joshua Ball, intending to test the limits of this façade. "What about eighteen and nineteen—are those unlucky for you as well?"

"Yes, sir. It doesn't improve until after twenty-eight and twenty-nine because the number two cancels the bad luck from then on."

Faucher stared at him and realized as more and more silent moments slipped by that Joshua Ball was perfectly serious.

"Are you of sound mind?"

"Yes, sir. I just fear for my well-being when anything pertaining to those numbers happens."

Faucher stared at the young man for another long moment. His student stood at perfect attention, his face neutral but his gaze earnest.

Looking to the sky, Faucher silently demanded the Gods explain what he had done so wrong in life to be given so many annoyances as of late.

"Mr. Ball, you will run eight laps. Then nine. Then eight again. You will do these laps while running the eight pattern, and by the end of those laps, I never want to hear about your featherheaded superstitions again, am I clear?"

The lad gulped.

Whether or not he was afraid of his new teacher or the idiotic theory of his, Faucher didn't want to know.

"What are you all standing around for? *Move.*"

The order succeeded in jolting the men into action, as they began running. It was at this time that Faucher saw a figure coming through the back doorway of his very own home. He soon recognized the Daxarian knight with whom he had recently traveled.

"Sir Cas? What brings you here?" Faucher faced the younger man with his brow lowered.

The knight had been far too sunny in his disposition for any Troivackian to take any true liking to him, but he had performed his duties well and without question, so he wasn't a total loss.

"I'm here to start as your assistant and help you prepare for teaching Lady Katarina Ashowan." Sir Cas proceeded to bow to the Troivackian, his light leather vest flapping open as he did so.

Faucher wasn't sure if he should be relieved or incensed.

"His Majesty sent you?"

"Yes, sir. He and Her Highness believe it will help Lady Katarina to have at least one friendly face while she trains. I apologize if my presence has made you uncomfortable."

Your apology is what has made me uncomfortable, Faucher snapped in his mind.

"Very well. I will show you what I have planned for her thus far. Tell me your thoughts after reading through what I've written and . . ." Faucher glanced at the future knights, who had already started jogging around the field that faced the back of Faucher's estate. "Don't mention about Lady Katarina joining them. Not yet. I'm still hoping that His Majesty will change his mind."

Sir Cas grinned. "I doubt he can do that from what I understand of the arrangement."

Faucher grimaced.

Yes, he had heard all about the absurd written agreement. He closed his eyes with a grunt as he tried to ignore the stinging pain in his chest that was surely thanks to his elevated stress levels.

"Come, I'll show you to my office. Don't mind the dogs."

Sir Cas followed behind Faucher as the man moved to enter his home once again.

"Ah, hunting dogs?"

Faucher hesitated. "Somewhat . . . They're my daughter's. She has near twenty-five now, I think."

Sir Cas halted in his steps, his eyes wide. "She . . . has twenty-five dogs?"

Faucher didn't say anything in response as he disappeared around the doorway and began striding down the corridor.

Sir Cas took another step to catch back up but glanced upward, suddenly sensing someone watching him. This was how he discovered what must have been eight dogs staring down at him. Hovering above them, with long frizzy dark hair and a wide, pale face was a young woman, who startled at his attention, causing her to hastily duck behind her hill of dogs.

Chuckling, Sir Cas turned back to Faucher's keep. *I suppose he isn't entirely unfamiliar with unusual women after all . . .*

CHAPTER 49

STAR STRUCK

Katarina sat in the windowsill of the north wing of the castle's second floor. The magnificent starry Troivackian sky enticed her from beyond the castle wall, which surrounded the castle and made it feel a little hard to breathe that evening for whatever reason . . .

Clutching a random book she had found in her chamber, Kat had attempted distracting herself from her abysmal day by reading, but it turned out it was a book about Troivack's noble houses, and, thanks to her mother, she had studied those enough to last a lifetime.

Leaning her head against the stone behind her, she relished in the quiet.

She had discovered the north corridor on the second floor wasn't as well traveled as the others, as the rooms were primarily used as storage to hold winter linens and other random items that would make the castle a cluttered mess year round if not stowed away.

All servants and nobility had gone to enjoy their dinners, and so the castle was especially quiet at that hour. Kat had been permitted to skip the meal under the private excuse of feeling under the weather.

She'd taken enough hardship for one day without having to suffer another uncomfortable dinner.

Sighing, she was forced to acquiesce that, in that moment, she deeply missed her home, and the admission brought both an ache in her heart and mind.

"For someone who attracts a lot of attention, sometimes you're really annoying to find."

Kat's eyes snapped up to stare at none other than Eric Reyes. He was holding a bowl and staring at her lazily with his head tilted over his shoulder before glancing at the book in her hand with a raised eyebrow.

"Didn't think you'd be the reading type."

Kat scowled at him as she crossed her arms and leaned her head against the window frame.

"It seemed like something that wouldn't get me in trouble for once. What do you want?" She gripped the book in her hand a little more tightly, as though considering throwing it at him.

Eric shook his head in response as he slowly knelt on the ground and set the bowl down.

"Have you washed the cuts yet?"

Kat felt her eyes widen in shock as she realized that he had in fact brought with him warm water and clean rags.

"It's not that bad. You know your sister isn't the mightiest of people physically, so—"

"I'm going to look at your legs now. Kick me in the face if you want, but I know from experience it's hard to see the backs of your calves." Eric cut her off before carefully lifting the hem of her skirt.

All words and coherent thought died in Kat's being as her face flushed, and her aura flickered briefly.

Eric pretended to ignore the magical glow he saw come and go, and instead noted the angry bloodied marks on her legs that had already stained the interior of her skirts.

"Godsdamn Kat, why didn't you clean up after?" Despite the chastising yet still relatively emotionless tone he used, Eric's hands were gentle as he handed her the hem of her dress and wrung out the rag in the bowl before dabbing at her wounds.

"Aren't you supposed to be avoiding me?" she mused instead when she realized her throat was beginning to feel uncomfortably tight.

"I'm usually great at avoiding people, aren't I?" Eric replied before shooting her a cheeky grin that succeeded in once again making the redhead freeze in surprise.

She liked the lines that appeared in the corners of his eyes when he smiled like that . . .

"So why are you so terrible about it now?" Kat managed while blinking a few times and looking over her shoulder, pretending to be cavalier, as Eric continued his soft strokes against her calves, the warmth from the cloth soothing. "Wait. If that feels warm to me, that has to be scalding for you!" Kat sat up in alarm as her eyes dropped to the bowl and noted that Eric's hands were red as beets.

"Don't worry. It feels good, actually. It stops me from noticing the blisters." He shrugged off her concern, sounding perfectly genuine.

Kat held his gaze for a moment, her emotions building in her chest to the point they created an uncomfortable, prickly burr.

"Why are you being nice to me?" she asked quietly as Eric resumed his work.

"You and your questions . . ." The prince sighed. "I'm being nice to you because I'm the only one who *can* be nice to you right now. Alina can't be seen tending to you or she'll spark discontent amongst the other Troivackian staff and nobility. Your handmaidens are banned from seeing you for the rest of today as you repent your actions—fantastic apology by the way," he remarked dryly before continuing. "I doubt the former Troivackian queen has much sympathy for you, and your maid, Poppy, I'm willing to bet has no idea this even happened because you like to be stubborn and ridiculous and keep things like this to yourself. So even if you wanted someone else, I'm afraid I'm all you've got right this moment."

"Lucky me." Kat tried to give a sardonic chuckle, but it didn't quite make it out of her throat as the tightness grew to an ache.

Eric didn't say anything as he finished cleaning her wounds, then produced a balm from his pocket that he uncapped and began to apply; the faint scent of peppermint and beeswax wafted up to Kat's nose. Despite his attentiveness and effort to not hurt her, however, the cool ointment still stung, and the redhead wasn't fast enough at hiding her wince.

"Sorry, can't help that effect, but at least by tomorrow your legs should feel significantly better. Just remember to tell Poppy to go easy on your bath oils—they can agitate the cuts."

Katarina couldn't say anything.

His unexpected kindness was making her fortifications crumble.

The pain and loneliness . . . being out of place . . . always feeling like if she wasn't making a mistake, she was about to . . .

She began to cry and so dropped her face to her hands, already embarrassed at the breakdown in front of Eric.

Kat could feel him wrap his arms around her then, could feel reassurance and safety as she allowed herself her moment of weakness.

Eric said nothing, only continued to hold her as he had once before when she'd been distressed . . . only this time she felt different in his arms. It didn't feel awkward and uncomfortable.

It felt . . . right.

Which in turn made Eric's gut churn and nausea rise from within his being.

What the hell is wrong with me? She's here crying, and I'm thinking about how I . . . Eric's thoughts trailed off.

He refused to admit it. It was nothing. A pesky moment of confusion that wasn't worth acknowledging.

He closed his eyes and forced any dangerous notions from his head.

No, Kat needed advice, or words of encouragement, and she'd be fine once more. Then he could return to his chamber and drink until whatever emotion regarding Kat that was threatening to rear its head was quenched and drowned.

Kat pulled away from him, her tears already starting to dry as she hastily wiped her face. She hoped she didn't have snot dribbling from her nose and that her eyes weren't as red as Satan's butt cheeks . . .

"You know, come to think of it, I think you've tried doing things the Troivackian way long enough. You keep trying to behave then explode because you can't help yourself." Eric's breezy, matter-of-fact tone succeeded in raising her gaze to him.

"So I've failed. Completely."

"Well, yes if that's the way you want to look at it. Then again, I wouldn't fault a horse for not swimming as fast as a trout. What I mean is, it's about time you just did things the Ashowan way, and if they send you home? So be it."

Kat stared into Eric's nonchalant face flatly. "You just want to get rid of me as soon as possible."

"That would be a fantastic bonus, but I'm serious, Kat. Your father always left the things he couldn't do to his familiar, Kraken. He always did things his way and that's how life turned out well for him. You already inherited his smart-arse comments and undeserved confidence. Why not try it his way?"

At this, the redhead couldn't think of a biting retort in response. Especially as her mother's advice the day of Alina's wedding drifted to the forefront of her mind . . . to always remember where she hailed from . . .

"While you figure out that I'm right, follow me. I have something you should see." Slowly Eric stood, the bowl with the dirty rags in one hand and his other finding its way into his pocket as he strode toward the east corridor.

"Are you taking me to the kitchens? I could probably eat at least five roast chickens." Kat pushed off the sill and stepped quickly to join Eric's side.

"The fact that I know you aren't exaggerating is unbelievable. If it isn't getting into trouble, it's about food with you."

"How is that a surprise? My father's the house witch."

"True. He did make the best cookies."

Kat turned to Eric, gently swatting his shoulder with the back of her hand. "Your Highness! That is the first nice thing you've said about my father in all my time of knowing you!"

He shot her a bemused side-glance with a brief raise of his eyebrow. "I can dispute how he handled things between us, but I will never be so dense as to lie and say he isn't the best cook in the world."

Kat beamed. "Have you ever tried his peach rum pie? It's my absolute favorite."

Eric chortled. "I'm not surprised that *that's* your favorite."

Perplexed, Katarina stared at Eric's profile, her question written across her forehead.

"When your mother was pregnant with you and your brother, she craved two specific foods. Drove your family cook half mad, I recall. Peaches and herb bread, she could never have enough of."

Kat's jaw dropped. "Really?! Tam's favorite food is herb bread! Or any bread with garlic, if I'm honest . . . I have never heard of that story though!"

The prince grinned but said nothing more as they continued walking side by side.

"So where is it you're taking me if not the kitchens? The cellar where they keep moonshine?" Katarina asked hopefully.

Eric's good-humored expression flattened instantly. "I haven't forgotten the state you were in this morning when you watched the duel; of course I'm not taking you to the cellar."

"Anyone ever call you a hypocrite?"

"You. Multiple times."

Kat let out an annoyed sigh at his blunt response, and she was about to fire back more barbs and criticisms when Eric suddenly stopped in front of a wooden door with intricate swirled iron hinges, positioned in the junction of where the north corridor of the castle met the east.

"What is this—"

Katarina's words were cut off as Eric pushed open the door and revealed . . .

A library.

An empty library. Its teak shelves that rose beyond what Kat could see from the castle corridors were flush against the cylindrical marble walls. In the room's center stood a long table capable of seating forty people, with candles lit around its four corners.

"Look I know I'm technically *holding* a book, but you might've been a little bit right that I'm not the reading type—"

Eric laughed a little before pressing his hand against her back and forcing her through the doorway.

Peering around, she noted the navy plush carpet beneath the thick table and its matching benches. She observed that there was no one else present, and the space was pleasantly quiet . . .

Eric strolled past her without even bothering to take stock of her unimpressed reaction as he set down the bowl with the warm water and dirty rags on the table.

"Er . . . thanks for the tour . . . ?" The redhead's tone was unabashedly glib.

Eric sighed and shook his head, then lifted his face toward the ceiling. "Young people. Never ever think to look upward in life."

"Pfft. You elderly folk always are so excited to look down on—oh."

Kat had finally followed Eric's eyeline, and when she raised her gaze found herself staring at a glass ceiling several stories above her that gave a breathtaking frame to the Troivackian night sky. Swirls of purples and blues wound together as the stars burned brilliantly against their canvas.

"You said your favorite thing about Troivack was the stars, if I recall correctly." The prince watched Kat's dazed expression. Her golden eyes sparkled with wonder, and then, she smiled.

A feeling Eric hadn't experienced in a very long time came burbling forward in his chest. It was a sensation of warmth, of goodness . . . happiness, even.

He stared at her blazing red hair cascading down her back, her eyes still lost to the beauty before her, and her face incandescently enraptured, as though beholding the heavens somehow made her a part of them.

She turned and locked eyes with him, and the horrible, jarring cold reality of a truth he had been battling for days besieged him.

"Eric, thank you. I really, *really* needed this tonight. I needed . . . well . . . everything. Everything you gave me."

Kat took a long breath, and unbeknownst to her, Eric's chest was constricting, making a deep pain from within ache more and more . . .

"I know you have issues, and I know you have your own depressing plans for your future, but right now? You're amazing. So, again . . . thank you. I mean it."

Eric's face was frozen, but his insides were a raging fire with no end to their intensity in sight.

Staring at Katarina for another long moment as she looked back to the sky with a small smile on her face, only a single thought managed to appear in his head.

Godsdamnit.

* * *

The wind sucked on the ruby curtains in Kat's bedroom chamber window, pulling them toward the chilly autumn morning then snapping them back to billow in the room.

Meanwhile, the witch slept perfectly comfortably in her bed despite the fire having extinguished early in the night. Her familiar, Pina, remained curled in the crook of her bent knees for warmth but was otherwise unbothered by the freezing chamber.

Her eyes slowly opening, Katarina felt herself smiling. She felt giddy and excited for the day ahead.

She would get up, have a proper meal, then meet with the ladies in the solar for only a small amount of embroidery before she would then help add the finishing touches to the throne room and banquet hall for the coronation in two days' time.

Her punishment in front of the Troivackian knights felt like a lifetime ago, despite it being less than a full day.

Sitting up with a stretch, Katarina happily swung her legs over the side of the bed and leapt nimbly onto the cool stones.

Despite the fact that Katarina knew her maids should have been in her chamber helping her dress hours ago, she didn't care. She didn't care that they'd neglected her or the fire in her hearth. If they were trying to distress her, they were going about it in all the worst ways.

The only reason Poppy wasn't by her side was that Kat had told her not to fight the orders she was given by the Head of Housekeeping to spend all her time preparing for the coronation. It was an entirely unfair request of the maid, as her primary duty lay with her mistress, however . . .

Kat didn't want Poppy to suffer just for the sake of serving her when really there was no point.

She loved being self-sufficient!

Humming as she slipped on a simple gray dress in hopes of appeasing Alina's beastly mother-in-law, she then began attacking her tangled hair with a brush, and had nearly finished taming the waving flames, when a knock on her door interrupted her daily preparation.

Standing and thinking it was some new form of discipline where she'd be escorted by some stone-faced Troivackian steward to her meal, Kat readied her somber expression.

When she opened the door however, she was shocked to see Alina.

Her best friend's face was red, tear soaked, and her gaze murderous.

"My brother's been taken. Those bastards in the rebellion . . . they took my Godsdamn brother."

CHAPTER 50

UNPLEASANT UNMASKING

Katarina watched her friend's pale face glower at the low table of the solar room, the dark bags under her eyes deep and purple.

Even Lady Sarah knew to hold her tongue despite the princess's poor posture and idle hands, though everyone knew the dark-haired woman with slightly drooping eyes wished she could.

However, the way Katarina looked at both Rebecca Devark and Lady Sarah Miller was similar to how a mother bear would eye two mountain cats around her cub.

"He was taken from within the castle?" Kezia asked carefully, noting the particularly tense parties in the room.

"Yes. Apparently two men took him and smuggled him out on a food waste cart," Alina ground out, her face becoming all the more sinister.

"How could they have possibly gotten him through the entire castle unconscious?" Wynonna managed to ask cautiously.

"No one is certain. It is either a massive hole in the castle security, a traitor, or His Highness left on his own," Alina supplied tersely.

No one said anything for several long moments.

Katarina was the first to stand.

"Eric is going to be fine. He's survived significantly worse odds. He's a wildly skilled swordsman . . . He'll come back in one piece."

Alina's gaze on her friend was neither kind nor appreciative of her optimism.

Instead, it was hard, and it took the redhead aback when she turned to her.

"My brother could've been drugged and rendered unconscious. Once word gets out—"

"You shouldn't let anyone aside from a few of our elite knights know anything, Your Highness," Rebecca Devark cut in suddenly. "My supposition is that this is a ruse from the rebellion to delay your coronation. They failed in trying to kill you on your way here and may be sending His Majesty demands imminently using the promise of the prince's safe return. It is most likely that they will insist you not be crowned, Your Highness.."

Katarina's eyebrows shot up. "They wouldn't, surely . . ."

Alina held up her hand and silenced her friend as she leaned forward in her seat, serious. "Could it be that one of the nobles in the castle directly interacted with my brother to kidnap him? If we retrieve him, will it be brought to light?"

Rebecca raised an eyebrow thoughtfully. "No. They wouldn't take the risk. The prince tended to visit the wine cellars at night; it is possible a servant tipped off the abductors of this habit. Of course that still means someone strong enough would have to have carried him once knocked unconscious. It most likely would be one of the knights, who is already displeased with Your Highness becoming queen."

Alina sat up straighter in her chair, her eyes brightening. "The new recruit my brother dismissed! His Majesty said that the prince found something odd about him."

"If he was dismissed, then he wouldn't have had the authority to enter the castle again," Kezia pointed out, as she, too, joined the discussion eagerly.

"Perhaps it wasn't the man he sent away then . . . Or perhaps there was more than just one suspicious new staff member," Lady Wynonna speculated, her eyes for once sharp and clear.

"It is a wise decision to look at the newest members of the knightage as well as other recent hires amongst the staff," Rebecca agreed, her face unemotional and her voice composed.

As Katarina sat back down and listened to the logic and possible motives of Eric's abductors, she concocted a few questions of her own, then she did what her mother had taught her from a young age . . .

She asked her gut whether Eric was alright.

While somewhat uneasy, the redhead did get the distinct impression that he was fine and that things would turn out . . . Even so . . . the memory of him smiling at her under the starry sky in the library the night before appeared in her mind and made her stomach drop unpleasantly.

"If they are traveling on horseback with the deadweight of an unconscious man, it means they are either noticeable, have a vehicle, have a hideaway nearby, or are using backroads. All those options mean they aren't moving quickly. Is the Coven of Aguas able to offer any air witches who could perhaps survey from the skies?" Katarina asked loudly, her index finger beginning its restless tapping against her seat under the window.

Alina turned to her mother-in-law, awaiting to hear the answer.

Rebecca Devark had stiffened at Kat's interruption, her natural dislike of the redheaded noblewoman as obvious as ever.

"The Coven of Aguas has only five members last I checked. They are not forthcoming, as most are slaughtered shortly after revealing their natures. Witches are mostly seen as demons here in Troivack."

Katarina blinked and was taken aback over the harsh report.

While she had known witches weren't the kingdom's favorites, no one in Daxaria had known Troivack's degree of hostility was at such a high level . . . Faucher and Sebastian had hinted, but to think the members had been slaughtered so thoroughly . . .

Kat glanced at Alina, whose expression showed her shared reaction.

"Who is the coven leader? We might be able to convince them to help if we don't publicly share their involvement," Alina queried patiently.

"I advise against involving the coven, Your Highness," Rebecca asserted firmly.

"We already have the disadvantage of not making Prince Eric's abduction known under your advice, and now you're adding another limitation? Do you even want him to be found?" Katarina snapped angrily.

Rebecca Devark's cold gaze did little to deter Kat's glare.

"I think it is more beneficial to seek the coven's help as well. Discreetly," Alina agreed before standing. "I will go ask His Majesty to—"

"His Majesty is busy with meetings pertaining to the coronation as well as overseeing your brother's rescue. You should have faith in him that he will take care of it and not burden him further." Rebecca stood and looked down her nose at Alina's profile.

Turning slowly, the princess's ominous expression only made a corner of her mother-in-law's lips twitch.

"It is my brother who is missing, and as you said, His Majesty is busy. I can help see to matters with regards to this abduction. Ma'am, we've touched on this topic before, but do you know exactly why your son chose me as his bride?"

Rebecca Devark frowned but said nothing.

"He chose me because he believed I was someone capable and who could share the burdens of leading a kingdom. He wanted that in a partner because, when he was growing up, he had wished *you* could have had the power to do exactly that should things have changed for the better here. He knew you were an intelligent and capable woman, and should men and women unite in their efforts, he saw the potential for even greater strength and accomplishments to be made. Now, are you going to attempt to go against me again? Or will you instead see how far our joint efforts can take us? Either way, with or without you, I will not sit by while my brother is in trouble." Alina took a step forward, any trace of kindness or warmth that normally rested naturally in her features was nowhere to be found.

The former queen didn't move, but it was clear from the slight rounding of her eyes that Alina had surprised her.

When no one said anything for several moments, Katarina stood, her shoulders straight and her eyes glinting predatorily as she stared at Rebecca and shifted forward lithely.

"Let's go talk to Mage Sebastian. He will know about the Coven of Aguas." Katarina allowed her gaze to linger on the queen for another moment, her aura flickering about her before her eyes moved to stare at the back of Alina's head.

The princess gave a lingering, icy stare at Rebecca before she headed to the door and took her leave.

Lady Kezia and Lady Wynonna exchanged a brief nod before they, too, rose and exited the room.

Once alone, Lady Sarah let out a huff. "It's absurd. Her Highness can't possibly mean to insinuate His Majesty would've proposed such an idea."

Rebecca closed her eyes briefly, her composure fixing itself firmly on her face and in her heart. "It is not for us to speculate what our king seeks to do. If Her Highness speaks lies, then she will destroy herself quickly, and there is no reason for us to stress. However, if she speaks the truth . . ."

Rebecca stared at the ground for a long moment before letting out a breath.

Then, reaching a decision, she, too, proceeded toward the door.

"Ma'am! You cannot possibly believe—if she is wrong, we will all suffer!"

The former queen stopped briefly before casting a somber side-glance at the young noblewoman.

"If she is right and we did nothing, I promise you, the suffering you will endure will be far greater. Though perhaps that notion won't be clear to you until you have sons of your own, Lady Sarah. If you wish to remain here, feel no guilt. I would've made the same decision at your age."

Lady Sarah opened her mouth to argue, but Rebecca Devark had already exited the room, leaving the Troivackian noblewoman alone with her fists clenched at her sides.

* * *

Sebastian stared at the princess and her three handmaidens, then at the former Troivackian queen in the otherwise empty castle corridor.

"I-I beg your pardon? You wish to summon air witches to search for the prince from the skies?"

"Yes," Alina replied calmly, though her pale face and unwavering gaze was more than a little disconcerting.

"I do not think involving them would be wise—"

"I did not ask for your opinion, I asked how I can contact the coven leader of Aguas," the princess informed the mage firmly.

Giving a small sniff before casting an uncertain glance at Rebecca Devark, Sebastian bowed.

"My apologies, but you do not have the authority to obtain that information, Your Highness."

"Oh, but *I* do Sebbie. As a witch from a foreign coven, it is in our own written law that I can seek refuge or counsel with *any* coven on *any* continent I'm on, and this is regardless of status or gender. I thought you knew everything?" Katarina stepped forward, her golden eyes and aura jointly burning a little brighter as she addressed the mage with a hint of sarcasm.

Sebastian shot her a flat look of disapproval.

"Is that true, Mage Sebastian?" Rebecca queried while tilting her head interestedly. "She can contact any coven?"

"It most certainly is," Katarina replied before Sebastian could, her gaze never leaving his face as she placed her hands on her hips.

The mage balked. "To summon the witches here puts everyone at risk."

"Well tell them not to wear bright pink and perhaps to leave the trumpets that announce their arrival at home, hm? I'm certain two or three witches can come without drawing attention," Kat countered while drawing even closer to the mage, whose forehead was beginning to look slightly damp.

"I-If you already know the law, then you know you can simply send a hawk with a message, so why bother coming to me?" Sebastian was forced to take a step back.

"Because if I go to the falconry and have to log that I'm sending a bird to the Coven of Aguas, a lot of people are going to find out. Believe it or not, I'm trying not to make a scene."

"You're doing a splendid job," Sebastian managed breathily as Katarina prowled closer. "Stop doing that! You look like a wild beast!" The mage seemed to have forgotten there were five other witnesses as he became increasingly agitated by the redhead's advancement.

"So, Sebbie? How do we contact the coven without raising alarms?" Kat asked again, finally stopping her movements, but her eyes still fixed upon her target.

The mage gulped, then briefly glanced at the group of noblewomen.

He didn't have any other choice but to comply.

He merely hoped that he wouldn't be caught up in whatever punishment would surely come after the haphazard plan blew up in their faces.

Eric recognized the faint blue and purple swirls drifting around him in the darkness. Though the ribbon of gold was new, he knew the friendly twinkling that came and went like fireflies in the darkness and the relaxed contentment in his being . . .

He was experiencing the effects of Witch's Brew.

When had he taken it?

The unpleasant jarring memory of a rough hand thrusting something into his mouth flashed in his mind, making his head give a small shake. As a result, the scrape of burlap across his cheek alerted him as to why things were so dark . . .

He had a sack on his head.

Ah . . . I've been kidnapped again . . .

Eric moved his hands with difficulty. They felt tingly and heavy . . . but they were unbound . . .

Clumsily, he pulled the sack from his head and blinked dazedly at his surroundings.

He was in a windowless stone room, and judging from the lack of damp musty smells, it was above ground. It then occurred to him that there was enough light that he could see despite there not being any openings in the stones, and so he turned to find that there was a small table and chair with multiple candles lit beside a heavy iron door, and seated in the chair, was a man around Eric's age with black hair that didn't quite reach his shoulders. His face was pale, his eyes . . .

"Tam?" Eric slurred while squinting.

The figure stiffened. "Look closer, Your Highness. I am not called Tam."

Eric blinked rapidly and saw that while the man had the same coloring as Katarina's twin brother, this stranger had a broader face and carried himself completely differently. He wore a black tunic that hung open enough to reveal his bare chest, with a scaly leather vest fastened around his middle, revealing that while he was lean, he was strong.

"Ah . . . you look like him . . . could be related," Eric murmured thoughtfully as his mind struggled to process any unpleasant thoughts.

"Are you referring to Tamlin Ashowan by chance?" the man raised a dark eyebrow.

"Yep. Kat's brother," the prince managed to say as he shifted positions. He realized then that his ankle had a steel cuff and chain around it that was attached to the wall.

A cold laugh drew Eric's attention back to his captor.

"I suppose, in a way, he and I *are* related . . . Oh . . . the Gods do have a cruelness about them . . ."

Eric didn't understand what the stranger meant, and so he didn't say anything as he comfortably slumped against the wall.

"You know, I wasn't going to reveal myself to one of the key players in this particular game, but I must say, the reports I heard about Lady Katarina made it hard to resist."

"What about Kat?" the prince asked blearily, his neck was starting to feel too weakened to properly support his head.

"My subordinate mentioned her aura consumes magic, they say she was a demon . . . and of course such a description drew my full attention."

"Leave . . . Kat alone. She's . . . good." Eric was struggling to stay in reality as a strange blue creature with wings appeared on the table beside his captor, its beady black eyes stared at him interestedly.

Noticing where the prince was looking, the stranger quirked an eyebrow. "Witch's Brew is a remarkable drug if it allows mere humans to see not only magic but also the ancient realm. I hear some humans even take on some of a witch's power when in close proximity. It was definitely one of her more ingenious inventions, I must admit."

"Whose . . . invention?" Eric asked as the little blue fellow grinned and revealed small, pointy teeth.

"Ah, you'll learn of her in due time. Now, tell me." The man stood, his hands in his pockets as he strode over to the prince and slowly crouched down so they were eye to eye. "Has Lady Katarina killed before?"

Eric tried to shake his head, but it sent the world spinning, and the colors and twinkling lights were making him go cross-eyed.

"Hm. Not sure I believe you. So I'll try a different phrasing for you. Do you think Lady Katarina is capable of fighting and besting a magical deity?"

"Fighting who . . . ?" Eric was barely able to keep his eyes open.

The man reached out and seized the prince's jaw.

Eric felt cold fear fill his being, and the bright magic around him faded.

The man smiled, his white teeth bright against the darkness.

"Wait . . . I remember you . . . you sold us . . . moonshine on our way to Troivack."

The man didn't bother masking his surprise. "I'm impressed your rotted brain has the capacity to remember such a detail. Then again, I see Lady Katarina's magic has attached itself to you. I imagine that is helping you a great deal as of late."

Eric couldn't move his eyes from the man as an ominous knowing slowly filled his gut . . .

"My name is Samuel, however, I do have a few others thanks to some of the more horrible creatures here." The prince's captor continued holding his face, his own smile growing. "Tell me, can you guess who I am thanks to Witch's Brew?"

Eric took in a breath to say he didn't, but then Samuel's eyes sharpened, and suddenly the prince's emotions surged forward.

His pain, his sadness, his anger, his fear . . .

"Your brokenness is extensive indeed . . . and . . . my, my, I see you are struggling with just how significant your feelings are toward Katarina Ashowan," Samuel mused, but . . . his lips didn't move. Instead, his voice echoed in Eric's head . . . paralyzing him. "Hm. Perhaps you are merely becoming addicted to her magic to replace your former vice . . . ? Ah, no, no, I see now. You truly do love her." He sighed as though disappointed and shook his head. "Oh well, with the amount of darkness in you, it will only bring about more destruction for yourself. Hopefully she is smart enough to run from you, though I have my doubts. I've seen many women shatter themselves in order to use their own pieces to fix the damaged men they fall for."

Eric could barely focus on Samuel's words, but he could feel his soul being scoured. Trembling at the unfathomable wave of power overtaking his senses, he could feel every dark impulse, every dent and scar it bore being inspected, even his heart that, until that moment, he hadn't realized was still somehow filled with love and goodness . . .

Samuel stood, finally releasing him. As though he were finally freed from a spell, Eric discovered he was gasping, and tears were rolling down his face.

"Well, I suppose as humans go, I've definitely met worse. I've seen enough. I'll come visit you again once you sober up."

Eric stared after him, his breaths still ragged and his tears still falling.

"Y-You . . . You are . . ."

Sam stopped and turned to look at the prince over his shoulder, his eyebrow raised indifferently.

"You're the devil. You're . . . Satan."

The corner of Sam's lips twitched closely to a jeer before he let out a small breath that was almost a laugh and turned back to the iron door.

He didn't need to answer because Eric could feel it all the way down to the depths of his exposed soul. This revelation was more unnerving than the prince could say, especially as it was the first time in a long time . . . he found he was fearing for his life.

CHAPTER 51

A LOATHSOME LINEAGE

Katarina, Alina, Wynonna, Kezia, and the former queen Rebecca Devark sat in a row, all staring at the coven leader of Aguas in the abandoned office where they had convened the day of the flowers incident, having deemed it one of the more inconspicuous places within the castle.

The coven leader was a slight man—uncommon for Troivackians—with gold-rimmed spectacles that weren't entirely useful in hiding his striking eyes. His left eye was a dark brown with a splattering of gray, while his right eye was a bright blue with flecks of light green and gold. Aside from this, he had long white- and black-streaked hair that he wore in a low ponytail. His clothes were mostly black aside from his worn cream wool coat that had seen better years.

"Mr. Kraft, thank you for your hasty arrival. I must admit I was surprised to learn that the coven was hidden so close to the castle here in Vessa," Alina began, her voice clear but her gaze somber.

"His Majesty has been kind enough to offer the castle as refuge should the citizens decide to attempt to mob us and wipe us out again," the coven leader informed Alina bleakly.

"Your restraint by refusing to counterattack the citizens is appreciated." Rebecca Devark gave a regal nod, whereas a look of outrage rose on Katarina's face.

"How could it have gotten to this point? There are only *five* members! Surely there are more witches throughout Troivack in need of—"

"Descendant of Helmer, I will not hear your criticisms." Mr. Kraft's icy voice and calculated stare silenced Katarina immediately.

Kezia, Rebecca, and Wynonna turned to Kat with rounded eyes.

"You . . . You are related to Aidan Helmer?" Lady Kezia asked quietly.

"Well, of course. My father is his son. This is public knowledge . . ." Kat attempted to sound dismissive, but her eyes shifted nervously to Alina.

Her friend, however, still had her attention fixed on the Aguas coven leader.

"Much has been forgotten since the Tri-War," Mr. Kraft explained, staring spitefully at Kat. "You take after both your father and grandfather a great deal in your looks."

The redhead grunted while shifting uncomfortably in her seat. "I take after my father more than my grandfather."

"I'd like to see if that's true." Mr. Kraft stepped forward and held out his hand to Katarina.

She stared at him, perplexed. Did he want to help her stand up for some reason?

Clasping his outstretched palm, Kat was about to rise, when his eyes glimmered magically.

She'd seen a similar sight in her father's eyes countless times, but when this man did it . . . her aura burst from her body and his eyes widened, dropping her hand immediately.

"You . . . You are nothing like your father." He stared at her in open fear and repulsion, and Kat's heart tripped over itself as she felt exposed.

"Your power . . . it consumes . . . it burns . . . it could kill many, many people, including yourself."

"I thought your magic only allowed you to have more energy and see in the dark?" Rebecca Devark asked sharply.

"I'm as surprised as you are," Kat informed her defensively, though there was the faintest flicker of doubt in her voice.

Mr. Kraft kept his unnerving gaze fixed on Katarina. "Your power . . . I have no idea what the Gods could've possibly been thinking when they made a being like you."

"Well, now you just sound like Alina's husband," Kat grumbled in a meek attempt at lightening the mood.

When her jest did not succeed, and instead all that followed was deathly silence, she acquiesced that she needed to change the topic quickly.

"We didn't summon you here to have you villainize me—though you're doing a fabulous job. Thanks for that," Kat added acidly. "We summoned you here to help search for the missing Daxarian prince. He was abducted from the castle, and given that he was taken against his will, the abductors must be noticeable. If an air witch were able to survey the area, it would be greatly appreciated."

Mr. Kraft stared at Katarina, his face stony.

"We would not let it be known that you are aiding us; you have our word." Alina's imperious tone at long last drew the witch's attention away from the redhead.

"I will have to politely decline, Your Highness, as the missing prince does not interfere with the well-being of witches." Mr. Kraft bowed.

"Yes, it does." Katarina stood, her eyes sparking dangerously, earning a look of hate and panic from the coven leader. "Prince Eric is my . . ."

Everyone in the room stared at her expectantly.

". . . He's my protector here in Troivack. Without him, I'll most likely be lynched within a day," Kat finished, her voice rising theatrically.

Mr. Kraft arched a skeptical eyebrow.

After a beat of silence, the redhead's expression deflated.

"I'm starting to understand how the witches of Troivack have been slaughtered so easily." Katarina's agitation was further enhanced by her magical aura that once again flamed to life.

The coven leader was unaffected by her argument, however, and instead redirected the conversation.

"Tell me, has your aura been appearing more and more as you've gotten older and become faced with more stressful situations?"

Kat's fierce expression froze.

"It has, hasn't it? You're struggling to remain in control of your magic. The day your aura burns endlessly? That's the day your magic consumes you and curses those unfortunate enough to be in its presence. You cannot deny your true nature in front of my eyes, Lady Katarina."

Kat stumbled backward, her knees weak.

He had seen straight through to her closely guarded secret . . . her biggest fear . . .

"We are not here to examine Lady Katarina's magic," Alina interrupted while she, too, rose from her seat. "We are here because my brother, the future king of Daxaria, is missing. You heard Lady Katarina—he is her protector while here. Does this not call for the Coven of Aguas's aide?"

Mr. Kraft gave a shallow bow to the princess. "Forgive me, Your Highness, but a witch flying in the sky is incredibly noticeable. We cannot risk the complete decimation of witches in Troivack."

"What if it were at night?" Lady Kezia asked earnestly.

Mr. Kraft regarded the beautiful woman with a small frown. "Then the air witch would not be able to see anything."

"If they are powerful enough to bring me up into the air with them, I can see perfectly well," Katarina added though still recovering from the coven leader's earlier confrontation. "Just one night. If we don't see anything tonight in Vessa or its surrounding area, we won't ask for more time."

Mr. Kraft's eyes slid to Kat, though his head didn't move.

After a brief moment of silence, he let out an aggravated sigh.

"Very well. However, the coven has terms. We request long-term lodging directly in the castle. At least through the winter. We will not let it be known who we are, but . . . times are hard enough."

Rebecca Devark was opening her mouth, the line between her brows deepening as she clearly intended to refute the request, when Alina cut her off.

"It will be done. I want this search to carry on throughout the night; is your air witch capable of handling that?" she demanded, her hazel eyes unwavering.

"Of course. Is Lady Katarina prepared for such a demanding task?" Mr. Kraft queried with a sidelong glance in Kat's direction.

She let out a slow breath that nearly ended in a growl. "Given that your mutated power is to see others' abilities, you should know that this will be easy for me."

The coven leader said nothing in response before he turned back to Alina. "I acquiesce but insist on the highest level of protection for our coven member afterward in the event someone sees her."

"I will see to it. Thank you, Mr. Kraft," the princess assured while gracefully extending her hand to the man.

Turning to face Alina, Mr. Kraft gave a respectful bow over her hand before rising once more.

"I will summon our air witch, though they may not be entirely willing once learning that Aidan Helmer's descendent is responsible for this summons."

Rebecca Devark looked to Katarina. "I remember Mr. Helmer. He convinced my husband that with his familiar dragon, victory was assured, and he led our kingdom to utter humiliation."

"How the hell is that my responsibility? I wasn't even born." Kat could feel panic rising in her stomach under Rebecca Devark's cold stare, but she tried not to let it show.

"Children bear the consequences of the sins of their parents."

Katarina's aura became tinted with red as she moved toward the former queen. "That's bullshit. If that were true, then His Majesty Brendan Devark would be charged for your dead husband's war crimes."

Rebecca Devark was on her feet in an instant, her ire for once entirely unrestrained.

"You vile devil—"

"*Enough.*" Alina rose, her commanding voice and sharp gaze cutting her mother-in-law off. "Lady Katarina's father, Viscount Finlay Ashowan, disowned his father long before she was born. All ties were cut even before his involvement in Troivack. There isn't a *crumb* you can stand on that calls for the injustice you are attempting to assign to her today." Alina turned to Mr. Kraft, whose hands had curled into fists at his side. "The pain of your past is directed to the wrong person."

The room rang with Alina's ferocious words, and Kat stared appreciatively at her friend as both Rebecca Devark and Mr. Kraft's attention remained fixed on her.

"Now, tonight, your air witch will leave with Lady Katarina. They will search thoroughly for my brother, and should they find anything, you will report it. Agreed?"

Mr. Kraft stared at the princess a long while before casting one last long gaze at Kat, though this time, there was less venom and more calculation present.

Kat felt her features fall into an unimpressed expression. "If your witch drops me from the sky, my parents will be infinitely *more* upset, believe it or not."

"We would never do something as—"

"You heard Lady Katarina. Now. Until this evening, good day, Mr. Kraft." Lady Kezia stood. While her voice was louder than usual, its tone, paired with her sparkling blue eyes, did much in gentling the interruption.

The coven leader let out a small sigh and barest shake of his head before he bowed again, the afternoon sun casting his gold-rimmed glasses ablaze for a moment as he righted himself and took his leave.

Once the women were alone, Alina gave a final disparaging look at her mother-in-law, but oddly enough did not glance at Kat before she left.

Rebecca Devark rounded on the redhead instantly.

However, Kat's expression gave her pause.

The redhead didn't look as formidable as usual. She didn't appear cocky or untouchable . . .

No.

She looked like a young woman, who had perhaps taken one blow too many, as her golden eyes appeared dulled and lingered on the floor for a moment before she lifted them toward the door.

"I'll go wait in my chamber until it's time."

"W-Won't you have to find a way to sneak out later? Your maids could—" Wynonna began tentatively while still eyeing the Troivackian queen, who, while silenced, still stared intently at Katarina.

"Oh no. Our former queen here has made sure maids aren't an issue." Katarina didn't bother looking at the other handmaidens or Rebecca. Instead she, too, departed without a second look back.

When it was only Kezia, Rebecca, and Wynonna remaining, Kezia faced her mother-in-law.

"What did she mean by that?"

Rebecca stared at the wall over her daughter-in-law's head but did not speak.

"You foolish, prideful woman." Kezia breathed, her hands cutting through the air emphatically as she realized *exactly* what Katarina had been inferring. "Putting aside that Lady Katarina is a *guest*, unmarried, and alone here without any other family, *she is one of the most well-connected women in all of Daxaria and someone who has been trying to protect your family*!" She seethed.

Rebecca finally lowered her eyes to her second son's wife. "I will not be lectured by—"

"A nomad? A commoner? Well, how about your *family member*, you viper!" Kezia threw her finger in Rebecca's face, and while the former queen did not take a step back, her eyes did flutter.

"*You* are one of the reasons I ran from Henry. I thought I could not hold my own against *you*. The moment I had a fighting chance, when His Majesty vowed to be on my side? I took it. I thought between him and Princess Alina, I could *survive*. Now I see a chance of happiness for many more people thanks to the woman who has been trying to bring back *any* sort of warmth or goodness and is far too powerful for even the likes of *you*, the *witch*, KATARINA GODSDAMN ASHOWAN!"

Kezia's scream ripped itself from her chest, accompanied by a small amount of spittle sent flying, as she stared at her mother-in-law, her chest heaving and tears in her eyes.

"What about being miserable is so Godsdamn important to protect here in Troivack? Is that all our kingdom is destined for? A land of suffering, because people who are bitter and hungry for control find it easier to rule over the broken?"

Rebeca's eyes looked suspiciously wet, and yet her face did not move.

"Everyone knows how you run your court ladies. How you play games. How you looked down on Henry . . . to the point where you made Brendan the only one protecting him. Not anymore. I'm here. The Daxarian princess is here, and the daughter of the house witch is here. Not Aidan Helmer. The woman who advocates for *smiling* in this tomb filled with the living."

Kezia finished her speech, turning to storm from the room.

"If you had to choose between the child you carry now and another, which would you pick?" the former queen asked softly.

The former nomad paused but did not look back at Rebecca.

"That is the choice I've had to make. You choose your battles in this court or lose everything. If you think I feel no guilt, then ask yourself why I am taking this risk now. I want my son's bride on the throne. I want to believe my son, His Majesty, is trying to find a way to be happy after everything he had to survive until this point. In my eyes, the only threat to all of that is Lady Katarina Ashowan. It was her kin who brought devastation to my family before, and I will not allow them to take more from me."

Kezia said nothing in response for several long moments. Eventually the door opened and closed behind her quietly.

Turning to the former queen of Troivack, Wynonna realized belatedly that she hadn't really wanted to be left alone with Rebecca Devark. Particularly in that moment.

"Lovely weather we're having!"

Rebecca shot the widow a wry glance before her eyes moved to the window and the overcast, drizzly day. Then she, too, retired from the room, her mind and heart filled with thoughts she acknowledged would require more than a cursory moment of time to process.

CHAPTER 52

DESIGNS OF THE DEITIES

Eric slowly came to, his expression gray, and his body cold and clammy as he peered around the stone room of his prison.

The effect of the Witch's Brew had finally worn off, leaving his mind sluggish, but at least present.

He had met the devil.

Or . . . had he?

Had it been a hallucination? Had he imagined the entire exchange?

"Welcome back, Your Highness."

Eric lifted his head from against the stone wall and nearly vomited.

After a moment of taking deep breaths, his eyes opened, and before him was the same man he recalled introducing himself as Samuel . . . but in actuality was the only son of the Gods.

Samuel sat in a dark red vest, white tunic, and black leather pants, cutting up an apple as he watched the prince disinterestedly.

"Are you really . . . the devil?" Eric managed to ask, though he wished he could have a drink of water as his throat rasped and burned at the same time.

"Mm. Well . . . that's what people began calling me thanks to my wretch of a sister," Sam explained before biting into the fruit and chewing idly.

The first witch had been created to maintain balance between man and nature. Her twin brother, the devil, had been created to help man master their own emotions that were of a higher caliber compared to the animals they lived amongst. However, the devil had become sickened by humanity, and in a fight about whether humans should be exterminated, he had slaughtered his twin.

"Your sister the first witch? The one you killed?" Eric asked, unsure if he were recalling the legend correctly.

"Yes, that one," Sam replied patiently as he continued eating.

"So . . . what . . . do you want with me?" Eric asked slowly. He again attempted to move and instantly was seized by another urge to be sick.

"To learn more about Katarina Ashowan. The man who wanted you kidnapped only requested you out of the way for a few days, but as I mentioned last night, the more I heard about the daughter of the house witch, the more intrigued I became. So here we are," Sam explained while placing his small dagger down on the table. He then proceeded to fold his hands across his belly and lean back to fix Eric with a long stare.

"Why Kat?" the prince shifted forward, raising his knees so that he could hang his head between them.

"Her powers intrigue me. I heard her magic consumed another witch's power, and I also heard she has enhanced strength and speed. She was even stabbed and did not bat an eye."

"What questions do you have?" Eric asked while at long last raising his head and fixing the devil with his bloodshot eyes.

After a moment of the two locking gazes, Samuel gave a small laugh. "Amazing. You meet the literal devil, I casually mention someone wants you kidnapped, and all you are asking about is what I want with the Ashowan woman. A love that will only end in tears . . . You seem addicted to making yourself suffer."

Eric said nothing, only waited.

"Does she have a weakness?" Samuel queried, tilting his head over his right shoulder and staring down at Eric with a small smile.

Still, the prince said nothing.

"That taste I gave you last night of what I am capable of was nothing compared to the hell I can make you live in for the rest of your life. You humans all seem to think some great torture resides in the Grove of Sorrows where my parents banish evil souls to repent. You think some kind of burning, drowning, or other unimaginable horrors await you. The truth is the torture comes from yourselves. Holding a mirror up and reflecting whatever damage you think you are inflicting to gain power or superiority. You humans are wildly efficient at bringing agony to yourselves, and I can see *you've* already been dosing yourself in pain. All I need to do is light the match."

"Why ask me about her weaknesses if you can find them just fine on your own?" Eric wondered, unmoved by the otherworldly being's ominous warning.

Samuel's smile faded then as he peered around the room casually. "Have you ever heard of the Lobahlan saying, 'By the hair of the Goddess'?"

Eric frowned but nodded.

"Everyone has their ties—their fates, if you will—that the Goddess and Green Man weave themselves amongst you humans. Some people have very simple hairs linking them to their destiny. A farmer marrying a woman, who will allow his crops to thrive for two generations is thought to be a simple one. Then, however, you get the ones with . . . intricate knots and multiple hairs."

"Kat is complicated?"

"My parents made her a mess of destinies. You see, there are outcomes that must occur, but there are also some that could branch off in two different scenarios, but the conclusion would more or less be the same. Getting close before understanding her more, means I could become tangled in those destinies, which would be . . . annoying, and problematic."

"What is Kat destined for?" Eric's chain jangled as he gradually shifted his feet until he was cross-legged.

"Uh-uh! Answer my question. What is her weakness? I will not ask a third time." Samuel's eyes glinted, and Eric felt his insides quake.

He swallowed slowly. "None."

Samuel stared at Eric with a rejuvenated smile. "Oh really? If she consumed all of a witch's power, including their life energy, does she also consume the curse that nature dictates should follow? Once she has consumed that power, does she gain that element? Or does she become a calamity that projects an even more powerful curse?"

Eric's heart pounded against his chest. "Kat isn't going to be a calamity. She's going to help Alina here and go home. Her father is more than capable in—"

"Tell me, did Lady Katarina find her familiar yet?"

Frowning, the prince once again resorted to silence.

"I see I'll need to encourage you." Samuel stood.

Eric's breath came out haltingly as fear and nausea brewed in his gut.

A knock on the closed door interrupted them.

"Master, our customer is here. He has news."

Sam let out a long-suffering sigh before turning to the exit, though he still addressed Eric as he moved. "I suppose you have your own destiny that is protecting you, Your Highness. At least for now."

Taking his leave and closing the door behind himself, Sam slid the bolt across the door, and wandered down the narrow hall toward the staircase that presumably led down to the main floor.

"They aren't reporting him missing! The coronation is *still* taking place, and apparently the princess remains in good health!" The infuriated voice of Duke Icarus drifted up to Sam, who stilled, his hand resting on the banister.

"I must admit, His Majesty seems to be quite determined to make her his queen," Leo cited lazily.

"Of course our brilliant king figured out what we're trying to do . . . and if we send a public notice for his ransom there is the risk of drawing more attention to us . . ." The duke seethed.

Sam watched as a shadow drifted back and forth along the plaster wall at the end of the curving stairs, surmising that the noble was pacing.

"You could always deliver the ransom request to the council alone. There are enough in support of the rebellion's cause that a vote to delay the coronation would take place," Manuel pointed out, though the timidness in his voice was audible.

"A temporary fix, you dullard! Unless we kill the Daxarian prince or princess, we become sitting ducks."

"We won't kill His Highness. Bringing the wrath of Daxaria to our shores won't—"

"What are you talking about?! It's perfect! We have our chance at rightfully conquering the kingdom of fools once and for all! We kill *both* the princess and prince and expand our control! The civil unrest in Daxaria as they battle for the throne will only help us," the duke reasoned, his pacing stopping as he began to revel in the idea of the glory of war.

"You want to risk another loss against the house witch?" Leo scoffed derisively. "They say he's only grown more powerful with time."

"He is one man! He cannot protect the whole continent, and his daughter is here on our lands, no less. We leverage her and—"

"Now see, Your Grace, we are beginning to have a conflict of interest." Sam descended the stairs, his hand still on the banister.

"What do you mean? And who are you?"

Samuel touched down on the floor and studied the duke, who had hired him to help prevent the princess from being crowned queen.

"I am another vested party in your plans. While I have no compunctions about Her Highness's death, I take exception to Prince Eric Reyes and Katarina Ashowan's." Samuel strode forward, the shadows in the darkened room casting menacing images along its walls.

Duke Icarus glared through his small spectacles at Sam, the lines in his forehead deepening.

"You don't know who you are trifling with, young man."

Samuel smiled as he continued drawing closer to the duke, while Leo, who was seated behind him, pushed the legs of his chair back until he balanced on only two and watched the entire scene with his expression no longer untroubled.

When Samuel finally came to a stop, his eyes fixed on the duke's.

The room became deathly still.

Leaning forward, Sam rested his hand on the nobleman's shoulder.

Sebastian Icarus grew pale, his thin lips draining of color as his knees began to tremble.

He was doused in iciness . . . Dark twisted shadows rose in the corner of his eyes that petrified him in place . . . Color faded from the world . . .

"How about you listen to *my* suggestions, Your Grace; I have a few good ones." Sam's quiet voice was like the stinging sharp edge of a blade against the duke's heart.

"A-Alright then."

The room once again warmed in the firelight, though sweat beaded along the duke's forehead . . .

Sam's dark eyes glittered. "Excellent decision. Why don't you have a seat, Your Grace."

Katarina stood in her black dress, her arms crossed and her boot tapping impatiently.

The air witch—a woman with silvery blond hair, translucent skin, and red eyes—waited, avoiding Kat's stare in the shadowed servants' exit.

"Mr. Kraft insisted on joining us, but he's late," Kat remarked dryly.

The air witch said nothing and instead studied the marble of the entryway with great interest.

"I swear, if he tries to back out of this deal—"

"I would never forsake my honor, Lady Katarina." Mr. Kraft's hushed voice behind her gave Katarina a small start, her hand jumping to her chest before she rolled her eyes.

"Is there a reason you are joining us on this search?" the redhead asked while watching Mr. Kraft give a bow to the air witch, who smiled shyly in return.

"To ensure you do not unfairly encourage Celeste to do things outside of our agreement," Mr. Kraft answered while tugging on his leather gloves.

"Gods, and I thought only mages could be this level of insufferable," Kat muttered while following him and the air witch, who she now knew was named Celeste.

"Bite your tongue," Mr. Kraft barked.

While Kat jeered at the coven leader's back, the air witch stepped forward in front of the both of them. She wore a plain black tunic and pants, knee-high boots, and her hair was braided.

"I can't fly three of us all night very well—it's hard keeping three larger figures level—but if we were to ride on a steady object, that could be of help." Her quiet, light voice reminded Katarina of an airy flute and almost made her smile.

How old was the air witch? She sounded young . . .

"What about a wagon?" Mr. Kraft suggested while peering around the servants' courtyard but only spotting overturned buckets, empty troughs, and rain barrels.

"I thought you were hell-bent on being inconspicuous," Kat pointed out, her golden eyes glowing in the dark as she peered at Mr. Kraft with a raised eyebrow.

"Those should work." Celeste walked over to a corner of the courtyard and procured two brooms and a mop.

"Are we dangling from these all night?" the redhead's voice rose in concern as Celeste handed her a broom without batting an eye in her direction or bothering to reply.

Kat, however, was rendered speechless when the broom in her hand suddenly swept itself between her legs and wrenched her high into the air with a great whoosh.

"Whaaaa . . . !" Kat's scream was stolen as she flew higher and higher over the castle, until she was at eye level with the highest tower windows.

In a state of utter disbelief, she turned her gaze out over Vessa and felt her jaw drop.

"Oh my . . . Gods . . ."

The city lay sprawled underneath the breathtaking sky, and beyond its reaches . . . the mountains created jagged peaks under the light of the full moon, which appeared from behind the clouds that had plagued the skies all day.

"If you are finished marveling at the view, we should proceed with our search."

Even Mr. Kraft's haughty voice next to Kat did nothing to take away from the spectacle before her. Even though she had gone on night rides with her father where he magically flew their horses, she couldn't deny the beauty of Troivack's landscape

"Gods, this is . . . incredible," she said breathily, turning back to the sights before her. She noted Celeste had joined them and was floating on the other side of Mr. Kraft. "Gods, I should show Eric this . . . I bet he'd . . ."

Kat trailed off.

In truth, she didn't know how Eric would react, but . . . she kind of wished to find out . . .

"Speaking of your *protector,* shall we begin to search for His Highness?" Mr. Kraft observed Katarina out of the corner of his eye, though as he watched her awestricken expression, the stoniness in his face softened ever so slightly.

"Of course." Kat bobbed her head. "Searching to the north and east of Vessa will take the most time; we'll start there!"

Mr. Kraft looked to Celeste, who gave a nod in understanding, and with the smallest turns of her head, she had the three witches sail across the night sky awash in moonlight.

Kat already had her glowing eyes cast back to the ground in hopes of seeing a cart or suspicious carriage. Though as they flew in the quiet cold air, realized she hadn't had a moment to truly be alone with her thoughts since learning of Eric's abduction. The more she thought about him trapped, suffering, with new horrors being added to his already extensive list, she could feel her grip on her broom handle tighten. She once again remembered the way he'd gently washed her wounds and the way he'd held her when she had succumbed to tears just one night before . . .

Please, Eric . . . Please be alright. I really . . . really *want to see you again . . .*

CHAPTER 53

A FAMILIAR FORCE

The moment the door had closed behind Sam, Eric dropped his sweaty face to his hands, rubbing it roughly as though trying to scrub away the last vestiges of the Witch's Brew.

The devil.

The actual devil . . .

And he was after Kat . . .

He wanted to know if she could kill a deity . . .

The first witch had been dead since times of legend, so the only reason he could be asking would be to see if Katarina was a threat to him.

Eric felt his stomach boil.

Kat needed to get the hell out of Troivack and back with her father, where she could be protected immediately . . .

Gods, will she even listen to me if I tell her to go home?

The prince found he already knew the answer.

She won't leave Alina . . . Fuck.

Raising his gaze once more to the table where the devil had sat, Eric stared at the space where he remembered seeing a blue winged creature sitting and staring at him.

The devil had said that it was a creature from the ancient realm, and he had also said people who had taken the Witch's Brew could see it . . .

Racking his brain back through his memories, the prince vaguely recalled that he used to see those types of creatures all the time when he first started taking Witch's Brew . . . When had they stopped appearing?

The last time he remembered seeing anything like them was the night that Fin had found him . . .

Three years ago . . .

"So, uh . . . So, after they threatened me, I uh . . . I had to kill them," Eric finished his sentence haltingly as he watched the dazzling sparkles twinkle around him, his back propped up against a small hoard of bejeweled colored pillows.

The seller of Witch's Brew had constructed an abode filled with thick curtains of Zinferan and Troivackian designs that blocked off rooms and cubbies. Choice pipe tobacco, moonshine, wine, and ales were offered to their patrons . . . It was also wonderfully quiet despite being a place of hedonistic vices.

"You know, it's nice to . . . to spend time with you like this." Eric turned and smiled dazedly at his companion, his hand reaching out to give their head a long stroke.

Kraken blinked up at him slowly. "*It sounds like a troublesome year, kitten.*"

"How it goes, I guess."

A flutter of movement drew Eric's attention to the far corner of the cubby.

Three creatures eyed him. One that was blue with pointy teeth and perhaps only two feet in height.

Another was a man . . . Or was it a man? The being had long, pointed ears, long black hair, and purple eyes that had the occasional dots of blackness. The third was what Eric thought to be a stump, but it had a face peering at him, its eyes like the hot coals of a fire . . .

"*Kitten, how long have you been seeing these?*" Kraken asked with a faint wary note in his voice, his tail swishing, as he stared from Eric to the mystical creatures.

"Hm? You see them too? I just assumed it was 'cause of the Witch's Brew . . ."

"*Aren't you tired, human? Don't you wish for a peaceful slumber free of worry?*" the creature from the corner asked, the black dots in his eyes shifting as he spoke.

Eric noticed this with laxed interest while the blue winged being smiled and once again revealed its pointy teeth.

"Hm . . . A good sleep . . . would be nice . . ." the prince murmured, his eyes growing heavy.

"*We know such a place, where everyone is safe, and you have no worries,*" the stump rumbled.

Eric smiled. "That could be nice, but . . . sounds too good . . . to be true . . ." His eyes began to close, and as a result, he did not notice the colors around him change to smoke and silver, or that they were slowly drawing closer to him, like fingers unfurling about to grasp him.

"*RARK*!"

The stump and man with pointy ears turned to the blue winged creature and stared in alarm at the large fluffy black cat that held him by the throat in his mouth.

After two flexes of his jaw, Kraken released the blue creature's limp body and glared up at the beings.

"*This is my kingdom. You will not steal* my *citizens.*"

The man frowned, the black dots in his eyes shifting quickly yet again.

"*Be gone, familiar. You have no power over—*"

Kraken rested his great paws against the stump, extended his claws, and pulled. He scratched all the way down to its broken roots. The stump roared in pain, making the long-eared man wince. The familiar then continued to treat the mythical creature as it deserved—as his casual scratching post. After a moment of the imp watching him in horror, Kraken raised his gaze.

"*I* am *power here, imp. Be gone. Or you may come to find your blood filling the bowls of my finest followers.*"

Kraken disengaged from the stump that had begun to weep, then prowled closer to the other ethereal being.

"*Y-You . . . beast . . . should not be able to touch us . . .*"

"*And* you, *foolish elder, should not be trespassing into this realm. There is nothing in my land I cannot touch. Now, little eel, be gone. If you try to take my kitten, I will follow you to the ancient world and bring my chaos.*"

"*Y-You couldn't possibly! I-I will bring the Goddess here to—*"

"*Why yes, why* don't *you summon the Goddess? I'm sure she gives the most* divine *cheek scratches.*" Kraken brushed against the imp's leg, making him shiver.

Slowly, the familiar rounded on the imp, his green eyes flashing.

"*Are we going to have a problem, imp? Or are you going to pass along my message? Whatever it is you are trying to do here, especially with this kitten, you will cease.*"

Swallowing with great difficulty, the imp straightened himself to his full height, the black dots in his eyes vibrating.

"*I call your bluff, you flea ridden beast. You can hurt my lessers, but there is no way you can—*"

A single chirp emanated from Kraken, and three cats entered the curtained cubby.

The imp looked at their gleaming eyes and lowered heads as they prowled closer. One of them was thick and shaggy and looked heavier than some breeds of dogs . . .

With his attention diverted, Kraken launched himself at the imp. With his claws digging into the being's chest, the familiar's weight managed to throw the creature against the wall, then half collapse against a small table . . . but the world around them shifted.

Suddenly, they weren't in the illegal tavern but instead a ring of deadened ash trees. Fog swept around the imp's ankles in the ferns, and beyond the ring stood several other creatures that eyed the scene with alarm.

"*My last warning, imp.*" Kraken leaned his wet nose forward, the mythical creature's eyes wide and his breath ragged. "*I will eat you as the eel you are if you do not make it clear to your allies that you are banned from my kingdom. That kitten you tried to steal gave me my name. Do you know what a kraken does?*"

The imp collapsed on the forest floor as Kraken's claws sank deeper into his chest, making the imp howl in pain.

"*The kraken comes from the shadowed depths of the ocean, and it swallows what disturbs the balance of man and nature. It is what rises above all forces in any realm. I, of course, as a familiar am more powerful. Now, what say you?*"

The imp began to sweat as Kraken plucked up his paws, tearing skin as he did so.

"I-I swear. W-We won't bother Daxaria." the imp's voice had shifted from its former ethereal warble once he returned to his own realm.

"*No one sets foot in my kingdom to bother so much as a tick without my permission.*" Kraken's pupils grew large, and the imp could see the chaos bottled within the small animal. He resisted the urge to weep as he nodded.

"*A wise decision.*"

Kraken cast one last look around the circle of trees and the creatures that were frozen at the spectacle before them.

He let out a single huff, then turned and sauntered through the ring, disappearing amongst the mists . . .

When the fog cleared, Kraken found himself back in the illegal tavern, and so he made his way over to where Eric drifted in and out of consciousness.

"*Are you faring well, kitten?*" Kraken asked as he leapt up and began to settle in beside the prince.

Blearily, Eric opened his eyes and smiled down at the fluffy black cat with his dash of white on his chest as he reached up and began scratching his cheek. "Yeah . . . Things have been rough . . . but maybe I can . . . sleep. For a bit . . ."

Kraken purred.

Then, the curtains to the cubby pulled open.

Finlay Ashowan stood in a simple black tunic and pants, his blue eyes magically aglow.

"Kraken, there you are, what are you doing here—Eric?!"

The prince gave his head a shake.

"Uh . . . hey, Fin!"

The house witch stared at Eric with a frown and stepped into the space hastily. He ensured the curtain was fully closed before he crouched before the young man.

"Eric, what are you doing here? I've been looking for you for two months!"

"Oh . . . I'm just . . . having a great talk with Kraken." Eric gave an extra-long scritch down the familiar's back.

"Yes, we've been having an excellent time catching up. I'm surprised it took you so long to find him," Kraken chirped while barely cracking open an eye.

"Well, to be fair, I have been traveling between the towns without giving my name," Eric contributed with a sage nod and weighty blink.

Fin drew back in alarm. "Wait. Eric . . . did you just understand and *reply* to Kraken?!"

Both Eric and Kraken stilled, then turned slowly to face each other.

"Kitten, I must admit, when you said cats could get influenced by the smoke in these places, I underestimated that . . ."

"Kraken, you can talk?!" Eric burst out startled. He relaxed again moments later. "Huh."

Fin stared back and forth between his familiar and the prince, a disturbing combination of worry and pent-up laughter mixing in his chest.

"Eric, just what have you consumed?"

"It's okay . . . just a good brew," the prince replied, his eyes fluttering as sleep wafted closer to his senses.

"Tea? What tea is—"

"It's Witch's Brew," Kraken supplied while his own eyes began to close. *"Now if you will excuse me . . . It is the Empurror's nap time."*

Fin stared at Eric's drawn tired face, already slack with sleep, and felt his heart drop to his stomach.

"Witch's Brew?! Gods, Eric . . . your father's a mess right now . . . And your sister . . ." he trailed off, tears rising in his eyes. "I know you're going through a bad time, but your family needs you."

Rubbing his face, Fin stared at the man, who had once been the little boy who had visited him every day and told him about his sword training . . . The boy who had played with Kraken for hours and had wanted him at his side for every birthday . . . The boy who had declared he'd protect his sister at all costs . . .

That boy had grown to become a master swordsman. When he wasn't training, he was teaching others how to improve.

Fin stared at the unconscious prince and remembered his own wife, who was devastated at home since the queen's death . . .

"I should have been there at least once or twice more for you, Eric. I'm so sorry . . ." Fin stood with difficulty and regarded Kraken for another thoughtful moment before turning and taking his leave.

The confrontation with his friend would have to wait, as neither of them were in any capacity to handle what needed to be said.

Present day . . .

Eric carved circles into his temples with his knuckles.

He couldn't remember the exact details, but Fin and Kraken had something to do with him not seeing those creatures anymore . . . at least until last night.

If that blue winged being was still in the room with Eric but he couldn't see them, it was possible they could warn the devil if he attempted escaping. Then that horrible sensation of his soul being openly probed would commence yet again, but this time it could be worse . . .

I still have to try and get out of here. I have to warn Kat. Giving his head a shake and shifting his attention to the table and chair, the prince eyed the forgotten knife the devil had been using to cut his apple.

He then dropped his gaze to the shackle around his ankle and surmised it was out of reach.

With a sigh, Eric stood and removed his tunic that was covered in dirt and his sweat stains, and he proceeded to spin the garment over and over until he'd fashioned a whip.

With a flick of his wrist the tunic snapped against the table corner, still inches too far from the blade. Inching forward until the chain connecting him to the wall was pulled tight, he spun the tunic once more.

Slapping it down onto the table, he sent the knife clattering to the floor.

Eric winced at the noise, and waited with his eyes glued to the door to see if anyone would burst in.

No one did.

Frowning, the prince reached down and grabbed the knife.

It felt too easy . . .

Seating himself on the ground, Eric slipped the tip of the blade into the keyhole, but the damned thing wouldn't open.

Staring around the room yet again, he tried to find anything that might be of help . . .

Then his eyes fell to the metal plate his chain was attached to.

It was screwed to the stone wall . . . but with the knife . . . maybe . . .

Eric stood and fought off the nausea and dizziness that once again plagued him.

There was no time to waste.

He was getting out of there, and he was going to make sure Kat was safe, no matter what.

And as far as being in love with her went . . . well . . .

He could figure out how to deal with that later.

CHAPTER 54

BREAKING AND ENTERING

Kat could feel her frustrations rising as they flew over the roofs of Austice. The moon was beginning to droop closer to the horizon, and panic was flooding her veins as the wind continued to whoosh past her ears.

"They most likely took him someplace already, and you won't be able to see through the walls," Mr. Kraft voiced beside her. He was astride the mop that Celeste had given him to ride, and his hands were pale around its shaft from the cold.

"The odds of finding him are ridiculously low," he continued slowly.

"Eric's a survivor. He may be a cockroach at times, and he may act like he doesn't give a rat's ass, but he *will* come back. Exactly like a cockroach, funny enough . . ." Kat's voice was firm as her eyes didn't raise from the ground below for a single second.

"The rumors around you two indicated an intimate relationship. I confess, I'm having trouble understanding your connection, but I can see it is indeed a meaningful one. Which is troublesome given your magic."

"Alright, first of all, other than being each other's dumping grounds for our nonsense and him saving my arse, we have no relationship. Second, I will not go on a killing spree," Kat ground out while frowning. Her eyes still never averted from her search.

"Your magic isn't controlled right now. It is growing in power with each passing year . . . It is hungry."

"For what?" Katarina snapped the question, but there was the hint of a crack in her voice at the end.

"I don't know. I only know that it seeks to feed off anything it can."

"But I . . . I thought a witch's power was based on their personality . . .

Am I a terrible person?" At long last Kat flit her gaze to Mr. Kraft, though only briefly.

It was then the coven leader realized that for all her hotheadedness and confidence, his words had genuinely terrified her, and it became clear to him then, that perhaps she was a mite more like her father than he had initially wanted to give her credit for.

"It has not happened often in history, but there are some instances where a witch is born with powers they never master; it often results in curses. In fact, the last time that happened sparked the hunting of our kind. Unfortunately, it also became the norm to kill a witch before their powers consumed them."

Katarina's shoulders stiffened.

"An archaic practice," Mr. Kraft added carefully. "What I mean to say is that these unfortunate souls were not evil, merely ill-equipped. If you truly wish to master it, I'm sure, as the daughter of the house witch, the resources will be offered. In truth, I'm surprised they haven't already been provided to you."

"No one has been able to see my abilities like you have," Kat informed him bluntly.

"The identifying spell should have—"

"It only indicated my primary element was clearly fire, but the others were all included as well. So I *am* a mutated witch to some degree . . . They also said my powers would grow as I did."

Mr. Kraft said nothing, but he was visibly perplexed by what she had just said.

After a moment of thoughtful silence stretching between them, Mr. Kraft began to open his mouth, but instead he sat up perfectly straight on his broom.

"Celeste! Go back! Do you see that tiled roof?" Mr. Kraft pointed to an inconspicuous building that was nestled between two grander homes. It was short and square, with no identifying shrubbery or flowers, its wooden shutters sealed tight . . . It could have been a servant's house belonging to one of the larger homes around it.

"What is it, Mr. Kraft?" Kat asked as she failed to notice anything amiss.

"There are creatures there. Ancient creatures that don't usually come out in swarms . . ."

"What has that got to do with Eric?" Kat demanded, her frustration making her aura flicker to life.

Mr. Kraft shot her a firm yet patient glance. "It is not something that is the norm, Lady Katarina. Anything that is out of place could have something to do with his disappearance. If I am wrong and we've wasted time, then I will promise you another night of our assistance."

Though still not entirely pleased, Kat couldn't help but admit to herself that another night of searching would be a significant help if they had, in fact, found nothing . . .

As Celeste brought them lower to the ground, the trio were unaware that one or two curious pairs of eyes had glimpsed them descending from the heavens.

Touching down quietly on the cobblestones, Mr. Kraft stepped closer to the house with Kat and Celeste following carefully behind him. Two burly men emerged from the shadows, swords on their belts, their faces menacing.

"Be gone," one growled at Mr. Kraft, freezing him in place.

Kat raised an eyebrow and shifted forward, the movement drawing both of the men's attention.

They both fell back a step, their faces paling.

"Y-You . . . You're that demon woman," the one with a shaved head, full beard, and silver hoop in his left ear managed to say.

"Oh, for the love of . . . What are you two guarding?" Kat demanded while placing her hands on her hips, her golden eyes gleaming in the night.

"Be gone, witch!" one of the men burst out, drawing his sword.

Despite Mr. Kraft falling back a foot, Kat didn't budge, though her eyes began to burn a little brighter, which succeeded in making the second man hesitate in freeing his own weapon from its scabbard.

"Lady Katarina, we should summon—"

"They'll run away by the time help comes," Kat replied over her shoulder before addressing the men, who were growing shiftier. "Now, you wouldn't happen to have a man in there, about so high, wavy dirty blond hair, hazel eyes, bit of a drinking habit—oh, he's also going to be the next king of Daxaria." Kat drew nearer, once again forcing the men to draw back and closer to each other.

"Leave! O-Or we will summon our master!"

Behind Katarina, Mr. Kraft eyed the ancient creatures that no one but he could see as they began to line the roof above them. He gulped as they turned their unnatural gazes interestedly to Katarina.

"I'll give you two choices. You could be courteous and open that there door for me, and we all have a splendid rest of our evenings . . ." Kat smiled at them, her aura fluttering from her skin like flames. "Or, I run a little experiment where I don't hold back and we see how much damage I can unleash. My companion back there says I show great potential in bringing about absolute chaos and death. Maybe even a curse." Her aura grew.

The men balked.

A tense moment in quiet stalemate passed, then two concussive bursts of air blasted the two men in their guts, knocking them against the stone walls of the small structure they guarded and rendering them unconscious.

Kat turned, startled, to stare at Celeste, who was rubbing her hands, appearing as untroubled as ever. It was as though she were merely trying to warm her hands in the chilly air.

"We really should summon the Troivackian knights at this point," the air witch said.

Kat's formerly fierce expression faded, and Mr. Kraft watched as a rush of pained concern and even fear replaced it.

"I . . . I don't think we should. My gut . . . my instincts are telling me that we need to go in there, right now. I understand if you don't want to come with me, Mr. Kraft and Celeste. Thank you for your help until now."

"Wait, my lady, we really couldn't leave you to—" Mr. Kraft's words were cut off as Kat opened the door and stepped in without another look back.

"Godsdamnit." Mr. Kraft exhaled while shooting a brief, anguished look at Celeste. The air witch appeared unperturbed, however, as she glided forward.

"I know I'm the only one who can deliver the message to the Troivackian knights, but it might be a bad idea if she goes in there alone," Celeste reasoned breezily while stretching her arms above her head. "Perhaps wait outside, Mr. Kraft."

Then she, too, disappeared into the building, leaving the coven leader of Aguas alone in the quiet street, his heart in his ears as he remembered with great clarity how terrifying the Troivackian king could be when angry . . .

Dropping his head to his hand, he let out a long breath. "Goddess, please protect them."

Kat stood in the open room with its slate floor and square posts, blinking at the sight before her.

Three men were on their feet, and a hooded figure was disappearing through a backdoor . . .

There was nothing in the room save for a table and chairs in its center and a great fireplace lit behind them.

A curved staircase in the right-hand corner of the room led to the second floor, and Katarina had yet another strong hunch that Eric was up there somewhere.

"My, my. Katarina Ashowan herself." A tall man with long black hair that he had partially tied back, and who wore a burgundy vest and black pants addressed her. His dark eyes roved over her with an interested glint.

Meanwhile the chestnut-haired man behind him slowly rose from his seat and folded his arms, his expression stony. The last of the three men openly cowered at the sight of her . . . He looked familiar . . .

"Yes, hi there. Afraid I don't have a lot of time, so if I could just pick up the prince of Daxaria so that we can be on our way, that'd be wonderful," Kat greeted, her voice casual, but her blood thrummed in her throat with its rapid steady pulses, making her aura burn a little brighter.

Silently by her side, Celeste stared at the three men with a casual tilt of her head.

"Well, now you see, we can't just do that. Her Highness's coronation seems to be proceeding as planned, which is an issue." The tall man with dark hair drew closer, his eyes never leaving Kat's face as he continued openly studying her.

"Prince or no prince, that coronation is going to happen . . . Though I'm not sure what everyone has against Alina. She's a lovely person," Kat babbled while folding her arms and trying to avoid the supposed leader's direct gaze as her insides began to tremble.

"Hm. I must admit, I wasn't intending on meeting you so soon." The advancing man's tone had lowered, his presence growing with each breath he took.

At long last he stood toe-to-toe with Kat, forcing her golden eyes to meet his dark ones as they called to her, drawing her in . . .

Then, the creeping awareness of his presence beneath her skin made her give a small start . . . almost like a small pinch of tingles . . . only the feeling grew uncomfortable as she became acutely aware that somehow . . . he was approaching her soul . . .

"Knock it off," Kat barked, though she faltered back a step and struggled to look away.

"Quite the guarded little thing, aren't you?" The man's soft voice sent shivers through Kat, and despite not sparing her a glance to warn her, even Celeste remained rooted to the spot as the two men by the table watched.

The one with chestnut hair and tinges of auburn was smiling coldly, while the shorter one was swallowing with great difficulty.

"I suppose your unfortunate hair of the Goddess tied to the prince drew you to me, or perhaps we have a fate of our own . . ." Sam's eyebrow raised as he noticed the red threads invisible to everyone else that began to rise and snake out to him.

He was becoming entangled . . . exactly what he had wished to avoid . . .

With a sigh, he straightened his head, and his eyes sharpened.

A thrum of power filled the air, and all at once everyone stilled as though stuck in time.

"I suppose if it's come to this, I will take a look to better understand just what my parents were planning when they created you."

Katarina couldn't breathe, the pressure around her was too much. Even more troubling, ravenous flames in her stomach began to rise . . .

It was then she bore the awful premonition that whatever strange magic the leader was about to perform, it was going to result in an outburst he was wildly unaware of . . . And it would be on a level Katarina had never allowed before.

"D-Don't . . . Whatever it is you're doing, stop—"

"I'll be quick this time around, so try to relax." Sam soothed, but the burning in Kat's belly was already traveling up to her chest.

His presence seeped further into Kat's being, drawing nearer to the burning magic in her chest that she was struggling to contain.

Her aura that had already been aglow when she'd first stepped foot in the room began to expand, its orange and gold reaching out farther and farther until red began to appear at its base . . .

"Master, are we sure that—" Leo's cold smile faded from his face as heat rose in the room and some sort of deeper sense welled up within him that something was about to go horribly wrong.

Sam did not react to the words, instead remaining unconcerned. That is, until he sifted through the final barrier Katarina Ashowan had carefully crafted to cage her magic . . .

What followed then . . . was an explosion.

CHAPTER 55

FANNING THE FLAMES

Brendan stared at Alina's shadowed eyes, then at his mother's bowed head.

With a single glance to his brother, Henry was set in motion, ushering forward and guiding the former queen out of the king's study.

Alina stood her ground, her formidable countenance never wavering for a moment.

"You summoned the Coven of Aguas without my consent in order to conduct a search of your own to find your brother." Brendan repeated what had been reported to him by Mage Sebastian.

For a moment Alina didn't move, but once she let out a short breath, responded.

"I did, yes. Katarina is out with the coven leader and an air witch right now."

"Are you aware I had arranged to send Faucher to perform a discreet investigation, starting this evening?"

"I was not because I haven't seen you since I was told this morning that my brother was missing." Alina's voice turned frosty.

Sensing this shift in his wife, Brendan leaned back in his chair and held her stormy gaze. "This arrangement presents new problems, Alina."

"On the contrary, this serves our objectives."

Brendan raised an eyebrow but didn't bother asking anything further.

"We had always intended to restore the Coven of Aguas in order to see better advancements in Troivack's economy, correct?" Alina asked, the edge still present in her tone.

Brendan nodded slowly, though his brows had begun to lower.

"In this recent exchange, they requested to reside here in the castle—of course without letting it be known who they are, but it is a great opportunity to start having them reenter the courts. It would be a way of easing everyone in. Part of what made Finlay Ashowan so widely accepted was that he lived for months amongst the nobility and servants, and they all got to know him before learning what he was." Alina paused and folded her hands in front of her skirts.

Brendan stared at her thoughtfully. "If I had heard this prior to you deciding for yourself, I wouldn't be angry."

"If you had told me what was going on through the day pertaining to my brother's rescue, I wouldn't have resorted to it." Alina's voice rasped, her ire barely contained.

Brendan stood, his expression darkening. "I needed to investigate more details of his disappearance before I could offer any conclusive information. You're aware that without you being crowned, if we tried to bring you into council meetings for this, it could completely destroy our plans."

"You could have sent missives updating me, and what do you mean you needed more details about his disappearance?" Alina's control was slipping as tears rose to her eyes while glaring at her husband.

Brendan let out a disgruntled breath before straightening and rounding his desk.

"I didn't want to tell you this, but . . . I'm beginning to see that it might be necessary." The king stood in front of his wife, and as he peered down into her glistening eyes, felt his expression soften. "I wanted to make sure your brother had in fact been abducted, and that he hadn't—"

"You wondered if he ran away." Alina exhaled in realization as her tears dripped onto her pale face.

Brendan reached up and gently brushed the droplets away with his thumb. "I wanted to make sure that was not the case. Because it would completely change how I approached the investigations."

Alina stared up at her husband, her eyes bright with pain. "Did he run?"

At this, Brendan gave a small, bittersweet smile. "No, he didn't."

Dropping her face to her hands, Alina let out a sob of relief mixed with anguish. "Gods, I don't know if that is better or worse . . ."

Wrapping his arms around his petite wife, Brendan dropped a kiss to the top of her head and held her close.

"When are Lady Katarina and the coven members supposed to be returning?"

Alina sniffled into his chest. "Just before dawn."

"Did my mother ensure no one would be out by the servants' entrance?"

"Yes."

The king held Alina a little more tightly as he debated whether to tell her that her brother had already tried to run while on his way to Vessa, or if he should mention that he was susceptible to soldiers spells, or whether he should reveal that her best friend had been stabbed again . . .

But the words of the physician that morning advising him to ensure she endured as little stress as possible during her pregnancy flashed in his mind.

His heart plummeted to his stomach as he lowered his head to breathe in her familiar scent of jasmine and lilies, and he closed his eyes tightly.

He needed Eric to return as soon as possible. He couldn't take the anxiety of anything happening to Alina . . . And with that wish came the acknowledgment that he wouldn't tell her any of what he had been keeping to himself for a long while yet. Not until their firstborn was in her arms and she was safe.

"I should have communicated with you what I was doing," Brendan admitted quietly.

While he had apologized to Alina once before, it was still not going to be the norm. However, he was improving in acknowledging his errors at the very least.

Alina squeezed him a little tighter. "I should have confirmed that what I was doing would be alright."

Brendan didn't respond. He had learned the hard way that when his wife conceded to a fault, further lecturing often resulted in another fight. So he simply appreciated that she had also reviewed an oversight in judgment.

After a long embrace, the two finally parted. Alina's eyes were red as she swiped at her face hurriedly with the back of her wrist. Brendan reached into his pocket and procured a handkerchief for her.

He had started carrying one around shortly after they'd married, knowing sometimes strong emotions (not just sad ones) made her cry.

Alina gratefully accepted the handkerchief, and once she felt she was presentable, wrapped her arms around her middle.

"The waiting is horrible . . . I truly hope they find something . . ."

A sudden thought occurred to Brendan that made him straighten, his formerly tender expression dropping.

"Lady Katarina knows not to attempt to rescue him herself if she *does* find him, correct?"

Alina's eyes widened. "It was just to search for some sign of him . . . It's unlikely they would find anything. I mean, it's been a full day since Eric was taken."

"If they *did* happen to find him, do you really think she would return for help?" Brendan asked, his mind already racing.

Panic rose in Alina's throat. "Oh Gods."

The couple turned toward the door and left as quickly as possible, both of them already well aware of what the reckless redhead with honorable intentions would do if she happened upon Eric and his abductors.

Light filled Katarina's eyes as her hand shot upward and seized Samuel by the throat, her aura had erupted out of her, tripling in size. The heat alone emanating from her made everyone present but her break out into a sweat.

"Master!" Leo drew his sword and rushed forward, but Katarina hoisted Samuel off his feet and threw him into his subordinate, sending them both crashing into the table.

Celeste, at last free of Samuel's power, bolted to the stairs.

Sprinting, the air witch checked the first door she came to and discovered nothing but a standard bedchamber.

As soon as she came upon the second room, she noted an unusually heavy deadbolt across its iron door. Seizing the bar and ramming it back, Celeste threw open the door. She felt a knife against her throat, and the front of her tunic was seized in a blur of movement that startled her.

Eric stopped himself from killing her at the last second as he stared into her red eyes, momentarily surprised.

"Your Highness! We're here to take you back to the castle!" Celeste whispered while gently laying her hand over his. She had nearly cut off his breathing . . . but once she glimpsed the wavy blond hair that clearly marked him a Daxarian, she had caught herself.

Hearing this, Eric released her, though his gaze was still skeptical . . .

"I am with the Coven of Aguas. I've come with Lady Katarina. She's downstairs dealing with your captors; we should hurry."

Eric's eyes widened at once in panic. He turned toward the stairs and began to run, but his shackle, chain, and the metal plate that had been attached to the wall encumbered his movements.

"Hold on!" Celeste called, stopping him as he turned to stare at her urgently.

She jogged forward and, leaning down toward the lock, blew into the keyhole. A moment later, the shackle fell to the ground.

Staring in surprise at the air witch, the prince opened his mouth to thank her, but he was interrupted by the echoing sound of a man being thrown with great force below them.

* * *

Katarina had shown no signs of registering Celeste's disappearance as she prowled closer to the two men.

Manuel was already tripping over himself to flee out the back door.

Leo was the first back onto his feet, his sword in one hand, and in his other, a circle of water began to magically form.

Katarina's burning golden eyes noted his power with a raise of an eyebrow and a laugh that reverberated unnaturally.

Despite this, Leo hastily sent the jet of water toward her eye, its glistening droplets moving fast enough to pierce through to her skull, but that didn't happen.

Katarina's aura swelled even more, easily consuming the missile as though it had never existed in the first place.

He sent another, then another, yet they all dissolved the same way.

Leo's eyes widened and sweat poured down his back as he shifted forward and began to swing his sword at her, but she moved with unnatural quickness. Her glowing eyes filled his vision, and with a single hand, she seized the front of his tunic and threw him against the stone fireplace, knocking him momentarily unconscious.

Katarina turned to Samuel, who was slowly rising, admiration and eagerness in his eyes as he beheld her.

"I see now. I see why my parents created you . . ." He smiled as she faced him directly. "You're the warning fire."

Katarina reached up, her burning hands about to seize Samuel's face, her thumbs sliding down to be in line with his eyes . . . her intention clear.

However, the face that appeared in her hands then, wasn't the devil who had unleashed her power against her will . . .

It was Eric's.

She stopped, her magical gaze staring blindly at him.

"Kat!" he called out desperately, his eyes sharp and his hands gently clasping her forearms. "Kat, stop now!"

Behind him, realizing that he had the perfect distraction to escape, Samuel gave a small scoff at the scene as though he'd known something like this was going to happen all along. He bent down, throwing Leo's arm over his shoulder as his subordinate's eyes blearily opened. While Sam casually took his leave, he cast a single glance at the air witch, who had stepped forward from the base of the stairs with the intention of stopping him. One final surge of petrifying fear, however, forced her to go still at once.

Meanwhile Katarina's glowing hadn't dimmed, but she wasn't attacking anyone with Eric in front of her . . .

Her hands slowly drifted away from the prince's face down to her sides, her head tilted as she continued staring at him without any emotion in her features or in her light-filled eyes.

"Kat, calm down, we're going back to the castle now, alright? I'm fine, everything is fine!" Shaking, Eric reached out and gently touched Kat's hand.

"Kat, come back—"

The prince was interrupted as Katarina's hand came up once more, her feverish fingertips brushing against his cheek as though she were an animal pawing at something curious.

Her aura began to burn brighter again, only this time it began to wrap itself around Eric.

"Your Highness!" Mr. Kraft's voice in the doorway came when Katarina had already begun to move. It was too late to stop the burning witch from doing what she saw fit.

She leaned forward, her aura whirling and flickering around them, the red tinges shifting to brilliant gold. When she closed her eyes, Eric's racing mind was only outmatched by his heart in his panic to stop her from hurting herself.

However, all semblance of thoughts simmered free of the confines of his mind the second that she leaned forward and kissed him.

Brendan, Alina, Henry, Kezia, Faucher, and Rebecca Devark stood in the servants' stairwell as dawn began to cast pale light above them, the stars dwindling and fading.

The small group stood in somber silence, their breaths quietly rising in plumes in the crisp early chill of the day.

Brendan eyed Alina worriedly, thinking how her lungs were not the healthiest to begin with. And he wasn't entirely comfortable with her losing sleep.

"There they are!" Rebecca Devark pointed, a note of relief that, while subtle, was still noticeable.

All gazes shifted toward the sky directly above them as four figures slowly descended until the quartet had their boots touching the cobblestones.

Alina's breath caught in her throat when she registered the two arrivals on the right.

Eric dismounted the broom, his face ashen, his cheeks sunken, but his eyes . . . They blazed.

His arms were wrapped around Kat, who wasn't riding astride like the others. Her eyes were only half open, and while she did manage to stand from the broom, it was apparent Eric was holding a great deal of her weight.

"Gods! What happened?!" Alina rushed forward. Upon reaching her brother, she began inspecting Kat's slackened expression and weakened body.

"She needs to rest," Eric responded firmly.

Alina's attention snapped to her brother's face, her worry and stress fervid.

"I'm fine, but I can't tell how much magic she used," the prince explained, his expression hard. He then proceeded to wrap one arm around Kat's waist while the other clasped her hand. He allowed her to lean heavily against him as they walked toward the group awaiting them.

Faucher approached them. "I can see that she reaches her chamber. Otherwise, unsavory rumors may begin if you are escorting her in such a state at dawn."

Kezia joined his side. "I will join as well to help make it seem less suspicious. We can say she came down with a flu."

Eric paused, his gaze not rising to meet the military leader's face before he gave a slow nod of assent and gently passed Kat's hand to Faucher. When the prince's arm disappeared from Kat's waist during the transfer, however, she stumbled. Immediately, Eric caught her and drew her to himself.

And in that moment, everyone froze.

The gentleness, the comfortable handling, the look on Eric's face . . . a look so filled with emotion that he was almost unrecognizable from his former hollow, passive self.

Carefully, Eric passed Katarina to Faucher, who made sure to have a firm grasp around her shoulders as well as her hand the second time. Kezia cast one final appraising glance at the prince before she followed behind without a word.

Everyone watched as the trio disappeared into the shadows of the castle. Once it was certain they were out of earshot, Brendan stepped toward Eric, whose attention remained fixed on Katarina's retreating back.

"What happened?"

His stare lingering for another breath on the castle entrance, Eric finally turned to the king, his usual flat expression gradually shifting back into place.

"The devil took me."

Brendan frowned while Henry and his mother shared confused glances.

"What are you talking about?" Alina drew closer to her brother, who regarded her with a strange coolness.

"The actual devil. Son of the Gods. He arranged for me to be taken to prevent you being crowned," Eric explained evenly before turning back to his brother-in-law. "He was especially interested in Kat. Wanted to know if she could kill a deity. He said someone else hired him to take me, but he was interested in her because of the rumors about her being demon-like."

Brendan's dark gaze shifted to his wife, and they shared in wordless alarm at the news.

"If you were drugged when they took you, it's possible you imagined it and—" Alina began.

"He didn't imagine it," the air witch with silvery blond hair and red eyes interrupted, her soft voice cutting in easily. "His power . . . He could control my soul without even looking at me. I couldn't move. I just felt fear and darkness . . ."

Everyone fell into a stunned quiet.

"How did you all escape the actual devil?" Henry asked sincerely, his shocked stare moving from Celeste to Eric.

"Lady Katarina." Mr. Kraft joined the discussion. The coven leader still held his mop in hand as he regarded them all with a small bow.

A heavy understanding settled over the group.

"Kat . . . fought against the actual devil?" Alina managed faintly.

"She did, and he escaped. He's going to come looking for her again." Eric's eyes sought out the king's.

When the two locked gazes, Brendan stiffened.

Ever since the Troivackian king had known him, Eric had been a bottomless pit of despondent resignation. He was at home in the darkness and more than willing to remain buried there until he himself was six feet down in the earth.

However, what he saw in the prince then was entirely different. A small light that had not existed before had been ignited.

Purpose.

It was clear that Eric Reyes, the lost prince of Daxaria, for the first time in four years, was prepared to face and battle the devil himself.

Yet the only factor Brendan was uncertain about was whether Eric was doing this for the greater good . . . Or whether he was doing this because of his concern for Lady Katarina Ashowan.

ABOUT THE AUTHOR

Delemhach is the author of the House Witch series, which they started in order to share with readers some of the warmth, fun, and love of food they experienced while growing up. Born and raised in Canada, Delemhach discovered their love of fantasy and magic at a young age, and the affair has carried on well into their adulthood. Currently, they work multiple jobs, but the one they most enjoy, aside from writing, is privately teaching music to people of all ages.

Get whiskered away

with updates on your favorite magical hijinks, the coziest content, and all things Delemhach!

Visit

laylo.com/delemhach

to sign up for Delemhach's newsletter!

Printed in the USA
CPSIA information can be obtained
at www.ICGtesting.com
LVHW040027191023
761517LV00002B/95

9 781039 429918